The Old Gun

Finding Sundance

A Novel by

Randal Benjamin

Copyright 2014

Published by: Young Lions At The Gate

Original Art: Randal Benjamin

Editing: Mary Ellen Gavin

Graphics: Miki Leathers

Acknowledgements

Many thanks to Joan Destino for the initial editing and her sage guidance.

To Maryellen Gavin for her expertise and professional insights.

I'd like to thank my wife, Pen, and the many friends and relatives who encouraged me in the long process of getting this novel to completion.

Prologue

Oklahoma 1921

~ ~ ~

It was sweltering in the hayloft of Gilbert Jackson's barn. With dust and hay particles lazily drifting around him, Gilbert labored at mowing away his freshly-cured crop of alfalfa. His back aching from the long days work, he relentlessly pitched his cured hay into a stack on the south side of the mow. Sweat, dripping from his chin, stained his plaid cotton shirt. Chaff stuck to the perspiration on his arms and drifted down the back of his neck to irritate and itch as it clung to his sweaty body. He'd been toiling all afternoon.

With each load of hay, he'd used a four-pronged hayfork to spear large clumps of alfalfa from the wagon in front of his barn. Using a system of ropes and pulleys hauled by a horse, Gilbert raised the hay up through a high door into the loft. After each load, he climbed a ladder to the hayloft through a hole in the floor. There he moved the hay with his pitchfork to the spot where it would be stored.

For the last ten years, Gilbert had labored and sweated on his small Oklahoma ranch. He took great pride in the place and, for once, it looked like he was going to have a pretty good year. It might even be good enough to buy Millie, his wife, a new dress; maybe good enough to buy new shoes for his two young girls and new boots for his boy, Gill Jr. The rambunctious six-year-old had all but ruined his last pair playing in the creek. Gilbert smiled as he mentally rehearsed the talk he'd give the youngster when he presented him with his new boots.

But Gilbert would never give his son that talk. For, as he toiled away, death was galloping toward him through the golden wheat field that blanketed the land behind his barn. Unaware of the danger, Gilbert was blissfully humming "Mary's a Grand Old Name," a George M. Cohan song he'd heard on the radio at the Hobard general store.

* * *

As five mounted killers neared Gilbert's barn, they cautiously slowed their horses and came to a halt. The leader, Travis Wilson, dismounted and looked around, casually pulling a .38 Smith & Wesson revolver from the black leather holster strapped to his thin waist. He checked the cylinder and holstered the gun.

Wilson's given name was Travis, but most referred to him as "Ratt." He'd earned the name because, when angry, his cold, pale-green eyes gave the impression of a rattlesnake about to strike.

With his men following closely behind, Ratt Wilson crept stealthily into the barn. As they neared the horse stalls, Gilbert Jackson's two mares began to snort and stamp nervously. Wilson silently signaled to his men and they paused to let the animals settle.

After a few tense moments, the horses relaxed and Wilson quietly led his four men to the foot of the ladder that led to the loft.

* * *

In the loft, Gilbert continued to hum and toil away. He hadn't noticed the nervous snorting of his horses below, nor did he hear the rasp of Wilson's boots climbing the wooden rungs of the ladder.

Slowly, Ratt Wilson's head and then his shoulders rose through the hole in the floor.

It was more the hairs on the back of his neck than a sound that alerted Gilbert to the fact that armed men were now standing behind him. Gilbert paused before he slowly turned to confront the intruders. "Wilson. What're you doing here?"

"Just passing by, Gilbert. Thought I'd pay you another visit."

Gripping his pitchfork to keep his hands from shaking, Gilbert turned his back on the men and began to work again. "You're w...wastin' yer time," he said, irritated at the slight tremor he could hear in his own voice. "I ... told you last time, even if Brooks were to give me a fair offer, I still wouldn't sell."

Hearing no response, Gilbert turned to face the men once again. Courage began to replace his fear. "You oil people ain't pokin' no holes in my land!" For punctuation, Gilbert stabbed his pitchfork into the wooden floorboards. "I don't want nothin' to do with Brooks or his damn stinkin' black goo."

"I know."

Wilson's softly-spoken words caused Gilbert to study the man's face. "Then what the hell are you doin' here?"

A cruel smile curled along Ratt Wilson's lips. He placed his hand on the butt of his revolver and whispered. "Just thought you might be able to help us persuade the other farmers to sell *their* land."

Gilbert looked at Wilson's gun. He squared his shoulders. "You don't scare me none, Wilson, and you can't scare the other ranchers either, especially ones like Harry Kidwell. You might be careful of that man."

Wilson smiled. "Kidwell? That old man don't look like much to me."

"He's quiet, but, like they say, still waters run deep," Jackson warned.

"Don't matter. It's you I'm here to see right now, Gilbert."

"You think you're gonna scare me or Kidwell or any of the others into selling or helping you, Wilson? You're wrong! Go ahead, pull your gun like you did the other day. Didn't scare me then. Don't scare me now. You can kill me but I ain't gonna help you.

Wilson shook his head. His laugh was like a snake weaving through dry grass. "Now that's where you're wrong. You see, that's exactly *how* you're gonna help us."

When Ratt pulled his gun, his men moved in. Gilbert didn't have a chance to even cry out before a cold clammy hand was clamped over his mouth and nose. Struggling for breath and kicking to get free, Gilbert was dragged by the thugs toward the opening in the floor.

Chapter 1

SOONERS BAR
Oklahoma 2001

~ ~ ~

"Shots fired at Sooners Bar on Route 9." The call came in over Sheriff Shepard's police radio. His brow furrowed. Any kind of disturbance was extremely rare at that out-of-the-way locals' tavern, but ... "Shots fired?" This was something he wanted to look into personally. It took him and his deputy only minutes to reach the bar.

Siren screaming and lights flashing, Shepard swung his dark blue sheriff's cruiser into the tavern's parking lot. Gravel popped and crunched under its tires as he punched the brake pedal and brought the vehicle to a skidding halt.

* * *

Less than an hour earlier, Big Bob, the Sooners' bartender, had been looming behind the tavern's large mahogany bar.

The luster of the varnish where he stood had been worn away by his ample belly. Polishing mugs with a frazzled old rag, Bob lazily gazed around the tranquil bar. Four aging wooden tables took up most of the floor space in the tavern. In a dark corner, glowing yellow and blue from its dust-covered neon lights, stood an old, mostly-ignored, jukebox.

Sooners wasn't a fancy place, but Bob knew that the half dozen or so customers seated around the room didn't come for the ambience. They came for the cold beer and a little quiet conversation.

* * *

Old Lee Kidwell sat at one of the wooden tables gazing at his aged friend Ernie seated across from him. Listening to Ernie talk, Lee rubbed the grey stubble on his chin with a hand that had darkened from years in the sun. He smiled patiently as his friend jawed on.

Absentmindedly, Lee unbuttoned the breast pocket of his flannel shirt and casually pulled out a silver pocket watch. The watch often brought back sad and tragically disturbing memories, but it was, nonetheless, one of Lee's most prized possessions. It had been a gift from his father eighty years earlier on Lee's thirteenth birthday. It was his habit to pull out the prized timepiece from time to time and lightly rub its face.

When Ernie finished his story, there was a long silence. Lee felt a tinge of sadness as he slipped the watch back in his pocket.

Ernie gazed at him pensively. "How's things out at the ranch, Lee?"

"Okay, I guess. Jist that Robert doesn't run things the way I used to."

"Lee, you knew when you turned it over to your sister's boy that he would probably want to do things different. Maybe you should sell it to him."

"Laura and I grew up out there, Ernie. Lot o' memories, some good, some bad... real bad. And the bad was mostly my fault. But it was my Pa's ranch. Hard to let it go."

Ernie nodded.

Lee rubbed his hand on the leg of his worn Levis. The denim was wearing thin as tissue paper at the thighs. About time to get new ones. He disliked the modern style of store-bought jeans that came threadbare and full of holes.

That was exactly what Lee was thinking as a blast of sunlight preceded two young cowboys pushing open the door and sauntering into the bar. Lee eyed the knee holes on the first young fellow as he looped his leg over a barstool.

The second cowboy called out to Bob as he settled in next to his companion. "Two cold ones."

Bob filled two mugs from the tap. "Jim. Billy. How you boys today?" He set the cold mugs in front of them with a warm smile. "A might hot out there, huh?"

The cowboy with the holes glared back. "Just pour the beer and keep yer comments to yer self. We ain't much in the mood fer chit-chat."

"Sorry, Jim," Bob said.

He mumbled something to himself as he walked away.

Lee caught Ernie's eye and nodded toward the young cowboys. "Rude punks."

On an old battered TV mounted behind the bar, an ice skating competition was being broadcast.

"Hey, Bob!" The second cowboy called out. "What the hell you got this ice fairy crap on for?"

"Tell me what you want, Billy." Bob grabbed the remote. He paused on a documentary. An archaeologist, being interviewed, was speaking. *"I followed the trail of Butch and Sundance to South America."*

"Leave it there," Jim said.

Old Lee was still staring at Jim's threadbare pants. "At least my nephew has sense not to wear...." Hearing the TV dialogue, he stopped to listen.

"The real history of these two outlaws is somewhat different than portrayed in the movie, 'Butch Cassidy and the Sundance Kid'."

"In what way?" The commentator inquired.

"For one thing, when they fled down to South America, they bought a ranch. I think they planned to use it as a base for their robberies down there. But, when word got out that the two famous American bandits were living there, the Argentinian authorities went to arrest them."

"That guy don't know shit!" Lee said under his breath as he clenched his fists.

The archaeologist continued. "I've been researching these two for over four years."

"You know," the Commentator said, *"before I looked into it, I thought they were fictional characters."*

"No, they were real. Butch's real name was Robert Leroy Parker and Sundance's was Harry Alonso Longabough. And like most outlaws of the Old West, they were just common crooks."

Old Lee gritted his teeth then took a deep breath to calm himself before addressing the bartender, "Would appreciate it, Bob, if you were to change that channel."

Jim and Billy turned and locked eyes with him. Jim growled, "We're watching it, old man. Leave it be, Bob!"

The TV interview continued.

"Were they anything like the characters portrayed by Redford and Newman?"

The archaeologist shook his head. "I believe they were just a couple of two-bit, murdering robbers and probably somewhat cowardly as well."

"Now that damn idiot has gone too far!" Lee muttered angrily. He pointed a shaky finger at the TV. "I'm askin' ya again, Bob, to change that!"

Billy turned back around. "Hey, old man, shut the hell up!"

On the TV the commentator asked, "So, did they die down there the way it was portrayed in the movie?"

"Not actually. Butch and Sundance got careless and were recognized in the town of San Vincente. They were reported to the authorities and the Federales showed up."

"So, there must have been a shoot-out like in the movie," the commentator said.

"Well, there were a few gunshots. But official documents indicated that, when they were trapped, they took the coward's way out and shot themselves."

Thrusting himself up, Lee slammed a fist down on his table with such a bang that it startled everyone in the bar. "I said shut that damn thing off!"

Billy turned to his friend. "Old fart's a nut case."

Jim stood up and blasted at Lee, "We're watching this and if you don't like it, get out!"

The patrons in the bar sat silently; their eyes nervously darted from the young cowboys to Lee.

Quivering like a covered pot about to boil over, Lee glared at Jim and then at the TV. For a second he wanted to take on the two. Instead, Lee gave them a malevolent look and headed for the exit. His body tingling with anger, he made up his mind what he was going to do. The solution was in the glove box of his truck. He threw open the door and stalked out. With a bang, the door slammed shut behind him.

* * *

Ernie sat silent, puzzling on Lee's outburst.

Jim and Billy turned their attention back to the TV.

"Now, the San Vicente graveyard is where Anne Meadows and Daniel Buck, the amateur archeologists, thought they'd unearthed the body of Sundance," the commentator said.

"You've done your homework. They found a body that seemed to match Sundance. Unfortunately, DNA proved it was instead a German miner named Zimmer," the archeologist explained.

"*So there is no concrete evidence that the robbers who died in San Vicente were actually Butch and Sundance?*"

The archeologist smiled. "You think maybe they didn't die down there?"

Ernie heard the front door open and quietly close, but paid it little attention.

"*Well,*" *the commentator said, "there was that interview with Butch's sister in the 1960s. She said Butch came to visit her years after he had supposedly been killed.*"

"*An old lady might say anything for a little attention. Believe me, Butch and Sundance died in....*"

An explosion shook the tavern. The television shattered.

In the close confines of the bar, the discharge of a Colt .45 revolver was deafening. Everyone, including Ernie dove for the floor. Looking up, he couldn't believe his eyes. With his ears still ringing, he stared incredulously at old Lee Kidwell holding a gun and standing in the middle of the room amid a cloud of billowing blue gun smoke.

Bob, looking every bit like a middle linebacker on a blitz, jumped over the bar and tackled the old man. Both men hit the floor hard. The gun in Lee's hand popped free and skittered across the hardwood floor and out of sight.

Later, after things cooled down, the patrons began talking quietly while waiting for the police. All eyes were on Lee who'd taken a seat off by himself.

Cautiously, Ernie went over and sat with his friend. Neither spoke.

Ernie was staring out the window when the first squad car wailed into the parking lot. He watched as two officers cautiously approached the bar. The large cop in the lead paused at the door to unsnap the holster strap that secured his weapon.

As the sheriff stepped inside Sooners Bar, his six-foot-four, two-hundred-forty-pound frame filled the door. Some eight inches shorter, his pipe-cleaner thin deputy followed. After a word with the bartender, they cautiously approached the table where Ernie sat with Lee.

Several minutes later, Ernie watched through the window as Lee was led to the squad car in handcuffs. Two more police cars with four deputies arrived.

Ernie could just make out the words as the sheriff addressed them. "This old boy doesn't seem like much of a desperado to me, but I want a complete report on what happened. They said he fired a gun. Didn't see it, so find it."

Once in the tavern, three of the officers took statements while the fourth clicked on his flashlight and searched the dimly-lit bar for the gun. As he searched, he addressed the patrons without looking in their direction. "Anyone know where the gun went?"

Bob spoke up. "I tackled him and it went flyin'."

"Anyone pick it up?" This time the deputy looked pointedly at each of the people in the bar. In turn they shook their heads no.

"Old man's crazy. Went postal over a documentary about Butch Cassidy and The Sundance Kid," Jim blurted out.

The officer searching for the gun leaned over to look at something under the jukebox. "There's something here." Using a pen he prodded and poked until he was able to extract and lift Lee's gun.

Holding the antique revolver by the trigger guard with his pen, the deputy stepped over into the light of the window to examine it. He was near enough for Ernie to see the old weapon quite clearly. There was a puzzling carving on the handle. "SUNDANCE" was engraved in neat clear letters on one side of the walnut grip.

* * *

Outside, Sheriff Barton Shepard, already planted behind the wheel of his cruiser, waited for Deputy Enid Phelps to settle into the shotgun seat. Then he put the car in gear and sped away.

Lee sat in back behind a steel screen. Glancing over his shoulder, the sheriff was puzzled and a little concerned by the blank look on old Lee's face.

"They told me your name is Lee. That right?" The sheriff threw the question over his shoulder at his prisoner.

* * *

Lee could faintly hear someone calling his name but he was floating back in time. Back to when he was thirteen, a time when he lived with his family on a ranch not far from here.

Somewhere in what seemed like a different place Lee could hear someone speaking. "Haven't I seen you around, Lee? Hey, I'm talking to you."

But Lee couldn't make sense of it. He was drifting away to another place and another time.

13

There it was again. "I'm talking to you, Lee. You hear me? Hey, Lee... Lee?"

Chapter 2

THE KIDWELLS
Oklahoma 1921

~ ~ ~

"Lee! Lee, get up! Lee! Breakfast is ready."

Lee drifted up from inside a foggy place of sleep and dreams. He could hear his name being called but it sounded so far away. As he awoke, he realized he'd been deep asleep and, for a minute, the voice was a part of the dream. He opened his bleary eyes knowing his mother's voice had been calling him from the bottom of the stairs. What had he been dreaming?

The shiny new pocket watch on the nightstand caught Lee's eye. His dad had recently given it to him for his thirteenth birthday. It was silver with a twelve-inch chain. Lee's most prized possession, he carried it everywhere. He reached over, grabbed the watch and clicked it open: 7:00. He'd overslept.

Usually Lee awoke at 6:00 a.m., and before breakfast he'd help with the morning chores. This morning his mother was calling him from downstairs and breakfast was probably already on the table. He wondered why he had overslept on this particular day. Yesterday his father had told him that today was going to be a big day.

"What's so big about tomorrow, Pa?" he'd asked.

"I'll let you know in the morning," his father had replied with a wink. "But be ready to work up a sweat over the next two or three days."

Quickly, Lee lifted his lanky legs over the edge of the bed and placed his bare feet on the cool wooden floor. With a sigh, he stood, crossed over to his bedroom door and yelled down, "Sorry, Ma, I'm up."

* * *

Lee's mother, Etta Kidwell, turned from the foot of the stairs and headed to the kitchen of their modest two-story wood frame house.

Laura, Lee's nine-year-old sister, was busy pouring hot coffee into three cups and cool milk into two glasses. She struggled first with the weight of the coffee pot and then with that of the pitcher. A minute later, Laura managed to complete the job without spilling a drop.

On the wood-burning stove, Etta had eggs, bacon, and hash brown potatoes waiting on a warming plate. From the oven came the unmistakable aroma of hot biscuits.

Etta had been up since 6:00 a.m. cooking. Any minute now her husband, Harry, would finish the early chores and head in for their morning meal.

Etta glanced at the food on the stove to make sure it wasn't burning. She watched for a second with pride as her daughter did her part to get breakfast ready.

Etta and Harry prided themselves on the fact that they seldom had to ask their children to pitch in with the chores. She smiled at the thought of Lee sleeping past his chance to help Harry with the morning work. Wiping her hands on her apron, Etta walked briskly through the kitchen before pushing open the door to the back porch.

She shielded her eyes from the early dawn sun and gazed across the barnyard. In the morning light, dew sparkled like diamonds on the yellow-green grass. Squinting into the glare of the sun, Etta saw Harry leave the barn and head her way. For a second she looked past her approaching husband toward a shed that was attached to the barn. Clarence, their hired hand, bunked in the shed. After helping Harry with the morning chores, he would probably be cleaning up before breakfast.

Etta called out, "Clarence! Breakfast is on!"

Harry stepped through the back gate and into the back yard. In his mid-fifties, Harry walked with the bearing and gait of a man twenty years younger.

"He'll be comin' directly," he said.

* * *

Harry Kidwell stopped at the porch steps and removed his brown fedora to smooth and straighten his thinning and mostly silver-grey hair. He smiled and looked up at his wife. There were small wrinkles around her pretty hazel eyes and at the corners of her mouth. The years of ranch life were taking their toll.

But, even at the age of forty-five, Etta Kidwell still shined with an uncommon beauty.

Stepping onto the porch, Harry used his hat to slap the morning's dust off his faded Levis and blue cotton shirt. Bending down, he pushed Etta's partially-graying hair away from her eyes and kissed her on the forehead.

With the hint of a smile, Etta playfully pushed him away. Harry winked at her and used his fingers to smooth his distinctive mustache. He'd sported it since he was a young man and now, pure silver, it contrasted strongly against his darkly-tanned face.

Over the last several years, the Oklahoma sun had etched deep lines in Harry's forehead and around his eyes, but he was proud that he had avoided the barrel that most men his age tended to develop around their waist.

Harry put his arm around Etta and opened the door to the house. Over his shoulder he saw the door to the shed open and a dark hulking figure stepped into view.

Clarence had hired on with Harry one summer, eleven years earlier. Since then he'd been a loyal and hard working ranch hand.

During the first fall, Harry and his new hired hand labored to attach a fine sturdy bunkhouse to the barn. It became a personal residence for Clarence.

The next year, Harry ordered a goose-feather mattress for Clarence through a Sears & Roebuck catalog. He still remembered the warm feeling that had washed over him when he presented the big man with the gift.

"Ain't never had no real store-bought mattress, 'afore, Harry," Clarence muttered as he'd gazed at his new possession.

* * *

Clarence Bell stood in front of his shed for a second looking at the clear blue Oklahoma sky. With a smile wide across his lips, he headed for the Kidwell house and the breakfast that awaited him. Mounting the back steps, he took a deep breath and smelled the pleasant aromas wafting through the screen door. The wood planks creaked under his weight as he walked across the porch. Clarence had always been built like an oak tree and, even at the age of sixty, felt little diminished in strength and vitality.

The big man gave the door a gentle rap before pulling it open and entering the kitchen. Lifting his nose, he sniffed the air again. "Somebody been cookin' up a mighty fine breakfast," he said.

Etta placed the last platter of food on the table and looked with a wry smile at their hired hand. "You say the same thing every morning, Clarence. I swear if I served pig slop for breakfast you'd still manage to complement it in some fashion."

"If you cooked it Mz Etta, I imagine it'd taste like baked sweet taders."

Etta flashed her special endearing smile to him.

Clarence cherished every sign of affection from her because he had a special place in his heart for Etta Kidwell. From the beginning, she'd looked after him with a kindness he'd not experienced since he was a young man.

"Have any laundry today, Clarence?"

"No, Mz Etta. Don't need none washed today."

"Don't need *any*," Etta corrected.

"Right. Don't need any, Mz Etta," Clarence corrected himself.

A small smile touched his lips. Etta did have one habit that mildly vexed him. She frequently corrected his manor of speech. He had to admit that he'd learned a good deal because of it. So, even though it was a bit irritating, he never could quite decide how he felt about the practice. At one time she'd offered to teach him how to read as well, but he declared that the effort would be a waste. "Cain't teach an old hound how t' hunt."

Standing by the table, Harry gave Clarence a wink. When Etta and Laura took their seats, he and Clarence took theirs. The oak chair gave a groan under Clarence as he settled himself at the table.

Looking around, Clarence asked, "Where's Lee?"

"Overslept," Etta answered.

At that moment footsteps could be heard flying down the stairs.

Chapter 3

OMINOUS NEWS

~ ~ ~

Still buttoning his shirt, Lee rushed into the kitchen, greeted everyone, and sat down.

As he settled into his chair, Laura gave him a mocking smile. "You overslept."

Lee flashed her a stern look. Sometimes little sisters could be a royal pain. He ignored her comment and looked at his dad. "Sorry, Pa, I don't know what happened this morning. I just..."

Harry gave his son a critical eye. "I'll let you make up for it, son. We have some fencin' to do."

So this is what his father had been talking about yesterday. Putting in fence was hard work. Hardwood posts had to be laid out along the fence line at intervals of ten to twelve feet. Holes would need to be dug, using a hand auger, to a depth of about two-and-a-half-feet. Six-foot long posts would be sunk in the holes. Dirt would then be shoveled in around them and tamped into place with a tamping stick. Finally, barbed wire would be attached to the posts.

Lee knew he would be more than a little tired before these next few days were done.

"I want the posts loaded and laid out along the line by noon," his father added.

Clarence spoke up between bites without taking his eyes from his plate of food. "Loaded most of them posts last night, Harry, 'afore I went to bed. Least ways, all I could get on the wagon."

Lee glanced over at Clarence, who often saw things that needed to be done and did them without waiting to be asked.

Harry smiled. "Might'a guessed that. I recon a couple of us just need to start dropping those posts off along the new fence line while *someone* gets busy diggin' holes."

When Harry turned to look at Lee, Clarence started to chuckle.

Lee shook his head. "Guess I've been volunteered. Teach me to get up late."

Etta and Laura were clearing the table when Laura happened to glance out the kitchen window. "Pa, rider comin'. Looks like Mr. Bevan."

* * *

Harry stood and looked over his daughter's shoulder.

Alva Bevan was a neighbor. Over the years he had become the unofficial harbinger of news for the county. He made it his duty to inform his neighbors of any and all news that would be relevant to their lives.

Alva rapped gently on the kitchen door. "Mornin' folks," he said as Etta motioned him inside.

Harry had grown to like Alva in spite of the fact that, as a young man, Alva had spent a short time as a sheriff's deputy in Missouri. At the turn of the century, when he was twenty-four, he moved from Missouri to Oklahoma, married a local woman and raised a family.

"Like some breakfast, Alva?" Etta asked.

"Kind o' ya ta ask, Miss Etta, but I already had mine, in there."

Alva had acquired a peculiar habit of ending most sentences with the phrase, "in there." No one knew just why. Some figured it was his way of making what he said seem important. Harry figured it was just a nervous habit.

"Well, sit down and have a cup of coffee then." Etta grabbed a cup from the cupboard.

"What's on your mind, Alva," Harry asked as his friend pulled up a chair.

"Guess you know that the city lawyer from Brooks Oil is still pressurin' people to sell their ranches."

Harry glanced uneasily at his son and daughter before he nodded. "He hasn't had much luck, I understand."

"Not at them prices." Alva took the hot cup from Etta and sipped. "Anyhow, now they brought in some rough lookin' men totin' side arms, in there. They been showin' up at the ranches that turned down the lawyer guy, in there."

"Heard some about that, too."

"Harry, the other day over to Gil Jackson's place, the leader o' the bunch unholstered his gun to make a point. Didn't shoot it, but. . .anyhow, you know how Jackson can get. He told 'em what they could do with their offer."

Again Harry glanced over at his kids. "I recon it might be best if we were to talk on this later Alva."

Alva seemed to miss the hint. "Head guy said he might just drop by again sometime. Could be bad, Harry."

Harry gave Alva a meaningful stare and his friend seemed to finally get the hint. "Maybe *could* keep, Harry. Just didn't know if you'd heard." He shook his head. "They got some o' the folk a bit nervous, in there."

Alva took a final swallow of coffee and stood up.

* * *

Once Alva had left, Lee looked at his father, not sure if he could be the only one to grasp the significance of this news. "Something needs to be done about this, Pa. We can't let these people come in here and push us around."

Lee saw his father glance once again at his young and impressionable daughter. "This isn't our concern, son."

"Pa, they'll be after our land next. *Then* it'll be our concern."

"That's enough, Lee. This isn't your business. Now, unless you want to be helping your sister and Ma do dishes, you best head directly outside and get the diggin' tools onto the wagon. That's what your business is today."

Lee choked back the comment that was itching to burst from his mouth. This attitude was typical of his father. Ever since he was old enough to think for himself, Lee had a growing suspicion about his dad. It started as a seed and it had grown. Small things fused together; things to which some would pay little attention, but to Lee they just seemed to add up to one conclusion.

First there was the gun thing. This was a ranch for Christ's sake. Ranchers needed to have a gun. Every rancher that Lee knew owned a firearm. But his father would have nothing to do with them, nor would he allow Lee to have one either. If it wasn't for the old .32 pistol that Clarence had, there would not be one single gun on the whole ranch.

Then there was the way his father always avoided confrontation. On many occasions his father had walked away from what Lee felt would have been a righteous fight.

Lee was especially rankled by an incident at the town picnic. A rancher named Cottrel had made a lewd comment about Lee's mother. He'd followed it up with an insult leveled at Harry. Lee could see his father's face burn red with anger. Still, Harry had gathered up his family and left. To Lee, this was another example of his timidity.

Surely, his dad could see that the oilman, Brooks, wanted all the land in the territory, including their ranch. Someone needed to stand up to that man, but Lee was convinced that it wasn't going to be his father.

Lee left the kitchen table and walked outside. Clarence stepped through the kitchen door right behind him. Together they headed for the barn to hitch up the wagon.

"Pa just don't understand, Clarence. Things are gettin' rough and somethin' bad's going to happen. I can jist feel it."

Clarence hoped Lee was wrong, but he too sensed something in the wind. The Kidwells had become his family and he would stand by them no matter what kind of trouble was blowing their way. After all, before he met Harry and his family, Clarence's life had been anything but ideal.

Chapter 4

CLARENCE

~ ~ ~

In 1861, Clarence Bell was born in Georgia technically making him, for a brief time, a slave. His mother, a young beauty named Ruby Bell, was fifteen when she gave birth to him. It was rumored that her master sired Clarence.

Not sure who his father was, Clarence was given his mother's last name. It was a name that she had chosen for herself when she was only ten. Clarence had once asked her how she'd come upon the name Bell. She'd looked at him with a wide smile and said, "Well, chil', it jist seemed to have a nice ring to it."

The Civil War ended when Clarence was only four years old. He could remember his mother's excitement and joy as she lifted him in the air and screamed, "You're gonna be free, chil'. We all gonna be free."

Of course, to four-year-old Clarence, this meant very little. But as he grew older, it all became ironically clear: he was no longer going to be anyone's property. Still, he would be slave to a life of poverty and hatred.

These thoughts did not often occupy his mind, though, as he toiled and sweated away the days in the cotton fields. Since the age of eight he'd been working. His share of the money went to his mother to help provide for them both. But as he reached a more mature age, he'd begun to struggle with the idea that perhaps he should keep a small portion for himself.

This is what Clarence was thinking one night as he sat across the dinner table from his mother in their small, shabby cabin. He set aside his spoon, pushed away his plate and shifted uncomfortably before clearing his throat.

His mother looked up at him. "What? What you thinkin', boy? You been chewin' somethin' in that mind o' your'n fer a week or more. So, jist out with it."

The nervous boy rubbed his chin with his thick meaty hand but could not look his mother directly in the eye. "Met a girl," he mumbled.

"What? You what?" The question came with the hint of a smile.

Clarence looked up from his shirt and met his mother's eyes. "Name's Rosa."

"When you have time to meet a girl? You work from dark to dark, same as me."

Clarence's eyes found his shirtfront again. "Ain't actually talked to her yet, Ma. Seen her at church on Sundays. She smiled a bit at me."

Ruby gazed at her son. "Rosa? That the little pint of a girl what always wears the blue ribbon in her hair?"

Clarence nodded.

"You'd make a strange couple, son. That girl would jist about fit in yer pocket."

A smile and a glint in his eyes lit Clarence's face.

"Clarence, you want I should talk to Rosa's ma?"

Shyly, Clarence looked up at his mother and nodded.

A year later, Clarence and Rosa were married. Clarence, though looking a good deal older, was just seventeen and his bride was the ripe old age of fifteen.

Clarence Jr. was born in 1879. A year later came Jeremiah.

It was a bittersweet life. Clarence worked long, hard hours to bring home just enough to get his family by. Rosa did the housework and looked after the boys. She also did laundry for several of the affluent white families.

No matter how tired he was, Clarence always entered the cabin at night with a smile and good word for his bride and sons.

After dinner, they would routinely settle in front of the fireplace and Rosa would read from the "Good Book." The Bible was a wedding gift from the people of their church. She and Clarence treasured it beyond any of their other possessions. Clarence couldn't read, but even if he could he'd have preferred to sit and listen to Rosa's soft, lilting voice.

Both boys were strong and healthy. When the influenza epidemic spread death though the area in 1887, neither boy was stricken. Not so with their mother. Rosa contracted the illness and lay delirious with fever for three days.

Almost every minute of that time, Clarence sat at her side. With a damp cloth he mopped her brow, trying to cool her fever.

"You gotta get better, Rosa. You gotta get well. Don' leave me, girl. I don' know how I can go on if'n you was to leave me."

It was the middle of the night and Clarence was holding her hand but fast asleep when she slipped out of his life. It was the coolness of her skin that finally woke him.

* * *

In 1891 Clarence married a woman named Cecelia. He needed someone to help him raise the boys and Cecelia reminded him a little of Rosa. But soon he realized that her looks were the only resemblance Cecelia had to his former wife.

A year after their marriage, Maggie was born and shortly thereafter, Cecelia's temperament took an ominous turn. It was almost impossible now for Clarence to enter the cabin at night with a smile. He was often greeted with scorn as soon as he opened the door.

"How I 'posed to get by on what money you earn? You spect me to look after them two brats o' yourn and take care of my baby, too?" Cecelia wailed on one typical night.

Clarence slumped down in his chair. "The boys do their chores. I leave word fer 'em to help you around here, too."

"Some help they is. I gotta do over most o' what they do. Them boys is worthless and you ain't much better."

Clarence looked at his wife and wondered how he'd so poorly judged her character when they were courting. Then he looked over at his daughter as she lay in the crib he'd fashioned for her. She was as sweet and mild-tempered as Cecelia was hateful and mean.

Over the next four years, as Maggie grew older, she became the honey that sweetened the sourness lingering in their small cabin.

Clarence's boys loved Maggie too, but the hatred that Cecelia bore toward them was more than they could stand.

Clarence Jr. sat down with his father one evening. "We been talking, Pa, Jeremiah an' me." He looked down at his shoe and rubbed the edge of the sole nervously on the floor.

"Speak yer mind, boy." Clarence suspected what was coming.

Clarence Jr. took a breath. "We gonna leave soon. We figure it's time to go."

"Where you gonna go? You neither one much more'n outa yer knee britches."

"We figure on joinin' up with the army. Goin' out West."

"Army? Thought you might be wantin' to head out on yer own, but can't say I 'spected the Army."

"Might find some adventures out West," Jr. said.

"Might find more than you want. It ain't easy out there for young boys like the two o' you.

"We don' wanna leave, Pa." Jeremiah had wandered over and taken his place beside his older brother. His eyes welled up as he spoke. "But we jist can't live here no more."

A year later, Clarence got a letter from them. Unable to read it himself, he held it for a week before he finally broke down and asked Cecelia to read it to him.

"They joined up with the Army, all right. Says here they joined a unit they call 'buffalo soldiers'. Now what the hell kinda name is that? I be tellin' ya, Clarence, them boys cain't hardly wipe they own ass. How they gonna keep themselves from gittin' kilt?"

Clarence gritted his teeth and said nothing. He knew she was just trying to rub salt. The Indian wars were all but over, and it didn't seem likely that the boys would get into any kind of trouble that could get them killed. So he just stood up and went out into the cool night to let the burning around his ears blow away with the summer breeze.

Clarence didn't hear from his boys for two more years. Then one day a letter arrived. But, it came from a Lieutenant Foster.

"Tode you," Cecelia said when Clarence finally asked her to read it. "They went to Cuba with them 'buff lo soldiers. They was in that Spanish War down there. They both dead."

Clarence had been standing near the fireplace and Cecelia's words felt like a gunshot to his heart. He crumpled into his chair. Anger and hatred for the callousness of his wife was smothered by his grief.

Maybe, as the shock wore away, rage would have welled up and he might have taken action that he'd have later regretted. But Maggie intervened.

Maggie had no idea that her mother had fueled the pain that she saw in her father's eyes. She only knew that he was in agony and she went to him. "Don' cry, Poppy. It be okay," she said as she got up into his lap and hugged his neck. The anger melted away but the pain would stay with Clarence for the rest of his life.

* * *

Clarence was working the day that the photographer showed up. The young man knocked lightly and straightened his store-bought suit. When Cecelia opened the cabin door, he gave her a broad smile. "How do, Miss? Name's Johnson. I do portraits," he looked her up and down. "Is the man o' the house to home?"

Cecelia gazed for a moment at the good-looking young fellow and smiled coyly. "He be workin'."

Johnson's smile widened. "I specialize in portraits of beautiful ladies like yo' self."

Cecelia had seen a few photographic portraits hanging in the home of the white people where one of her friends worked as a maid. However, she'd never heard of a black man doing portraits for black people. That intrigued her, but it wasn't the only thing that motivated Cecelia to welcome the man into their cabin.

"Would you like some coffee, Mr. Johnson?" Cecelia cooed.

When Clarence came home that night he was greeted by a much different Cecelia. She sweetly bid him to sit in his chair by the fire as she tenderly rubbed his back. It didn't take her long to put forth her request.

"It ain't much money, Clarence. He charge less'n half what the white picture-takers do."

"What we gonna do with no photo-graph, Cecelia?"

Cecelia had been expecting resistance. Still, she wanted that photograph, if for no other reason than to keep Mr. Johnson coming around. And she had an ace up her sleeve. "Don' you wan' a picture o' Maggie?"

Clarence set aside a penny each day, and in time, he had enough to pay for a seven-inch portrait of Cecelia and his beloved daughter.

As Clarence toiled, Cecelia did not stay idol. She worked her charms on Mr. Johnson and by the time the portrait was taken, she'd managed to capture his heart or, at the very least, an organ located a bit lower on his anatomy.

* * *

The day after the portrait was completed, Clarence came home to find the only remnant of his wife and daughter to be the photograph. In her haste to vacate the premises with Mr. Johnson, Cecelia had gathered up her belongings and ten-year-old Maggie, but had forgotten the photo.

A week later, when Cecelia hadn't returned, Clarence took the only two things that were of any value to him and went looking for his wife and daughter. With the photograph of Maggie tucked firmly in his bible, Clarence wandered though the South...searching.

It was a tough life for a man of color. On several occasions he narrowly escaped the wrath of vengeful whites that still resented the freedom granted to the Negroes after the Civil War.

After several years of searching, he realized that it was unlikely he would ever see Cecelia or his daughter again. Still, he never stopped thinking of Maggie and wondering what had become of her.

When he met Harry Kidwell, things began to change for Clarence. He'd seen Harry harvesting a crop of wheat in a field that bordered the road. Clarence asked if he could work for a meal. Eleven years later, he was still working for him.

Chapter 5

THE FENCE

~ ~ ~

Under a crystal blue Oklahoma sky, Harry drove his horse-drawn wagon along what would be the new fence line. Standing in the back, Clarence periodically unloaded fence posts, one at a time. Each wooden post landed with a thump, stirring up a small puff of dust that was gently whisked away with the morning breeze.

About halfway through the load, Clarence tossed a post that thumped down on the hard earth and came to rest in a particularly thick patch of weeds. There was a rustling and ominous movement in the grass that went unnoticed by the men in the wagon.

* * *

Lee took a final turn of a wooden-handled auger. Sweat dripping from his chin and nose dropped into the hole he was digging, where it splattered onto the steel head of the auger. The muscles of his arms tensed as he pulled the tool from the ground and thumped its head down on the pile of dirt he'd already excavated. Red, moist soil broke free from the auger and spilled over the mound.

Lee gazed back along the fencerow at the posts he'd already planted. Arching his back, he stretched his gangly limbs, took a long deep breath, and sat down. This was Lee's fourth post and he felt he deserved a minute's rest.

That's when he heard the unmistakable putter of his father's truck approaching.

Damn. He didn't want his dad and Clarence to think he was shirking.

The truck crested the hill before he could stand up. Quickly, he retrieved a post from where it had been dumped earlier in the day.

After unloading their posts, Harry and Clarence had driven the empty wagon to the barn to get Harry's truck. A 1915 Model T Ford Pickup, it was the first and only vehicle that Lee's father had owned. It had an open cab with doors but no glass windows, only a flat glass windshield. The truck had a cloth top that Harry kept on the cab year-round.

From the corner of his eye, Lee watched Harry and Clarence as they stepped from the truck amid a cloud of dust.

Clarence ambled in his direction. The big black man was wearing his usual straw hat covering most of his wooly white hair. The hat had a wide brim that slumped down in the front to cast a shadow over the upper half of his face. There was a smile on his lips.

Stuck in the waistband of his grey cotton trousers was the old Smith & Wesson revolver that Lee had counted as the only gun on the ranch. Clarence always carried the revolver when they worked in the field and Lee admired him for that, even though the .32 did look rather small when stuck in the belt of such a big man.

In Lee's mind, carrying a gun was what a man on a ranch should do. This was often a subject of conversation among the boys at his school. It embarrassed Lee that he had to admit to the other kids that his father didn't own any firearms.

Harry took a few minutes to check the posts that Lee had already set. With an almost imperceptible nod, he walked back to join the boy and Clarence.

"How you holdin' up, son?"

"Fair enough, Pa. Hit some pretty big rocks in that hole over there, but got through 'em."

"Take a break."

"Ain't tired, Pa. Don't need a break."

"Up to you, but at least get a cool drink from the water jug in the truck."

Lee stepped over to the truck while Clarence grabbed the auger and started to work on the next hole. Harry kicked some dirt into the hole around the post Lee had just planted and began to tamp it. As they worked, not far away there was another ominous rustle in the deep dry grass.

* * *

When the sun rose to mid-day, Harry paused from his work to gaze off across the field.

Right on time he saw Etta riding their way. One hand expertly handled her mount while the other carried a basket lunch for the men.

A short time later, she sat on a blanket with the men while they talked and ate. When they were finished, Etta stood and motioned Harry off to the side.

"Have some sad news, Harry." Etta spoke quietly so as not be overheard by Lee. "Alva sent Slim Moore by a short time ago to tell us. Millie Jackson found Gilbert dead in their barn last night. When he didn't come in for supper, she went looking for him. Looks like he slipped and fell from the loft and broke his neck."

Harry took a moment to absorb the news. "Gilbert wasn't a careless man. Not likely he'd slip and fall from his own barn like that. I was afraid of something like this. Looks to me like that Wilson fella made good on his threat to pay Gil another visit." Harry looked over at Lee and Clarence. "Let's keep it a secret between us for now. No reason to upset everyone. We'll talk on it tonight.

* * *

As the afternoon wore on, Lee proceeded to goad Clarence into stepping up the pace. Clarence knew it was a game Lee liked to play with his dad, each trying to one-up the other. Soon he and Lee were digging several holes ahead of where Harry was setting posts.

A short time later, with his shirt soaked with sweat and plastered to his large frame, Clarence reached into his front pocket for a flat, brown, unmarked whiskey bottle. On occasion, when he thought Harry wasn't looking, Clarence pulled it out and took a sip. He drank so sparingly that usually the same bottle would last him a week or more.

Clarence had never seen Harry take strong drink. He'd once confided to Alva that he didn't think Harry approved of hard liquor.

As was his custom when Lee was around, Clarence made his usual off-handed remark. "Powerful dry work. Think I best drink some o'my condensated water." Clarence smacked his lips as he carefully twisted the cork free of the bottle.

Lee shook his head. "Don't you think it's about time you changed your story? I may o' bought that hog wash when I was a kid, but I'm smart enough now to know there ain't no such a thing as condensated water."

Clarence looked at Lee with surprise.

"Don't look so shocked. I know you thought I always swallowed that story like a slick oyster. Go ahead, take a slug of whiskey, if you want."

"Don't believe I will," Clarence said. "You went an' took the pleasure out'n it."

Clarence placed the cork back in the bottle and gave it a decisive whack with his palm.

* * *

Toward evening Harry had fallen far behind Clarence and Lee. The boy sauntered over to his father.

"Looks like you're laggin'' behind a might, Pa. Must be your old age. Guess I best be helpin' you out or else you might be still plantin' posts in the middle of the night."

Harry looked up to see his son smiling with a canary-eating grin. Straightening up slowly, Harry looked as though he was put off by the insult.

"Okay, smart guy, go grab that post over there. A man of my advanced age doesn't need to be hauling a big old heavy post around."

The post Harry had been referring to was the one that had come to rest in the tall grass. Nearly hidden, Lee had to search with his eyes for a second to spot it. Still smiling, he ventured into that tall grass to retrieve the partially-hidden post. A rustle in the grass froze the smile on his face.

The snake was coiled in the grass no more than a couple of feet from Lee's left boot. Its rattle vibrated with a loud sickening sizzle, almost like the sound of bacon frying.

Lee knew that, depending on their size, rattlesnakes were deadly. This diamondback was not small by any means. Measuring about five feet in length, it looked to Lee like the mother of all snakes. He also knew that rattlers are very defensive. With its head rising a few inches above its coiled body, this one was poised to strike.

Lee stood as if planted like one of his fence posts. Easily within striking distance of the serpent, he was too afraid to back up. He wanted to call for help but his throat was dry and choked with fear. He had seen a number of rattlesnakes in his lifetime, but never so close and so sudden. Lee needed help but he couldn't get the words to come out.

* * *

Even at fifteen feet away, Harry heard the rattle and saw his son freeze. In a split second, Harry's right hand moved toward his hip. He realized that his instincts had made his hand reach for something that, in fact was not there. Quickly he grabbed his tamping stick, the only thing available to use as a weapon, and moved toward his son.

Lee's raspy voice finally whispered, "Help me, Pa. Hel...help me!"

"Stay calm, Son. No sudden moves," Harry cautioned as he crept slowly toward the boy. When he got within five feet of Lee, the snake stepped up the tempo of its rattle. Harry stopped. He was not close enough to reach the snake with his stick.

"Pa, you gotta do something! Please, Pa!"

* * *

Clarence had taken a turn on the auger, but paused to remove his hat and wipe his sweaty brow with his already damp sleeve. It was then that he noticed Lee standing as stiff as a Fredrick Remington statue. He watched as Harry moved cautiously closer to the boy and then he watched as Harry stopped dead in his tracks. That was when Harry turned to look desperately in his direction.

"Rattler, Clarence!

The big man grabbed his little gun, threw down his straw hat, and covered the distance between them quicker than anyone could have expected from a man his age and size.

When Clarence closed within seven feet he slowed to a stop. Moving like a stalking panther, he crept to Harry's side.

"Pa...Pa. Do somethin', Pa!" Lee pleaded.

Clarence lifted his gun while Harry tried to calm his boy. "It's going to be ok, Son. Stay still. Clarence, go for the head. Take your time."

As Clarence sighted down the barrel of the .32, he was wishing he had practiced with the weapon more. He'd fired it once, at the time of its purchase, and once to make sure he could come close to hitting what he might aim at. The ammunition was so costly, he'd never fired it again.

Sweat beaded Clarence's forehead and dripped from his chin. Tension and apprehension covered his face like a frozen mask as he focused on the head of the snake coiled in the grass a few feet away. Somehow he managed to hold steady as he pulled the trigger. The gun let out a deafening bark as it jumped in his hand.

Snakes have several acute senses, but hearing is not one of them. So, when the bullet passed within inches of the snake, it didn't know it had been the object of a failed attempt to separate its head from its body.

* * *

Harry had known that it was going to be a difficult shot, but he'd hoped Clarence would get lucky. Seeing Clarence pull the trigger, he realized that his friend was not as familiar with firearms as he had hoped. Harry wrestled with the idea of asking Clarence to let him take the next shot, but Clarence had already cocked the gun and was taking aim again.

"Try squeezing the trigger a little slower, Clarence." The words came from Harry like a quiet breeze.

Clarence nodded and slowly squeezed the trigger a second time. The retort and the kick were the same as the first time, but the result was different. When the gun spoke this time, the bullet hit the head of the snake and it exploded like someone had put a firecracker in its mouth and lit it. The reptile had been raised up and ready to strike. When its head exploded, the rattler dropped like a sock full of sand.

Lee sank back and collapsed on his butt in the tall grass. A dark stain had formed on his trousers around his groin. He looked down at it and then at his father.

Harry saw it, too, and his eyes locked for an instant with Lee's. He saw the embarrassment and shame written in his son's glassy eyes.

Stepping closer to the boy, Harry offered his hand to help him up. "It's all right, Son," he said. That was when he saw the look in Lee's eyes change to anger and then contempt. Lee ignored Harry's hand and hoisted himself to his feet. Without a word, and with tears in his eyes, he stalked off.

Harry took a few steps to follow his son, but Clarence stayed him with a touch to his arm. Without a word between them Harry knew that Clarence was right. He should let the boy be.

Lee stopped some distance away from his father and Clarence. With his back to them, Lee steadied himself on one of the posts he had set in the ground only a couple of hours before.

The silence was broken as the bell began to clang. Etta was calling supper. Every evening at suppertime, Etta stepped out of the house and down the porch steps to ring the bell hanging on a post in the back yard. Weighing about twenty-five pounds, it was rusty with age and gave off a clang that could be heard for miles. When the bell tolled, no matter where her men were located on the ranch, they could hear it.

Today it was more than a call to supper. It was an important diversion that gave relief.

Harry and Clarence began putting their tools in the bed of the truck. Wiping his eyes quickly on his shirtsleeve, Lee walked toward the Model T. Harry could see he was doing his best to walk naturally in spite of the cold dampness that had to be chaffing against his inner thighs.

Since Harry's truck was not one of the newer versions of the Model T, it didn't have an electric starter. Harry had heard of the new invention and actually thought it was a bit silly.

In order for Harry to start his truck, he had to manually retard the spark and then use the hand crank at the front of the vehicle. There was always the chance that the engine might kick back, so Harry used an open hand to turn the crank. On the first turn the engine popped and chugged to life.

Easing himself behind the wheel, Harry could see his son heading their way. He knew Lee was embarrassed and probably angry. Still, the boy was doing his best to regain his composure. Harry waited for him to reach the truck, open the passenger door, and slip onto the seat beside him.

* * *

Clarence climbed into the back of the Model T and sat himself down in the bed of the truck. The big man usually gave the passenger seat to Lee and once had told Harry it was best that a boy sit beside his father.

So it was with a mildly-surprised look on his face that Clarence watched Lee walk past the passenger door and jump into the truck bed with him.

Inside the cab, Clarence saw Harry make an almost imperceptible shrug before engaging the gear of the truck. Then, using the lever on the steering column, Harry throttled up the engine. The truck jumped forward and began its bouncy journey toward the house.

Back in the truck bed, Lee gave Clarence a sideways glance and then turned his head away. For a few minutes, there was only the sound of the truck's engine and the wheels rolling over the dirt and grass.

Clarence was the first to break their silence. "You got nothin' to be 'shamed of, boy."

Lee sat quietly then turned to Clarence and nodded toward his father up front in the cab. "He'd a had a gun, he wouldn't of had to count on you to save me, Clarence."

"Well, Lee, that may be, but you know your Pa ain't never had no use for guns."

Clarence could sense the anger and contempt as the boy replied. "That's because he's scared of 'em. Won't touch one and won't let me have one, neither. He just stood there, Clarence! He froze! I think he was more scared than me. If it hadn't been for you...he just ain't much. 'Fraid a guns and more than that. He just ain't much of a man, that's all."

"Whoa up there, boy. You're dancin' to the wrong tune with them words, Lee Kidwell. I knowed your Pa nigh on eleven year. He's a good man and the kind of fear you're talkin' about ain't in him. You'll see that someday, boy."

Clarence knew that Lee had heard his words, but the skeptical look in the boy's eyes said it all. Lee lowered his head and mumbled under his breath. "Still think he was afraid. Ain't much, that's all. Just ain't much."

Chapter 6

THE DIME NOVELS

~ ~ ~

The Model T bounced over the rough ground as it approached the Kidwell homestead. It entered the barnyard and came to a stop near the white fence running along the backside of the house.

It was Harry's plan to eventually surround the house and yard with that same fencing, but time and expense had limited his labor to just this one side.

The back door to the house opened and Etta stepped onto the porch. Wiping her hands on her light blue apron, she smiled a warm greeting.

Harry walked up to the porch while Lee and Clarence were jumping down from the truck bed.

Once on the porch, Harry suddenly stopped and took a long questioning look at the woman standing before him. Harry had pulled this stunt many times, but he knew that like most women, Etta never really tired of the attention. Before Harry spoke he took a quick look back at Clarence now reaching the steps.

"Who's this woman here, Clarence?"

Clarence had enjoyed a speaking part in this act before.

"Looks to me like it's your wife, Harry," he recited.

"Damn if I remember her being so all-fired pretty."

Etta couldn't quite repress a smile. She was about to give a witty retort when, without a word, Lee blew past them like an Oklahoma dust devil and charged up the steps. The heard-it-all-before smile vanished as a look of concern clouded her face. She looked questioningly at Harry.

After a second or two, Harry shrugged and gave Etta her usual hug. When he released her, she was still looking at him with a question in her eyes.

He sighed. "He'll be fine."

Having said that, Harry nodded, more to himself than anyone, and stepped into the kitchen. Over his shoulder he could see that Etta had shifted her attention to Clarence. Their hired hand gave an almost-imperceptible shake of his head before speaking. "There was a close shave with a rattler. Boy's upset, that's all."

A flicker of fright lit up Etta's face.

"He's okay," Clarence said soothingly. "Just a might shook up is all. My guess is, won't neither of 'em be wantin' to talk on it much fer a spell. Might be best to let it pass fer now."

* * *

In the kitchen, Harry turned to watch Laura as she busied herself at the stove. So intent was she on her task, she hadn't noticed him enter.

With the sound of the door closing, she looked around and a smile touched her lips.

"Hi, Pa"

"Hey, Polliwog. You been helping your Ma fix supper?"

"Paaa, I ain't no polliwog," she said, still smiling.

"No, I guess maybe you're not. Gittin' too big, I recon."

Laura nodded at Clarence as he and Etta entered the kitchen. Then she returned her attention to her father. "What's eatin' Lee, Pa? He stormed by a minute ago lookin' mighty upset."

The question from his daughter caused Harry to get another look from his wife. "He'll be fine, Etta."

Harry stepped over to the kitchen washbasin. Without looking back at Etta, he began pumping water from the well into a ceramic basin. When drained, the used water flowed into a tile that emptied into a nearby creek.

As yet, they didn't have running water in the house, but Harry had plans. What he really wanted to build was a water tower that could be filled by their windmill pumping fresh water from their well.

When Harry and Etta had first settled on the ranch, the well had taken Harry three weeks to dig by hand. Thinking back on those days, he wished that he'd had Clarence back then to help.

As he dried his hands, Harry looked again at his daughter who'd returned to her tasks at the stove. He watched her brush her long brown hair back from her face with one hand while working with the other.

"What ya workin' on, Sweetie?" He asked.

"Makin' mashed potatoes, Pa. Did them from the start by myself." she smiled with beaming pride.

Harry was certain that Laura had been a baby just yesterday. How did they grow up so quickly? He did a quick calculation and came up with the fact that she soon would be ten years old.

"Made them yourself? Well, if that's the case, I guess I may have to get on the outside of a *big* helping of those potatoes tonight," He said.

Laura beamed at her mother with a hint of pride and her mother smiled back.

* * *

Etta was aware that both of their kids had their challenging days. But all in all they were raising two very fine children. She shifted her gaze to the hallway beyond the kitchen. "Where'd your brother go when he came in, Laura?"

"Upstairs to his room, I guess."

Etta stepped into the hallway, stopped at the foot of the stairs, and called out, "Lee! Supper's on! Come on down!"

From upstairs she heard him call back in a glum voice. "Ain't hungry, Ma."

Etta was an educated woman and was in the habit of correcting her children when they used improper English. Actually, she had to do it considerably more often than should be necessary. It was mostly Harry and Clarence who set the bad example. Figuring this wasn't the best time to correct him, she mumbled, "Am not hungry, not ain't hungry."

So she could be heard, she said, "We fixed your favorite for supper: pot roast and mashed potatoes."

There was no answer. Etta turned and went back into the kitchen.

Harry and Clarence were standing behind their chairs, waiting for the women to put the food on the table and take their seats.

When Etta entered the kitchen, she gave Harry a meaningful look. No words were needed. Etta knew that Harry understood exactly what was required of him. He gave Etta a nod and headed for the stairway.

* * *

When Lee stormed into his room several minutes before, the first thing he did was to change his damp pants. As he dropped his Levi jeans on the floor, he felt the weight of his prized possession, the silver watch. He reached down and pulled the watch from his pocket and threw it on the bed. For a while he glared at it as though it were spoiled meat. Finally he snatched it off the bed and stuffed it in a dresser drawer. He no longer had a desire to carry the watch his father had given him.

His pitcher of water and bowl stood on his dresser and he sponged himself off before donning clean pants.

Plopping down on his bed, he reached under it to a box he kept stashed there. In the box were half-a-dozen or so dime novels. They were mostly stories of daring-do by infamous characters of the Old West. Billy the Kid, Jessie James, and John Wesley Hardin were his favorites. According the stories, Lee learned that these men knew how to handle a gun and they weren't afraid to use one. When things got tough, they shot their way out. These were men of action who shot with speed and acted with bravery. Maybe they broke the law now and then, but Lee read where they'd been driven to it by rough times and circumstances.

As he lay there, Lee heard the clomping of his father's footsteps mounting the wooden staircase. Listening to his father's approach, he couldn't help but compare the man's actions today to what one of his dime novel heroes would have done.

When his father knocked on the doorframe and stepped in, Lee couldn't bring himself to look at him.

* * *

Harry saw the stack of dime novels Lee had on his bed. He had never admonished his son for his choice of literature. He was glad that the boy was reading, even if the subject matter left a lot to be desired. Harry gave Lee a small allowance each month and this was how the boy sometimes chose to spend some of it.

Harry hesitated, searching for the right words. Finally, keeping his voice low and calm, he said to Lee, "You most mad at me or at yourself?"

After a pause, Lee looked up and glared at his father. "I could have been bit, Pa!"

"You weren't."

Quick as a snake strike, Lee grabbed one of the dime novels and held it out to his father. As he spoke, Harry could tell his son was choking back the anger from his voice. "Billy the Kid would'a shot that rattler's eye out in half a blink."

"Clarence did all right," Harry replied.

Tears formed in Lee's eyes, but he managed to keep them from running down his cheeks. He set the novel aside. "Pa, you didn't do nothin'. You had to call for Clarence. If it wasn't for him having a gun ..."

Lee pointed to the novel he'd just set down on his bed. "Nobody around here could hold a candle to one of these guys. *They* would have known how to handle things."

Harry gritted his teeth and the back of his neck turned red. Finally he spoke. "Not everything is as clear-cut as you might think, Lee. There is more at play here than you know and than I can tell you. I know that you're having doubts and concerns. You just need to trust me."

"I got eyes, Pa. I can see." Lee put his hand on the dime novels. "And I can read, too."

Harry waited as the redness slowly drained away from the back of his neck. "Son, you work hard here on the ranch. I value your contribution and that's why I give you a small wage every month. I don't tell you how to spend it. These here books are, I guess, a form of entertainment for you, so it's up to you if you want to buy them."

Lee was listening but he shifted uneasily on the edge of the bed. Harry could tell that the boy was aching to say something, but instead, his son just looked the other way and kept silent.

"Son, don't be putting store in what is written in dime novels. Most o' what you read there is lies and made-up stories. Those men weren't heroes. They were killers and thieves. In some cases, circumstances may have driven them to do what they did, but they made the choice to keep doing it and, in the end, they died because of it."

Lee snatched up the whole stack of magazines. "You don't know anything about these men. You don't know anything about what it is to be brave. You ..."

Harry looked at his son with deep sadness. A moment of uneasy silence filled the room before Harry spoke again. "Your Ma has supper ready."

"I ain't hungry," Lee said with his head bent low.

Harry could see that much of his son's anger and spite had melted away.

"Your mother and sister work hard to put meals on the table for us. You gonna make them feel small by refusin' to eat it?"

Lee took a second before speaking in a soft voice. "I'll be down in a minute."

* * *

Supper was quiet that evening. Lee had regained his appetite, but not his good spirits. He ate without looking up from the table or uttering a word. There was tension in the air. Laura kept looking at her parents. Harry smiled at her from time-to-time, but didn't speak.

It was up to Clarence to finally break the silence. "That t'were a powerful fine meal, ladies." And with a wink at Laura he added, "Best taters I ever et."

Laura shined.

Etta got up to start clearing the dishes and, with a smile still on her face, Laura started to help her.

Harry pushed back from the table, looked at Clarence and signaled him to follow as he headed out to the porch.

After Harry settled himself down on the porch steps, Clarence eased down beside him. Before he spoke, Harry looked over his shoulder to make sure the women were not in earshot. "Could I have a sip o' that 'condensated' water of yours, Clarence?"

The surprise on his friend's face caused the old rancher to smile. Clarence looked into Harry's eyes and cocked his head. With a wry grin, he pulled out the bottle and handed it over.

Harry twisted out the cork with a pop and took a long swig. Smacking his lips, he handed it back. Clarence grabbed the bottle with his powerful black hand, took a gulp, and then replaced the cork with a whack of his palm before shoving it back in his pocket.

In a quiet voice, Harry said, "Thanks, Clarence."

"Anytime, Harry. Didn't know you took strong drink or I'd o' offered you some 'afore now."

"I know you would of, but that's not what I meant. I meant thanks for what you did out there." Harry motioned toward the field where they'd run up against the snake.

"Not yo' fault, Harry. I know you don't have no use fer guns an' the like. Glad I was able to help." Then he stood. "Think I'll turn in. Night, Harry."

Harry watched as Clarence walked to his shed and, a second later, the flickering light of a lantern illuminated his window.

Harry went over to sit in the porch swing that, at Etta's bidding, he'd made six years before. A few minutes later Etta came out and joined him. They often sat in the swing during the evening hours. It was a quiet time for them, a time to just sit and talk.

"You finished the dishes pretty quick," Harry said.

Etta smiled. "Laura and Lee are doing them."

"Lee? Scrubbing dishes?"

"I think he's feeling a bit poorly about the way he acted earlier." Etta had a smile as she spoke, but then it was replaced with a more sober look. "Harry, I'm sorry about what happened out there today. Clarence told me some and I guess I can figure the rest. But it doesn't change anything. You know that, don't you? We agreed about the guns and how it was going to be."

"Doesn't make it any easier, Etta."

"I know," she said as she snuggled in closer to Harry and gave him a kiss on the cheek. A moment passed as they swayed gently back and forth, listening to the nighttime crickets chirping in harmony with the rhythmic squeaking of the swing.

Finally Etta spoke in a soft voice. "We haven't had a chance to talk much on it, but you were right when you said it wasn't likely that Gilbert Jackson fell out of his own barn and broke his neck ... at least not without help."

Harry had suspected that Brooks was a ruthless man and this was the proof. "Been fearful that something would happen. Just didn't expect anything so ... deadly."

Etta touched Harry's arm. "We're going to have to tell Lee and Laura that Gilbert died. Laura may not understand the significance of it, but Lee certainly will."

Harry nodded. "We'll tell 'em in the morning at breakfast."

Etta nodded then said, "Alva came by again this afternoon. Said there will be a special service after church meeting tomorrow. I imagine they'll be passing a hat. Poor Millie and the little boy, and the girls. They're so young. Now, to be without a father...."

There was a pause, and then with a wry smile, Harry said, "Sometimes I wonder if Alva ever does any work on his ranch."

"Don't change the subject, Harry. Don't you think someone should go to the law?"

"You know what I think about the law. Besides, I'm pretty sure Brooks has already bought the sheriff off. I hate it, but we'll just have to wait a bit to see what happens."

Chapter 7

SUNDAY MEETING

~ ~ ~

Sunday morning came like any other Sunday on the Kidwell ranch. Except that this morning there was an uneasy pall over what was usually a festive day.

On Sundays, Harry outfitted the truck bed with two bags of corn meal that he covered with a blanket. This was where Lee and Laura would sit for the ride to church.

Before marrying Etta, Harry had not been much for churches or organized religion. It was not that he was against religion, it was just that he had never felt comfortable in a church. When they married, Etta had convinced him that, if for no other reason than the children, Harry and she should attend the local Christian church.

As it turned out, Harry had found it a good deal less burdensome than he had imagined. However, he often wondered why the pews had to be so damn hard and uncomfortable. But, that aside, he had gotten so he looked forward to the socializing that took place after the services.

The sermons, on the other hand, were routinely every bit of what Harry had expected. He could have forgone that hour of preaching, but the rest was unexpectedly pleasant.

After breakfast, Harry pulled the truck up near the gate at the back of the house and waited for the others. His family always dressed in their best clothes before loading into the Model T.

Lee came out of the house, jumped into the bed of the truck, and sat waiting for the ladies to make their appearance. Etta and Laura always came last. It was the duty of women, Harry figured, to make the men wait.

Five minutes later, Etta and Laura approached the truck. Harry jumped out to open the door for Etta and then, as was his routine, he picked up his daughter and hoisted her into the truck bed where she took a seat next to her brother. Then Harry jumped behind the wheel and put the truck in gear.

As the truck began to lurch forward, Clarence came out of his bunkhouse and gave the Kidwells a wave. Etta waved back then glanced over at Harry with a question on her face. Looking back at Clarence, she was about to yell something when Harry stopped her short with a subtle hand motion and an almost silent, "Don't."

"Harry...." Etta protested.

"Etta, you'll only embarrass him. As many times as you've asked, he's never joined us. He feels certain that there are a few people there who would not welcome him. And truth be known, he's right about some who come to my mind."

"I know who you mean and those people are no account anyway," Etta snapped back.

Harry knew that the people at their church were, for the most part, good, charitable and unprejudiced. But there were a small few that still advocated the Jim Crow laws of the Deep South.

The rest of the congregation tolerated these views because the subject seldom arose.

Etta had made several attempts to get Clarence to join them at the Sunday church meetings but he had always declined.

Harry suspected that Clarence knew how some would be cordial, but inwardly uneasy at his presence and that there were others who would likely cause trouble. Trouble for himself, Harry knew, was not what worried Clarence. It was the trouble that could rain down on Harry and his family that concerned his friend.

"Look after things, Clarence." Harry called out as he waved from the truck.

* * *

Clarence smiled as the truck drove down the lane. He turned and entered his bunkhouse. Clarence knew that Etta wanted him to join them, but he was content to sit at home and relax on Sundays. He had his "Good Book" that he kept in his room. He couldn't read it. Still, it gave him comfort to just hold the book while he sat bedside, remembering the lilting voice of the one who used to read the words to him. Then, there was the picture wedged between the pages. Torn and ragged, Clarence still took great comfort in gazing at it on Sunday mornings, smiling at the face of the little girl smiling back at him.

* * *

As he drove along the road to the church, Harry couldn't help but notice in the distance that a new oil derrick had joined the half-dozen or so that he'd seen dotting the horizon the week before. He supposed that he'd be seeing more rise up on Gilbert Jackson's ranch in the coming weeks. Thinking about it, Harry could feel the hairs rise up on the back of his neck.

Harry and his family arrived at a tall white church nestled among a grove of trees on a rise that overlooked the surrounding countryside.

Behind the church was a cemetery with several dozen headstones standing chalky and cold against the blue Oklahoma sky. On Monday morning, Gilbert Jackson would be laid to rest there and his headstone would take its silent place among the others.

From the high vantage point of the church, Harry gazed out over the landscape. The sight of more oil derricks standing like burnt sticks against the warm cerulean sky irritated him.

Harry parked among the vehicles and carriages that had already gathered for the Sunday meeting. There were a couple of Model T passenger cars, a red 1919 Chevrolet 490 touring car, and a six-passenger, six-cylinder Buick Touring Car. The most impressive was a 1916 Willys-Overland Knight Touring Sedan with retractable glass windows and the quieter sleeve valve motor that Austin Peese had recently bought.

Sometimes Harry wondered if this trend toward machines and away from the good old reliable horse was all that wise. It was probably for this reason that he was not all that impressed with Austin's highfalutin automobile.

Austin Peese, on the other hand, was a different matter. Harry was impressed with Austin and liked him a good deal.

Austin and his wife, Edith, were standing by his automobile when Harry and his family arrived. Austin unbuttoned his Sunday suit coat and took a breath. The coat had become a bit snug over the last couple of years.

"Mornin', Kidwells. Sad day." Austin shook Harry's hand and bowed to Etta. There was a look of deep concern in Austin's eyes.

Mrs. Peese took Etta's arm and together they walked ahead of the men.

Austin rubbed his graying beard in thought as they walked. "The Widow Jackson and her kids arrived just a minute ago." Austin spoke in a quiet voice. "Pretty damn sad, Harry."

As they entered the church, the organ was playing. Pews, oak benches with hard backs and harder seats, lined either side of the center aisle. In a pinch, the church could seat about 120 people. The high vaulted ceiling with large exposed rafters gave the small church a sensation of grandness. The stained-glass windows that lined the walls added to the impression.

Harry and his family found an empty pew where they could settle in and still have room for Austin and Edith to join them. Harry glanced over at the short rotund man as he settled into his seat. It bothered him to see this particular rancher unnerved. He was not a man to be easily rattled.

Austin had been among the hundreds who had taken part in the Oklahoma Land Rush of 1889, one of the most bizarre episodes in the settling of the West. Those who had taken part in it were called Boomers, although there were many who were called by a different name. Actually, Austin was one of the latter.

* * *

Austin Peese had been a young drover working in Kansas when he first heard the news of the Oklahoma land rush. A fellow cowpuncher had seen posters in Dodge City.

"No, not sellin', givin' it away."

"Nobody gives land away," Austin said.

"I ain't foolin'. The Government is givin' away land in the Oklahoma Territory," the cowpuncher insisted. "All you gotta do is go down there and git it."

At the first opportunity, Austin rode over to Dodge City and read the posters for himself. Of course, it wasn't quite as easy as his friend had led him to believe. Still, the Government was indeed offering free sections of land in the Oklahoma Territory. Those interested would have to gather along the border on Monday, April 22, 1889. At noon of that day, the Army would open the way and the rush would be on.

It was the spring of 1888 when Austin first saw the posters and, for a young man with a bleak future, this was a dream come true. Determined to get a piece of that good fortune, Austin began to learn all he could about the incredible give-a-way.

Prior to April 22, prospective settlers would be allowed to wander around and peruse the land. Then, several days before the kickoff of the rush, the U.S. Army would clear the territory. All settlers would be moved back to the borders and held there until the bugles blew at noon to signal the opening of the land. On horse, on foot, in buggy or wagon, the hopeful could charge into the territory to try to claim their future.

Although Austin was a reasonably honest man, his desire to become a landowner soon outweighed his integrity. He began to plan a way to give himself an edge.

Ever since Austin began working cattle at the age of fourteen, he'd always been frugal. While others gambled and squandered their pay on loose women and strong drink, Austin had scrimped and saved.

Learning of the land rush, he doubled his efforts to accumulate a nest egg. Being shrewdly aware that just showing up and claiming a section would not guarantee the ability to keep it, he accepted that it would take money and grit to make it through the first year.

Austin began to look for ways to earn extra money when not herding cattle. He was a talented horseman and knew of an outfit in Dodge that sold mustangs to cow hands as well as the Army. He went to see the boss about a job taming horses.

"You look a might young, boy. Sure you can handle a wild mustang?" Austin stood before the man who was surveying him from boot to hat. The big hat sat low on Austin's small head, bending his ears like pieces of folded jerky.

"Show me a horse. I'll break it in ten minutes."

The boss smiled and hired the confident young cowboy.

By March of 1889, Austin had accumulated $220. That was when he put his plan into action and left Dodge City, Kansas. He arrived in the Oklahoma Territory on the twenty-seventh of March. It took more than a week of searching before he found a desirable section of land that he wanted to claim as his own.

Then he rode his horse out of the territory and sold his exceptionally fine steed to anxious Boomers, as the prospective settlers were now being called. By now they were gathering in the thousands at the border. Many were eager to get their hands on most any mount, but fine animals like Austin's were demanding grossly-inflated prices. He added this money to his already sufficient bankroll.

Late on April twenty-first under the cover of darkness and carrying a pack of supplies and a Winchester repeating rifle, Austin crept back over the border. He traveled on foot all night using the stars and other skills he'd learned as a drover to guide him.

Austin figured that traveling on foot would afford him a better chance to hide from the soldiers patrolling the territory. And he was right. Five hours into his trek he heard troopers on horseback scouring the area for unauthorized citizens. Quickly, yet silently, he scurried into a gully. As the soldiers approached, he burrowed in among a clump of bushes where he froze like a hare being stalked by a fox. One of the horses almost stepped on him as the soldiers rode into the gully and up the other side. He waited until they were long out of sight before he crawled out and continued his journey.

Covering almost five miles every hour, Austin made his way to his chosen section of land. Near to total exhaustion upon arrival, he collapsed inside a grove of trees. There he hid until 12:30 p.m. on the twenty-second when he mustered the strength to rise from his hiding place and lay claim to his land. Because he got there sooner than those who had waited at the border, Austin Peese and others like him became known as "Oklahoma Sooners."

Soon after claiming his section of land, a group of men consisting of three rough-looking, well-armed individuals, rode up. At a glance, Austin knew what they were after. He greeted them by cocking his Winchester.

The men gauged the steely look in the small cowboy's eyes and the way he held his weapon. They nodded back at him, turned their mounts and rode away.

Austin had obtained his land by dubious means but he was not, by far, the most dishonorable of those who had schemed to secure sections of land. Some, like these men, simply took it by force from those who had already laid claim to a section.

A large number of the Boomers came into the territory without proper provisions or money. They made claims on fine sections of land, but they had no way to support themselves until they could profit from its resources. They ended up selling their claims to people with means for a fraction of the actual value.

To his credit, Austin didn't use this practice to his advantage, though he had opportunities to do so. Instead, he actually helped a neighbor and his family who had claimed a section next to his by loaning them enough money to get them through the first year. He could have waited and bought their land when they were forced to sell. But Austin, though not without fault, was nonetheless caring and generous in nature.

Thirty-two years later, with their two children grown and moved away, Austin and Edith still owned the same section of land and ran it with the help of two ranch hands. Now on this day, with the news of Gilbert Jackson's "accidental" death, Austin, was concerned about his property for the first time since claiming his land."

* * *

Harry looked up to the front of the church where the minister stood behind a lectern on an elevated platform. On the left, the organist was seated at the new organ.

At the conclusion of the hymn, the part of the service began to which Harry was particularly ambivalent. The minister cleared his throat to quiet the congregation.

Harry tried, in vain, to get himself comfortable in the unforgiving oak seat. It wasn't the hard seats, nor was it the sermons themselves that made Harry most uncomfortable. It was more the fact that the good Reverend Michaels delivered his sermons with a drone that could put a bride to sleep on her wedding day.

A long hour later, Harry found himself outside the church amidst a group of his neighbors. They all watched as the widow Jackson left the chapel. Millie was holding the hand of her little tow-headed boy while her daughters followed in her shadow. The men removed their hats as she walked to her horse and buggy.

After the main service, everyone had passed a special collection plate for the widow and her kids.

Gilbert Jackson's wake would be later that afternoon and Harry and Etta planned to attend.

As was their custom after a church meeting, Harry and the men separated themselves from the ladies while the children went off to play.

Recently, Lee had taken to joining the men after church instead of playing with the kids. He'd explained to his dad he was old enough now to be with the adults. Harry advised him that it would be best if he just listened until he earned the older men's respect.

On this day there was a group of a dozen men. Among them, besides Harry and Lee, were Alva Bevan and Austin Peese.

Slim Moore was there, too. Slim was a tall young man whose slight frame gave rise to his nickname. His given name was Frank, but no one called him that. Slim was a nervous man prone to seeing a bear behind every tree. Harry suspected that one of the reasons Slim was of such a slight build was because he worried himself thin.

Slim shook his head after Millie and her kids walked by. "What's she gonna do now, you suppose, what with Gilbert getting dead an' all?" Slim question went out to no one in particular.

"Her brother is coming later today from Illinois to take her and the kids with him back to Peoria, in there," Alva answered.

"Hadn't heard that. What about the ranch?" Austin asked.

"Sellin' out to Brooks, I 'magine. Can't do much else, in there. She can't run a ranch by herself and raise three kids to boot," Alva answered.

Slim shook his head again. "That's just plain sad. Gilbert swore he'd never sell. It's a shame, that's all. Had to go and get his self killed. Now that bastard Brooks will get his hands on Gil's ranch."

"What makes you think he got his *self* killed, in there, Slim? Takes a careless man to fall from his own barn. Gilbert weren't a careless man, in there."

"And a mighty-unlucky man to break his neck when he fell only ten feet." Austin turned to Harry, "What do you think?"

Harry knew that most of the ranchers looked up to him because, in most matters, his opinions were considered perceptive and wise.

"Mighty convenient," Harry replied. He could see that his son was itching to put in his two cents. He gave Lee a "keep quiet" look.

Alva cleared his throat before speaking. "Brooks and his thugs been after Gil's ranch all along, in there. After all our ranches, for that matter. They've paid a visit to me. They come to you yet, Harry?" he asked with agitation in his voice.

Harry was becoming concerned that the women and children might overhear this ominous discussion and he thought it best to wait for a better time. He only shook his head to Alva's question. If he thought his example might quiet the rest, he was mistaken.

Slim rubbed thin fingers on his narrow chin. "Brook's lawyer came by my place t'other day. *Seemed* right friendly. But it worried me nonetheless."

"Yeah, first time's real friendly like. Next time they send that Ratt Wilson fellow by with a few gun hands, make it clear they ain't foolin' none," Austin replied. "Two days before he died, they visited Gilbert."

Slim's eyes widened. "Well, I told them I couldn't afford to sell. I made it right plain that what they offered wouldn't hardly cover what I owe the bank." Slim turned to Harry with a worried look. "You don't really think that Wilson fella killed Gilbert, do you Harry?"

Harry looked out toward the oil derricks in the distance. He let Slim's question hang in the air as the others followed Harry's gaze.

Chapter 8

THE THREAT

~ ~ ~

The hot mid-day sun was beating down when Harry turned his truck onto the dirt lane leading home. It was almost 12:30 p.m. Usually the Kidwells returned from Sunday meeting by half past eleven. On this Sunday, discussions concerning the plight of Millie Jackson and her kids had occupied a good deal more time than the usual polite after-meeting conversation.

"Somebody's at the house, Harry," Etta said, looking at a vehicle parked in the barnyard near the gate.

Harry could see a lone figure planted in the front seat of a 1920 blue Cadillac 57 Victoria Coupe.

"Looks like he's alone. Never seen the automobile before. Mighty fancy though," Harry observed.

"I don't think I like it, Harry. Look, Clarence is sitting on the porch and he's got his gun in his lap."

Harry nodded. He'd noticed the same almost as soon as he'd seen the automobile. Harry pulled the

Model T to a stop several yards away from the Cadillac and, as he jumped out, he addressed the kids in the back. "Stay where you are for a minute."

To Etta he cautioned, "Best wait here, too."

Harry wasn't really worried about the presence of the stranger, but figured it was always best to be cautious. Besides, he kind of hoped to get Clarence to put the gun away before the kids noticed it. As he approached the stranger in the Cadillac, Harry made a subtle motion to Clarence suggesting the gun go back in his belt.

Sporting a coal grey suit minus the jacket, the man in the Cadillac slowly opened his door. With a wary look at Clarence, he swung his feet to the ground but remained seated. Keeping an eye on the porch, the man extended his hand from where he was sitting and gave a greeting to Harry.

"Sure glad to see you, Mr. Kidwell."

As Harry reluctantly grasped the extended hand, he noticed the man's drenched shirt and sweaty brow. He was clearly suffering the heat of the early afternoon sun.

* * *

An hour-and-a-half earlier when he first arrived at the Kidwell ranch, Melvin Howell had been met by Clarence, who stepped out of the bunkhouse holding his revolver. Howell informed Clarence that he was there to see Mr. Kidwell, but Clarence told him Harry wasn't home yet from church.

Howell suggested to Clarence that he be allowed to wait at the house in the cool of the porch. Clarence would have none of it. He told him that, if he wanted to wait, he could wait in his fancy "auto-mobile."

Within the hour, the searing noonday sun had done a pretty good job on Mr. Howell. He removed his jacket within three minutes of returning to his sedan and within another fifteen, his white linen shirt was nearly soaked with sweat.

Twice he tried to get Clarence to let him sit on the porch, but was met each time with a shake of the head and the brandishing of Clarence's .32 pistol. After the second request, Clarence punctuated his refusal by walking over to the porch and setting up sentry on the steps.

Now, even with Harry's arrival, Howell was a bit reluctant to leave the safety of his sedan.

"Sure glad you're back. This damn nigger here has been keepin' me holed up in my auto for the best part of an hour." The man almost spat out the words. Then, shifting to a polite tone, he said, "My name's Melvin Howell."

* * *

At the first sight of the man, Harry didn't like him. He had a slick, oily look about him and now, with his insult and disrespect for Clarence, Harry's opinion was quickly confirmed.

"I don't much care for the way of your talk, Mr. Howell."

"Sorry, no offense meant. It's just that ... well, it's a mighty hot day and your boy there wouldn't so much as let me out of my automobile."

Harry suspected why the man was here and he was of a mind to just kick him off the ranch. But, a bit of wisdom he'd picked up from one of his best

74

friends years before came to mind: "Know as much as possible about your enemies."

"What do you want?" Harry asked.

Howell smiled with cold, dead eyes.

"I'm an attorney for Mr. Scott C. Brooks of Brooks' Oil. I've been sent here by Mr. Brooks himself. Matter of fact, Mr. Brooks wants me to give you this little gift as a token of good will."

As he spoke he cautiously stepped from his auto, all the while keeping a wary eye on Clarence. He moved around to the back of the Cadillac and opened the rear compartment. Bending over, he struggled to pull out a case of whiskey.

"This here, Mr. Kidwell, is the finest sippin' whiskey money can buy," Howell offered.

On the porch, Clarence was watching as Howell produced the case of whiskey. He licked his lips.

Harry glanced at the porch and saw the look on Clarence's face. A wry smile touched Harry's lips.

When he turned back to the lawyer, the smile was replaced with a hard, cold stare.

"I don't believe I care for any gift Mr. Brooks has to offer. Anything else I can do for you?"

Howell shrugged and lowered the case back into the compartment.

At the Model T, Etta turned to her kids. "Go on into the house," she said before going to join her husband. Laura obeyed, but Lee hesitated, then joined his parents at the lawyer's auto. Howell nodded at Etta then turned his attention back to Harry.

"You see, Harry ... mind if I call you Harry?" he smiled.

Harry ignored the question and the smile.

"We were hoping maybe you could help us out some, you being older than most of the other ranchers and maybe a lot wiser. We thought you would be more reasonable: see things in a sensible way."

"Get to the point, Mr. Howell," Harry demanded with an obvious tinge of irritation.

"All right, we'd like you to help us convince these ranchers it would be in their interest, as well as ours, to sell their land to Mr. Brooks. No sense in fighting the future. What's going to happen will eventually happen anyway. You can see that, Harry; you're a smart fellow. They might as well face up to it and get what they can. We're offering a fair price, given the circumstances," Howell smiled again.

From the corner of his eye, Harry could see his son ball his fists and step forward. Harry reached out and gently pushed Lee back.

"Your boss has a peculiar notion of what 'fair price' means," Harry observed. "You've spent a long hot hour in your fancy automobile for nothing, Mr. Howell. You best be on your way."

"We're prepared to make it worth your while to help us out, Harry. We'll pay extra for your place. Maybe ... twice what we pay the others." Howell gave Harry a conspiratory wink. "Just between us, you know, Harry."

"Mr. Kidwell," Harry pointedly corrected the familiar use of his first name. His next words flowed softly, but with controlled anger; he said, "I don't believe I will be selling out my friends and neighbors today. Tell your boss, Mr. Brooks, he'd best look for some other land for his oil wells. He won't be buying any more land around here for the price he's offering."

"That's not a very friendly attitude, Mr. Kidwell." Howell's eyes were cold and lifeless and his use of Harry's formal name was anything but respectful. Slowly, he turned his attention on Etta and Lee, then on Clarence and Laura who were standing next to each other on the porch.

"You have a nice family here, although you should teach your nigger some manners." He saw the anger welling up in Harry's eyes but continued, "Too bad about the accident your neighbor had the other day." With this last statement he spotted Clarence pulling the .32 back out of his belt.

Howell jumped into his Cadillac and started the engine.

"Think about what I said, Harry," he yelled over the roar of the motor. "You and your family can avoid a lot of trouble by co-operating." He hit the accelerator and his tires spun on the dry grass until they caught hold.

Once Howell was out of sight, Harry motioned for Etta and Lee to go to the porch and take Laura inside. As his family disappeared into the house, Harry gave Clarence a look that told him he wanted to talk. They strolled toward the barn.

"I appreciate your lookin' after things, Clarence," Harry said. "You must have figured pretty quick when you saw him drive up that he was sent by Brooks."

"Never seen that fancy auto 'afore, Harry. Figured to be a Brooks man in a fancy rig like that. Didn't see much reason to make him comfortable.

Scum, but kinda wish ya'd kept the whiskey jist the same." Clarence smiled as he spoke. Then with a more sober look he continued. "This figures to be the start of it, I guess. Am I right, Harry?"

Harry nodded solemnly. "Going to get a lot worse. It's a good bet that they killed Gilbert and that means they won't stop short of killin' again. Things are going to get rough, Clarence. You might want to consider your options."

"Options? What you talkin' about?"

Harry paused in front of the barn door.

"You hired on to be a ranch hand, not to fight my battles. You've already done a lot more than I would have expected."

For a second there was a flash of hurt in Clarence's eyes. "Kinda feel like it's my fight, too, Harry." He looked down at the ground. "Know it ain't my ranch or nothin', but come to feel like I got a stake somehow. Anyway, don't plan to run from no fight, Harry. More'n a little sorryful that you'd think I might want to."

Clarence looked Harry straight in the eye as he tapped the gun that was stuck in his waistband. "Know you ain't much fer firearms, Harry. This here gun is the only fightin' tool we got on this ranch. I ain't gonna be 'fraid to use it if'n I have to."

Harry nodded. "Obliged, Clarence. Jist hope you won't regret it."

Actually, Harry was a bit conflicted. If Clarence had chosen to pass on this fight, Harry would not have been upset. He was not anxious for his friend to get hurt. But he also suspected that he might need

Clarence's help at some point. "Wanted you to know how it's liable to be."

Clarence tapped the butt of his gun. "I'll be ready."

Harry smiled affectionately at his hired hand. He was struck by the thought of Clarence being their *knight in shining armor* standing guard over him and his family with his trusty .32.

"You got a plan, Harry?"

The smile faded. "Not even the makings of one. 'Fraid this is one of the places they talk about: the one that's between a hard spot and a rock."

"We'll work somethin' out, Harry. Don't reckon them fellers are all that tough."

Harry had not told anyone, but he'd looked into Wilson and his men. They were gun-hands, men who carried firearms and knew how to use them.

Before Gilbert was killed, Harry had hoped they were just for show, a bluff if you will. But now he knew Brooks was deadly serious and would stop at nothing to get his hands on all the land in the area.

He looked sadly at Clarence and his old worn revolver. "Let's hope we won't have to use your gun, Clarence."

Chapter 9

THE LETTER

~ ~ ~

The Kidwells returned from Gilbert's wake around 8:30 p.m. in the evening. It had been a somber event, as was to be expected. The inevitable whispers of Brooks and his hired guns created an additional specter that lay like a dark blanket over the whole affair.

Harry was relieved, however, that no one brought up the suspicious manner of Gilbert's death. He didn't want Millie or her kids hearing talk of that nature. Harry hoped Millie would never learn that her husband was probably murdered, since it would serve no purpose. No one would ever be brought to justice for the crime. The ranch was being sold and the Jacksons were moving on.

Since they had returned so late, Etta opted to make a simple supper of pork'n beans and corn bread. The same dark specter that had hovered over the funeral followed them home. It was there to join them as they sat down to eat.

For the better part of the meal, everyone ate without speaking. Silence lay over the meal like oil on stagnant water.

Finally, Clarence tried his usual tactic to slice through the gloom. "Well, all I can say is that was some very fine-tastin' cornbread." But tonight his words landed as flat as unleavened bread.

Harry gave the big man a half-hearted smile for the effort and nodded.

Earlier, at the funeral, Lee had just moped around. Now, at the dinner table, he sat looking morose. He fidgeted in his seat and picked at his food. Finally he slammed down his fork. "We gotta do something, Pa! They killed Mr. Jackson! Don't that mean anything to anyone?"

Harry looked at his son with compassionate eyes. Then he saw the confusion on his daughter's face. "Not a good time to talk on this, Lee."

"That's what you always say. When is there a good time, Pa? When someone else is murdered?"

"That's enough of that talk, Son." Harry glanced once again at the worried look on Laura's face.

"I just want to know," Lee persisted.

Laura looked at her father. "What's Lee talking about?"

"Nothing, Honey. Eat your supper." He turned to Lee. "What happened is water under the bridge. Best let it be for now." Harry spoke evenly trying to control his anger.

Lee glared at his father. "That Brooks' man; he was threatening us today. Well, wasn't he? That ain't no water under the bridge, Pa!"

Harry set a firm jaw as he leveled his gaze at Lee.

"It's my problem, Son. It's for me to handle. Besides, this isn't the time to be discussing it." Harry glanced meaningfully in Laura's direction.

Lee was too upset to notice the hint. "All I know is, if we had a few guns and a little backbone, those oil people would think twice about trying to buffalo us!" He was shouting now.

Harry's neck and face turned crimson.

Etta stepped in to lower the heat that was rising in the room. "There are other ways to handle things like this, Lee. Guns are not always the ..."

Harry cut in. "I don't like your disrespect, boy! Now, you'll apologize for shouting."

"What I said is true. No one has any backbone around here. If Uncle Leroy were here he'd know how to handle those slimy snakes." Lee spoke without shouting, but the words had an even stronger effect because he spoke with conviction, not anger.

Harry was caught off guard. "Where? What brought him to your mind? In your lifetime you've met your Uncle Leroy one time. And that had to be at least ... what, seven years ago? You were just a kid."

"I remember him well enough. Besides, Ma told me about him. She says he's one of the smartest and bravest men she ever knew. Doubt he'd be afraid of those Brooks men."

"Well, your Uncle isn't here. And even if he ..."

Lee jumped in, shouting once again. "He carries a gun! I saw it. And, unlike others I know, I bet he knows how to use it!"

"That will be enough!" Harry shot to his feet, his chair tipping over behind him as he spoke.

But Lee couldn't seem to stop himself. "I'll bet he wouldn't sit still and let those people push him around! Bet he's got some backbone!"

Red-faced and gritting his teeth, Harry somehow managed to keep from shouting. "Lee, that's all I will hear from you tonight. You will leave the table and you will go to your room. Now!"

Lee pushed back and stood up. With anger in his eyes, he stalked past his father. "You're afraid of them, that's all! Afraid of guns, afraid of fights, afraid of most everything!" Lee shot this over his shoulder as he headed for his room.

Etta went to stand by Harry. She put her arm around him and leaned her head on his shoulder. "He didn't mean it."

Laura looked with confusion at her parents. "What's going on?" What's Lee talking about?" Tears streaked down her cheeks.

Etta moved near her daughter and put a soothing arm around her shoulders. "It's all right, Honey. Lee's just been upset some lately. Everything's going to be just fine."

* * *

That night, a magnificent full moon illuminated the Kidwell ranch house with a creamy golden glow, while the glimmer of a kerosene lamp emanated from Harry and Etta's upstairs bedroom window.

Harry sat up on their ornately-carved walnut bed with his back against its six-foot-tall bedstead. Etta had bought it when she was living in Texas before Harry had asked her to marry him. It was the most prized possession that she had ever owned. Wearing a modest nightgown, she crossed the room and slipped into the bed beside her brooding husband. Snuggling close, she put her arms around him in a compassionate hug.

"Sorry, Harry. I suppose you should blame me for the way Lee feels," she whispered.

Harry gently placed a finger on Etta's lips. "We both agreed to the way things would be," he said. "And you were right. This was the only way things could have worked for us here, or anywhere for that matter."

"What should we do, Harry? We can't fight these people. Brooks has hired professionals."

Harry slowly nodded in agreement. "Thought about trying to organize the men around here, but ..."

"No match for the men Brooks hired, are they?"

Harry slowly shook his head.

There was sadness in Etta's eyes. "Can we sell and move on? Find another place somewhere?"

Harry felt a flash of anger. "I won't sell to Brooks, even for the extra he's offered. For one thing, it would give him leverage with the others. Besides, it's more than the betrayal of our friends, Etta. Selling would be giving in. And I won't give in to a man like that."

"Maybe we could find someone else to buy our place?" Etta asked with a tinge of desperation in her voice.

Harry saw the concern in her eyes. "There's more to this than you know, Etta. I've kept my ear to the ground and there's more going on here than even Alva knows. I don't want to alarm you, but you deserve to know everything. Brooks has a stronger grip on things than anyone knows. He's locked out all the other prospective buyers."

Harry stared into her eyes. "No other buyer is going to touch our land or anyone else's around here."

A cloud of hopelessness drifted across Etta's face as she took in this information. Suddenly, a spark lit up her eyes. "Harry, if there's oil on our land, maybe *we* could drill for it."

"Crossed my mind, but, I'm no oilman. I have no idea how to even begin. Only thing that I do know about drilling for oil is that it takes a lot of money."

Harry paused before he continued. "All we had from the old days went into this ranch. If we wanted to even think about drilling ourselves, we'd have to find a way to get more money."

Etta noticed his pause and, for a second, she gazed into his eyes. "I've seen that look, Harry. What are you thinking? Better not be considering what I think you are, Harry. Don't even think it!" There was a bit of panic in Etta's voice.

"Don't look so worried." He gave her a reassuring smile. "I'm too old, and besides, it wouldn't be as easy as it was in the old days. I was just remembering, that's all."

As he spoke, Harry could see the tension slip away from Etta's body.

"So, what do we do, Harry? We can't run and we can't fight. That man, Howell, coming to our ranch was just the beginning. They'll be back."

Harry nodded. "True. And I won't run."

"And we can't fight, right?" Etta repeated.

Harry ignored the question and altered the subject.

"They won't come back right away. They're likely to let what happened to Gilbert soak in a bit. Gilbert was a stubborn man and that's why they picked him as an example. Now they've come to me because they figure, if they can buy me off, the rest of the ranchers might fold."

Etta nodded her understanding.

"What worries me is that, since I wouldn't go along, their next move will probably be to start working on one of the weaker ranchers. My guess is Ned Jones or maybe Slim. They're the most likely to spook, but we'll just have to wait and see."

Harry reached over to turn out the lantern that sat on the night table next him. Etta gently touched his arm to stop him.

"Harry, about Lee; I know it bothers you the way he's been acting. Do you want me to talk to him, explain about the guns?"

"What would you tell him...the truth? Can't do that. You're right though when you say it bothers me. It's hard to hear the things he says and to see the way he looks at me. But that's not really so important. What is important is that he learns there is more than one way to figure the true measure of a man."

Etta gave Harry a coy look. Her hands reached under the covers and found her husband.

"Now, figuring the true measure of a man is something I know how to do," she purred.

"Not at all what I meant," Harry spoke seriously, but a mischievous smile cracked his lips. He pulled her into his arms, kissing her long and hard.

* * *

When the light finally went out in Harry and Etta's bedroom, a lantern in Lee's room still cast an orange glow on the trees outside his window. Sitting on his bed, he held a pen as he tried to think how to word his letter. It was obvious that his father was not up to the task of standing up to Brooks and his hired gunmen. The only thing to do was to ask for help. After a long pause, he dipped his pen into the inkbottle on the nightstand. Slowly and carefully, Lee began to write. "Dear Uncle Leroy," the letter began.

After fifteen minutes he set the pen down and looked at his writing. Nodding to himself, he folded it to fit into the envelope he had taken earlier from his mother's writing desk in the sitting room downstairs.

He picked up his pen once more and wrote down the post office box in Oregon his uncle had given him during his visit several years before. Lee had taken a liking to his uncle immediately and Leroy told Lee that if he ever wanted to get a hold of him, he could write to that address.

Lee didn't know if the letter would still reach him or if Uncle Leroy would come to help if it did. In any event, now that he'd written it, he felt better and was ready to go to sleep. He stuck the letter under his pillow, pulled the covers up and turned out the lantern.

Lee was sure that writing to his uncle for help was the right thing to do, but he planned to keep the letter secret. There was a good chance his father would stop him if he knew.

The Kidwell mailbox was located at the end of the dirt lane that led from the house to the road. The mailman was due tomorrow. In order to secretly mail his letter, Lee decided he would get up before anyone awoke.

* * *

Etta jumped when the back door opened and Lee stepped into the kitchen. "Oh, my!" she gasped. "You scared me, Lee. I didn't know you were up. What were you doing outside so early?"

Standing in front of the stove, his mother was fixing scrambled eggs.

Lee had awakened at 5:45 a.m., later than he'd planned. He'd rushed to mail his letter hoping to get back before anyone was up. He too jumped with a start when he opened the kitchen door and saw his mother already fixing breakfast. "Oh! Morning, Ma. Thought I heard something... outside ... spooking the horses in the barn. Went out to take a look. Wasn't nothin'."

"It wasn't 'anything'." Etta corrected.

"Right, 'anything'," Lee said, glad for any diversion from explaining further why he was outside so early.

"Well, as long as you're up, help me with breakfast. You can fix biscuits." Etta offered Lee an apron.

Under most circumstances Lee would have acquiesced to this womanly chore only after showing at least a modicum of manly resistance. This morning, he was too preoccupied with his deception to protest. He was about to take the apron when his father and sister entered the kitchen.

"Well, you're up pretty early, Son," Harry said. He'd obviously heard the last of their conversation.

He gave Lee a wink. "Ready to help me with the morning chores?"

Etta saw the wink. "Ok, here, give me back the apron. You two go outside to do your chores and we women will fix the breakfast." She reached out briskly and grabbed the apron. Etta gave the impression of being put out, but the twinkle in her eyes gave her away.

Chapter 10

THE MISSING CATTLE

~ ~ ~

Etta and Laura were busy cleaning house when they heard the sound of an approaching horse. Etta looked out the kitchen window and saw a rider heading their way. A shiver ran up her spine. She and Laura were alone.

Looking around the kitchen for a weapon, her eyes spied a large butcher's knife. Grabbing it, she peered out the window once again. The rider was closer now. Etta let out a sigh as she recognized the small figure of Alva atop his large fifteen-hand gelding. Feeling foolish, she set aside the knife.

Alva reined in his horse near the gate and gave a shout. "Hello in the house."

Etta opened the door and stepped onto the porch.

"Alva. Nice to see you this morning. What brings you this way again?"

"How do, Mrs. Kidwell? Mighty nice to see you too, in there. Would Harry be t'home?" Alva took off his hat and wiped his shiny bald head with a blue handkerchief.

"The men are all out laying fence, Alva. Can I get you a cool drink? Why don't you step down from your horse and come up on the porch?"

Etta could see that Alva had something on his mind by the way he looked out toward the fields. It was as if he wanted to find the men and talk to them. But Alva was a polite man, and besides, she could tell she'd hit the mark with the offer of a cool drink.

"Have a seat in the shade of the porch, Alva. I'll fetch some lemonade. I just made a fresh batch."

This was a little white lie. Etta liked Alva and knew that he would likely decline the drink if he knew she didn't have it on hand. When she got into the kitchen, she quickly began slicing the lemons.

When Etta came in to fix the drinks, Laura went out to the porch. Through the screen door she heard her daughter say, "Hi, Mr. Bevan."

Alva had made himself comfortable on the porch swing and she went over to join him.

"Well, hello there, Sprout. How you been, in there?"

"Fine. Bring us some news, Mr. Bevan?"

Alva shifted uncomfortably in the swing. "So, what year you gonna be in school this fall, Laura?"

In the house, Etta finished squeezing the lemon juice into a pitcher and stirring in sugar and water. She grabbed three glasses from the cupboard and set them on a tray along with the pitcher filled with lemonade.

"Here you go. Hope it's not too tart," Etta said as she stepped onto the porch.

Alva licked his lips as Etta poured the cool drink. He took a long sip and shook his head.

"Mighty fine. Sure hits the spot on a hot day, in there."

Etta smiled and then asked, "So, tell me, Alva, what brings you out this way?"

Alva looked around nervously. "The men are out working in the field, huh?"

Etta nodded, but raised her eyebrows waiting for an answer.

Alva squirmed a little before he spoke. "Maybe I best jist mosey on out and talk to Harry."

Etta enjoyed Alva's discomfort. She understood that whatever information it was that he wished to convey, he felt it was something that should be shared directly with the men. She could tell that Alva was just now realizing that his thirst had gotten him trapped.

* * *

Harry, Clarence and Lee were laying fence when they heard the sound of horse's hooves in the distance. They looked up to see Etta riding their way.

She reined her horse to a stop in front of Harry and handed him a jar of lemonade.

"I just happened to have a little lemonade on hand." Etta smiled as Harry helped her to the ground. She gave him a kiss on the cheek and went to retrieve four tin cups from her saddlebag.

A few minutes later, Etta, Harry, Clarence and Lee were sitting in the grass drinking lemonade.

Clarence licked his lips. "That sure did cool the sun, Mz Etta."

"You're welcome, Clarence," Etta said with a smile. Then her smile faded as she looked meaningfully at Harry.

Harry knew without her saying anything that she wanted to talk, so he stood up and helped her to her feet. Together, like two lovers out for a stroll, they walked away from Lee and Clarence.

When they reached a safe distance, Etta spoke softly. "Alva stopped by just now. He told me that Brooks' man, Howell, slithered by at least three other ranchers yesterday. He made mention of Gilbert's "accidental" death to each of them."

"Not surprised." Harry spoke softly and looked over at Lee to see if he was listening. "Imagine that must have put some fright in them."

Etta followed his gaze and kept her voice low. "Alva said they're getting worried, but none of them wants to sell. Alva thinks the ranchers should all get together this Sunday after church-meeting and talk about what to do."

"Waste of time as far as I can see."

"Don't say that, Harry." Etta raised her voice causing Lee and Clarence to look their way.

Harry put on a smile for show and slipped his arm around Etta's shoulder. "Don't get excited," he whispered. "Alva's a good man. If that's what he wants then it won't hurt to oblige him."

Etta nodded then paused before she spoke again. "That brings something else up, Harry. I suppose, under the circumstances, it's not that important but it just rankles. Alva *is* a good man but I get mighty tired of him, as well as most of the other men around here, with their *it's-a-man's-world* attitude."

Harry could just about imagine what had taken place when Alva stopped by at the house.

"He didn't want to tell you about Howell trying to scare the ranchers, did he?" Harry smiled.

Etta's eyes flashed a hint of irritation when she gazed on Harry's smile. Holding her temper, she said, "He wanted to tell you directly, said it was 'man's business'."

Harry could see it all playing out in his mind. "Imagine you set him straight."

A smile touched Etta's lips. "I guess I did, 'in there'."

Harry chuckled.

"Jokes aside, Harry, so far the ranchers don't seem to be giving in. You think that maybe Brooks will give up if no one bends to him?"

Harry searched Etta's eyes as he shook his head. "You know better than that. When he killed Gilbert, Brooks showed us how far he's willing to go."

* * *

In the evening sky above the Kidwell ranch, clouds hugged the setting sun like soft quilts of pink and orange.

The workday was done and inside the house, Clarence washed his hands in the sink as he gazed out the kitchen window. He could hear Etta and Laura talking behind him as they busied themselves putting food on the table for supper. For just a second, Clarence caught a glimpse of movement out the window in the distance but his attention was distracted when he heard Harry enter the kitchen.

"We almost have the fencing done, but we need to take tomorrow and cut hay." Harry looked at

Clarence as he spoke. "Can finish the fence later. Hay's more important right now."

Clarence nodded his agreement just as Lee entered the kitchen.

"Rider, Pa!" Lee exclaimed.

"I hear him," Harry said as he stepped over to the window next to Clarence. Together they peered out and saw a lone rider silhouetted against the setting sun.

Lee looked over his father's shoulder. "Just one horse, Pa. Think it's one of Brooks' gunmen?"

Harry stared hard at the lone figure. As the rider drew closer, he shook his head.

"Now, what does he want?" Harry sighed. "It's Alva."

Harry stepped over to the door and opened it.

Etta peered out the window. "Again? What could bring him out here twice in one day?"

"It can't be good, whatever the reason," Harry whispered to himself as he stepped onto the porch.

Clarence and Lee followed while Etta and Laura waited just inside the door.

Alva dismounted. When he saw the women looking out from inside the door, he took off his hat and nodded. "Evening, folks.

Harry watched as Alva approached the house. He wasn't sure, but he suspected that this second trip was unrelated to the visit he'd paid them that morning. "Evening, Alva," he said. "Etta told me you were by this morning. She already shared your news."

Alva scraped a little dirt off his boot on the porch step. "This ain't about that, Harry. Least not directly, in there. It seems that Slim Moore's fence was cut, a pretty big section. A mess of his steers went and wandered off."

Clarence took a step forward. "Any idea how many?"

"Pretty near the whole herd, in there."

"When did this happen?" Harry asked.

"Early this mornin'. Slim was cuttin' hay on the other side o' his ranch and he never realized it 'til late this afternoon. You know how Slim is, always so nervous an' all, so you can imagine how he's takin' all this, in there. Asked me if I could help round 'em up. Thought maybe you'd be willin' to give us a hand too, Harry. It's a big bunch of cattle. Could use a little extra help, in there." Alva glanced at Clarence as he spoke.

Harry nodded. "Could you saddle a horse for me, Clarence? I'll grab a bite of food to take with me."

Harry turned to go back in the house. "Hungry, Alva?" he asked over his shoulder

"Don't fix nothin' fer me, in there, Harry. I already et."

Clarence turned to head for the barn. "Think maybe I'll saddle up two horses, Harry, if you wouldn't mind packin' a little extra grub for me?"

Harry cracked a smile and nodded at his friend. He suspected that this job was going to entail a bit more than just rounding up cattle.

As he entered the house, Lee followed him. "I'd like to go too, Pa."

Harry was glad to have Clarence join him but he didn't want Lee along. "I need you here, Son. Someone has to look after your mom and sister."

Lee stared at his father, ready to argue. Then he glanced at his sister and mother. "Okay, Pa."

It was just about dusk when Alva, Clarence, and Harry rode away from the Kidwell ranch. Each of the men carried food, water, and a kerosene lantern. Alva had a Winchester rifle in the sheath on his saddle and Clarence had his .32 stuck in his waistband.

Chapter 11

THE SEARCH

~ ~ ~

It took about an hour to reach Slim's ranch. Slim was waiting on horseback near the section of cut fence. He rode out to meet them as soon as he saw the approaching glow of their lanterns.

Harry could see a pale mask of worry etched in Slim's features.

"They're gone! All of 'em just plain gone," Slim wailed.

Harry looked beyond Slim. More than twenty feet of fence had been knocked down and the wire cut.

Alva reached out and put his hand on Slim's shoulder. "We'll find 'em, Slim."

Harry left the group and began to ride back and forth along the section of cut fence. He held his lantern low as he searched the ground.

The others started to shadow Harry as he moved his horse along the line of broken and cut fence. He pulled up abruptly and turned to his friends. "Hold back there, boys. Let me work this myself." The others nodded and retreated a few yards. After a bit, Harry rode outside the broken fence and away from Slim's land.

Harry had been born in Pennsylvania, but had migrated to Colorado at the tender age of fifteen. There he had met Charlie Redcloud a mixed Caucasian and Cheyenne Indian.

Charlie liked Harry from the start and taught him much of the skills that were a part of the Cheyenne culture. Among them were tracking and reading sign. They were skills that Harry learned well, but had little use for over the last several years. But the ability was still with him.

As Harry scoured the ground, trying to read what he could barely make out in the dim light, he wished that he had the superior skill of his old mentor. He struggled for several minutes until he was confident in what he was reading.

Turning his horse, he rode back to his companions.

"What do ya see, Harry?" Slim's voice cracked a little.

"I figure about ninety head, Slim. Sound about right?"

"Pretty close, Harry. Ninety-four and them's all the cattle I got. I need 'em bad, Harry. Can't pay the bills and such without sellin' a bunch of 'em this fall."

Alva asked, "What can you make out, in there, Harry? Looks like they was scattered pretty good I'd guess."

"Didn't scatter 'em," Harry said, looking off into the night.

"What do ya mean, Harry?" Slim looked bewildered.

"Can't say for sure, but it looks like four or maybe five riders and they're driving the cattle North."

"Drivin' 'em?" Slim questioned. "You sayin' they rustled 'em, Harry?"

"That sounds crazy," Alva said. "This here's the twentieth century. Even when I was workin' as a deputy back in Missouri, in there, we didn't get no cattle rustlin'.

"You was a deputy, Alva?" Slim asked, looking puzzled.

It had slipped Harry's mind about Alva's short stint as a sheriff's deputy. Because of things in his past, Harry had little use for lawmen. Still, he liked Alva and had long ago decided not to hold this against him.

"Fer a year and a half," Alva declared with pride. "Anyway, people don't go around rustling cattle any more, in there. I mean, do they? Least ways not around here."

Harry was sure what he'd seen: four or five riders herding the cattle away from Slim's ranch. He spurred his horse and motioned for the others to follow.

"One way to find out," he said.

Lights from their lanterns danced to the gait of their horses as the four men rode slowly through the inky black night.

Holding his lantern and bending low in the saddle, Harry led the way. He searched the ground for signs of the riders who were driving the cattle.

The signs were there and Harry was sure now that there were five rustlers.

Although Harry hated to admit it, his adrenaline was flowing and, in a perverse way, he was enjoying this chase. It brought back old memories of long ago. He wished that some of his friends from those days were with him now. They would have come in very handy.

As it was, Harry wasn't sure what he would do if the four of them caught up to the herd. The rustlers would be armed and experienced whereas his little posse was ill-equipped to deal with thieves and gunfighters. Harry figured that was a bridge he'd cross when they came to it.

They had been following the tracks for almost half an hour when Harry began to suspect where they were being herded.

Ten minutes later, Alva came to the same conclusion. "Believe they're driving this herd to Gilbert Jackson's place, in there. What do you think, Harry?"

"My guess too, Alva."

"You track pretty good, Harry. Where'd you learn to read sign so good?" This was the first time Slim had spoken since they'd started out.

"Friend of mine taught me some when I was a boy. He was a sight better than me, though."

"Must o' been mighty good," Alva said.

"He was. But, to tell the truth, as good as he was I knew of a fellow who might just have been a bit better."

"Who was that, Harry," Slim asked.

"Lawman named Stillman. Could follow a horse with bagged hooves over bare rock." Harry had a far-away look as he spoke.

"Harry, I do believe I heard tell of him. Did he teach you some too, in there?"

"No, never actually met up with the man. Though I imagine he was anxious some that we should get together back then. At the time, I just didn't feel much in the mood to spend time with him." Harry said this with a hint of a smile on his lips.

A little while later they approached a low hill. Harry pulled up and signaled the others to do the same.

"Gilbert's ranch house is just over that rise. Might be best if we lead our mounts on foot and without these." Harry pointed to their lanterns. He dismounted, extinguished his and led his horse to the top of the rise.

* * *

Clarence had been quiet during the ride. He'd kept an eye on his friend and wasn't surprised when Harry took the lead on this venture. Most people saw Harry as quiet and low-key, but Clarence had long suspected that there was something just under the surface that was always waiting to burst out of Harry.

The thing that did surprise Clarence was the ease with which Harry had tracked the rustlers. However, Clarence sensed there would be more things revealed about Harry before the night was over.

Chapter 12

THE RUSTLERS

~ ~ ~

As Harry and the others reached the crest of the rise, they stopped and peered down on the ranch that had once belonged to Gilbert Jackson. Laid out below them, under a low-hanging half moon, were the ranch house, barn, and Gilbert's corral. Milling about inside the corral were Slim's cattle.

Slim stomped his foot and got so made he could hardly keep his voice down as he pointed a thin, shaking finger. "Damn! Look there! They got my cattle packed in right there in Gilbert's corral." He started to lift a foot to his stirrup.

Harry had been studying the layout below them, but at Slim's first move he grabbed the excited man's reins.

Alva had seen Slim's angry movement also and grabbed him by the arm. "Whoa, Slim. That sure as hell is your cattle down there, but those are Brooks' men guarding 'em, in there. Let's think about this," he cautioned.

Harry directed his attention back to the ranch below. "Five men were herding the cattle. I see only four."

Alva gazed over Harry's shoulder. "Wilson had to be behind this. Once the cattle were corralled, in there, he probably left to go report back to his slimy boss."

"Could be. But, even with him out of the picture, these four could be a mess o' trouble," Harry said.

Alva nodded. "Can't argue with that. These four are packin' iron. We go rushin' down there and we're liable to run into a gun fight."

Harry peered down through the darkness at the corral and the men standing guard. Two rustlers were standing in the light of a fire they'd lit and two others could be seen in the glow of their lanterns on the other side of the corral.

Harry looked pointedly at Slim when he spoke. "They each have a revolver and that one over on the other side is carryin' what looks like a shotgun. We have your rifle, Alva's rifle, and the .32 Clarence is packin'."

"What we gonna do? I can't just leave 'em have my cattle, Harry." Slim looked shaken. "I wasn't thinkin' on no gun fight, though."

"We go charging down there and we'll sure enough get us one," Alva said.

Harry was trying to figure a strategy when Slim spoke again. "Best thing to do, I'm thinkin', is to go to Hobard and get the sheriff. What do you think, Harry?"

Alva spoke up before Harry could answer. "Slim could be right, Harry. From here it ain't so far. We could ride on over and get Sheriff Rafter, in there."

Harry was certain that Rafter was bought and paid for by Brooks and this would be a waste of time, but he also saw this as a solution to his problem. He needed to get Alva and Slim out of harm's way if he was going to have any chance to get the cattle back without getting his friends hurt or killed. At the same time, he didn't want to seem too anxious to get rid of them.

"I don't hold much with most lawmen," Harry said. Then, giving Alva a sideways glance, he added, "Present company excepted, Alva."

Alva nodded.

"Anyway, that Rafter fellow is tied to Brooks like a watch fob. May not get as much help from him as you think."

"Worth a try, though, Harry." Slim sounded desperate. "Can't likely win a fight agin' these hired gunmen."

Harry appeared to consider this before he spoke. "Maybe you're right, Slim. Clarence and I can keep an eye on the cattle while you two ride over to Hobard."

"We should be back before dawn," Alva said as he mounted his horse.

Slim mounted up, too, and they both rode off into the charcoal night.

After they left, Harry and Clarence crouched in the darkness, holding their horse's reins and gazing down on the ranch. They were well-hidden in the dark. The milling and bawling of the cattle covered any sounds they might make.

"What ya thinkin', Harry?"

"I'm thinkin' they had to suspect we'd follow 'em here."

"So you thinkin' it's a trap?"

Harry shook his head. "I'm thinkin' that they figured we'd go to the sheriff."

"They don't look like men who is worried much about a visit from the law."

"They're not."

"Sheriff's in with Brooks, ain't he, Harry?"

Harry nodded.

"Then why let Slim and Alva run off on a wild goose chase? I mean, if he won't help, what's the use in them ridin' all the way over to Hobard?"

"I'd just as soon they were out of the way, Clarence. Don't wanta take a chance on 'em gettin' hurt."

"You figuring on us takin' them bastards ourselves, Harry?" There was a slight trepidation in Clarence's voice. "Ya know we only got my gun. Alva 'n Slim took the rifles."

"Those boys down there aren't expecting anyone to have the nerve to confront them. That's our edge."

Clarence nodded.

"You'll need to take my word for this, Clarence, but we stand a better chance just the two of us. I have a plan. But first, we'll wait a bit. Let them rustlers get tired and slack." As he spoke, Harry lay back in the soft grass.

Clarence looked at him for a second and then lay down as well.

Closing his eyes, Harry began to hone his plan by reflecting on what he'd observed at Gilbert's ranch.

The barn and ranch house were dark and appeared empty. The four rustlers were staked out at intervals watching the cattle now crowded into the corral.

Each side of the corral was about fifty yards or so long. The two sides furthest from the house and barn were being guarded by two of the rustlers, one on each side. They had lanterns to push back the darkness and they were both packing revolvers. Besides the revolvers, one man was carrying a shotgun.

The other two rustlers were squatting at a campfire that had been lit near the corner of the corral closest to the barn. They were brewing coffee to help ward off the slight chill of the long night.

Harry decided he and Clarence would take an hour or so to grab some shut-eye while the rustlers got more tired and were lulled into further laxity. Then he'd put his plan into action.

* * *

Travis "Ratt" Wilson had planned his theft with cunning and precision. He'd made his men work most of two days expanding the corral at Gilbert Jackson's ranch to hold Slim's ninety-some head of cattle. Then they'd ridden boldly to Slim's ranch, cut his fence, rounded up his herd and drove them away.

Wilson knew that Slim would be busy on the other side of his ranch cutting hay, so he'd been confident that he and his men would not be spotted.

He also knew that, if somehow Slim tracked the cattle to the Jackson ranch, the rancher would balk at any kind of confrontation with him and his well-armed men.

When Wilson and his gang returned to the Jackson ranch with Slim's cattle, he staked out his men more as a show of force than as a means of defense.

The two men he stationed on the far side of the corral were brothers: killers out of Missouri named Wes and Frank Murphy. They'd started their outlaw careers some years before as petty thieves and had worked their way up to murderers for hire. They had built a reputation that had caught the attention of Ratt Wilson and he'd suggested them to Brooks when they were putting together their crew.

The other two members of his outfit were Josh Howard and Pony McCauley. They'd come from Texas and had been recommended by an oilman who was an acquaintance of Brooks. They'd been doing similar work for that man in Western Texas. However, they had been forced to leave the man's employ, as well as the territory, when they'd become suspects in the deaths of three ranchers.

All four men were ruthless and knew how to handle a gun. They practiced often and fancied themselves shootists.

Wilson figured that these men guarding the cattle would encourage Slim and anyone riding with him to go high-tailing it to the only law within forty miles, Sheriff Rafter. And, of course, his plan had been formed with this in mind all along. A smile touched his lips.

With the cattle secured in the corral, his men deployed to guard them, and their horses bedded in the barn for the night, Wilson confidently strolled to the Jackson house to take what he considered to be a well-deserved nap. Carrying his bedroll, he mounted the steps and opened the door.

He was mildly surprised when a cat followed him in.

"Jacksons leave you behind, cat?" He looked down at the feline as it rubbed against his leg. He reached in a pocket and pulled out a sliver of jerky. "Here. Now beat it and leave me be." He threw the jerky to the gaunt cat and the grateful animal snatched it before rushing out the door. Wilson's eyes followed it as the cat disappeared into the darkness. He'd once had a cat when he was a boy. Old memories stirred in the gunman as he lay down on his bedroll and closed his eyes.

* * *

Travis Wilson had been raised solely by his father. His mother had died at his birthing, something for which he knew his father had never forgiven him. The anger and loss that Travis' father felt was not motivated by love for the woman. Instead, it was because he felt he'd been robbed of the one person he most delighted in mistreating.

His father's abuse was soon redirected toward Travis. As a result, Travis had endured a harsh childhood. It hadn't been made any easier by the fact that his father frequently imbibed a form of home-made corn liquor which tended to put him into even more grievously foul moods. These moods led to more brutal beatings and on one occasion, to the demise of Travis' only pet.

The old man kicked his son out of the house when Travis reached puberty and had become too big and strong for him to mistreat.

After that, Wilson saw his father only one time. He was nineteen and had returned home for a visit that proved fatal for the old man. Wilson put a single .38 bullet in his father's forehead and rode away.

Chapter 13

THE PLAN

~ ~ ~

On the hill overlooking the ranch, Harry was still resting. He'd never really slept. Clarence, on the other hand, was snoring lightly when Harry decided it was time to go. He touched his friend on the shoulder and the snoring ceased.

"Ready to go, Harry?" Clarence asked as he rubbed the sleep from his eyes.

Harry nodded and walked to his horse. Retrieving several strands of rawhide from his saddlebag, he said, "This is what we will do."

* * *

Below them at the corral, Wes Murphy was tired of listening to the damn cattle bawl. In his mind, at this late hour, there was no chance that anyone would show up to challenge them for the cattle. He was getting cold from the late-night chill and the dampness wasn't helping, either. His thin frame offered no insulation and he was tired. He had half a notion to walk over to his brother and suggest that they say "screw it" and go join Josh and Pony by the fire.

A few seconds later, when Wes saw the shadowy figure walking toward him, he thought his brother was reading his mind and was coming to suggest they go in together. It was only when the figure was a few yards away that Wes realized it was not his brother, nor was it any of their gang.

"Hold it right there!" Wes pulled out his revolver. "Who the hell are you?" The light from the lantern at his feet only penetrated several feet into the darkness.

"Put yer hands where I can see 'em and step into the light," Wes Murphy demanded.

* * *

Earlier, covered by the noise of the restless cattle, Harry had worked his way down the hill and had quietly started his approach to the rustler. He planned to get as close as possible before being seen.

"Whoa. Take it easy there, Mister." Harry slowly put up his hands before adding, "I'm not armed."

Turning around with his hands still in the air, Harry demonstrated that he had no gun before advancing into the light.

Wes Murphy had been leaning on the fence before Harry showed up and he was still standing within a couple feet of it. The rustler suspiciously looked behind Harry into the darkness.

"You alone?"

Harry nodded and stepped closer.

"Close enough." Murphy held up his left hand. "Now, what the hell do you think you're ...?"

Wes stopped mid-sentence when he heard the click. At the sound, recognition and defeat registered in his eyes.

* * *

A few minutes before Harry had started his descent, Clarence had wormed his way in the dusty darkness down the hill.

With his dark clothes and ebony skin, Clarence was almost invisible in the dark night. He'd learned from an early age how to move quietly and unseen whenever it was necessary and it had been necessary on many an occasion during his lifetime.

Approaching a point between the two brothers, he slipped under the bottom fence rail and quietly crawled along the inside of the coral, slowly working his way to a position within a few feet of Wes Murphy.

Harry had appeared right on cue. Distracting the rustler had given Clarence the opportunity to get close and reach over the fence with his .32. Pointed at Wes's head and less than six inches from the rustler's ear, he cocked the revolver. That was the click that Wes Murphy had heard and recognized.

An ominous whisper issued from deep in Clarence's throat. "Twitch a whisker and I'll blow yo brains out'n your other ear. Now, drop dat hog leg!"

Wes had neglected to cock his gun when Harry had approached. But even if he had, with Clarence's .32 pointed straight at his head, he was without options. He dropped the weapon.

When the gun hit the ground, Clarence said, "Kick yer piece over ta my friend there."

Murphy clenched his fists and kicked the gun. He glared at the two men but said nothing.

Harry picked up the pistol. "Don't even think about calling out to the others," he said. "Do as you're told and you'll live to see tomorrow."

* * *

Five minutes later, the outlaw was bound with rawhide and sitting on the ground next to the fence. He'd been relieved of his brown derby hat and long, tan duster.

Harry replaced his own hat with the derby and slipped on the duster. For a second he gazed at the gun he was holding. Finally making up his mind, he stuck it in his belt. Adjusting the derby, he looked questioningly at Clarence.

"Looks perdy good. In this pitch dark it should do jist fine."

Harry looked at the rustler sitting on the ground and then at Clarence standing over him. He gave his friend a meaningful nod. Then to the rustler he said, "Good night."

Clarence thumped down on the man's head with the butt of his gun. The resulting crack was somewhat louder than Harry had expected. As Wes Murphy toppled sideways into the dirt and lost consciousness, Harry glanced around to see if the loud crack had been heard by anyone.

"You think you thumped him hard enough there, Clarence?"

Clarence looked sheepishly at Harry and then bent down to check the rustler for signs of life.

"Maybe a might, but he'll live. Should have a sizable headache in the mornin', though."

* * *

Wes Murphy's brother, Frank, was leaning against the wooden fence, struggling to stay awake. The boards bent under the weight of his rotund frame. Wes often berated him for carrying too much weight but on this cool night, the extra fat gave Frank a layer of insulation.

Though not feeling the cold, he was nonetheless aggravated that he and his brother had been left out there to guard a bunch of smelly animals against the unlikely chance that their rightful owner might make a play to get them back.

Frank's 12-gauge shotgun was propped against the fence and his lantern was on the ground at his feet. His head bobbed as he slipped in and out of a light doze. For a second he almost fell over before regaining his balance. It was at this moment that he spotted his brother, Wes, lantern in hand and heading in his direction.

He had been hoping that Ratt would send word for them to come in. It was almost four in the morning and no one had showed up yet to try and reclaim the cattle.

It looked like Wilson had been right. The chicken-shit rancher who owned the cattle wasn't about to confront armed gunmen and, if he hadn't already, would surely run off to town for help from the sheriff.

"Ratt Wilson send word for us to come in?" Frank Murphy called out to the shadowy figure he assumed was his brother. He stooped to pick up his lantern and shotgun.

The approaching outline of a man stopped about twenty feet away. In the darkness, Frank could only make out a slight nod. As the dark figure turned and walked away, he motioned for Frank to follow.

"Well, it's about time. Can't believe the bastard left us out here this long." Frank stomped after the man he still thought was his brother.

Walking close to the fence, he heard a sound behind him. He turned to look into the darkness, but the inky night flashed red. Then coal black came over Frank Murphy.

* * *

As Frank fell, the shotgun slipped from his hand and the lantern clattered to the ground.

Harry watched as Clarence climbed over the fence and checked his victim for vital signs.

"Better, Harry? Thumped him a might softer than the other'n." Clarence smiled as he spoke.

Harry smiled too, but said nothing as he began to bind the unconscious rustler. He tied Frank's hands with rawhide and ran a strand down to bind his feet, leaving him hog-tied.

He had not gagged either man after tying them. He'd learned from experience that men who are knocked unconscious tend to vomit when they come to. If they were gagged, they could easily choke to death on their own puke. It was not Harry's intention to kill any of these men. Their deaths would give Brooks a legal excuse to come after the ranchers. Tonight, Harry simply wanted Slim's cattle returned.

"What now, Harry?" Clarence asked in a low voice.

Harry kept his voice low as well. "This one and the other will keep long enough for our purposes. Now, we'll pay a visit to the other two. You can do the inside work again." Harry gave Clarence a wry smile. "You seem to have a way with those cows. Take the scatter gun." Harry looked guiltily at the revolver in his belt. "I have the first one's pistol."

"Careful with that thing, Harry." Clarence nodded at the pistol.

Harry's plan did not call for the need to shoot any weapon. He'd made the plan with that in mind. It vexed him some that he was going to even handle a gun considering his promise to Etta. Still, he figured just using it for show was marginally within the intent of the vow.

"Don't worry, Clarence, it's just fer show. Do your part with the scatter gun an' it'll be fine."

Clarence nodded. Then he climbed back into the corral with the fidgety, bawling cattle. "See ya over there," he whispered.

Harry had been kidding when he told Clarence he had a way with the cows, but the truth was Clarence was good with cattle. It would be dangerous for most men to work their way through a herd of cattle that had been driven for several hours and then confined in an unfamiliar corral, but Clarence had a way. His presence often soothed them.

For a moment, Harry watched him move with ease and confidence through the restless animals, calming them by stroking their shoulders as he duck-walked toward the campfire and the other two rustlers.

* * *

The fire crackled and sparked as Josh Howard and Pony McCauley soaked up its warmth. Sitting on cut tree stumps, they smugly sipped hot cups of steaming coffee.

Just before Wilson went into the house for his nap, he'd told Josh and Pony to exchange places with the Murphy brothers in an hour or so. But the fire and coffee had proved too much of a comfort for these two rustlers to waste on two "Missouri mules," as they often called the Murphy boys when they were out of earshot.

It was with a little guilt as well as surprise that Pony looked up and saw what appeared to be Wes Murphy in his derby hat and long duster heading their way. He carried his lantern low and he had his head bent down. The brim of his hat and the cap of the lantern cast a dark shadow across his face. Pony nudged Josh and nodded toward the approaching figure.

Pony decided it was best to go on the offensive instead of sounding guilty for hogging the fire and coffee.

"What you doin' over here?" Pony challenged as he and Josh stood up. "Thought Wilson told you to stay on the other side until he said different."

"Could use some coffee," Harry spoke with a hoarse whisper.

Stepping into the firelight, Harry lifted his head. His right hand moved forward out of the shadow and Pony could see a revolver pointed at them.

Josh dropped his coffee and pulled his gun. At the same time Pony reached for his.

There was an explosion and the dirt in front of the two rustlers burst up in a cloud of grass and dust. They stumbled back and froze in place.

"That was just one barrel," said a dark, menacing figure standing on the other side of the corral fence. Smoke drifted lazily from a barrel of his shotgun. "Drop those irons or I'll use the other'n to blow a head off."

Harry cocked the hammer on his revolver. "I'd advise you to do as he said."

Pony looked at his companion, sighed, and then both men dropped their weapons.

Still leveling his shotgun at the two, Clarence climbed over the fence. "Not too bad, Harry. You'd a made a good law man."

* * *

Ratt Wilson was jarred from his sound sleep by a loud explosion. He shook his head and looked around the room. At first he thought maybe he'd been dreaming. He rubbed his eyes and peered out the kitchen window.

What he saw near the corral was something he could not quite get his mind around. It looked like the Murphys were holding guns on Josh and Pony.

He watched as the two Texans dropped their guns and unbuckled their gun belts. Then one of the Murphy's stepped closer to the fire. He was a black man. And then he saw that the other man, though dressed like Wes Murphy, was not a Murphy either.

Anger welled up like gases building in an oil well. Wilson quickly pulled on his boots and strapped on his gun belt. Checking his revolver, he pushed through the ranch house door and slipped into the dark night.

* * *

At the corral, Harry stuck the gun he'd taken from Wes Murphy back in his belt and kicked Josh's and Pony's pistols well out of reach.

Clarence kept the shotgun pointed at the rustlers while Harry reached for the final two strands of rawhide he had in his pocket.

"Now, you two turn slow, so's yo' backs are toward Mr. Kidwell there and put yo' hands together 'hind yo' backs," Clarence barked.

As the two men slowly turned around, Harry stepped forward to tie their wrists.

There was a slight noise in the darkness behind Harry and then came the sound of a revolver hammer being clicked back.

"A fine idea," came a voice from the darkness. "Only let's have you two do it instead. Drop that shotgun, Darky! And both of ya drop your pistols and kick 'em away."

Ratt Wilson stepped into the light. He stood just behind Harry and was shielded from Clarence's aim. Harry shook his head as he pulled the revolver from his belt, dropped it, and kicked it away.

"Gettin' old," he whispered as the gun skittered into the darkness.

Chapter 14

THE SHERIFF

~ ~ ~

A few parked automobiles lined the streets of the sleepy town of Hobard. It was a town that was just beginning to find its way into the Twentieth Century. In this part of Oklahoma, the horse and buggy was still the prevalent mode of transportation, but it was slowly giving way to the horseless carriage.

Brick buildings, reaching as high as four stories had begun to replace the wooden structures of the last century. Electricity lit many of the homes and businesses that only a few years before had been illuminated with oil or kerosene.

* * *

The clip-clop of horse hooves on brick pavement echoed in the still night as Alva rode with Slim along Main Street. Their shadows alternately shortened and lengthened as they passed under the electric lamp posts lining the street. It was almost 3:30 in the morning.

"Looks like the town's asleep." Slim looked around as he spoke. "You figure the sheriff's office will be open, Alva? What if the rustlers move the cattle somewheres before we get back with the law?"

"Relax, Slim," Alva said calmingly. "If it's closed, I know where Rafter lives and, if they move the cattle, Harry and Clarence will follow 'em and send us word, in there."

Alva could well imagine the panic that Slim was feeling. His cattle meant his livelihood. To lose them would be his ruin.

A few minutes later they approached the sheriff's office. It was a new two-story brick building with jail cells on the second floor. On the ground floor the street-side windows were dark.

Slim sprang down from his horse and pounded on the door. After a few seconds, he pounded again. Finally, a light came on and Alva could see the movement of a shadow through the door window. Slim continued to pound.

"All right, I hear ya," hollered a voice from inside.

With a click of a lock, the door eased open a few inches.

"Office's closed. You'll have to come back in the morning," a male voice said.

"This is important. I need to talk to the sheriff." Slim pleaded.

"Sheriff ain't here."

"It's important."

"Anybody been killed?" the voice asked.

"No, but...."

"Then you'll have to come back in the morning."
The door went shut.

Slim was about to pound on the door again when
Alva intervened. "Forget it. We'll go directly to the
horse's mouth, in there."

Slim took a last look at the door then turned
away. He climbed on his horse and the two rode
slowly down the street.

"Sheriff lives above the hardware store." Alva
pointed to a store several buildings away from the
jail.

There was a wooden side stair attached to the
building and Alva led the way as the two men
mounted the steps. Their cowboy boots clacked on
the hardwood and echoed though the night. At the
top, Alva rapped on the sheriff's door. A light came
on.

* * *

Several minutes later Alva and Slim followed as
Sheriff Rafter led them back to his office. His sleepy
deputy stepped aside as they entered.

"I told them you weren't here, Sheriff, and they
should come back in the morning," the deputy
whined as the three men entered the office.

Rafter nodded and gave him a dismissive wave
as he sat down behind his desk. The deputy retreated
to one of the back rooms.

"All right, give it to me again, gentlemen."
Rafter rubbed the sleep from his eyes.

"It's like I told you, Sheriff. They stole my
cattle," Slim squawked. "We followed 'em to Gilbert
Jackson's place. They got 'em in the corral there. It's

a pure case of rustlin'!" He punctuated the last sentence with a bang of his fist on the sheriff's desk.

Rafter looked disapprovingly at Slim's balled fist and then at Slim. "Afraid it ain't that simple, fellas," he began. "You see, Melvin Howell and that Wilson fellow came in here yesterday mornin'. Said there just might be some trouble with you, Mr. Moore, in regards to some cattle they bought. Showed me a bill of sale."

Red-faced, Slim shouted, "Bill 'o sale! What the hell you talkin' about, Sheriff? I didn't sell no cattle!"

"Well, that's just what Mr. Howell said you'd say. That's why he brought the bill o' sale with him and showed it to me. Looked legal and proper. Had your signature on it and Mr. Travis Wilson witnessed it."

"I'm tellin' ya, I didn't sell no cattle and I didn't sign no bill o' sale! Those cattle were rustled off'n my place yesterday," Slim yelled.

"Ease up there, Mr. Moore. No sense in yellin'. Where did you say those cattle were now?" Sheriff Rafter spoke softly.

"They're over to the Jackson place in Gilbert's corral." Slim calmed a little.

Rafter shook his head slowly. "That right? That ranch belongs to Mr. Brooks, if I'm not mistaken. Seems rather peculiar that these so-called rustlers would take your cattle and then just leave them right there where everyone can see 'em. Seems more like what someone would do if they bought those cattle."

Slim balled his fists and moved toward the sheriff. "You think I'm lyin'? What the hell's goin' on here! What kinda..."

From the very first Alva could see where this whole thing was headed and a fight with the sheriff would only make matters worse. "Whoa, Slim! Take it easy, in there." Alva put a hand on his friend's shoulder and eased himself between Slim and the sheriff. "This ain't gettin' us nowhere."

After waiting a second or two for Slim to calm a little, Alva addressed Rafter. "You sayin' you ain't gonna do nothing, in there?"

"I didn't say that. What I'm saying is I'll have to look into it. In the meantime you can file a complaint, and I'll take it to the County Judge."

"File a complaint? Take it 'afore a judge? This ain't right!" Slim wailed. "Alva, this ain't right! Them cattle are mine!"

Alva moved Slim to the other side of the room and sat him in a chair. "I know, Slim. I know."

Anger and frustration radiated from his friend like smoldering ash. Alva put his hand on Slim's shoulder and waited. Slowly the anger was replaced by exhaustion and a look of hopelessness.

Seeing that Slim had calmed a bit, Alva turned back to the sheriff. "Where's this complaint form we gotta fill out?"

Rafter smiled as he rifled through one of his desk drawers. He pulled out a piece of paper. "This should do. You'll need to give me some information, Mr. Moore."

A few minutes later, Slim signed the paper that Rafter had prepared.

By now, Alva could see that Slim had regained a little of his fight. Pulling himself to his full height, the rancher looked Rafter in the eye. "This here piece a paper better get me my cattle back. Them fellas stole my whole herd."

"I'm afraid that will be up to the judge, Mr. Moore. But to tell you the truth, possession is what usually counts in these cases." As he spoke, a crooked smile crept across Rafter's lips. "And since they have the cattle, well, they have the upper hand you see."

Slim was beginning to heat up again. Alva stepped in and ushered his friend toward the door. "Come on, Slim. We've done all we can here."

"Now, don't you boys get any foolish ideas about taking the law in your own hands," Rafter warned. "Best stay away from the Jackson ranch and those cattle until this is settled."

Alva grabbed Slim by the arm and dragged him out the door.

Chapter 15

MISDIRECTION

~ ~ ~

Harry couldn't believe how foolish he'd been. This was the kind of mistake his old partner had always managed to avoid. "Prepare for every possibility" had been his motto. Why hadn't he thought about the possibility that Wilson was sleeping in the ranch house? That had to be where he'd come from.

Wilson stepped closer and took a look at Harry. "Well, damn if it ain't old Harry Kidwell." Then with a glance at Clarence, "And this here must be your nigger."

Harry hated that term and he felt his neck begin to burn.

Wilson smiled. "Howell said you were a might touchy when it comes to your boy, here. Well, won't do you no good to get riled up. I'm the one with the gun."

Wilson waved his .38 at Clarence. "You! Come a might closer."

Bravely squaring his shoulders, Clarence stepped forward, stopping just to Harry's right.

Wilson glanced at his men who were still standing by the fence. "What you two idiots doin' just standin' there? Get your guns!"

As his men moved to retrieve their weapons, Ratt Wilson stepped closer to Harry and put his gun in Harry's face. The .38 was still cocked and the barrel was about twelve inches from Harry's nose.

It was all that Harry could do to keep from smiling at the mistake. Obviously, Wilson didn't consider him much of a threat. Now, if he wasn't too rusty, Harry figured he could take advantage of that mistake. But there were problems. One, he wasn't sure if he still had the skill to do what he planned. And, if he did, Clarence would see it all. Well, he'd have to deal with that when the time came.

"Now, both of you slowly raise your hands above your heads," Wilson sneered. "I like to see brave old heroes with their hands in the air."

Harry realized Wilson would soon tire of playing with them. Any second now, he'd just shoot them and later claim self-defense.

Harry looked into Ratt Wilson's cold pale green eyes and slowly raised his hands by extending them to his sides.

It was when his arms were parallel to the ground that Harry's expression changed. His face took on a distorted look, like a strange face in a fun-house mirror. Slowly his eyes moved to gaze at his right hand. That hand had taken on palsy-like contortions.

Harry could see the puzzlement in Wilson's eyes. The gunman couldn't help but follow Harry's gaze with that of his own. In that split second, Wilson was misdirected and Harry acted. In cases like this, a gunman expected an opponent to grab for his weapon.

Instead, Harry brought his sharp-toed cowboy boot up into Wilson's unprotected and sensitive groin.

When the boot connected with Ratt Wilson's testicles, his eyes popped open like giant marbles. The air rushed from his lungs with a half-gasp and half-scream. Instinctively, he bent forward and reached to protect himself.

At that instant, Harry brought his left hand around in a lightning-fast arch that slipped up from beneath Wilson's gun hand, striking with brutal force and blinding speed. With the impact, the gun pointed skyward and discharged. The bullet passed by Harry's left ear, missing it by less than two inches. The force of the impact wrenched the .38 from Ratt's hand and sent it flying into the air.

The bullet buzzing past Harry's ear didn't distract him. His attention was focused on the gun as it spun upward. In his peripheral vision he sensed the movements of Howard and McCauley who had quickened their attempts to retrieve their weapons.

As Ratt's gun descended, Harry snatched it expertly out of the air and, in a continuous motion, brought the butt of the weapon down hard on Wilson's head. The resulting crack seemed even louder than the one Clarence had dealt Wes Murphy. Wilson crumpled unconscious to the ground.

Josh Howard was the first to reach his gun. He lifted the revolver to fire. Harry fanned off a shot.

Harry had little sympathy for these men. Nonetheless, he didn't shoot to kill. Killing them would surely bring the corrupt law down on him and Clarence, as well as Alva and Slim.

His bullet slammed into Josh Howard's gun hand, taking off his little finger and spinning the gun across the corral fence and into the darkness.

Pony McCauley retrieved his gun, but fired too quickly. The bullet went wide.

Harry fanned his gun twice. Both bullets struck Pony McCauley. The first went straight through his right wrist. The second plowed into his lower right forearm, shattering muscle and bone before exiting through his elbow.

Pony took one look at his damaged right arm and fainted.

Clarence stood dumbfounded. The look on his face read as a mixture of amazement and disbelief.

"Clarence, grab your gun and then see to that last one I shot. He looks to be bleeding pretty bad. See if you can find something to bind his wounds."

Josh Howard seemed in shock at the loss of his pinky finger. He was dumbly looking around as if he might find it on the ground somewhere in the darkness.

Harry smiled a little at the thought of the murderer looking for his finger like a little boy looking for a lost marble. "Just sit down over there with your back to the fence," he ordered.

As Josh numbly obeyed and sat on the ground, Harry stuck Wilson's gun in his belt and retrieved the one he'd been forced to drop earlier.

A few minutes later, Clarence emerged from the ranch house with rags to bandage Pony's and Josh's wounds. He looked over at Harry as he wrapped them around the arm of the still-unconscious Pony McCauley.

"What the hell jist happened here, Harry? How...? Harry, I ain't never seen nothin' like that a'fore."

"It might be best if you were to get it in your mind that you didn't see it now. I just got lucky. Nothing more, okay?"

Clarence nodded slowly. Still, Harry could see a look of suspicion in his dark brown eyes.

* * *

A little later all five rustlers – attended to, bound, and somewhat dazed – sat in the dirt next to the corral.

Wilson watched with murderous eyes as Harry and Clarence drove the cattle through the corral gate, past him and his trussed-up gunmen. "You'll regret this, Kidwell. You an' your nigger, both."

As the last steer exited the corral, Harry tipped his hat at Wilson and his hired guns. Then he spurred his horse and took out after Clarence and the herd.

They were barely over the rise with the cattle when Alva and Slim rode into view. They galloped over and pulled up next to Harry.

"What happened, Harry? How the hell...?" Slim gazed out at his herd and then, confounded, he looked at Harry and Clarence.

"Long story, Slim. Fill you in later. Right now let's get these cattle of yours back where they belong." Harry turned his attention to the herd.

As he drove the cattle away from the Jackson ranch, Harry couldn't help but feel guilty. He'd broken his long-time promise to Etta. And if it came right down to it, the thing that made him feel the worst was that he'd enjoyed it.

He was thinking about this and about Etta as he pulled Wes's and Wilson's guns from his belt and let them fall to the ground to be trampled by the cattle.

* * *

It was midmorning by the time Harry and Clarence returned home. Etta stood with Lee on the porch looking anxiously down the lane. It was Laura, playing in the back yard, who saw them first. She called to her mom and watched as her father and Clarence dismounted and led their horses into the barn.

Harry and Clarence were busy unsaddling their mounts when Etta and the kids burst into the barn. Harry didn't look up from his task. He had fully intended to get back the cattle without shooting a gun. Unfortunately, he'd gotten Clarence and himself into a situation that would have been lethal if he'd not fired one. But that didn't change the fact that he'd broken his promise to the woman he loved.

Trying to keep his eyes from Etta's, Harry carried his saddle into the tack room.

"Did you find them?" Lee followed his father to the door, eager to hear the details.

Harry came out and returned to his horse. He said nothing as he used a brush to rub it down.

Lee stood patiently, waiting for an answer.

Etta gazed at her husband and waited as well.

Finally, Clarence answered the question. "Found 'em over to the Jackson place."

"How in the world did they get over there?" Etta asked Harry, who continued to curry his horse.

When Harry didn't answer, Clarence spoke up again. "Some men took 'em, Mz Etta. Herded them over there and put 'em up in Gilbert's corral."

"You mean they rustled 'em?" Lee asked.

Etta was still staring at Harry, suspicion clouding her face. Walking up to him, she put her hand on his shoulder.

"Where are they now, Harry?"

Keeping his eyes averted, Harry stopped work on his horse and said, "Slim's got 'em."

Etta looked puzzled. "Slim has them?"

"How'd you get them back, Pa?" Lee interrupted.

Etta gently turned Harry to face her. "How much trouble was there?"

He finally looked into Etta's eyes. "Not much," he said before going back to grooming his horse.

Clarence broke the silence. "We pretty much snuck 'em outa there, Mz Etta. I don't believe the men who took 'em expected anyone to be comin' after 'em in the middle of the night."

Etta looked skeptical. Her eyes questioned back and forth between Harry and Clarence. "So they rustled them and then they let you waltz in there and take them back."

Again an uneasy silence and again, it was Clarence who finally spoke. "For the most part they was kinda sleepin'. The ones who weren't, we convinced 'em it would be best to just give 'em up."

"That right, Harry? They just gave the cattle back?" The accusation in Etta's voice was like lemon on a cut.

"More or less that's the way it happened. We had to do a little convincing, but they turned out to be reasonable. Important thing is we got them back without anyone getting killed and that's the end of it." Harry spoke in a way that told everyone that the subject was closed.

* * *

Lee was puzzled. He knew there was something going on between his mother and father, but he couldn't figure out what it was. His mother was both suspicious and angry and his father seemed embarrassed and evasive.

A thought struck Lee. His father was embarrassed because it was Clarence, Slim and Alva who had confronted the rustlers and made them give back the cattle. They were the ones who would have had guns. His father was afraid of guns and probably backed away when it came time to confront the rustlers. He'd let the others do all the dangerous work. That must be it. His pa was ashamed of himself and he was evasive because Lee's mother suspected as much. It all made sense.

Lee glared at his father then turned away and ran back into the house.

Chapter 16

SCOTT C. BROOKS

~ ~ ~

Scott C. Brooks had an office on the fifth floor of the Brooks Petroleum building in downtown Oklahoma City. Although not the tallest building in the city, it was one of the most recently built.

From his office, Brooks could hear the sound of the trolley cars rattling below on their steel tracks. And, on the brick street, he could hear the din of the autos that had nearly surpassed the numbers of horse-and-buggies in Oklahoma City.

Brooks sat behind his large walnut desk smoking a fat Cuban cigar. Squinting coldly at the men seated before him, he took the cigar out of his mouth with pudgy fingers and flicked its ash into a solid silver ashtray.

Brooks had started in the oil business only three years before. He'd bought into a small oil company in Pennsylvania. A year later his sole partner died unexpectedly. The death was ruled "natural causes," but the only things natural were the castor beans Brooks had used to poison the man.

He'd re-christened the company with his own name and expanded it through criminal means no less lethal than those he'd used to become sole owner.

Scott Brooks had been born Salvatore Cappaletti in Brooklyn, New York. A thief, at the age of fourteen, he ran with a few small-time crooks. Eventually, he worked his way into the notorious Five Points Gang. It was there that he became acquainted with a young tough named Alphonse. They developed a mutual respect.

When Cappaletti left Brooklyn to muscle his way into the Pennsylvania oil business, he didn't lose touch with the young tough. He kept track of Al's career as he followed Johnny Torrio, their mentor, to Chicago.

With his new line of work, Cappaletti changed his name to Brooks. It was partially to create a different identity and partially because he didn't like the name Cappaletti, which, in Italian, meant 'little hat'. Brooks was a name that gave him a new identity but still reflected, in a sly way, his ties to Brooklyn.

The new Scott C. Brooks was cunning, as well as lethal. He made friends with those who were on their way up in the rackets, like Alphonse, and he eliminated those who might stand in his way.

He could put on a congenial face and he knew how to use money to curry favor or grease palms when it was to his advantage.

During his days back in New York, Brooks had been impressed with Alphonse. Although not close friends, he and Al had maintained a professional relationship that was mutually beneficial.

Eventually Al's mentor, Johnny Torrio, had become the top Chicago mafia figure and Alphonse Capone was his right-hand man.

When Brooks first got word that Ratt Wilson was encountering more resistance than anticipated, he immediately got in touch with Al. A good deal of money exchanged hands and the best "enforcer" in the Windy City, along with his team, had been hired.

Brooks was content to use a billy club to do a job if that were all that was needed. If a billy club was inadequate, he would not hesitate to bring in a cannon. Serpente, the man Al had recommended, was the cannon.

Sitting comfortably behind his desk, Brooks eyed what he considered his billy club.

Ratt Wilson, the Murphy brothers, and Josh Howard, with his hand bandaged and looking pale, sat in chairs facing Brooks' impressive desk. Pony McCauley was not there. He was so badly wounded that he would no longer be of any use.

Sun streaming through the window cast shadows from the "Brooks Imperial Petroleum Company" sign on Wilson and his men.

Brooks finally spoke. "Well? I'm waiting."

Wilson looked defiant and was about to say something when Josh blurted out, "It was that rancher. What's his name ...?"

Wilson cursed under his breath and gave Josh a deadly look. Josh seemed to get the message and shut up.

"Look, everything went like I planned." Wilson turned his attention from Josh to focus on the fat man behind the opulent desk. "We had it all worked out with your friend, Sheriff Rafter. They go to him, they get nowhere. If they get dumb enough to try and get the cattle themselves, we're ready. This old rancher named Kidwell was foolish enough to make a play for the cattle. We got the drop on him easy enough. Then outa nowhere his black-ass hired hand showed up and started blastin' away with a .32. He couldn't shoot for shit, but he got lucky and shot Josh in the hand and Pony in the arm."

"What the hell were you doing during all this?" Brooks' eyes bore into Ratt Wilson.

For a second Wilson's face went blank. Finally, he shrugged. "I was knocked out. They got lucky. Hadn't been for that darky slippin' up on us.... Can't see them sons o' bitches in the dark."

Brooks eyeballed the four men. He said nothing for a long while and the room grew heavy with tension.

He blew forth a plume of cigar smoke before he spoke. "Seems maybe I overestimated you and your men, Wilson. I've decided to bring in a man from Chicago. A man named Serpente. He comes with a crew."

"There's no need for that. They got lucky this one time, that's all." Wilson's snake eyes stared unblinking at Brooks. "We can handle this."

"I've seen how you can handle it. Doesn't matter, though. I sent for Serpente day before yesterday when I heard about what happened at the Jackson ranch. This man and his boys come well recommended by my friend in Chicago."

"Look, we have these two-bit ranchers on the edge," Wilson declared in a hiss. "Just a little push and they'll fold. I know just where to push."

Before Brooks could answer, there was a knock on his door. He looked impatiently at his secretary as she stepped into the room.

This was the third personal secretary that Brooks had hired in the last year. She was an attractive young woman, as had been the others. She nervously fidgeted as she spoke.

"Sorry to bother you, Mr. Brooks, but that man is here. The one you wanted me to tell you when he arrived."

Brooks waved her away and she quickly closed the door. As the door shut behind her, Brooks returned his attention to the men before him.

"Do what you like, Wilson. I'm still going to back you up with this man from Chicago." Brooks dismissed them with a wave of his hand. As they walked out, he followed them to his office door.

* * *

As Wilson led his men into the reception area, he was aware that the attractive secretary had repositioned herself behind her desk. But, as attractive as she was, his attention was drawn to the man sitting alone in a chair looking cool and calm.

Walking past him, the man stared back locking eyes with Wilson for a moment before he turned his attention to Brooks, looming in his office doorway. Standing up, the man straightened his finely-tailored suit and nodded. Brooks motioned him into his office.

Waiting with his men in the hall for the elevator car to arrive, Josh looked quizzically at his boss. "What the hell was that all about?" When Wilson didn't answer right away, Josh continued. "I'm talkin' about that shit where you said the spook came out o' the dark blastin' away. It wasn't like that at all."

Wilson shot Josh an evil stare. "I wasn't about to tell Brooks that some old grey-haired farmer got the drop on us. And you can keep your yap shut about it, too. Next time I meet up with that old bastard he won't get lucky like he did that night."

"You didn't see what he did, Ratt. He ain't just some old farmer. I'm tellin' ya, there's somethin' just ain't right about that old guy. You was out cold. You didn't see ..."

"Shut the hell up! I heard it all before!" Wilson was fed up with Josh and the others. They'd been harping on it for two days now. With fire in his eyes, he stuck his finger in Josh's face. "I'm tellin' you, he got lucky! You men can say that shit about him bein' special all you want, but no old, over-the-hill rancher could'a done what you say without gettin' lucky. Now just drop it."

The elevator arrived and the door slid open. Wilson's men hesitated. He looked at them as though their fears of this strange box that transported people up and down the tall building were silly and unwarranted. He squared his shoulders and bravely stepped aboard. Warily, his men followed.

The elevator operator moved the handle and the car dropped a few feet before it started its slow decent. Wide-eyed, all four *brave* gunmen stood with their backs pressed to the walls. Finally, the car jerked to a stop on the ground floor. The door was thrown open and, with an audible sigh, the men exited.

As they left the building Wes Murphy was the first to speak. "That guy who went into Brooks' office just now? Do you think he was the fella Brooks hired from Chicago?"

"Maybe. But, if it is him, I didn't much like the way he looked at me," Wilson said.

* * *

When he let the stranger into his office, S.C. Brooks made himself comfortable behind his imposing desk. He liked to be the dominant figure in any situation and always sat in a chair six inches higher than the others in his office.

The oilman put on his congenial face, motioning for the stranger to take a seat. He was a little irritated when the man declined and continued to wander about the office, inspecting Brooks' pictures and framed documents on the walls.

To cover his irritation, Brooks directed his attention to paperwork that the man had placed on his desk. After perusing it, he shoved the papers across his desk.

"Impressive." Brooks once again motioned for the man to sit.

* * *

The stranger ignored the gesture for a moment as he stood looking out the window. Turning slowly, he moved toward one of the chairs.

As a man who knew the subtleties of control and dominance, he'd purposely remained standing until now. He did not let Brooks feel comfortable until he'd established a little dominance of his own.

Casually, he slipped into one of the visitor's chairs. He leaned back and studied the oilman before him.

"I need to ask a few questions about your organization. More importantly, what exactly do you have in mind?"

Chapter 17

GROWING ANXIETY

~ ~ ~

On the Sunday following the return of Slim's cattle, Harry piled his family into the Model T and headed for church as usual.

An hour later, the congregation's voices, raised in song and filling the solitary white church, could be heard harmonizing with the strains of the new organ.

The singing reached a crescendo as the final hymn, "Rock of Ages", came to an end. The Parson recited a prayer. Then, after walking down the aisle, he addressed the crowd from the rear of the sanctuary.

"That concludes our services. I understand that the ranchers have business they'd like to discuss. If the children would go out to play and the ladies would like to gather outside to socialize, I'll turn the premises over to the men-folk."

Harry knew that Alva believed it was the men's job to provide and protect. Alva had arranged for this meeting and that meant the men were the ones expected to handle these situations.

For Harry this presented a problem. None of the ranchers knew his and Etta's history. If they had, they would have known that there was no way Etta would allow herself to be excused from this meeting.

At the Parson's announcement, the children cheered and rushed outside. The women began to file out, whispering among themselves as they walked down the aisle and out into the bright sun of a beautiful day.

The Parson, as usual, had positioned himself just outside the church doors to shake hands with those who were not staying for the meeting.

Inside the church, Etta was still in her seat. She gave Harry a look that said, "You best back me in this."

When Laura and the other children filed out, Lee started to leave, as well. But, when he saw his mother still sitting, he stopped.

Harry nodded at Etta and looked up at his son who was still standing in the aisle.

"Pa, I want to stay. I do a man's work and I think I'm old enough," Lee blurted out.

Harry thought on it a minute. "You will just listen. No comments. You may think you're old enough, but the men here will not take kindly to a boy giving comments."

Lee looked his father in the eye and nodded.

A low murmur had already begun when Alva rose and started toward the front of the church. The eyes of most of the men-folk had turned toward Etta.

As Alva came even with Harry's pew he paused and looked from Etta to Harry.

"Harry ... you think maybe it would be best ..." Alva started.

"No, I don't, Alva." Harry cut him off with a steely look and sharp-edged tone.

Alva paused then continued on toward the front of the sanctuary.

He had turned to address the crowd when Slim stood and cleared his throat. "Before you start, Alva, I have somethin' I'd like to say. Wanna say how grateful I am for what Harry and his hired-hand, Clarence, did for me t'other night. Grateful to you too, Alva. Mostly 'cause of them I got my herd back and for that I'm mighty grateful." Slim nodded shyly at everyone. Before he sat, he added, "Just wanted everyone to know."

Harry's neck turned red as he felt Etta's eyes on him. A soft round of applause didn't make things any better. He nodded and mumbled, "Didn't do much."

"We're grateful to you both, in there. Woulda liked to of thanked Clarence again in person. Too bad he don't attend on Sundays." Alva said.

"Clarence makes his own mind on things like Sunday meetin'." Feeling Etta stiffen beside him, Harry regretted his words before they were completely out of his mouth.

There were sparks in Etta's eyes as she bolted up to speak. "Now, why don't you just tell these fine gentlemen the truth, Harry? Tell them why Clarence doesn't come here on Sundays."

When Harry didn't answer, Etta decided she would. "Clarence feels that there are some folks here who wouldn't welcome him because of his color. He's a mild man and not one to make waves, especially if they might cause trouble for our family."

There was a long silence before Slim finally spoke up. "Well, all's I can say is my welcome wagon's out anytime and anywhere, 'specially after what he done for me."

"Same goes for me," Alva said.

Austin was seated among the attending ranchers and he chimed in, as well. "Me too. I feel a might 'shamed that some here would hold a man's color agin' him. From what I hear Clarence risked his life to help not jist Slim, but, in a way, all of us the other night."

There were murmurs of agreement, but Etta saw that a few of the men were conspicuous in their silence.

* * *

Buford Bauer turned to look at the man next to him. Buford knew that there were at least two others in the room who felt the same as he. One was Martin Bowen, seated next to him, and the other was Darnell Hutton.

Buford had come by his predisposition toward blacks in the most common of ways. He was the youngest of seven brothers and sisters and had been born in 1883 in Pulaski, Tennessee. His father was thirty-nine at the time of Buford's birth and Buford's mother was thirty-one.

During the War between the North and South Buford's father, Elijah, had fought for the "cause," and he'd never let Buford or any of Buford's siblings forget it. He was a bitter man and resented the fact that the South had lost.

After the war, Elijah had joined a group of like-minded men dedicated to putting the "darkies" of the South in their place and righting the wrongs brought on by the occupation of the South by Union Troops.

This group called themselves the Ku Klux Klan, a name that was derived from imitating the sound of a bolt-action rifle racking a bullet into place. Hiding beneath their white robes and covered faces, these men were ruthless in doling out their concept of justice to the Southern Blacks.

Federal troops eventually targeted the group for doing what Elijah thought was just and proper. In the end, the KKK was destroyed by President Grant's passage and enforcement of the Force Act of 1870.

Although further embittered by this second defeat, Elijah had continued to live in Tennessee with his family until shortly after Buford was born. Then he'd picked up and moved everyone to Texas.

During his entire life he never tired of regaling any who'd listen with his adventures and exploits during the war against the damnable Yankees.

In 1899, with Elijah's health failing and his children grown, the ailing old Bauer and his wife had been invited to move with their son, Buford, to a ranch in Oklahoma. Elijah and his wife had reluctantly agreed to make this one last move. Their final years were spent in Oklahoma with Buford and his family.

It would have pleased Elijah greatly had he lived long enough to witness the revival of the KKK in

1915. But, as it was, he died of cancer in 1913. Five years later Buford's mother passed away, as well.

Both now rested side-by-side in the church cemetery that lay twenty yards to the west of where Buford now sat.

To be fair, Buford and the others in the church, who were of a like mind, were somewhat less ill-disposed toward people of color than Buford's father had been. Nonetheless, they harbored certain opinions as to what should be the Negro's proper place in a white man's society.

The three men looked back and forth at each other as seconds ticked by in awkward silence.

* * *

Sitting in his pew, Austin felt the tension. In an attempt to change the subject, he addressed Alva who was still standing at the head of the sanctuary. "Alva, you figure, after getting' Slim's herd back, that Brooks and his gunmen will back off a might? I mean, we stood up to 'em, right?"

"Don't imagine they'll give up that easy, in there. I seen me plenty o' outlaws when I was deputy back in Missouri. I'll tell ya true, I can spot an outlaw anywhere and those men are gunfighters and outlaws. I can't prove it but I surely believe they murdered Gilbert."

There were murmurs of agreement.

Alva let things quiet a little before he continued. "As you all know, the other night they rustled Slim's cattle. I think they're determined and not likely to back off. Matter of fact, I believe things will just get worse, in there."

Austin stood up and looked around at his fellow ranchers. He pulled himself to his full five-foot-seven inch-height. "Then I think we should fight. Band together."

Mild arguments broke out and the church buzzed with voices. Finally, Slim stood and asked to speak.

"I understand how Austin feels but we got women and kids. Least ways most of us do. Like Alva said, these men Brooks brought in here are paid gunmen. I jist can't see us gettin' mixed up in a gun war with 'em. As for bandin' together, we can't always be in the same place. They'll just bide their time and pick us off one by one."

Slim's words seemed to resonate with many of the men and, for a time, the small sanctuary was filled once again with the sound of voices all talking at once.

"Let's have a little quiet," Alva intervened. When things settled, he looked pointedly at Harry then asked, "What do you think, Harry?"

Eyes turned toward him and Harry spoke softly. "My guess is Brooks is already thinking about bringing in more guns. He felt a little sting the other night and I imagine he doesn't like it. He'll up the ante."

Pausing to look around the room, Harry said, "Most here are just ranchers. No match for professional gunmen. Not sure it would be wise to take them on with guns."

Lee was sitting next to Etta and had listened in silence to everything that had been said. But, with this last statement from his father, he slapped the pew in front of him and sprang from his seat.

"If you don't stand up and fight, you're just cowards! Plain cowards!" Lee looked pointedly at Harry as he spit out the last words. Then, red-faced, he bolted from the church.

Harry watched his son with sadness as he stormed out the door. For a second there was silence and then whispers rustled through the sanctuary like wind through autumn leaves.

Harry was about to speak when Etta stood and addressed the men. "Please excuse our son. He's young and impetuous." She looked around the room before continuing. "You have all spoken of different ideas and possible solutions, but no one has talked about what I think should be obvious. Go to the authorities."

The room erupted with impatient protests and Etta put up her hand to quiet them before she continued. "I know, I know, the sheriff can't be trusted. Even Harry says that he's in Brooks' pocket. But, what about the Governor? Surely we could go to him."

Alva spoke up. "Ain't that simple, Etta. Brooks is a very influential man with a lot of money. He helped elect the Governor, in there, so it ain't likely that the Governor's gonna give us much help."

Slim blurted, "We gotta do somethin'. I damn sure as hell can't...." He stopped and looked sheepishly around the sanctuary. "Sorry, didn't mean to profane in church. What I mean is, I can't afford to sell out. Not at the price Brooks is offerin'. Don't imagine anyone else can either."

"Maybe we can organize some kind of alarm system," Austin suggested. "You know, like the minutemen. Be ready to come together if any one place is threatened."

There were nods and more murmurs of agreement.

"Sounds possible." Once again Alva turned to Harry. "Harry?"

"Might work. Guess it won't hurt to set something up. But, if I read Brooks right, he's just getting started."

Chapter 18

THE STRANGER

~ ~ ~

It was a quiet ride home. Lee felt fortunate to be in the back of the Model T where he didn't have to look at his father and mother. "I was right in what I said," he mumbled to himself. Still, he felt shame knowing he had humiliated his father and had angered and embarrassed his mother.

Neither had scolded him when they loaded up the truck and pulled away from the church; then again, he had not expected them to say anything in public. His rebuke and punishment would be doled out when they got back to the ranch. His parents would not embarrass him before his neighbors, which was more than he could say for himself.

Lee sighed, knowing he would have to apologize and take his punishment when they got home.

As they sat on their makeshift seats in the back of the truck, Lee felt Laura's eyes on him. She'd been outside during his outburst in the church, but Lee had seen her look up from her play when he'd burst out of the doors. There had been puzzlement in her eyes as he'd plopped himself down on the church steps.

Now her puzzled eyes were on him once again.

"What happened in the church, Lee?"

He lowered his head and looked away. "Nothin'." There was sorrow and pain in his simple answer.

Laura leaned into him and gave him a hug. Slowly he put his arm around her and hugged her back.

* * *

The next day, Clarence and Harry began working to put up a crop of hay, about ten-acres worth that had been cut two days before.

Near noon, after the dew was burnt off, Harry went to the field to check the alfalfa. He wanted to see if it was well cured. Twisting a stalk to see how dry it was, he took a small chew. The hay had to be dry, but not brittle. It had to bend without breaking and it had to have a moist taste. But it couldn't be too moist. If a man were to gather and put up hay that was too "green," it could mold in the barn. Worse yet, if "green" hay got stacked too tight, it could spontaneously combust and burn down the barn.

The alfalfa, by Harry's reckoning, was just right for "puttin' up." He and Clarence hauled the hayrack to the field and began loading the finely-cured crop.

Forty minutes later they returned with a full rack and parked it in front of the barn. Harry climbed into the mow and waited as Clarence plunged the forks into the hay and started the pulley system that took it up to the hayloft door and on into the mow.

As the first fork-load was delivered into the loft, Harry heard Clarence's voice above the sound of the pulley. Harry poked his head out of the hayloft door and looked down at his hired hand.

"Harry!" Clarence nodded toward an approaching vehicle. "Someone's comin', Harry."

Harry stared off to the east and watched as an automobile turned off the road and started up the long dirt lane. The fast-moving vehicle stirred up a cloud of dust as it sped toward the ranch house and barn.

Harry squinted. After being in the dusky hayloft, his eyes were having trouble adjusting to the bright sun. "Ya tell who it is?"

"No. Never seen this auto-mobile 'afore. Don't like the looks of it, Harry."

"Got your gun?" Harry called down.

Clarence pulled his revolver from his belt and offered to throw it up to the loft.

"That's all right. Keep it. Be right down."

A few seconds later, Harry stepped from the barn and joined Clarence next to the hayrack.

Across the barnyard, the back door of the house opened and Etta stepped onto the porch. Behind her, Lee and Laura followed.

"Keep them in the house, Etta," Harry shouted above the sound of the rapidly-approaching automobile engine.

Etta motioned Lee and Laura back inside. Then, shielding her eyes, she stared down the lane at the vehicle kicking up a trail of dust as it headed their way.

At the time, Harry could not have named the make of vehicle that was approaching. In fact, it was a 1921 Dodge Brothers convertible. The cloth top was up and bright sunlight was reflecting off the windshield. Harry noticed the auto's vivid color – maroon with black fenders and a black cloth top.

The glare of the windshield made it impossible to make out the man behind the wheel.

Pulling into the barnyard at a high speed, it skidded to a stop. The car's door burst open and the driver stepped from the vehicle. Dust following in the auto's wake caught up and enveloped the stranger in a billowing cloud.

When the air cleared, an ominous figure dressed in an expensive dark suit was revealed. It was the man who had been in Brooks' office on the day Wilson and his men had been there. In the stranger's hands were two matching nickel-plated Colt .45 automatic pistols.

At sight of the Colts, Clarence brought his own revolver into view. Harry put his hand on Clarence's wrist and gently urged him to lower his weapon.

On the porch, Etta got her first good look at the stranger. She let out a gasp. "Oh, my God!"

The man turned the guns in his hands. A smile touched his lips. "You ever seen anything like these here automatic pistols, Mr. Kidwell?"

Chapter 19

THE REUNION

~ ~ ~

Harry couldn't quite believe his eyes. "What are you doing here?"

The kitchen door burst open and Lee came rushing out.

"Uncle Leroy!" he yelled. With Etta following close behind, Lee bounded down the steps and ran to greet the man he knew as his brave and gallant uncle. The boy came up short and shyly stood before his uncle. Etta, on the other hand, blew past her son and into Leroy's arms. She kissed him on the cheek and gave him a robust hug.

With the two Colts still in his hands, Leroy returned the hug as best he could. When Etta finally released him and stepped back, he thrust the guns back into his waistband.

"You are a sight for sore eyes." Etta's words had an almost musical lilt.

Harry gazed onto the scene impassively.

Laura came running from the house and stood before Leroy looking curious. She had been a toddler when her uncle had last visited.

Clarence had looked with bewilderment at the finely-dressed man until Lee called out the man's name. Then he broke into a broad grin.

"I'be! He exclaimed. "Yo shoa look different in that fine store-bought suit, Mr. Leroy. Din't hardly recognize ya. Some fine auto-mobile yo got there, too."

Leroy smiled and took a bow. "Thank you, Clarence."

Harry was the only one who stood solemn. "Don't get me wrong. It's not that I'm not glad to see you, Leroy, but what the hell are you doing here?"

Leroy glanced at Lee, who had suddenly found the ground at his feet to be of extraordinary interest. Then he looked back at Harry and smiled.

"Well, Harry, I was thinkin' that maybe Etta here might be gettin' a might tired of your sorry old ass. So, I figured I'd come by and offer to take her away from all this."

Harry nodded. "Okay, take her then." There was just a hint of a smile as he said this.

"You mean you're not going to put up a fight?" Leroy asked.

Harry shook his head.

"Then I ain't sure I want her."

"Thought that was why you came," Harry stated flatly.

Etta sighed and shook her head.

"Listen, while you two argue again over who doesn't want me the most, I'm going back inside to start fixing dinner. I assume you're staying, Leroy."

Etta turned to Lee. "You can come in with me, young man. You still have work to do. You too, Laura."

For a second Harry saw a flash of fire in Lee's eyes. It was quickly replaced with resignation. Nonetheless, he gave one feeble attempt to resist.

"Ma, I haven't seen him in years. There's some things I want ..."

"You can talk to him later," Etta directed. "He and your father have business to discuss."

As Etta and the kids headed into the house, Leroy turned to Clarence. "So, Clarence, I see your still here. Thought you'd have found someone who'd pay you a fair wage by now and left this sorry son'bitch."

Clarence smiled. "Nice to see yo too, Mr. Leroy."

Harry smiled and then motioned for Leroy to follow him to the barn. To Clarence he said, "Got a few things to talk over with Leroy, Clarence."

Clarence nodded and headed for his bunkhouse.

As Harry led his old friend toward the barn he asked, "Now, why are you really here, Butch?"

Leroy looked over his shoulder at the house. "How come you got Lee doin' housework? Thought he'd be workin' the ranch with you."

"Punishment. Now, answer my question." Harry replied.

"Punishment?

Harry stopped walking and gave Leroy a look.

"All right! Damn, Sundance, you don't have to get riled."

Leroy reached into his pocket and pulled out a crumpled letter. He handed it to Harry.

As Harry took the letter, he and Leroy stood in front of the barn thinking they were pretty much out of earshot of Clarence.

* * *

They were not. Clarence was now standing in his bunkhouse doorway trying to make sense of what he'd just over heard. He was perplexed, not by the conversation, but by the names they'd used to address each other.

Clarence peered around the door and watched Harry take the letter from Leroy, unfolded it, and read what Lee had written to his uncle.

"Damn! That young...." Harry cursed.

"Now, don't get mad at the boy, Sundance. He was only trying to help." Leroy smiled and added, "Besides, looks like he's already in enough trouble."

Clarence could see Harry trying to cool down before shaking his head and putting his hand on his old friend's shoulder.

"Wasn't expecting you, Butch, but I'll have to say it's good to see you."

The two men entered the barn away from Clarence's eyes.

Still looking confused, Clarence stepped into his bunkhouse and closed the door. Sitting next to his bed, he tried to get his mind around what he had just heard. Putting this new information with everything that had gone on at the Jackson corral, it started to make sense. And, when he thought back about things that had puzzled him for years, he knew the truth of the matter.

Since Clarence had never learned to read, he didn't know what was in newspapers. Nonetheless, he knew the names Butch Cassidy and The Sundance Kid. He'd heard about their reputation. He'd also heard they'd been killed.

"Damn." He said to himself. "I been workin' all these years for an outlaw." He smiled wryly. "And a dead one, at that."

* * *

When Etta entered the kitchen, her elation at seeing Leroy was quickly replaced by puzzlement. What had caused him to show up now of all times? She turned and watched as first Laura and then Lee followed her inside.

Lee was still looking over his shoulder at his father and Uncle Leroy.

"Tell me, Lee, just what was it you wanted to talk to Uncle Leroy about?" Etta asked.

Lee looked at his mother like a puppy who'd been caught chewing on his master's favorite shoes. "I just ... I mean, I haven't seen him since I was a kid. I just wanted to say hello ... that's all."

Etta had her answer. "You wrote to him."

Lee lowered his head. "You wanted me to carry those apples down to the fruit cellar. Best be doin' it," he said as he slipped away from her and out of the kitchen.

"I think your father may want to talk to you later, young man." Etta's words followed Lee.

Etta sighed. There would be time later to talk about how Butch had heard of their trouble. The fact was, Butch was here and Etta wasn't quite sure how she felt about it.

For almost fourteen years, she had tried to keep the violence from skulking back into their life. But this situation with Brooks and his gunmen was roaring into their life like a charging bull.

Nonetheless, Etta still hoped they could avoid getting drawn in further. She had not given up on the idea of getting help from the authorities and planned to talk to Harry about it again that night.

Now that Butch was here and the two men were together again, Etta wasn't sure of her hold on Harry.

She knew that Lee had done what he did with the best of intentions, but Etta was afraid he'd only made things worse.

* * *

Lee quickly busied himself with his chores. The fruit cellar for storing fruit, vegetables, and canned goods was under the house. It could only be accessed through the trap door in the pantry. Lee carried the last of the apples into the cellar. He was glad to have an excuse to get away from his mother's probing eyes, but he was not happy to be shut away in the house doing chores while his Uncle Leroy was out in the barn. It was his letter that brought Leroy here. Lee felt he should be out there helping to make plans to deal with Brooks' gunmen.

His father wouldn't have much of an idea of how to handle the situation, but Lee could work with Uncle Leroy. They could formulate a plan to teach those thugs a lesson. He cursed under his breath. For now, he was resigned to apple toting. Tomorrow he'd get Uncle Leroy alone and fill him in on just what needed to be done.

* * *

A little while later Etta called the men into supper. It was a fine meal of baked ham, sweet potatoes, green beans, and apple pie for dessert. Leroy brought everyone up-to-date on life in Oregon. He'd met a woman there but hadn't yet found the proper time to pop the question. She was a fine woman and quite different than some of his conquests of the past.

As Leroy told his stories, there was a good deal of laughter all around, but Etta couldn't help but notice that Clarence was unusually quiet and kept looking back and forth at Harry and Leroy.

The subject of what had brought Leroy to the Kidwell ranch in such a timely manner did not come up. But Etta noticed that Harry would, from time to time, turn a rather malicious eye on his son.

After dinner, Clarence excused himself and went to his bunkhouse. Etta and the kids began clearing the table while Harry motioned for Leroy to follow him back to the barn.

* * *

Harry led the way as they entered the barn and headed for the tack room.

The Kidwell's barn-raising had followed the usual practice. Harry and Etta provided the materials while their neighbors gathered to help build their oversized barn. Harry's barn consisted of a lower level for animals, equipment and a tack room and an upper level for storing hay. It was larger than many because it also had a granary, a small depository for oats that he used to feed his livestock.

In the tack room, Harry retrieved a bottle of Scotch Whiskey that he had stowed away in a cupboard. Since Harry seldom drank, it had been there a long while and was still nearly full.

Harry sat down on a tack box and motioned for Butch to do the same. After uncorking the bottle, he offered his old friend a drink.

Butch took a long slug and smacked his lips. "Now that was exactly what I needed," he said. He took another swig and passed the bottle back to Harry.

Harry took a sip and set the bottle down between them. He paused as he looked his friend up and down.

Harry had seen Butch dressed in a suit on a number of occasions, but this outfit seemed especially fine and probably quite expensive. It reminded Harry of the time in the old days when they had dressed to the hilt in order to get their pictures taken. That had been the biggest mistake of their lives. The law had gotten hold of those photographs and pretty soon every lawman in America knew what Butch Cassidy and the Sundance Kid looked like.

"A little overdressed, aren't ya, Butch?" Harry asked, still gazing at the extravagant suit.

"Just dressin' the part." Butch flashed his signature smile, making him appear so innocent.

"Part? What part you talking about?"

"A wealthy investor from San...fran...cisco." Butch stood and made an exaggerated forward bow and a flare of his right hand. "You see, I paid a little visit to your friend, S.C. Brooks. Let him think I was interested in putting a massive sum of money into his oil company. He's still waiting for my final answer after he made me a rather shabby counter proposal."

Harry smiled. "I should have known. You always find a way to investigate the other side," he said.

"I visited some of his competitors, too, those that were left to visit. This is not a pleasant man, Sundance. Evil is a word that comes to mind."

Butch sat back down. "What's the situation here, Harry? These ranchers, any of 'em know how to fight ... use a gun?"

"They're ranchers, just cattle herders and hay cutters. Good men, Butch, but no match for Brooks' hired guns. Besides, most have families."

"So do you, but I don't imagine that's going to slow you down none," Butch said.

Harry sighed and shook his head.

Butch smiled at his old friend. "You mean Etta's still holding your feet to the fire on that old promise? She's got to know this is serious."

"Etta's mighty strong-willed and you know it, Butch. I made her a promise. She won't take it well if I break it. You know she left me twice before."

"That was a long time ago. You weren't married and besides, you didn't have kids then."

Harry smiled back at his friend. Butch didn't know as much as he thought he knew. Harry considered enlightening him but said nothing.

Butch continued. "Her leavin' was all because of Villa Mercedes. That was a mess and I'll admit we were lucky to get out 'o there."

Harry was pensive, but Butch was right. The robbery in Villa Mercedes had been a debacle and that was when Etta had made up her mind to return to the States. But, as he sat there, Harry began to think back – back to his youth and to how his whole life as an outlaw had started.

PART II

THE OUTLAW YEARS

Chapter 20

BECOMING THE SUNDANCE KID

~ ~ ~

Harry's life of adventure on the wrong side of the law began when he was nineteen. Prior to that, he'd been a fun-loving honest young man. He enjoyed being a Montana ranch hand working with livestock on the N Bar N Ranch near Miles City.

He learned young how to ride and rope as well as shoot, skills at which he'd become quite proficient and for which he was earning a reputation. Through his friend and mentor, Charlie Redcloud, he'd adopted to some of the ways of the Native Americans.

In 1887 everything changed. Two tough winters put him out of work. After an unprofitable venture into the Black Hills of South Dakota searching for work, Harry wandered into Wyoming.

It was a beautiful Appaloosa stallion that helped to send him down his infamous path. The horse belonged to Alonzo Craven, a ranch hand working for the 3V Ranch.

The Old Gun

A full moon shined brightly on a crisp, cold night as Harry approached a popular tavern in the small Wyoming town of Sundance. That was when he spotted the majestic Appaloosa tied to a hitching rail outside the saloon. The magnificent stallion stopped him in his tracks. For a full minute he stood in the freezing night, admiring the horse as it stood there snorting puffs of frosty air. Finally, he pulled his coat tighter up around his neck and mounted the steps of the saloon. He was down to his last ten dollars when he stepped though the door.

Like bear prints in fresh snow, Harry's boots made tracks in the sawdust that covered the pine wood floors. Sauntering up to the bar, he ordered a beer. When the bartender slid a tall glass across the bar to him, he took a sip and gazed around the room. At a table in the corner, four cowboys from the 3V ranch were engaged in a game of draw poker.

Harry strolled over. "Mind if I sit in?"

The four cowboys looked up.

"As long as you got the where-with-all," a thin dark-haired fellow said, "Your name's Longabough ain't it?"

Harry nodded.

The dark haired man stared at Harry's gun. "Heard about you some. Feel a bit more comfortable if'n you was to hang that piece o' yours with the rest o' our guns before ya sit down."

Harry took a long look at the man before unbuckling and hanging his holster and gun on a peg with the others.

The man nodded and reached to shake Harry's hand. "Name's Alonzo Craven."

Harry sat down and the cards were dealt. During the first hand, Harry drew to an open straight. He filled the straight and beat the other better who was holding three kings. From this point on, Harry could do no wrong. An hour later, two of the cowboys had given up. Harry was sitting across from Craven and one other player.

Harry picked up his cards and found himself looking at four dealt sevens. Craven made a bet, the other player folded and Harry called. Harry drew one card to disguise his hand, while Craven drew two.

Looking up from his draw, Craven couldn't quite hide a hint of a smile. He made a rather large bet and Harry raised. Craven's hint of a smile broadened as he wagered his appaloosa stallion to sweeten the deal. Harry called and Craven showed three aces full of jacks.

When Harry showed his four sevens, Alonzo Craven's eyes blazed with fury, but he said nothing. A few minutes later, Craven's ears burned red as Harry left the saloon and collected his prized appaloosa.

Harry rode away that night with Craven's stallion, a pocket full of money, and a Smith & Wesson revolver he'd won from one of the other players.

* * *

For the rest of the night Alonzo Craven fumed. The next day he had convinced himself that Harry's incredible run of luck had not been by chance. It was more a matter of chicanery. That very day, Craven filed a complaint with the sheriff for the theft of his horse as well as his friend's pistol.

* * *

Harry's reputation with firearms was well known in Wyoming. Because of this, the authorities were given to believe that Harry was someone who should be approached cautiously.

With warrant in hand, Sheriff James Ryan went looking for the young thief. He found him in Montana.

The young desperado was in a café having dinner when Ryan eased up behind him. "Harry Longabough?" he asked as he pulled his gun and cocked the hammer. "You're under arrest for grand larceny."

Harry looked at Ryan with bewilderment. He surrendered without resistance.

The sheriff decided not to transport his prisoner alone and on horseback all the way to Sundance, Wyoming. Instead, he booked them on a train. It was to be a rather circuitous route, but one the sheriff deemed much safer.

* * *

It was when Harry was on the train and he had time to think that he began to realize the seriousness of the situation.

During the journey, the sheriff told him that the boys from the 3V were backing Craven in the accusation. In his mind Harry had been thinking it would be his word against Craven's. But now his situation had begun to look dire. Escape seemed to be his only option, so Harry formulated a plan.

"Sorry, Sheriff, 'fraid I need to use the water closet."

The sheriff looked warily at his charge and then at the rapidly-passing countryside as the train rumbled along on the iron rails. He drew his gun and motioned for Harry to stand up.

With his gun stuck in Harry's back, Sheriff Ryan herded him to the toilet at the end of the car. When they reached the door to the privy, Harry smiled and motioned to the handcuffs that were securing his wrists. "Guess I need you to take these off, Sheriff, 'lest you want to do the cleanin' for me."

Again the sheriff glanced out the window as the wheels of the train rapidly clicked off the distance.

He cocked his gun before he unlocked one of the cuffs.

"Don't get no ideas," he warned. "I'll put a bullet in yer head just as soon as look at ya, kid."

The sheriff opened the door and allowed Harry to step into the cramped space. Leaning back against the wall next to the door, he settled in to wait.

As soon as Harry stepped into the small cramped space, he was sure of one thing: this was his only chance to escape. He knew that the toilet was less than four feet from the exit door at the end of the car. Pausing, he gathered his nerve before throwing open the water closet door. Sheriff Ryan yelled his name, but in two seconds, he was through the exit and standing between his car and the next.

Harry took a deep breath and jumped. Flying through the air, he caught a glimpse of the lawman standing between the cars. Harry hit the ground and a searing pain stabbed his left ankle. He began to tumble through the deep grass and weeds along the track.

Finally, he rolled and skidded to a stop. Blood flowed from a gash in his forehead. His left ankle was sprained, his clothes were torn and dirty, and his knees were cut and bruised. Still, he was alive.

* * *

Ryan had charged after Harry the second he realized his prisoner was making a break. But he was seconds too late. Now he stood helplessly watching as the pulsing steam engine rapidly carried him away from his prisoner. "This isn't over, Harry!" he shouted into the wind.

* * *

Had Harry kept running, things might have turned out differently. Unfortunately, he convinced himself that if he could speak to Alonzo Craven, he could persuade the man that it would be in everyone's best interest to retract his accusation. So he returned to Wyoming.

Alonzo, having heard of Harry's escape, had gone into hiding. Harry also learned, to his misfortune, that some of Alonzo's friends had informed the law that he was back in the vicinity.

Several days later Harry was arrested again and taken directly, and with a good deal more precaution, to the jail in Sundance, Wyoming.

His initial escape and then his re-arrest made a sensation in the newspapers. The reporters made him out to be the new Jessie James.

Harry was appointed a youthful, inexperienced lawyer who convinced the young desperado that the notorious escape and adverse publicity would weigh heavily against him at trial and that, if convicted on all counts, he would spend several years in prison.

With little hope of an acquittal, Harry agreed to a plea bargain. He pled guilty to horse theft and was sentenced to a year and a half.

It would have been normal for Harry to serve his time in the Wyoming State Prison. Had this happened, it would have been doubtful that he'd have been given the nickname that followed him throughout his lawless years. As it turned out, he was incarcerated in the local jail at Sundance.

As a result, Harry became thereafter known as The Sundance Kid. A name like that can create destiny, but for the Sundance Kid, bad luck played as much of a role in his destiny as the name.

A day before he was to be released from jail, the Governor of Wyoming, who'd heard that the Kid had been practically railroaded into jail, gave Sundance a pardon. He thought he was doing the young man a favor and normally it would have been. In this case, it only served to focus attention on The Kid and to bolster his reputation.

* * *

In spite of his notoriety, Harry wanted to start over. He got a job as a ranch hand not far from the town that had given him his name. It was to his misfortune that Laurence Jepson, one of the men Sundance was working with on the ranch, was wanted for murder.

Later that spring, he and Jepson were mending fence when the local sheriff and his deputy rode into view. Harry saw them approaching and recognized them as lawmen. Unfortunately, so did Jepson. He immediately drew his revolver and started shooting. Had Harry joined in, his speed and accuracy with a gun would have assured a markedly-different outcome. As it was, Harry, having no desire to get involved, dove out of harm's way.

As the lawmen galloped toward Jepson, the desperado continued to fire. Even though he was a poor shot, one lucky bullet did hit the deputy's horse. It went down, catapulting the deputy over its head. He landed hard and skidded to within a few feet of the wanted man.

Jepson stepped forward and took point-blank aim at the deputy as he lay on the ground. The young lawman would have died there if the sheriff hadn't, at that very moment, gotten off a lucky shot of his own. Shooting from horseback with a pistol, the sheriff was very limited in his accuracy. Nonetheless, his bullet caught Laurence Jepson in the middle of his forehead.

Even though he hadn't drawn his gun or taken any part in the shoot-out, this incident along with his reputation caused Sundance to find himself at odds once again with most lawmen.

The Kid moved away and, for a time, worked on his cousin's ranch near the Canadian border. But the authorities were constantly harassing him. Eventually, he decided to move on once again.

It seemed as if he was marked. No matter where he went the law was constantly harassing him. The big outfits were reluctant to hire him and it became harder and harder for the Sundance Kid to make an honest living. Having already been branded an outlaw, desperation eventually drove him to that very way of life.

For a while, Sundance teamed up with two other desperados, one named James Punteney and one named Harvey Logan. Logan would later be a part of Butch's Hole in The Wall Gang.

For several years Sundance and the others were successful in a number of robberies. But after a while, their luck ran out.

* * *

It was a cool misty morning. Sundance, Logan, and Punteney were camped in the shelter of a box canyon near a small stream. Sundance was pouring a cup of coffee when he caught a glimpse of movement in the trees near by. A posse had caught up with them.

The lawmen fired on the three without warning. The first shot wounded Logan and he threw up his hands in surrender. Sundance realized that he could shoot his way out, but only by killing one or more of the posse. Reluctant to do this, he threw up his hands, as well. Punteney did the same and the shooting stopped.

The three outlaws were taken to Deadwood City, South Dakota. The jail they were held in was the same one that had held Jack McCall, the killer of Wild Bill Hickok, more than a decade earlier. Even back then, that old calaboose wasn't very secure.

As soon as the rusty lock on the old cell was clicked shut by the sheriff, Sundance began to take measure of his surroundings. Looking at the floor he spotted a loose nail protruding from a plank near the wall.

Waiting until the middle of the night, he used his belt buckle to loosen and pry the nail from the floor. When he finally extracted it, he jammed it between the cell door and the metal frame and bent it into the shape of a hook.

Sticking his arm through the bars, Sundance used the hooked nail as a pick to work on the primitive door lock. It took well over an hour but the tumbler moved and the bolt slid back. Sundance spent the next hour re-locking the door.

Escaping from his cell would not free Sundance from the building. He would also have to go through another locked door to get to the office and then get by three armed guards. Sundance decided to bide his time.

Two days later, on Halloween, his opportunity arose. The entire town was gearing up for the festivities. There would be contests, music, dancing and plenty of food. Even the sheriff and deputies didn't want to miss out on the food and desserts that were always the center of the celebration.

As the evening wore on, the sheriff left one of his deputies to guard the prisoners while he and the other deputy took a short break.

"Half an hour and we'll be back. I'll bring you some pie," the sheriff said as he stepped out the door.

"Make it apple," the deputy called back. After the door went shut, he mumbled, "Asshole. Leaves me here while they go have fun."

Harry heard the two depart, which left only one deputy in the office. He had little time, but over the last three nights he'd been practicing on the lock. He had reduced the time to open it to eleven minutes.

Immediately, he got to work. Fifteen minutes later, with sweat dripping from his chin, he was still working. In his haste and under pressure, he'd dropped the pick twice.

Punteney and Logan were in two separate cells on either side of Sundance's. They'd been watching the Kid each time he'd practiced during the last few nights. Seeing him struggle now, they showed their impatience. "What's the matter, Kid? You're runnin' outa time." Logan whispered.

Sundance gave him a look and kept working. A few minutes later the tumbler finally turned. Sundance gave a sigh then turned to Punteney who was in the furthest cell from the office door. "Now, do what we planned. Make like you're sick. Call for the deputy," he whispered.

Punteney nodded and after several moans and cries for help, the deputy opened the office door. He cautiously moved along the cells. "Sick or not, I ain't comin' in that cell. I weren't born yesterday," he declared as he passed Sundance heading for Punteny's cell.

The deputy's attention was focused on the moaning prisoner in the last cell. He didn't notice when Sundance slipped open his cell and quietly stepped up behind him. His first clue that he was in trouble was when his gun was pulled from its holster.

After cuffing and gagging the deputy, Harry placed him in a cell. The three fugitives stole horses from outside the jail and rode away. Just outside Deadwood they split up. Although the Kid and Logan got away clean, Punteney was caught the next day.

Once again the Sundance Kid made headlines.

Chapter 21

BUTCH AND ETTA

~ ~ ~

The next year Sundance met the amiable outlaw, Butch Cassidy, in a saloon in Johnson County, Wyoming. The two took to each other immediately. Soon after, Butch organized The Hole in the Wall Gang.

For several years, they enjoyed complete impunity as they plied their trade throughout the West.

Times were good for Sundance and Butch, but occasionally the Kid wondered about the bad luck that had brought both him and Butch to the outlaw life. Like Sundance, Butch had claimed that events beyond his control, as well as bad luck, had put him on the wrong side of the law. But the excitement and easy money were too alluring to allow much time for such thoughts.

After their robberies, it was customary for the gang to separate and join up later. Usually, they went back to their hideout at Hole in The Wall in Johnson County, Wyoming. At times they met at Robbers

Roost in Utah, and occasionally they re-grouped in Fort Worth, Texas where they could lay low and take a vacation from their outlaw ways.

It was on one such trip that Sundance met Etta.

* * *

It was a warm summer day in Fort Worth. Having just finished a steak dinner, Sundance and George "Flat Nose" Currie were stepping out of the Lone Star Café. Etta was strolling by, carrying a new hat in its round cardboard box. Sundance was talking to George while Etta was concentrating on her new acquisition. When they slammed into each other, the collision knocked her hatbox to the ground and Sundance accidentally stepped on it.

Fire burned in Etta's pretty eyes as she glared at Harry standing on her hatbox.

After staring at her for an awkward moment, Sundance managed to speak. "Sorry, so sorry, but if you'd let me, Ma'am, I'd be happy to buy you another hat."

For several seconds, Etta just glared at the tall handsome man before her.

"It would make me happy if you'd just take your foot off this one. Any replacing I will do myself," she barked.

Etta realized that the collision was as much her fault as his, but that didn't diminish her anger. However, that wasn't the reason she refused his offer. She was not able to explain why, but nonetheless, Etta felt an underlying danger from this good-looking man.

Sundance tipped his hat as she stalked away.

Etta would later confess that, in spite of her wariness, she had never met anyone so striking and confident. Her existence up to then had been common and, to tell the truth, quite boring. The men who vied for her attention were lacking any kind of fire or bravado. As time went on, she found Sundance to be everything that her former suitors were not.

* * *

All that day Sundance couldn't get her out of his mind. She was surely the prettiest female he'd ever seen. By late afternoon his obsession with her compelled him to visit the store where she'd bought her hat. The salesman told him her name was Etta and she lived at a boarding house a few blocks away. Sundance purchased a fine new hat and delivered it to her that very evening.

"I told you that I buy my own hats, thank you very much." Her words stung like dry ice on bare skin.

"Make me feel a might better if you'd accept it, Miss. Real sorry about ruinin' your other one."

Sundance could see her eyes begin to soften. She looked at the bow-tied hatbox in his big hands and a smile began to form on her full lips. After a long pause, she accepted the gift and tried on the hat. Soon after, Etta accepted Sundance as a suitor as well.

* * *

Several months later, when Sundance asked her to join him in his adventures, it took Etta only a second to consider before she agreed. But it wasn't Sundance alone that influenced her decision. There was Butch also. She'd gotten to know Sundance's best friend quite well. It wasn't that she cared for Butch romantically. What she found captivating was his fun-loving nature and carefree attitude. As much as she was delighted to fall into the arms of Sundance, she also found a great deal of enjoyment being around Butch. He became the fun-loving brother that Etta never had.

From the first, Etta was enthralled by the adventure and excitement of the outlaw life. It seemed as much of an addiction for her as it was for Butch and the Kid. But, as time went by, the danger involved in their line of work began weighing on her. She was beginning to worry that Sundance and Butch would get caught or, worse yet, killed.

When things got too hot and Etta became exceptionally worried, Butch and Sundance would take the gang and head back to Texas where Etta felt there was less danger.

While in Texas, the Hole in The Wall Gang stayed in the finest hotels, ate the best food, and drank the finest wines. Down there the gang was free of worry and Etta could relax.

* * *

On one such trip, Sundance and Butch were having such a good time that, when one of the boys suggested they all get one of those new-fangled portraits, neither of them stopped to think about the hazards of such a rash act.

Part of the reason they had been successful over the years at eluding the law was because the authorities didn't know exactly what they looked like. Of course Sundance and the others didn't plan for anyone outside the gang to see the photograph. They planned to pose for the portrait then buy the photo and they would be the only ones to ever see it.

The five gang members who posed for the portrait had never looked more dapper. Sundance wore the finest outfit he'd ever owned. From the dark-tailored suit to the crisp derby hat, he looked every bit a well-to-do gentleman.

"Those are some mighty fine duds you're sportin', gentlemen. You must be very prosperous," the photographer observed casually as he posed the gang.

Butch slapped the fellow on the back and smiled. "We have interest in banking and have some in the railroads, as well. Good money in banking and railroads."

* * *

Stepping behind the camera, the man smiled and accepted the remarks at face value. When he took the photograph, he had no idea how infamous the well-dressed men were who had assembled in his shop. Nor did he know how famous the portrait would later become. It was after the session, as the men were talking among themselves, that the photographer overheard the names Butch and Sundance.

At the time he didn't let on to the outlaws, but once they left, he proceeded to make a copy. The next day he displayed the portrait with pride and prominence in his shop window, along with a title in large print that said, "The infamous Hole in the Wall Gang."

The Old Gun

Actually, the photographer didn't do it with any malice. He simply was excited and proud to have been the one to photograph the notorious robbers. Still, as innocuous as his actions were, they turned out to have dire consequences for Sundance, Butch, and the others.

* * *

Sundance was the first to realize the danger posed by the photo. He learned that a lawman passing the photographic shop had glanced into the window and been shocked to see the Hole in the Wall Gang staring back at him. The lawman quickly obtained copies and sent them to law enforcement throughout the United States.

During their robberies, Sundance and Butch had never allowed killing. Unfortunately, some members of their gang had less scruples. Kid Curry and Harvey Logan had pulled off a few jobs on their own and had not been very conscientious about avoiding lethal gunplay.

When it came to murder, Sundance knew the law didn't make any distinction between members of their outlaw gang. Therefore, he and Butch were considered not only robbers but murderers, as well. For the Hole in the Wall Gang there would be little difference between being killed and being caught. Capture would surely mean a date with the rope.

With this effective tool to use against them, lawmen like Charles Seringo and Samuel Stillman were on their trail and things were getting way too hot.

On two separate occasions, these two lawmen had come so near to the gang that Sundance and Butch had been able to get a close look at them.

The diminutive Charlie Seringo, with his distinctive blood-red bandana and the towering, powerful Sam Stillman, dressed all in black including his distinctive four-corned hat, were unforgettable.

Butch was the one who eventually suggested South America. "We can lose ourselves down there and start over. Go straight and buy a ranch. Live the good life."

Sundance wasn't so sure, but Etta had immediately warmed to the idea.

In August of 1900 they robbed the Union Pacific Train near Tipton, Wyoming. After the job the gang split up and headed by different routes, to Texas.

Back in Fort Worth, they gathered in a bedroom at the boarding house. A kerosene lantern cast flickering shadows on the candy-striped wallpaper. They were there to split the loot.

Sundance looked on as Butch sat down on the lumpy feather bed and cleared his throat. "Fraid it's time, boys. Gittin' a might too hot around here for me and the Kid. This here was our last job."

Murmurs of protest filled the room until Butch held up his hand. "You boys split up an' lay low for a while, you'll likely be all right. You're wanted men but they ain't so all-fired-set on catchin' you like they are me and Sundance. The two of us will be hunted from here to Maine and back. We gotta get outa this whole dang country."

There was more murmuring, but it subsided when Butch laid out their take from the Union Pacific robbery. He divided the bills into equal shares and passed them out.

Sundance and Etta headed out the next morning. To make things more difficult for any lawmen on their trail, Butch took a different route out of Texas. They were to meet up in New York City in one month. From New York the plan was to set sail for Argentina where they would buy a ranch, leave the outlaw ways behind and start new lives.

Chapter 22

THE DEBACLE

Villa Mercedes, Argentina
December 1905

~ ~ ~

Things had not gone at all as Sundance had hoped in Argentina. Circumstances had not allowed the three to live the peaceful ranching life that they were hoping to acquire there. And now, five years later, they found themselves once again preparing to rob a bank.

Sundance, accompanied by Etta, rode into the small town of Villa Mercedes. It was mid-morning and a bright golden sun had burned through the clouds that had hung over the town since dawn.

Etta turned heads wherever she went. Therefore, this morning, she wore men's clothes and had stuffed her beautiful auburn hair into a worn tan sombrero. To conceal her feminine curves, she wore a red and black poncho that fell almost to her knees. The last thing Harry wanted was to attract attention.

Unfortunately, with his gringo attire, including a brown Catera Stetson cowboy hat, Harry stood out a little more than he sometimes realized. Today, that small oversight would create a monumental debacle for the bandits.

Harry and Etta casually rode up to the Hotel de la Mercedes and dismounted. They tied their horses to a hitching rail before climbing the steps and entering the lobby. From there they stepped through a set of double doors into the hotel's small cantina. Harry quickly scanned the room, his eyes slowly adjusting to the dim light.

Butch was sipping a cup of coffee near a window that looked out onto the street. The remnants of a nearly-finished breakfast lay before him. He smiled when he saw the two. Graciously, he stood, pulled out a chair, and held it for Etta.

"Nice to see you this morning, Mr. and Mrs. Place."

Place was Sundance's mother's maiden name and it was the alias that Sundance and Etta had used when they registered at the hotel two days earlier. Butch routinely registered at hotels under the name James Ryan. The alias was a private joke between him and Sundance. James Ryan was the name of the Sheriff who had first arrested Sundance back in Wyoming for "stealing" a horse.

Etta sat down without saying a word. A look, cold as a glacier, frosted over her face. Ignoring Butch's greeting, she turned her head to gaze out the nearby window.

Butch seemed not to notice as he settled into his chair. "You two want some breakfast? You must be hungry after that long night," he said.

Etta continued to stare out the window without answering.

Sundance had known for some time that Etta was not happy. Butch seemed to know, too, but he kept telling Sundance that she'd get over it. Sundance wasn't so sure. He'd never seen her quite so unhappy. Even when she'd left him to go back to the States two years before she'd not been this despondent.

Butch ordered two breakfasts from the hombre behind the bar and then turned back to his cup of coffee.

Sundance peered out the window at the Banco de la Nación across the street. That same old tingle rose up from somewhere deep inside; it always seemed to surface before they did a job. Sundance welcomed the sensation because it helped to give him an edge, but, for years now, it had been tempered by a shade of self-reproach.

The life that he and Butch were leading had once been full of adventure and thrills. Now it lay on him like a heavy blanket. Added to that was Etta's mounting discontent. Because he felt a measure of the same discontent, Harry could empathize. What were they to do? They'd done their best to change things. That was why they'd come down here to South America.

But, here they were, sitting across the street from another bank in another town and sometimes Sundance wondered how he'd gotten here. Looking back, he wasn't sure if he would trade away the past even if a genie in a bottle popped out and offered it; most of the memories were too good. But he certainly would trade away the present. The problem was they were inseparable.

The breakfast arrived and Sundance started sawing away at a tough piece of beef. He finally cut through the stubborn slab of meat and took a bite. He chewed for about a minute before he spoke.

"Yours this tough, Butch? They must feed their cattle iron weed and thistle."

"Try the eggs. They're all right."

"I'd hope so. What could they possibly do to mess up eggs?"

Butch was about to reply when Etta sighed in disgust and pushed her plate away. She gave Sundance a look that told him their small talk was more than a little annoying.

Sundance changed the subject. "We put the relief horses and supplies in the draw where you suggested, Butch."

Butch nodded.

Sundance continued, "But it seems like a lot of extra trouble for nothing. Every time we hit a bank, we stake out the relief horses. But we're never chased. Least ways not far enough to where we need a second set of horses."

Butch smiled. "Chances are they won't chase us that far this time either. But I always figure, better safe."

"Planning's what you're good at Butch, but it just seems ..."

Butch cut in, "They never chased us much in the States at first either. Then along came lawmen like Serringo and Stillman."

"There ain't no Charlie Serringo or Sam Stillman down here," Sundance replied.

"True, but I just have a feeling that things are about to heat up. Having all these other Yankee bandits down here doesn't help any, either."

Finally, Etta spoke up. "That's just fine. You think things are about to heat up. Why wouldn't it? They hear up in the States that the great Butch Cassidy and The Sundance Kid are down here having free reign and easy pickings. Suddenly, there are legions of would-be Wild Bunch Bandits down here. What do you expect?"

"The price of fame," Butch said with a smile.

"Smile if you want, Butch, but you're pushing your luck. We didn't come down here for this." Etta spit out the words and looked pointedly at Sundance.

"They didn't really give us much of a choice, Etta," Sundance said. "I mean, we did try to go straight."

Etta sighed and looked out the window again. An uneasy silence fell on the three.

Finally, Butch checked his watch. "It's time," he said. "You ready to dance?"

Sundance nodded and the two stood up. As an afterthought, The Kid asked, "You pay the hotel bill, Butch?"

Butch rolled his eyes and sighed. "Not this again?"

"We owe lodging for two rooms for two nights." Sundance insisted.

"Why do you always do this? We're robbers, Sundance."

"Like to pay my way."

Butch sighed in resignation and pulled out a few bills. With an exaggerated flourish he offered them to Etta. "Would you be so kind, Mrs. Place, as to use this to settle our account with this fine establishment? Mr. Place and I will head on over to the bank." Butch bowed slightly to Sundance then continued, "We have business with the manager."

Sundance smiled inwardly. He knew the game. Had he not insisted that they pay for the rooms, Butch would have quietly slipped Etta the cash and whispered in her ear to pay the bill. Both men had a lopsided idea of honesty, only Butch refused to display it openly. They each had no problem with robbing a train or bank, but to skip out on a bill was considered by both outlaws to be dishonest.

They'd checked into the hotel two days before and had spent a day checking out the Banco de la Nación: its schedule, security, and the proximity of the law. Later, posing as wealthy mine owners, they'd made a ten o'clock appointment for this morning with the manager, ostensibly to make a large deposit.

During the night Etta and Sundance had ridden out of town to an isolated spot twenty miles from Villa Mercedes where they'd stashed three fresh horses. As always, they planned to switch to these fresh mounts to give them an advantage if they were pursued.

As Etta took the money from Butch, she maintained a sober look. But, as she counted it, a fraction of the anger seemed to melt away. It was her part in the game to make a show of not completely trusting Butch to give her enough to cover the expenses, so she made a show of counting it twice.

"How long?" she said after finishing the count.

"I'd say ten minutes." Butch pulled out his pocket watch and looked at it. "Make it ten-ten on the button. Have the horses right in front of the door to the bank."

Etta had a small gold pocket watch of her own that she pulled out and clicked open. "Just now ten."

"On the nose." Then Butch looked at Sundance. "Let's dance."

Sundance smiled and nodded. This was a catch phrase that he and Butch had used to signal the start of every venture since 1898. It had started after they robbed a Saloon in Nevada. Their take in that robbery was so small that Butch commented they'd have gotten more out of it if they'd gone in there to dance, a euphemism for having sex with the saloon girls.

Two months later, just before they robbed the Union Pacific train in Wyoming, Sundance looked at Butch with a wry smile and asked, "You ready to dance?" The phrase stuck and the two outlaws used it from then on before every venture.

Now, as they headed for the door, Sundance glanced over his shoulder and caught a look of fear flash in Etta's eyes. "Be careful. I have a bad feeling," she whispered.

* * *

Juan Garcia owned and operated a small general store situated near the hotel and across the street from the Villa Mercedes bank. Juan was a naturally curious man. He spent much of his day looking out the window, observing the comings and goings of the town people.

Two days before, he had watched as three gringos rode into town. This, in and of itself, did not alarm him. Nonetheless, he might have paid much less attention to them if it were not so obvious that they were gringos. Peering though his shop window, he'd watched as they entered the hotel.

It was what had happened during their second night that particularly intrigued him. Living above his store, he was awakened late at night by the sounds of horses. Looking out his bedroom window, he saw two of the gringos riding out of town.

Then, this morning as he was tending his store, he saw them return. Why would they pay for rooms in the hotel and then spend the whole night somewhere else?

He'd heard a number of stories recently about banditos Yankees who had been robbing banks in Argentina as well as in other South American countries. He didn't really have strong suspicions about these particular foreigners. Still, he was concerned enough to load the rifle he kept behind his counter and to keep an eye out for the three gringos.

When two of the gringos left the hotel, Juan watched as they crossed the street and climbed the stone steps leading to the bank entrance. Wearing tan jackets that came below their waists and carrying two leather bags, they entered the bank. If they were planning to make a deposit, the bags could likely be the method used to transport the money. Still, it made Juan wonder.

* * *

As Sundance and Butch stepped into the bank, Ricardo Lopez, the bank manager, looked up from his desk behind the teller's cage. He immediately smiled and greeted the two Americanos in Spanish, "Hola, hola, mis amigos. La recepción, viene adentro."

Sundance and Butch had visited the bank the day before, saying that they would come this morning to make a large deposit.

Lopez's grin widened as he stood up and came out from behind his desk. "I talk the English with you, yes? Come, come," he said, motioning for the two men to join him behind the cage.

Butch gave him a big warm smile. "Thank you, Señor Lopez. Always impressed when an hombre can speak more than one language."

Lopez looked at the two bags that Sundance and Butch were carrying. "You have los depositos, the deposits. No?"

"I'm afraid, Señor Lopez, that there has been a small change of plans." Butch was still smiling, but the smile on Ricardo Lopez's face froze when he saw Sundance pull a gun from under his jacket.

There was only one patron and one teller in the bank. Butch pulled his gun also and ordered the single customer to join everyone behind the teller's cage. Then he ordered everyone to lay face down on the floor.

Sundance cocked the hammer on his Colt and spoke in a cool, calm voice as he placed the gun barrel next to the manager's ear. "El dinero por favor, Puesto le todo en el bolso."

In compliance, the manager began stuffing money from the vault into the bandit's two leather bags. Small droplets of sweat broke out on his forehead and from time to time several of the bank notes slipped from his nervous hands and fluttered to the vault's floor.

* * *

The time was ten-oh--nine and outside Etta cantered up to the bank leading Butch and Sundance's two mounts. As she rode to a halt before the stone steps, she noticed a woman and her little girl strolling along the walkway in front of a store next to the bank.

The morning light glittered on the woman's coal black hair as she led her daughter by the hand. Her little girl was chattering. The mother stopped and bent over to hear what her daughter was saying.

For just that moment, Etta smiled at the scene. But, her smile was instantly replaced with a look of anxiety as the bank doors burst open. Butch and Sundance were backing their way out into the morning sun.

* * *

From his store, Juan Garcia watched as the small figure rode up to the bank leading two rider-less horses. Of the three gringos, this one seemed the youngest, perhaps a boy of only fourteen or fifteen. The activities of these three gringos were looking extremely suspicious.

Juan stepped quickly behind his counter and retrieved his Mauser bolt-action rifle. Juan's pride and joy had been purchased from a peddler in the spring of 1900. The peddler told him it had been used against the Americans when they'd fought the Spanish in Cuba in 1898. Juan had fired it only a few times but he considered himself a fair shot. In truth, he was not accurate in the best of circumstances.

If there was any doubt in Juan's mind as to the intent of the three Yanquis, it was quickly dispelled when Butch and Sundance backed out of the bank, each carrying a bulging leather bag in one hand and a revolver in the other.

* * *

Sundance and Butch bounded down the stone steps where Etta waited, steadying their two horses. Holstering their guns, the two men quickly secured their bags to their saddle horns and began to mount up.

Just then Sundance saw the manager burst through the doors of the bank wielding a pistol. "Banditos Yanquis! Banditos Yanquis!" he shouted as he took aim and fired.

The bullet whizzed by Sundance's head close enough for him to feel the breeze of the passing projectile. The startled horses stomped and pranced. The manager fired his second shot. This one was further from the mark; it plowed into the dirt some fifty yards down the street.

Sundance had fully seated himself on his prancing steed. Focusing on the manager, he drew his Colt 45. With his reins in his teeth, he fanned off two shots. The first shattered the back of the bank manager's hand. There was a shriek of pain and the gun flew from the man's grasp. The second shot caught the gun in mid-air and sent it flying several feet away from the wounded banker.

The dark-haired woman on the walkway had flattened herself against the store wall. Her child began to scream and instinct caused her to pull the little girl close and try to shield her.

At this instant Sundance saw a storekeeper step from his doorway and take aim with a Mauser rifle. He was aiming at Butch. But when he fired, the bullet grazed Sundance. Pain flashed across his left side like a hot poker. Sundance grabbed at the wound, but somehow managed to keep his jaw clamped down on the reins.

The storekeeper racked another round into his bolt-action Mauser and fired again. This bullet buzzed past the bandits and buried itself in the store wall, just missing the little girl's head. The storekeeper racked and fired one more round. This bullet also sped past the outlaws, striking the little girl's mother in the collarbone and slamming her against the wall. Immediately she collapsed onto the walkway. The little girl fell to her knees, grabbed her mother, and began to wail.

The horses continued to buck and prance. The acrid smells of gun smoke and dust filled the air. Butch took a few seconds to turn his horse in order to take aim at the shopkeeper. It was during these split seconds that the man had been able to fire the first two shots.

Finally, just as the man was pulling the trigger for the shot that tragically hit the little girl's mother, Butch drew and fired two times. He aimed first at the doorframe by the shopkeeper's head. Wood splintered next to his left eye. He turned and ducked. Butch fired next at the frame on his other side. Splinters flew on all sides of the terrified man, who dove for cover inside his store.

Across the street, the child was still screaming while trying to rouse her unconscious mother. Etta sat frozen on her horse staring wide-eyed at the little girl.

Unaware that Etta had fixated on the wounded woman and her traumatized child, Sundance and Butch spurred their horses and raced off down the street. Sundance clutched his burning wound with his left hand and looked down to assess the damage. Looking up again, he realized Etta was not following them. He reined in his mount and skidded to a stop. Amid a billowing cloud of dust, Sundance turned his horse and galloped back toward the bank.

In the distance he saw Etta look in his direction and spur her horse.

The shopkeeper stepped out of his store, chambered another round, and fired.

Sundance saw the bullet from the shopkeeper's rifle strike Etta's fleeing horse, smacking into its right shoulder just in front of Etta's leg. The animal collapsed and Etta was catapulted over its head. She hit the street, rolling in the dust and dirt. She lay there for a moment before staggering to her feet. Another shot from the Mauser and the dirt exploded next to her.

A curtain of dust blasted into the air as Sundance skidded his horse to a halt next to a dazed and disoriented Etta. Dismounting, he pulled her to her feet and threw her onto the back of his mount.

* * *

It had taken Butch a moment to realize his friends were missing. He turned his horse and hastened to their defense. As he arrived to give aid, another shot rang out from the Mauser.

Butch drew his weapon and fired. It hit the same doorframe again splintering more wood. The man spun away from the flying fragments. This time, his precious Mauser was exposed to a full side on view. Butch's next two bullets slammed into the stock and then the barrel near the bolt. The Mauser split in two and fell to the ground.

Sundance nodded and a smile curled his lips. As Butch put his spurs to his horse, he smiled back. Butch knew that most people underestimated his skill with a handgun; Sundance was not among them. Truth be told, Butch knew that he was only a fraction less skilled than his friend.

The outlaws raced out of town. But as they sped away, the pounding of their horses' hooves did not drown out the wails of the terrified little girl as she sat on the walkway clinging to her injured mother.

* * *

Etta bounced along on the back of Sundance's horse as the trio rode away in silence. Looking down, she realized that her poncho was smeared with blood. She checked herself for a wound, but a quick search revealed none. Seeing the blood on Sundance's hand and on his left side, she screamed above the pounding hooves and panting horses, "You're hit!"

"Just took some skin is all."

"Pull up and let me look at it!"

"It'll be fine."

"I want to take a look!"

Butch glanced over his shoulder. "You two can have coffee and chew the fat later. Right now we have company."

Six riders were in pursuit.

Sundance shouted to Butch, "With Etta and me riding double, I think they'll catch up before we get to the relief horses. Maybe I should stop and send a few shots their way."

Butch looked at the Kid. "Couple shots should do the trick, but best if it's me. Take that pretty woman of yours and high-tail it outta here. If I have to, I'll take out a couple o' their mounts."

With this, Butch reined in and pulled a Winchester from the scabbard fitted to his horse.

A few moments later, Etta heard gunshots. Looking over her shoulder, she could see that one pursuer's horse was down and the rest of them were scattering. As she watched, Butch spurred his mount and hurried to catch up.

Together they retrieved the relief horses from the dry streambed where Sundance and Etta had stashed them. Wasting no time, they rode away on the fresh mounts leading their spent horses.

When they were sure no one was following, they headed for the small valley they had chosen to be their hideout.

Several days before going to Villa Mercedes, they had established a camp there. After the robbery, they planned to hold up in the valley for a week or two and then make the long trip to La Paz, the capital city of Bolivia. There, they knew they could lose themselves in the large town, relax and spend some of the money.

* * *

It was late in the evening when the three rode into the secluded valley. They began to settle in. Etta laid out a bedroll on the lush tall grass and helped Sundance to lie down. Butch started a campfire. It was dusk, so the smoke was unlikely to be seen beyond the surrounding hills.

With the fire going, Butch directed his attention to the horses. After the long hard ride, they needed to be rubbed down and watered. They also needed to be fed. And for that, they had stashed feed in the valley when they'd established the hide-away.

While Butch tended to the horses, Etta attended to Sundance's wound. Using hot water from the fire and a clean cloth, she began to wipe away the dirt and blood. Sundance gritted his teeth and managed not to make a sound as she worked. Once cleaned, Etta stopped to gaze at the wound.

Sundance read her thoughts. "Told you it wasn't serious. Hardly a scratch."

This comment brought sparks to her hazel eyes. She set her jaw and said nothing as she splashed whiskey on the wound. Heating a needle in the campfire, she used thread from her sewing kit and began to stitch up the open gash. She was none too gentle as she worked, and each stitch burned like she was putting a branding iron to his skin. When she finished, Sundance looked into her eyes and saw the burning anger.

He knew that she had been holding a lot inside. Now, her anger was about to boil over. He wanted to say something to sooth her fury, but no words would come to mind. So, he lowered his head and turned away.

Over the last two months Sundance had seen a profound change come over Etta. She'd become distant and moody. He figured that it was because of the way things had turned out in South America. But damn, it wasn't his or Butch's fault. Why did that damn bank have to get robbed in Rio Gallegos? Everything had been fine until then, but that robbery was what had changed it all.

Chapter 23

THE RANCH IN ARGENTINA

~ ~ ~

In the beginning things in Argentina had gone exactly as they had planned. Butch, Sundance and Etta had set sail on the British ship, Herminius, from New York in the spring of 1901.

On the second day of the voyage, as the Herminius plowed its way through the blue-green waters of the Atlantic Ocean, Sundance strolled casually with Butch along the ship's promenade. A cool breeze blew up a mist of sea spray, filling the air with the taste of saline and the smell of ocean brine.

Butch stopped and leaned on the polished wooden rail. "Etta still feeling poorly from the roll of the ship, Kid?"

Sundance nodded. "Her first venture onto the open sea. Recon she'll get her legs in a day or so."

Butch looked off toward the horizon. The setting sun glittered like gold and diamonds as it reflected off the rippling sea.

Sundance realized that, during the voyage, a seed of enthusiasm for their new venture had begun to germinate within Butch.

"You know this could really work out," Butch said, almost to himself. He turned to Sundance. "A couple of highfalutin Argentine land barons raisin' beef cattle and horses. Life o' luxury. I think I could get used to that." Butch broke into a broad smile. "You can call me Baron Cassidy. What do you want to name the ranch, Kid?"

"Maybe we should wait, Butch, 'til we actually find a place and buy it."

Butch didn't seem to hear him. His eyes wandered out over the sparkling sea.

By the time they landed in port at the capital city of Buenos Aires, Sundance could see that Butch's seed of enthusiasm had germinated and bloomed like a meadow of wild flowers. As soon as they stepped off the gangplank, he started looking for a land office.

"Maybe we should get us a couple rooms first, Butch," Sundance suggested a little testily. "Etta and I don't plan on carrying these bags all over this damn town."

"You two get the rooms, Kid. I want to find a land office. I want a big spread where we can graze and breed cattle and horses. And you said you wanted a few sheep, right, Etta?"

Etta, who still looked woozy from the voyage sighed. "I said that, Butch, but it could wait until we get settled. I need a bed and a bath."

"Like I said, you and Sundance get us a couple o' rooms. I'll find a land office."

It took several days, but eventually Butch settled on a 15,000-acres section of land on the east bank of Rio Blanco near a place called Cholila, Argentina. Their newly-acquired homestead was a sprawling, vast grassland with towering snow-capped mountains in the distance. To get there the trio took a train to the Chubut territory of Patagonia near Cholila.

Standing on the land that was now their new ranch, Sundance put his arm around Etta and gazed off into the distance and their new future.

Soon after they arrived, Butch made a deal to buy cattle, horses and a few sheep from a transplanted Texan named Jones who was now their new neighbor.

The first week, they began work on a fine sturdy log cabin that Sundance eventually furnished with the kinds of amenities he felt would please Etta.

The ranch work was harder than imagined, but Sundance and Etta adapted well to it. On the other hand, Butch spent more time in town at the taverns and bordellos than he did on the ranch.

Still, Sundance and Etta didn't seem to mind. They enjoyed their time together working the ranch and tending the livestock.

Sundance and Butch had paid more than a fair price for the large ranch, but in time they built up an impressive herd of cattle and over fifty head of fine horses.

Now that they were settled in their new home, Etta was as happy as Sundance had ever seen her. But, just to make sure she didn't get homesick during the first year, Sundance booked passage on the SS Soldier Prince to New York. He thought that it would please her if they went home for a while. It turned out to be unnecessary. During the trip back to the States, Etta, ironically, become homesick for the Cholila Ranch. It didn't help either that they were constantly looking over their shoulders for the law. After a short stay, they returned to Argentina.

* * *

Butch, as well, was content with their new way of life, especially that part of it that involved the nightlife in Cholila. He had a favorite tavern where he liked to throw back a few cool beers. The place was a bit dingy and smelled of stale alcohol, sweat, and strong tobacco. Actually, he might never have gone back after his first visit if he hadn't met Ed Humphreys there. At the time of their meeting, Butch had no idea that the big Welsh Argentinean was the local sheriff.

Butch nuzzled in next to the mountain of a man as Humphreys was leaning against the tavern bar. With not quite enough room to get comfortable, Butch smiled up at the massive fellow. "I do believe you're bigger than a pile o' rocks. Man would have to hire a team o' oxen to move you if you didn't wanta move."

For a moment the tavern went silent. No one had ever talked that way to Big Ed. The large Welshman gazed down on Butch, now smiling up at him. After a second, he threw back his head and let out a laugh that was as big as his immense frame.

"You're a bloke with more pluck than you got brains. Anybody with all that mettle has to be all right in my book. Let me buy you a pint, stranger."

Butch stuck out his hand. "Only if I can buy the next one, big fella. Name's, Butch."

Even after Butch found out that Humphreys was the sheriff, he still spent most of his time in the Welshman's company. Together they hunted, fished, drank and even, occasionally, spent time chasing women together.

Surprisingly, when Ed found out just who Butch was, he also continued their friendship. Ed told Butch that his past was just that and it didn't matter here in Cholila.

Nonetheless, Sundance was quick to voice his disapproval of the friendship.

"He's the law, Butch."

"That may be, Kid, but he's my friend."

The look Butch gave Sundance said it all and, in time, the Kid let it go.

Life was good and all three were well-liked and respected in the territory. Butch believed it would have continued that way had it not been for a robbery in Rio Gallegos.

As it often had, Butch's gregarious nature and winning personality were what ended up saving their hides. He had not developed his friendship with Humphreys for any particular reason other than the fact that he genuinely liked the big Welshman. But, the friendship turned out to be fortuitous.

Humphreys had told Butch the Argentine authorities had a vague idea that the gringos living on the Cholila Ranch were possible fugitives from the USA, but never had any reason to investigate the three.

What Butch didn't know was that, when a bank in Rio Gallegos was robbed, even though it was two hundred miles from the Cholila Ranch, the authorities decided to do some investigating. They contacted the Pinkerton Agency in America and within a short time, it was determined that the two ranchers were none other than the infamous American outlaws, Butch Cassidy and The Sundance Kid.

When the Pinkertons learned that the two outlaws were living on the Cholila Ranch, they assigned an agent to assist the Argentine authorities in making an arrest. However, it was the rainy season and in typical South American fashion the arrest was postponed until more favorable weather.

During the hiatus, Sheriff Humphreys became aware that Governor Lezana had issued an arrest warrant for Butch and Sundance. For three days he did nothing.

Then, on the evening of the forth day, Butch saw him walk into their favorite hang out. He grabbed two whiskeys from the bar and clumped over to the table where Butch was sitting.

"Best drink this," he said as he slapped one drink down on the oak table in front of his friend.

Butch looked at the glass as whiskey splashed over the rim.

Humphreys pulled back a chair and sat down with a sigh. He threw back his own drink and then said, "I been pondering on this for some time, Butch. And, truth is, I shouldn't be telling you, but I have a bit o' bad news."

* * *

The Old Gun

Etta was devastated when Butch brought home the news. Realizing their time in Cholila was up, the outlaws went on the run. They left their ranch in the hands of a neighbor with a promise that, when things cooled down, they would steal back to Cholila and make a deal with him to buy it.

They kicked around in Chile for a while doing odd jobs but unfortunately the meager pay could not support them. When they were able to return to Cholila and sell their ranch, the price settled on was anything but satisfying. Eventually, they turned to the only thing they knew how to do other than ranching. They started by robbing two trains during the spring and summer of that year.

For Etta it was a return to the life she'd been so relieved to leave behind in the United States. She'd been happy on the ranch at Cholila. Now the carefree life was just a memory. It was during these worrisome times that she began to grow more frustrated.

Chapter 24

THE SPLIT

~ ~ ~

Several months later, with things getting a little hot for the outlaws, Butch suggested they lay low for a while in the town of Tupiza in Bolivia.

The first night was long and restless for Etta. Sleep was kept at bay by her troubled mind. Finally the dawning sun peeked through the hotel window where she and Sundance were staying. It cast a golden glow on the faded, flowered wallpaper of the small room.

Etta sat up in the creaky, paint-chipped iron bed and gazed past her feet at the pine washstand, the only other piece of furniture in the dingy room. Worn and battered, it sat snuggly against the far wall. On it rested a porcelain bowl and pitcher. The once ivory-white bowl was now stained yellow from the iron-saturated wash water supplied each day by the establishment for the hotel guests.

The old bed let out a loud plaintive creak as Etta sat up and lifted her legs over the edge. Next to her, Sundance stirred and opened his eyes. He peered through the window at the early morning sun as it broke free of the distant mountains.

"What time is it? Anything wrong?" he croaked.

"Early," Etta said as she heaved herself from the bed. At the washstand she bent over the porcelain bowl, cupped her hands and splashed water onto her face. Turning to look at the Sundance Kid she said, "I'm going back, Harry."

"Going?" Sundance shook his head as though trying to shake loose dust that sleep had deposited on his brain. "Going? Where?"

"Back. This just isn't working for us, Harry. I need some time to think. Alone. Away from here. Away from you. I'm going back to Texas."

Sundance put his feet over the edge of the bed and sat there in his gray woolen long johns.

"It won't be like this always, Etta. All we need is one good score ..."

Etta sighed. "You're starting to sound like Butch." She picked up an old battered towel from the washstand and absentmindedly dried her face. She set the rag aside with a sigh and turned to face the Kid. "You can take me to the train tomorrow morning."

Sundance started to say something. Instead, he stood up and began to get dressed.

The next morning Etta boarded the train. She watched Sundance standing on the platform, through a smoke-stained window, as the train pulled away from the station. With every click of the wheels, his image grew smaller in the distance. When he was out of sight Etta began to realize that he was still with her. Settling back in her seat, she closed her eyes. Just before she dozed off, she felt his arms close around her and his lips press against her forehead. She heard him say, *Sleep tight.*

Etta woke with a start. Although she was looking into the face of a stranger seated across from her, Sundance's dark eyes were gazing back at her.

When she boarded the steamship for America, she noticed a young couple holding hands while mounting the gangplank. For a moment she closed her eyes and could feel Sundance reach out and grasp her slender fingers in his strong hand.

The sensations of Harry being with her didn't diminish when she reached Texas. In Fort Worth, she often imagined spotting him in the crowds on the street or in the restaurant where she often ate.

Now that she was back in Texas, Etta realized many of her friends had moved away, and those who were still there had changed, or so it seemed. Many came across as dull and tiresome, like pennies that had lost their luster.

On her third day in Fort Worth, she found herself sitting alone in her hotel room. She felt no desire to spend the day with any of her old friends who still lived there.

Even when an old beau named Walter had asked her out to dinner, the idea of spending an evening with him left her cold. She'd politely declined the offer.

The following days were much the same. After a month of this daily routine, Etta realized it wasn't her friends whom had changed. Her heart longed for the company of the one man who brought excitement into her life and made her feel happy.

The next day, she began her journey back to South America, back to Sundance.

* * *

Sundance waited on the pier at Mollendo after he'd received her wire. Even though it was a cool day, sweat formed on his brow as he watched the steamship tie up at the dock. As soon as the gangplank was lowered he found himself standing closest to its foot.

When he saw her, it took all his self-discipline to keep from rushing up to her. Instead, he stood there displaying what he figured was the proper amount of disinterest. That all fell away when Etta stepped off the ramp and stood before him. He took her in his arms and tears filled his eyes.

For the next year she stuck by him, but it was still obvious that she was unhappy. He knew that she longed for the ranch and the full life they'd enjoyed there. This unfulfilling life they were enduring now was not only dangerous, but it was also harsh. Cold misty nights on damp ground under the stars and meager meals of beans and tortillas were all too common.

During this period, Etta began to spend time each day away from Butch and Sundance. Often, in the mornings Sundance would awaken to find himself sleeping alone.

One day at dawn, shortly before the near-disastrous robbery of the Banco de la Nación in Villa Mercedes, Sundance awoke to discover her bedroll empty. He found her sitting by herself near a small stream running through the valley not far from their campsite. She looked up with sad eyes when he approached.

"You all right, Etta?"

She nodded, stood and took his hand. Together they walked back toward camp. She snuggled close as they walked, but didn't say a word until they were almost at the camp.

"Sometimes I just like to be alone to think," she said in a small, sad voice.

Sundance didn't know what he should say. It seemed no response could be the right one so he simply said, "It's okay."

All that day, Etta's apprehension over the upcoming Villa Mercedes job was obvious. Something had made her more fearful than usual of the possible dangers.

On the night Sundance and Etta were going to leave the Hotel de la Mercedes to stake out their relief horses, they had a late supper in the cantina. Looking across the table at Etta, Sundance tried to reassure her. "You had that same feeling before the train job we did two years ago, and there was no trouble that time."

Etta raised her eyebrows. "There wasn't any money on that train, Sundance."

Sundance smiled. "We know there's money in this bank."

Etta gave him a worried look.

"It's gonna be just fine."

* * *

But it hadn't been fine. In the Villa Mercedes robbery Sundance had been wounded, an innocent woman had been shot and a little girl had been terrorized.

Now after the robbery, and safe in their secluded valley, Butch started to make coffee.

Sundance was not necessarily fond of Butch's brew. He tended to make it more bitter than raw dandelion juice. But, on this night, Sundance was too weak to complain.

When Butch approached Etta and Sundance with two cups of steaming coffee, he glanced at his partner's wound. "It doesn't look too bad, Kid. Guess I won't be able to keep your share after all."

Etta slammed down her cup. Coffee splashed out and hissed on the hot coals of the glowing fire. "This isn't funny, Butch. This could have been a lot worse."

Butch tried to calm her. "It could have, but hey, everything worked out."

Etta's eyes flashed. "Yes, we're fine! Everything is just dandy. What about that woman back there, Butch? Is she fine? And her little girl, you think she's going to be 'JUST FINE'?"

Sundance tried to come to Butch's defense. "Be fair, Etta. We didn't shoot that poor woman."

Now, Etta turned on Sundance. "Oh, so that's supposed to make a difference. You think that woman gives a damn who shot her? She had no choice in what happened. She didn't choose to put herself and her baby in danger. She didn't choose to risk her child's life." Tears began to stream down Etta's cheeks. "I can't do this, Sundance. This time I really can't do this anymore. I do have a choice. I won't...I keep seeing the terror in that child's eyes. I hear her screams as she watched her mother laying there with blood flowing out on the walkway."

Butch and Sundance were mute. Sundance couldn't argue because he knew she was right.

Etta finally quieted and wiped her tears. With sad eyes, she turned to Sundance. "I'm going back, Harry. You can stay here with Butch if you want. I'm leaving and going back to the States. And this time it's for good."

The words hit him like a punch to the stomach. It wasn't that he hadn't seen it coming, but it was a powerful blow nonetheless. He knew the woman, and he knew there was no use arguing with her. Besides, she'd called him Harry. Etta only did that when she was very serious.

Calling him Harry always reminded him of his mother. As a child, when his mother got cross with him, she used his full name. "Harry Alonso Longabaugh, get yourself in here...right now." When Etta wanted to make a point, she used his given name the same way.

Butch made a futile attempt to reason with her. "We never had a woman get hurt before. Not likely to ever happen again either."

"You think that's all there is to this, Butch?" Etta was calmer now. "Can't you see? You're reaching the end and you just don't know it. I'm not going to stay here and witness it. I'm not going to see you two die. And that's what's going to happen. They may not have lawmen like Charlie Serringo or Samuel Stillman down here to hunt you from one end to the other of this damn country, but they will find a way and they will get you both. I won't watch it and I won't put my..." Etta stopped. She pondered for a second. "I just won't!"

With these final words Etta lay down on her bedroll, pulled her blanket up to her neck, and turned away.

Sundance grimaced from the pain in his side as he sat up. He wanted to go to her and hold her and was struggling to get up when Butch put a staying hand on his shoulder. "Leave her be, Kid," He whispered. "You're in no condition to be moving around. Besides, she'll get over it."

"She's a hard woman when she makes up her mind ..."

"She'll calm down by morning. You'll see. I'm bettin' she won't leave at all and even if she does, she'll come back."

Etta did leave. Sundance agreed to escort her back to the States. He did so partially because he felt it his responsibility to see her safely back to the States and partly because he figured the longer he was with her, the more chance there was that she would change her mind.

Lately, the three had been spending time in Bolivia. So, two weeks later, Etta and the Kid went to La Paz. Once there, they boarded a train that took them to Lake Titicaca and then on to the port town of Mollendo in Peru. From there Sundance booked passage on a ship to San Francisco.

There was little conversation between them on their journey. Etta seemed to have her mind set and Sundance was too proud to beg her not to leave him. As the journey continued and Etta didn't change her mind, Sundance actually began to get angry. Surely she didn't expect him to stay in the States with her?

Sundance could not just settle in with the woman he loved. Every minute spent in the United States put him under the shadow of a gallows. What good would it do to stay with Etta only to be arrested and hanged? On top of all that – Sundance hated to admit it – but the bond between him and Butch was very strong.

When he and Etta arrived in San Francisco, Sundance immediately bought a ticket on the next ship back to Peru, which was leaving the next day.

The two of them spent a civil, but strained night, at a hotel in the city. The next morning, Etta accompanied him to the wharf. Once again, there was little conversation during the ride.

When they got to the gangplank Etta said nothing. She simply gave Sundance a cool hug before he boarded.

With a cold invisible fist clutching at his chest, Sundance slowly trudged up the gangplank. When he reached the deck, he turned to wave. Etta had vanished.

Chapter 25

THE CONTRAPTION

~ ~ ~

The sun was a mandarin glowing orb that seemed to dip into the shimmering waters of the Pacific Ocean as his ship pulled into the dock at Mollendo. Sundance trudged down the gangplank and stood on the dock like an abandoned orphan. Finally, he wandered off to find a place to lodge.

There was no sleep for him that night. Before the morning sun broke free of the surrounding mountains, he found himself at the Mollendo harbor.

Since a ship from California was scheduled to dock at noon, Sundance sat on a wharf piling and waited. It was an hour late when it finally steamed into view. Later, with the gangplank lowered, the passengers began to disembark. Sundance stood eagerly watching and waiting. When the last passenger stepped onto the wharf, Sundance turned away and, with bowed shoulders, wandered back to his hotel.

Sundance continued to meet each ship arriving from the U.S. hoping Etta would come walking down the gangway; she never did. Nor did she write, even though he'd given her a post office box in Mollendo.

Sundance knew that Butch would be wondering about his whereabouts. He figured his friend would be staying in Tupiza. So, after three weeks he sent a wire to him there. Reluctantly, he told his partner he needed to wait a while longer to see if Etta might return.

Finally, after four dismal months, Sundance gave up and headed back to meet up with Butch.

* * *

During Sundance's absence, Butch moved from Tupiza to La Paz where he could enjoy the finer saloons and bordellos in that city. In La Paz, there was one particular saloon where he liked to hang out. The place smelled of cheap perfume and cheaper beer, but the girls were so attractive he had trouble choosing his companion each night.

Even though his time in La Paz was enjoyable, after three months he began to get restless. He'd heard of a bank on the outskirts of Santa Cruz that was often loaded with cash and had not yet installed modern security devises, causing trouble for people of his and Sundance's occupation.

Butch decided to do some reconnoitering. He grew a scraggly beard and, wearing a faded serape, threadbare trousers, and a shabby straw sombrero, he wandered into the town leading a bedraggled burro. Few paid attention to what looked like a down-on-his-luck miner as he sat outside the bank holding the lead to his donkey and smoking a corncob pipe.

Each night he bedded down on a straw pad that could be rented nightly for ten Bolivian centavos. Butch was not above getting down and dirty for information about a prospective target. By the time he left the place, he had a pretty good idea of all the bank's strengths and, better yet, all its weaknesses. With this information, he went to Tupiza to await word from Sundance.

Tupiza was not only a good town to hide out from the law — it also was close to the target town of Santa Cruz. When the Kid finally returned, it would be Tupiza where they would meet.

As soon as he saw him, Butch could see a change in his old friend. There was sadness in his eyes and a forlorn appearance in the way he carried himself.

Later that night, they dined together at a small restaurant near their hotel. They seated themselves at a battered wooden table covered with a red-and-white-checkered tablecloth. A waiter wearing an apron stained with grease wandered over and took their order.

Butch had been pondering Sundance's melancholy. Neither of them spoke. Butch gazed around at the dull ochre wall with patches of coralline brick showing where the plaster had flaked away. After a bit, Butch shifted his gaze to his friend and saw a distant look in the Kid's stare.

Finally, their food arrived.

"Are you ready to get back to work?" Butch asked as he swallowed a chunk of rare steak. When Sundance didn't answer right away, Butch took a long drink of beer and continued. "I found a bank that's ripe and ready."

Sundance set down his fork and gave Butch a seemingly interested look. "You checked it out?"

"Down to the number of tiles on the floor." Butch looked straight into the eyes of his friend and could still sense a certain detachment. He suspected that Sundance was trying to look interested, but was still lost in thoughts about Etta.

Butch took another bite of his steak. Chewing thoughtfully on it, he decided the only way to get Sundance back to being his old self would be if they could get back to business.

But as the days went by, Sundance seemed to find one reason after another for postponing the job in Santa Cruz: he could use a little more time to clear his head, he needed a better horse, the timing just wasn't right, he hadn't practiced much with his Colt and could use some time to get reacquainted with the weapon.

The excuses were as lame as an unshod horse, but Butch didn't challenge him. He knew the real reason: the Kid needed time to forget Etta before he could focus on business. After a month of Sundance's stalling, Butch decided to sit back and wait.

In the meantime, to help make ends meet, Butch found a job for them as payroll guards for the Concordia Tin Mine in Tres Cruces. It amounted to riding guard over a donkey train that traveled back and forth between a bank in La Paz and the mine. But, after a few short months, worry that they might be recognized plus the fact that the pay was meager caused them to leave the job.

* * *

The moon was shaped like a golden cup ready to spill wine when the two out-of-work bandits rode back into the sleepy town of Tupiza.

They dismounted in front of a cantina and sauntered inside. Butch inhaled the sour smell of beer and smoke as if it was the aroma of expensive toilet water.

"That's a hell of a lot better than donkey shit," Butch observed as he put an elbow on the bar. "Could sure use a beer." The homemade structure he was leaning on appeared to have been slapped together from used packing crates and was the color of pale slate. After a casual glance at the frail wooden bar, Butch removed his elbow and brushed his shirt.

"Dos cervezas, Amigo," Butch said as he reached into his pocket. The hand remained in the pocket for a second as a pained look crept across his face. "You mind buyin' this round, Sundance?" he said under his breath.

The Kid smiled and pulled out a handful of coins.

"Maybe it's time to take care of that little matter at the bank, Butch."

Butch gave his friend a grateful smile.

The next day Butch made a final trip to Santa Cruz to reconnoiter one more time. When he returned several days later, they made their plans.

* * *

It was a quiet, sunny morning in front of the bank on the outskirts of Santa Cruz. A dust devil whipped up dirt and swirled past the outlaws as they rode along the street. Sundance and Butch dismounted and tied their horses to a hitching rail in front of the bank. A few minutes earlier, Butch had ridden behind the bank to tend to a matter he said needed to be taken care of.

Sundance took a minute to gaze up and then down the street. When he was sure there were no signs of women or children, the Kid nodded to Butch who was scanning the street for signs of the law. With the coast clear, Butch smiled and the two outlaws mounted the steps of the bank.

They had decided this job would be straightforward: go inside, pull their guns, demand the money, and leave. The closest Policía Nacional was six blocks away. As long as no random officers came wandering by, it would take four to five minutes for the policía to respond. By then Butch and Sundance would have a good head start. With the usual precaution, they had stashed two relief horses outside of town.

* * *

Days earlier, while making the final recon of the town, Butch had noticed something unusual. It was an interesting contraption parked near the office of the Policía Nacional He had a pretty good idea of what it was used for and, seeing it, a sly smile had touched his lips.

Now, he and Sundance stood before the large wooden doors to the Santa Cruz Bank. The scene around them was calm and quiet. A shopkeeper was casually sweeping the walkway in front of his store next to the bank. A lone, one-horse wagon moved leisurely along the street. A stray dog roamed with his nose to the ground, taking his time to mark his territory.

Giving the impression of costumers, the outlaws entered the bank.

A few minutes later they slammed out of the double doors firing their pistols into the air.

At the sound of the gunfire, the dog yelped in fear and scampered off. The shopkeeper dove into his store and the horse pulling the lone wagon reared up and almost unseated the driver before lunging forward and racing down the street.

These were precisely the reactions that the firing of their pistols was designed to evoke. Butch and Sundance counted on fear and panic to give them the time needed to escape. They threw the saddlebags over their horses, mounted up, and sped off down the street.

A teller came rushing from the bank. "Bandidos Yanquis! Bandidos Yanquis," he yelled, pointing at the fleeing bandits.

* * *

Inside the bank, the manager was rapidly turning the crank on the bank's newly-installed telephone frantically trying to place a call to the policía. After several attempts, he slammed the receiver against the box in frustration.

He would later learn the line was dead because, minutes before the robbery, someone had cut the single phone line that ran from the back of the building.

When the manager realized he could not get through on the phone, he rushed outside and ordered the teller, who was still screaming "Banditos Yankees!" to run and get the law.

At his fastest speed, the portly teller took a full seven minutes to reach the office of the Policía Nacional. It was five minutes more before the law was mobilized and the manager saw the policía gallop by, in pursuit.

* * *

As the two outlaws reached the edge of town, they took time to look back to see if they were being pursued. They saw no one. With the town fading into the distance, Butch looked at Sundance. "Looks like they aren't comin' after us, Kid."

"Hope you're right."

They were several miles out of Santa Cruz when Sundance spied a plume of dust in the distance at the edge of town. "Hate to loosen yer cinch, Butch, but take a look."

Butch glanced over his shoulder. "Damn!"

Some minutes later they realized that the plume was growing closer.

Usually the two robbers spared their horses when first leaving a scene. If not being pursued immediately, there was little reason to unduly exhaust their mounts.

"Appears they've got some mighty fine horses, Sundance," Butch shouted. "Best put the spurs to these nags."

When Sundance looked again, the posse was still gaining and were close enough now where he could see the individual riders. He tried to count their numbers.

"Count seven riders, Butch. But, there's something else." Sundance looked perplexed. "Thought at first it was a wagon, but ... it's some other kinda contraption."

Butch shouted back, "Been lookin' at it, too. Ain't no wagon. It's an auto-mobile."

"Automobile?"

* * *

Behind them, seven riders spurred their fine steeds, closing the gap. Among the riders motored a 1903 16-24 Hp Fiat Coupe-Sedan that had been modified and outfitted for police work.

Inside the rear compartment, two policia tried to keep from hitting their heads on the roof as the vehicle bounced and jolted in an attempt to maintain pace with the galloping horses.

On top of the rear compartment was a flat deck where a single man lay prone with a rifle. A rack that went around the edge of the deck and a belted contraption that went around the waist of the rifleman helped keep him from sliding off the top. Nonetheless, the man on the deck struggled franticly to keep himself firmly planted in the middle of the bouncing platform.

In the open cab, the driver wrestled to keep the vehicle pointed in the right direction. Captain Vasquez sat next to him in the passenger seat.

Vasquez was a determined and ambitious man; this was his big chance. He'd been assigned as Captain of a station on the outskirts of a small town, but he saw himself as someone who should be the Captain of Policía in La Paz. He was not going to let these gringos get away. Whatever it took, he was going to hunt them down.

The terrain over which the posse followed the robbers was extremely rough. The rifleman riding on the top tried in vain to draw an accurate bead on the fleeing bandits. Though the vehicle was capable of greater speeds than the horses, the rough ground was making it difficult to even keep up with the police mounts.

* * *

"There's somebody on that thing shooting at us, Butch," Sundance observed. "Want me to pull up and take a few shots?"

The relief horses had been hidden among a grove of trees in an arroyo not far from the fleeing bandits.

Butch yelled back over the thunder of their galloping horses. "Let's get to the fresh mounts. Arroyo's just ahead."

"These horses are about played out," Sundance shouted back. "Theirs must be spent too."

By the time Sundance and Butch reached the arroyo, their horses were wheezing and covered in lather. Bullets whizzed by as they entered the grove and goaded their exhausted mounts into the shallow gully.

The policía were much closer now. Several of the mounted lawmen were taking pot shots from horseback. Dirt flew up near the two robbers as bullets slammed into the ground at the edge of the arroyo.

Quickly, Sundance and Butch dismounted and transferred the money-laden saddlebags to their awaiting horses.

Butch looked sadly at their spent mounts. "May have killed these two nags. No time to tend 'em."

Sundance glanced at the horses they'd been riding. He gave a sigh of regret, then his attention shifted back to the approaching posse. "Good cover here, Butch."

"Thought about that too," Butch said as he mounted his prancing horse. "Kill any of these Policía Nacional and we'll bring down more heat than we can handle. Besides, their horses are played out. No reason to make a stand."

More bullets plowed into the bank of the arroyo. The two men spurred their new mounts up the other side of the gully and resumed their flight.

Butch always reserved their best animals to be used as relief horses. If it became necessary to use them in an escape, the chances were that the original mounts would have to be left behind.

As Sundance looked over his shoulders he was not surprised to see the mounted lawmen come to a stop just after crossing the arroyo. Butch smiled and gave Sundance a wink.

The Kid smiled, too, and gave the pursuers a final look back. That was when he spotted the automobile that had skirted the arroyo and was still in pursuit.

"Butch, that contraption's not stopping," he called out.

"Saw that damn thing when I was checking out the town," Butch yelled back.

"You knew about it?"

Butch smiled and gave Sundance a wink.

Five minutes later, the two outlaws approached a steep, seventy-foot deep gorge. They pulled up to the edge and looked down. Below them rushed a small, rapidly-flowing river that appeared to be a few feet deep.

Butch smiled. "I figured, when I saw the damn thing at the office of the Policía National, it might be used ta chase us. That's why I come this way. That contraption ain't getting' down this gorge and across that river."

Sundance looked at the steep grade before them and glanced back at the pursuing automobile. He smiled and both men goaded their horses to drop over the edge. Dust flying and stones tumbling, the horses skidded and pranced their way down the steep grade. The two riders fought to stay mounted as they slid down to the foot of the gorge.

When they reached the bottom still in their saddles, they hesitated only a moment before plunging their horses into the cold rushing water. Although the river was shallow and the animals didn't have to swim, the rushing current was strong enough to move them downstream before they reached the other bank. The frigid water stung like sharp needles stabbing at their legs. Soon the horses leaped free and bounded up the low bank on the other side.

With legs still dripping river water, Sundance and Butch urged their mounts into a small grove of trees. From there they could see the other side of the gorge and observe, unseen, the actions of their pursuers as they reached the edge of the precipice.

They didn't have long to wait. The Fiat came skidding to a halt at the rim only seconds after hiding themselves among the trees.

"Ten miles, maybe fifteen for them to go around," Butch observed. "Take at least an hour to get to where we are now."

At the top of the steep gorge, the Captain exited the vehicle and took a look over the edge. Even at this distance, Sundance could hear the shouting and arguing that ensued. The officer was yelling at the driver who seemed to be voicing a strenuous objection. Finally, the driver was ordered from the vehicle and the shooter on top of the platform was ordered down. Then, much to Sundance's surprise, the captain got behind the wheel of the Fiat.

With the driver and the rifleman left standing at the edge of the precipice, the captain engaged the gears and eased the automobile over the side. Locked by the brakes, the back wheels stirred up dirt and dust as the auto skidded down the dizzying decline. The two other lawmen, remaining in the back seat, extended their heads in order to better observe their slide down the steep gorge. Shouting above the noise of the dragging wheels and rushing stream below, they gave advice and warnings as the vehicle began its treacherous descent.

For the first thirty feet or so, it looked to Sundance that the idiot officer might just pull it off and reach the bottom in one piece. Then, slowly, the vehicle began to slip sideways.

Shouting increased from the men inside. Yelling erupted from the observers at the top of the gorge, then the auto began to tip. With the first roll, the captain jumped free. The screaming of the men left inside harmonized with the cacophony of metal crashing and banging as the automobile began to tumble.

Dust and rocks catapulted skyward as the wreck spun over and over. The men inside were trapped and helpless as the Fiat tumbled and crashed down the embankment. Finally the mangled vehicle came to a stop on its side at the bottom of the gorge.

After jumping free, the captain rolled and slid until he finally came to rest next to the battered automobile.

There was deadly quiet as dust settled around the wreck. After several minutes, the two men inside the auto slowly began to crawl, bloody and bruised, from the battered vehicle.

Sundance and Butch waited long enough to see that no one was killed before turning their horses and riding away.

"Don't you just love modern technology, Sundance?" Butch asked, wearing a sly grin.

Sundance smiled back. "Yeah, but I think they're getting a bit more determined, don't you?"

"In spite of what Etta said, they gotta get up mighty early to catch ol' Butch Cassidy."

The smile disappeared from the Kid's face. Turning away from his friend, he rode on. Talk of Etta still stung.

Butch cursed and spurred his horse to catch up.

"I still say she'll be back, kid."

"Been almost a year, Butch. Never shoulda let her go."

"Look, couple more jobs we'll be set. After that, if you want, we'll go to the States and look for her."

"What about Serringo and Stillman? We go back there and we won't likely live very long."

"We'll figure somethin' out, Sundance."

"It's not just losing Etta, Butch. I feel like things are closing in. Can't put my finger on it, but something's in the wind."

Chapter 26

THE TALL MAN

~ ~ ~

Director General Francisco Diaz, in charge of all law enforcement in Bolivia, bowed as he was escorted into the office of El Presidente de Bolivia. The Presidente, a small man, looked even smaller in his richly-appointed, spacious office. Standing behind his massive desk, he smoothed his thinning black hair before extending a hand to Director Diaz. "Sit down, Director," he spoke in Spanish. "We must talk."

The Presidente got to the point. "For some time now you have failed to capture or kill the two bandidos Yanquis."

"I have shame, El Presidente."

The Presidente sat in his large chair and gazed at Diaz. Finally, he spoke. "Diaz, I appointed you as Director General because I knew you were a man who gets things done. I know you have done your best, but this situation with these bandidos cannot go on any longer. Something must be done. It isn't just the two famous outlaws that are causing all the problems," he said. "It is also the numerous imitators who have migrated to our country during the last two years."

Francisco Diaz leaned forward in his chair and nodded. "El Presidente, I estimate that at least a half dozen other bandidos Yankees are now operating in Bolivia and there are more in other South American countries."

For the next hour the two men discussed their options. The Director gave advice, but he knew that the final say was up to El Presidente. They finally, but reluctantly, agreed on the most obvious course of action to resolve the problem. The plan was simple, but for the Director and El Presidente it would be humbling.

The Director General returned to his office and later that day put the plan into action.

* * *

Using public transportation, there are two ways to get to La Paz from North or Central America. One is to land at the seaport of Mollendo in Peru and make an arduous journey by train to Arequipa, a picturesque town nestled at the foot of the towering snow-capped volcano, El Misti. From there the train travels to the town of Puno at Lake Titicaca, one of the highest lakes in the world. A ferry takes travelers across the pristine lake to connect with a railway known as La Ferrocarril Guaqui a La Paz that ends its journey in the city of La Paz, the administrative capital of Bolivia.

The second method is to sail further down the coast of South America to the small port of Mejillones sitting on the rocky, but sparkling coast of

Chile just north of Antofagasta. The Ferrocarril de Antofagasta a Bolivia Railway climbs up the front range of the Andes to Ollagüe on the Bolivian border, then continues across the Bolivian pampas to Oruro and on to La Paz.

Both methods are long and arduous; both meet meet with problems and delays on a regular basis. It was for this reason that Diego Sanchez had, for the last four days, met every train arriving at the La Paz station, whether from north or south.

He had been given a photograph from his boss, Director General Diaz, along with instructions to meet the man in the picture when he arrived at the train station. The distance from which the man was traveling and the unreliability of the railway system had caused Diego to be disappointed, thus far, at every arrival.

Diego was not informed as to the nature of the man's business with the Director, but he knew that it was important. He had been impressed upon to make sure he met the man when he got off the train and he was to spare no expense to accommodate and make the man welcome.

Diego was extremely loyal to his boss. He'd worked for Director General Diaz for two years and genuinely liked him. This job had been given to him and he would wait as long as necessary to greet the man in the photograph.

On this afternoon, he was waiting as the train from Chile arrived. The shrill whistle pierced his ears as the locomotive pulled into the station. Diego held onto his brown bowler as the exhaust steam from the engine blasted across the platform.

As was his routine now, Diego pulled the worn photo from his suit jacket and began to compare it with each of the gentlemen who disembarked from the train. He'd been told he was looking for an exceptionally tall individual. After several minutes, Diego saw what appeared to be the last passenger, a frail elderly man, stepping down from the last car.

Diego sighed and turned to leave, figuring he would just have to go back to his hotel and return in the evening in time for the train from the North. Something caught his eye.

A tall man dressed from hat to boots in black stepped down from the last car. A distinctive, large, western hat added to the stature of the man who already towered above the diminutive locals. The man set down a single cloth travel bag and, with cool grey eyes, scanned the platform from one end to the other.

The tall man's eyes locked with Diego's. Diego glanced down at the photograph; a smile lit up his face. Looking up, he saw the tall man snatch up his travel bag and nod. Only a hint of a smile crossed the tall man's ruggedly sun-weathered face.

As he once again compared the man to the picture, Diego was amazed at how these new photographs could capture a person's looks so accurately.

"Buen día, señor. Usted habla español?" Diego said as he rushed up to the tall man.

"Only 'nough to get by if'n I have to, little fella. I'd just as leave talk American if you know the lingo." The tall man pulled a cigar from the inside pocket of his long black jacket and stuck it in his mouth.

"I speak the English, Señor. I am so pleased that you have arrived safely. I am Diego; the Director General has sent me to meet you."

"Mighty good to hear, but tell me, Die-go, how'd ya know I'd be on this here train?" The tall man snapped a match with his thumbnail and when it flared to a bright yellow flame he held it to his cigar.

"This train? Señor, I did not know. I have met all the trains for four days. The Director General is very anxious to meet with you."

"Well, I'll be happy to meet with him but first I believe I'd like to rest up a might. Ya know a hotel where I c'n lay up?"

"Sí." Diego picked up the tall man's bag. "With your permission, I carry your bag. We make accommodations for you at one fine hotel in La Paz. Perhaps this evening, after you rest yourself, you will have the dinner with His Excellency, the Director General."

The tall man took a long drag on his cigar and looked at the small man holding his bag. "If'n it's all the same to you, Die-go, I'd just as leave wait 'til tomorrow to meet with your boss. It's been a right long trip t'get here."

For a second the smile faded from Diego's rusty brown face. He knew that Director General Diaz expected Diego to bring the man as soon as he arrived. But as intimidating as Señor Diaz could be, this stranger exuded an air of authority that Diego dared not challenge. He would have to deal with the Director later.

A half hour later, Diego led the tall man into the marble festooned lobby of the Hotel Real de La Paz. At the reception desk, he collected a key and escorted his charge up a grand set of stairs to the second floor.

The tall man looked around at the accommodations as he and Diego entered his suite. If he was impressed with the plush and fine furnishings he didn't show it.

Diego went into the bedroom and set the man's bag on a small table near the bed.

"I hope you have the good rest," he said pleasantly as he returned to the main room. "I will come in the morning for taking to the Director General, señor."

"Noon," corrected the tall man.

Diego paused for just a second. "Of course," he agreed as he nodded and backed out of the suite. "Noon."

* * *

While laying low in a small hotel in Tupiza, Butch had noticed that Sundance finally seemed to be putting the loss of Etta behind him. He was still not prone to any excessive mirth, but he was definitely less maudlin.

As usual, Butch was not reluctant to spread around the fruits of his labor. His money flowed freely and so did the beer and wine. Butch was by no means a drunkard but he did like a good time. Since Tupiza was somewhat lacking the fancier establishments that Butch most-enjoyed, he had grown bored with the small town. To humor him, Sundance agreed to travel with him to La Paz.

As a result, several days before Diego met the stranger at the La Paz train station, Sundance and Butch had checked into a secluded hotel in that same city. It was a small elegant hotel on the edge of the city and they registered under their usual aliases, Ryan and Place.

* * *

On the morning he was scheduled to meet with the Director General, the tall man awoke at nine o'clock. He'd slept for an extra three hours in an attempt to regenerate his energy, but the extra sleep had only been partially successful.

He wasn't quite sure why he'd agreed to make this journey. The money that had been promised was, undoubtedly a contributing factor, but there was more to it than that.

It was such a long journey and the customs of Bolivia were far removed from what he was used to. The language was troublesome. The legal system, especially the police system, was unfamiliar. On top of that, he had no idea what role he was going to play in the overall scenario. Still, this was unfinished business and he hated to leave things unfinished.

Hunger took him downstairs where he spotted a bustling café off the main lobby.

Struggling with the breakfast menu, he elicited help from the waiter to describe some of the items listed. In his profession it was necessary for him to know at least a little Spanish, but his knowledge was limited.

Since Diego was not due until noon, he took his time to enjoy the breakfast. After eating, he lit up a cigar and tried to work his way through a local newspaper.

Something caught his attention. An article on the second page detailed the exploits of a number of North American bandits who were robbing banks and payrolls in Bolivia. Two bandits in particular were featured and their names were more than a little familiar to him.

After setting aside the paper, he leaned back to finish his Cuban cigar. The food had helped to revitalize him and, as he puffed, he began to look forward to the meeting with Francisco Diaz, the Director General.

Chapter 27

EL VERRACO NEGRO

~ ~ ~

D iego arrived at the hotel with a hired carriage at precisely twelve o'clock to pick up the tall man. Their destination, Diego told him, was about three kilometers from the hotel.

The tall man gazed out from the carriage as they moved up and then down the rolling hills. All around them the sights of the city slowly slipped by to the sound of wooden wheels chattering on the cobblestone streets.

As they passed a small street market, he was struck with the pleasant smell of local fruits: Acai berries, achachairu, a small Bolivian orange, and carambola or star fruit as it is sometimes known, all combining to create a powerfully, fresh, tart aroma.

The women selling fruits and vegetables from the open stands were costumed in colorful dresses and blouses of indigo, coral, aquamarine, lavender and other striking hues. Some wore the typical bowler hats while others sported small straw hats festooned with ribbons of blue or green.

Moving into the interior of the town, he noticed how La Paz was slowly becoming a modern city. Here and there he observed automobiles puttering along the streets. He also noted that electricity, though not common, was evident in some of the buildings.

They came to a stop and left the carriage. The tall man followed Diego along a noisy street to the entrance of "El Verraco Negro," a popular restaurant.

The first room of the establishment was a dimly-lit beer parlor. A large, ornate mahogany bar sat parallel to the wall opposite the entrance. Behind it was a long mirror that tended to give an illusionary expansion to the small parlor. There was standing space for at least ten people at the bar and there were several tables that could accommodate maybe fifteen more.

The tall man could see into the adjoining restaurant and noted the only women present were the waitresses. He surmised that, during the day at least, this was a businessman's restaurant.

In the restaurant's main dining room, Diego paused to speak with the maitre'd. With a nod, the maitre'd led them through the dining room and outside to a veranda where there was a single large round table.

The veranda was situated on one of the more elevated hills of the city and had a view that looked out over the tile roofs of the surrounding buildings towards the lavender mountains in the distance.

Seated at the round table was a dark-haired gentleman with a crisp thin mustache. He was alone and had before him a very sumptuous meal.

Director General Francisco Diaz was fully-absorbed in his lunch and didn't see Diego and the tall man as they stepped onto the veranda. When he did, he immediately stood and wiped his mouth with the napkin that had been tucked in his shirt collar.

"Estoy tan contento que usted nos ha honrado, Señor Stillman," said the Director General as he extended his hand.

Samuel Stillman took off his distinctive black, four-cornered hat and reached out to shake the Director General's hand.

Stillman could be a very tough man when he wished, but he was also courteous. He wanted to speak the language of his host. "Ah...Director, de la buena tarde...I...."

The Director General smiled. "If you have no objections, Señor Stillman, we will speak English. I am very comfortable with your language." Then he bowed and said, "I'm so pleased that you have honored us, Mr. Stillman."

"You folks made it a might hard to refuse."

The Director nodded with understanding. "Sit, sit; I will order food for you. The food here is quite excelente."

"Thanks, but I already et," Stillman said as he pulled up a chair and sat down.

Diego also pulled up a chair.

"Then a glass of wine, Mr. Stillman? You must try our wine," the Director insisted. "It, too, is quite good."

"Wine will be fine, but a beer would go even better."

Some time later, with the food gone and the glasses empty, the three men sat quietly at the large table. Stillman took out a cigar and offered one to each of the men. "Cuban."

"Gracias." The Director General reached for one of the cigars; Diego politely refused. Stillman struck a match with his thumbnail and lit the Director General's cigar before lighting his own. Sitting back, he waited expectantly.

"Let me come directly to the point, Señor Stillman," the Director General began. "It must be obvious that we are desperate. To admit that we need to bring here a lawman from another country ..." The Director sighed and looked off toward the mountains before he continued. "Forgive me, it is somewhat embarrassing. But these two gringo banditos have caused for us a great deal of trouble. They not only robbed and plundered our country; they inspired imitators who are causing additional mayhem. I, that is we, El Presidente and I, want them eliminated."

Samuel Stillman took a drag on his Cuban cigar before he nodded. "I understand, Sir. Butch and Sundance have left me a might frustrated, too."

"Perhaps, but I believe that no one knows these two bandidos as well as you, Señor Stillman. I understand that it was because of you that they fled from the United States. Obviously, they fear you and I believe you are the one man who can help us catch them." The Director General paused and, as he did, his anger built. "They make fools of us. I want to see them dead. I want their heads stuck on poles for all to see. We chase them and chase them, but they always are one step ahead."

"That's the problem," Stillman said.

The Director gave Stillman a questioning look. "I do not understand."

"We never caught 'em' 'cause they were always one step ahead," Stillman explained. "If I learned anything over the years while I was after those two, it is that you cain't catch 'em by chasin' 'em. I realized it too late."

"I see. So, you have now the way to catch these men?" The Director still seemed puzzled.

"Believe I do."

"You will help us then?"

"I'll tell you a little secret there, Director General, Sir. I don't hate these men the way y'all do. In some ways I guess I even tend to give 'em their due. But I see this here as unfinished business. At first, when I come down, I was wonderin' what I was doin'. But this morning I realized that, even for a damn sight less than you're payin' me, I'd a probably come down here anyway."

"This is good news, Señor Stillman. Now what do you suggest we do?"

Stillman took another puff on his cigar. "The way I see it, if you want to catch 'em, there's only one way to do it; you gotta get ahead of 'em."

* * *

Samuel Stillman had come as close as anyone to catching Butch and Sundance during their years in the United States. He had missed them by only one day on one occasion and by a matter of hours on a second.

The first near-miss had come in Texas. At the time, Stillman was working for Pinkerton's National Detective Agency. They had been hired by the Union Pacific Railroad to hunt down Butch and Sundance as well as the rest of the infamous Wild Bunch.

Stillman had worked, at that time, hand-in-hand with Charlie Siringo. Together, they had tracked the outlaws to a boarding house near Fort Worth. They arrived twenty-six hours after the gang had left.

A year later Stillman tracked Sundance and his girlfriend Etta, to New York City. Good detective work allowed him to learn of their plans to leave the States on the steam ship Herminius, bound for Buenos Aires. As soon as he received the information, he rushed to the port only to arrive in time to see the ship disappear over the horizon.

Instead of being hailed as the man who had nearly captured the outlaws, Stillman had been denigrated among his peers at the Pinkerton Agency as the man who had let them slip through his fingers and was unofficially demoted.

A year later, he resigned from the Pinkerton's and took a post as a US Marshal. For four years he held that position with honor and distinction.

When the wire came from Francisco Diaz, the Director General, he deliberated on Bolivia's proposal for nearly two weeks. Going to that South American country, beyond all the hardships of the journey, would require him to resign his post as US Marshall. The money he'd been offered by Diaz was more than he could make in several years but the decision was still a difficult one.

In the end Stillman agreed to go down there and hear them out. He informed his superiors of the offer and took a three-week temporary leave from his post with the promise to let his superiors know of his final decision by the end of that time.

This morning, before he even met with Diaz, he had made up his mind. The newspaper article that he'd read over breakfast had fanned the fires. He didn't hate Butch and Sundance, but he firmly believed that they needed to be stopped.

However, unlike many of his peers, Samuel Stillman was of the opinion that Butch and Sundance were not murderers. He had interviewed dozens of associates and friends of the outlaws as well as numerous victims. It both rancored and bemused him that even their victims had good things to say about the two outlaws, especially Butch.

On the other hand, two members of the Wild Bunch, Harvey Logan and Kid Curry, had killed on several occasions. These murders had often been attributed to Butch and Sundance, but Stillman had learned that this was one of the reasons they split with Logan and Curry.

* * *

Sitting on the veranda of El Verraco Negro, Stillman leaned back in his chair. Murderers or not, he was determined he would finish the job that he'd started nearly a decade ago. He took a moment and gazed out across the rooftops towards the snow-capped lavender mountains in the distance. Returning his eyes to the Director General he said, "I'll be needin' about two dozen of yer best carabineers."

Chapter 28

THE IDIOTS

~ ~ ~

Shortly after arriving in La Paz, Butch received a letter addressed to his alias, James Ryan. It came from a man named Dick Clifford. Though Butch had only briefly met him once in Texas, he knew him to be a friend of Harvey Logan. Clifford had written of a mine payroll delivery that could be carrying up to $250,000.

Under normal circumstances, Butch would have ignored the communication. But boredom and curiosity, combined with a desire to replenish his dwindling bankroll, caused him to respond to the man. He made arrangements for him and Sundance to meet with Clifford and his partner at a popular restaurant near the center of La Paz.

The day before the meeting Butch informed Sundance of the rendezvous.

"It's a lot o' money, Kid," Butch said.

"You don't even know these guys, Butch."

"Friends o' Harvey," Butch explained.

Sundance raised his eyebrows. "And you call that a reference?"

"I know. I know. Jist humor me a little on this. I need you to go with me to meet these guys. You always have a good sense about people. I need your intuition," Butch pleaded.

"This isn't like you, Butch. You gotta be pretty bored or pretty low on cash to want to meet up with fiends of Harvey."

Butch smiled and ignored the comment. "Knew you'd go along. Thanks, Kid."

* * *

It was a hot and sunny day as Sundance and Butch climbed up a steeply-graded street in La Paz. Their finely-tailored and vested wool suits were a bit warm for the searing heat. Before they had trudged more than a hundred yards up the steep hill, they removed their jackets. Finally, with a sigh, Butch came to a stop in front of the agreed upon restaurant. He took off his derby and wiped his forehead with a linen handkerchief. Sundance looked up at the sign above the door. "EL VERRACO NEGRO ... this the place?"

Butch nodded and led the way through the doors and into the beer parlor. He and Sundance eased through the crowd to the ornate, mahogany bar where they nudged between the patrons already standing there.

"Doesn't look like much. Crowded, though," Sundance observed as he looked around.

"Suppose to be a well-liked eatin' joint," Butch said as he caught his image in the huge mirror behind the bar. "Best in the town, I was told."

Sundance pulled out his pocket watch and compared the time to a clock hanging to the left of the mirror.

"Quarter to three, Butch. Appears we're a bit early."

"That's all right. I wanted to get here first. Let's stay at the bar and have a drink." Butch wiped his damp forehead again with the handkerchief. "Could sure use one."

Butch called down to the bartender who quickly drew two cool beers and slid them down the bar.

"You told 'em three o'clock, right?" Sundance asked as he took a long swig.

Butch drained his mug in one long chug. Wiping his mouth with the back of his sleeve, he let out a sigh. "They aren't here by three o'clock on the nose we're outta here." Butch turned and yelled back to the bartender, "Uno más."

"Besides them knowin' Harvey, what do you know about these fellas, Butch?"

"Did meet Clifford once, but don't know much more than that." Butch shrugged. "Just want to check it out, that's all,"

"Still seems like a mistake to me," Sundance mumbled.

* * *

On the veranda of El Verraco Negro, the meeting between Samuel Stillman and Francisco Diaz was coming to a close. Stillman had conveyed to the Director General his plan for catching the troublesome duo and the Director, for his part, had promised the famed lawman his complete co-operation.

The men stood and shook hands. "I am grateful for your assistance, Señor Stillman," Diaz smiled. "Diego will take you back to your hotel. He will provide for you anything you require."

Samuel nodded, then leaving the Director to enjoy the rest of his siesta on the veranda, the lawman led the way as he and Diego stepped into the restaurant.

It was two minutes to three when Stillman and Diego entered the beer parlor. They pushed their way through the crowded, smoke-filled room and headed through the double doors leading to the street. Exiting the bar, Stillman donned his distinctive, four-cornered hat.

* * *

Sundance was checking his pocket watch and Butch was eyeing the clock on the wall. As he turned away from the clock, Butch caught a glimpse in the mirror of the tall man and the hat as the doors shut behind him.

"Hey, did you see....? I thought I saw...."

"What?" Sundance looked up from his watch.

Butch shook his head. "Nothin'. Couldn't be. Never mind." Still, the image stuck in his mind. He was about to push his way through to the street and look when the door opened and two young men entered. At a glance, Butch recognized Dick Clifford. The image of the two obvious Yankee cowboys immediately made Butch regret his decision to meet them.

When Sundance got a look at them, he looked questioningly at Butch who sheepishly nodded. Sundance rolled his eyes.

It was bad enough to be obvious gringos in a town where most people were natives, but to dress in such a way as to stand out as American cowboys could only draw attention – the one thing that Butch wanted to avoid. Both of the young men clomped into the bar in their hand tool boots. They didn't even bother to remove their cowboy hats as they stood near the doorway.

Butch could see that Sundance was staring at the Levi's and colorful western shirts that almost glowed among the somberly-dressed natives.

The Kid turned to Butch. "Damn, let's get the hell outa here, Butch."

Butch nodded and motioned for Sundance to follow him as he started to move surreptitiously toward the door. But, it was too late. Clifford spotted them and approached.

"Hi there, Butch." Dick Clifford extended his hand. "Mighty nice to see ya. Been a long time," he said. "And this here must be..."

Butch cut him off. "We can save the introductions for now. Let's get us a table in the restaurant." Butch had stopped the gringo from saying "Sundance" in the crowded bar. It was bad enough that he'd used his name, but if he'd blurted out his partner's name the chances were that someone would have taken notice.

Sundance's eyes were blazing as he stared at Butch.

A few minutes later the four men were escorted to a table in a secluded corner of the restaurant. As they sat down, Clifford started talking again.

"This here's my partner, Harry Nation. We can't say how much we is honored to meet with you two. You might say as how we admire you a powerful lot," Clifford said. "We worked some in the States with Harvey, but when we heard how well you was doin' down here…" Clifford shrugged.

Butch nodded with a patient smile. He wanted to get this over as quickly as possible and leave, but, first he figured he'd hear them out. On the other hand, Sundance was steaming and hadn't said a word. He kept sending daggers at Butch.

The four men ordered and Butch suggested that they save their business until after they ate. In the meantime he engaged them in conversation about what had been happening in the States over the last several years. Finally, with their meal concluded, Butch wiped his mouth and set down his napkin.

"Now, just what did you gentlemen have in mind?" Butch ignored the hot glare from Sundance.

Clifford pulled his linen napkin from his shirt collar and used it to blow his nose. Then he leaned across the table and spoke in a whisper. "You ever heard of the Aramayo payroll mule train?"

When Butch shook his head no, Clifford continued, "It's a payroll that's delivered by mule twice't a week. A man name o' Pero is in charge. Now we been studyin' on this here job for a month." Clifford stopped and looked around to see if any ears were eavesdropping.

"There's three guards," he went on when he thought it was safe to speak. "We done picked the best spot for a ambush. We got inside information that puts up to $250,000 U.S. being shipped on a certain day. It's supposed to be a specialized shipment."

Clifford puffed himself up and tried to look confident before he continued. "Now, we could do this here job ourselves. But we figured two more guns would make it a sight easier. Like I said, we'd admire to work with the likes o' you two. You might say as how you're our idols."

Butch didn't know much about these two men, but he'd heard a couple of things and one kind of rankled him.

"Admire us. Nice to hear. So, Dick, that why you been going around usin' the name, Cassidy?" Butch's tone snapped like a whip.

Butch knew that Clifford was a Wild Bunch-wannabe. He'd been acting so much like Butch that he'd actually tried to make some people believe he was Butch Cassidy. Butch was mildly amused, but also angered by it.

Clifford's face turned scarlet. He'd been caught and stumbled for an excuse.

"No matter. Forget it." Butch said.

For a moment there was an uneasy silence. Then, for the first time, Sundance spoke. "What's your getaway plan?" He glanced at Butch while waiting for the answer.

Butch had known Sundance for so long he often knew what his friend was thinking. Sundance's look had said, "These guys are idiots and dangerous and this answer will prove it."

"That there is the beauty of the plan." Harry Nation, who had said very little up to now, spoke up. "I got that figured out down to the nubs. The area is so remote, we don't figure on the law chasin' us none. Least ways, not fer a while. We plan on takin' the mules with the payroll to a little town name o' San Vincente. It's about half-day's ride from the ambush place. We'll hole up there overnight and head out over the mountains at daylight the next day. Slick as you please," he concluded with a big grin.

Again, Sundance glared at Butch. The two wannabe outlaws had been too focused on Butch to see the side-glances Sundance had been blasting at his partner.

"Sounds like a pretty big haul." Butch stood up and extended his hand. "We'll study on it some. I'll be in touch."

Clifford shook Butch's hand and then reached out to Sundance. Sundance hesitated, but, seeing a quick plea from Butch, he extended his hand.

Butch and Sundance sat back down as Nation and Clifford left the restaurant. As soon as they were out of earshot, Sundance snapped at his friend. "They don't figure on being chased! What were you thinking, Butch?"

Butch smiled, shrugged his shoulders and made a surrendering gesture with his hands. "What can I say? I was getting bored."

"They plan on keeping the payroll mules. That's like carryin' a sign. Even Harvey's smarter than these two."

Butch was as convinced as Sundance of the folly it would be to team up with these two, but he couldn't help putting Sundance on a bit. "$250,000 is a lot o' loot, though. Maybe we could set 'em straight some, Sundance. You know, take 'em under our wing, so to speak."

Sundance paused. Anger welled up until he saw the slight twinkle in Butch's eye. "This ain't funny, Butch. Those two guys could have got us caught just by meeting up with us."

"I don't see any lawmen bustin' down the doors to arrest us." Butch smiled. "Guess we'll be all right."

"I'm serious, Butch. I had my doubts all along about those two but, anyways, I was hoping that maybe they could steer us onto something. I know you. You're running out of cash so we need to find something. It's a sure bet you won't be wantin' to go back to working at the Concordia."

Butch looked Sundance in the eye. "Don't fret. I'll find something. I just need one good job."

Sundance shook his head sadly. "That's your trouble, Butch, always needin' one good job."

The next day, Butch began to put out feelers to his contacts. He was sure that, eventually, he would find something worth their attention.

In the meantime, Nation and Clifford had become restless. When they didn't hear back from Butch and Sundance after a few days, they contacted Butch once again.

Butch met with them one last time. The young outlaws pitched their plan again and repeated the amount of the rewards that Butch and Sundance could reap by joining up with them.

Butch didn't want to tell them straight out that they were idiots, so he made it sound as if he and Sundance were content to work alone, and were in fact thinking about hanging up the outlaw business altogether. He was pretty sure they didn't believe the last bit, but they seemed to accept the idea that he and Sundance preferred to work alone. At any rate, they shook hands and went their way.

But it would not be the last that Sundance and Butch would hear of Dick Clifford and Harry Nation.

Chapter 29

THE LAST BANK

~ ~ ~

A week later, Butch got word from not only one, but two of his most reliable contacts. There was an unusually large amount of money going to be held in the Tupiza National Bank. He brought it up with Sundance at supper that evening.

"Tupiza? I don't know, Butch. That's kinda like takin' a crap in your own dining room."

"It's just a town, Sundance, like any other. We stay there some when we're hiding out, that's all," Butch replied.

"Just my point. It's a refuge, Butch. If we rob a bank there it'll be pretty tough to lay low in that town anymore."

"May-be true. But, if this is our last job it won't matter. There's going to be payrolls for three area mines in that bank all in one day. That figures to be at least $350,000. It doesn't matter how fast I can go through money. That much will last a long time, Kid."

"How reliable are your sources?"

"Damn sight more reliable than Clifford and Nation," Butch shot back.

"I'm serious. How reliable?"

"This comes from my best contacts. I paid a lot for the information and I trust them more than any of the other contacts I have."

"Still don't like it, Butch. Just too close to home."

"Let me do the research. It'll take a couple of days. Then I'll lay it all out for you and we'll see what you think."

* * *

Sundance pondered the situation that night as he lay in bed. He knew that if Butch put his mind to it he could come up with a master plan for robbing the Bank of England. But, he wasn't going to like doing this job no matter how well it was planned. It seemed as if robbing a bank in Tupiza meant they were coming to the end of their rope.

Tupiza was a place where they could go when things got hot. They had a few friends in high places there to whom they had made donations. Those friends might not be willing to look the other way if one of their main banks got robbed.

The next morning Butch left for Tupiza. When he returned three days later, the prospects had him as enthused as a kid on Christmas morning. He was so excited that Sundance didn't have the heart to tell him no. Besides, he knew how much Butch needed the money. Butch had gone through almost everything they'd stolen since selling the ranch.

Maybe with this money, Sundance thought, he could convince Butch to go someplace in Europe like Spain or Italy and settle down there. He could even try to get a letter to Etta and convince her to join them there. But, then again, getting in touch with Etta was more dream than plan. His letters kept coming back. He couldn't safely go to the States and search for her in person. Half the lawmen up there were on the lookout for Butch and him. It wasn't likely that he would ever see her again, but it was a nice dream. Thinking about settling down with her again in a far away place like Spain ... maybe on a rancho.

* * *

The Tupiza National Bank was situated in the center of the gritty little town on an open square with a small marble fountain in the middle. The bank was on one side of the square. A number of stores and other buildings, including a cantina, made up the other three sides.

Tupiza was not a large town and the streets, in the early afternoon, were usually deserted because most people tended to take a siesta after their noon meal. It was for this very reason that Butch had chosen the early afternoon for the robbery.

The cantina was a one-story adobe building with a pine bar and a few wooden tables. Several locals were lolling around either sipping cerveza or quietly dozing.

Sundance sat at a table near a window that looked out onto the square. He could see and hear the fountain's water trickling from the mouths of three marble cherubs and splashing into a shallow pool. Other than the sound of the water, the square was deadly quiet.

Beyond the fountain, Sundance could see the bank and had a clear view of the rest of the square. He had been nursing the same glass of beer for nearly half an hour while patiently waiting for his partner.

Butch was doing recon: checking the policía to make sure they were where they were expected to be, looking for anything that could cause problems. Butch was generally making sure that everything would go as planned.

Gazing out the window, Sundance's attention was captured by a cat stalking a bird perched in a low-hanging branch. This drama had caught his attention because it was about the only moving thing in the square. "Mighty damn quiet," he mumbled to himself.

Sundance looked away when the cantina door opened and a flood of noonday sunlight streamed in. For a second, a lone figure blocked the sunlight as he filled the door. A large sombrero sat on his head, the brim flopping down over his face. The door squeaked shut and the man strolled over to the table where Sundance was seated.

Butch took off the sombrero and pulled up a chair.

"Beautiful, just beautiful. Like a ripe plum," Butch whispered. "And quiet as a grave yard."

"Quiet, yes, but I could do without that particular comparison," Sundance observed.

Butch ignored the comment. "Far as I can tell, there's only one or two policía in the whole town. The rest were sent down to Villazon. Some kind of border trouble there. Three-hundred-fifty big ones just sittin' there for the takin'." Butch was too excited to respond to Sundance's gloomy face.

"I'm still not convinced this is a good idea, Butch," Sundance whispered.

"Relax. I got it covered." Butch pulled out his watch and snapped open the cover. He noted the time then glanced up at his sullen partner. "Look, Kid, there's enough green backs over there to set us up for life. You gotta snap out of this thing with Etta."

"Miss her."

"Sorry, Kid, guess I was wrong. Doesn't look like she's comin' back. But, after this job we can retire. You can go find her."

Sundance didn't say what he was thinking, but there was no way he could go back to the States and look for Etta no matter how much money he had. He nodded and thought for a second. "You see any automobile contraptions around town, Butch? I don't take much to being chased by those damn things."

"Haven't seen a one," Butch smiled.

"Alright, then I guess we might as well get it over with. You ready to dance?" Sundance almost smiled.

Butch gave him a grin. "Almost. Where's the privy?"

"Through that door and out back," Sundance pointed, indicating a door in the back of the cantina to the left of the bar.

"Finish your beer. I have to shake a bit o' dew off'n my best friend," Butch chuckled as he headed for the toilet.

"Hey," Sundance called out after him. "I thought I was your best friend."

Butch turned around. With a wide smile he said, "I will admit that I'm a might attached to ya, Kid. Jist not in the same way."

As Butch disappeared through the door, Sundance took a sip of his warm beer. Making a sour face, he pushed the tepid brew that had gone flat aside and gazed out the window. The bird and the cat were both gone.

A few minutes passed before he spotted something that caused him to shoot up straight in his chair. Two horsemen were riding into the square. They passed right by the window Sundance was looking out of. It was obvious from their gear and the way they were surveying their surroundings just what they were: bandidos Yanquis.

"Damn!" Sundance swore under his breath.

At that very minute Butch re-entered the cantina, still buttoning his fly. "Ready? Let's dance."

Sundance held up his hand and pointed out the window. "Look!"

Butch leaned over and took a gander through the lead glass. "Now who the hell are those guys?"

"Can't say who 'cause I never saw 'em before but I sure as hell can say what they are. Take a close look."

Butch stared at them for a second. "No, oh no. Oh no! That's my bank. What the hell they think they're doin'? They're not gettin' away with this. Come on, Kid."

Butch's neck had turned beet red. He motioned for Sundance to get up and follow. Sundance understood, but he also knew that a cooler head was needed right now.

By this time, the two interlopers had reached the bank and were starting to dismount.

"What are you going to do, Butch, go over there and tell 'em you saw it first?"

"Damn right, and you're comin' with me. They ain't about to get away with robbin' my bank. Come on." Butch spoke loud enough to wake up one of the patrons dozing at a nearby table. The drowsy man looked around and then laid his head back down.

Sundance nodded toward the man and raised his eyebrows to Butch.

"I don't care!" Butch lowered his voice a little. "I planned too hard for this."

"We can't very well have it out with them in the middle of the square." Sundance was still looking out the window. "Besides, they already went into the bank."

"I don't care!" Butch said again.

Sundance saw Butch take a step away from the table but, at the same time, his attention was drawn to something outside.

"Wait a second, Butch."

"You're not going to talk me outa this, Kid. If I have to, I'll wait 'til they come out and then rob *them*. You gonna help me, or not?"

"Wait! Take a look at this."

Butch had already started for the door.

Sundance stood riveted by what was going on in the square. "I'm serious. You gotta see this." He waved Butch over.

Butch reluctantly stepped back to the table and peered out the window.

In the square, two carabineers had materialized. A few seconds later, like ants when their mound is disturbed, nearly two-dozen more carabineers swarmed into view.

The two outlaws watched through the window as the well-armed men took up positions surrounding the entrance to the bank. Butch drew in a breath of air at the sight of the military riflemen leveling their weapons at the door.

"I thought you said there were only one or two policía in the whole town." Sundance said.

"Someone must a had 'em damn well hidden." Butch whispered as he slowly exhaled. Then, the air was suddenly sucked back in.

Wearing his distinctive, black, four-cornered hat, and a long black coat, Samuel Stillman stepped from the entrance of the building next-door to the cantina. With his back to them, he stood not more than forty feet away.

"Butch! That looks like ..." Sundance gasped.

Butch stared at the tall man's back. "Can't be. He wouldn't come all the way down here ... would he?"

"If that ain't him, Butch, I'll eat that damn black hat he's wearing."

"What could they be payin' him? I mean...I wouldn't come all the way down here for Marshal's pay. They have to be payin' him a fortune."

As Butch rambled on, Sundance kept his eye on the door to the bank.

A few seconds later, the two bandidos backed out through the doors holding saddlebags and brandishing their pistols.

"Serves 'em right. Tryin' to rob my bank," Butch snarled.

The bandidos were reaching for the reins of their horses when Stillman shouted out from across the square.

"ALTO, HALT! Drop your guns! Drop your guns and put up yer hands! You're surrounded."

Sundance could see the hesitation and the defiant look in the outlaws' eyes as they turned their heads. He had seen the look before and he knew what it meant. Unfortunately for the two robbers in the square, Sam Stillman recognized the signs as well.

"Oh, no. They can't be thinkin' about ..." Sundance started to say, but before he could finish, the bandidos spun around and fired.

Almost before they had begun to turn, Stillman gave the order. "Dispara! Fire! Carabineers, dispara sus armas!" The square erupted in gunfire. The sound, even inside the cantina, was deafening. Butch and Sundance turned away from the window as dozens of bullets tore into the hapless bandidos.

"Owww. That was dumb." Butch said.

A few seconds later, a profound silence settled over the square. A cloud of blue grey gun smoke veiled the scene like a gauze curtain. The two bandidos Yanquis lay face-down and motionless in the street. Their bodies were riddled and torn. Blood pooled around them and seeped into the red soil.

The patrons in the cantina were awake now. With the gun battle finished, they peered out the windows into the square.

Sundance and Butch resumed their positions at the window and watched as Stillman approached the two bodies. Using his foot, he turned over first one outlaw's body and then the other. He gazed at them long and hard.

A small dark-skinned man stepped from the same building where Stillman had been laying in wait. The little man walked over and stood in the shadow of the tall lawman. After a few seconds, Stillman shook his head and looked at the small man.

"It's not them, Diego" Stillman declared.

"Are you sure?" Diego asked.

Stillman simply nodded and walked away.

Inside the cantina, Sundance and Butch backed away from the window.

"That was supposed to be us, Butch." Sundance turned to look at his partner. Raising his eyebrows he said, "Now what?"

* * *

Sundance and Butch hid out for several days in their little secluded valley. They needed time to analyze their situation and decide a plan of action. Sundance knew that Butch would not give up easily. They'd realized that, as long as they weren't robbing anything, Stillman wouldn't be able to track them. Stillman's plan was to trap the two outlaws, not hunt them.

Butch was not one to give up easily. He spent the first day running though scenarios that would allow them to keep robbing but he could see no solution. If they robbed another bank in Bolivia, or anywhere in South America for that matter, Stillman could be setting a trap for them.

Butch had a few ideas for other countries where they might start fresh robbing banks. Sundance shot the ideas down.

The evening of the forth night, they sat beside their campfire drinking hot coffee and watching the glowing embers float slowly toward the stars.

"The situation's not good, I know, Butch," Sundance said as he stirred the fire with a stick. More embers flew up into the cool night sky. "But, it may not be as bad as you think."

"Looks pretty bad, Kid," Butch said with a sad grin.

"I know you're low on cash. But to tell the truth, Butch, it's because you spend it like water rushing over Niagara Falls."

"Can't argue with you there, Kid, but this is a hell of a time to bring it up."

"Just hear me out. Since we sold the ranch I've been saving most of what we've been getting from the robberies. I have a pretty good nest egg set aside."

"You never told me that. I thought you were in almost the same shape as me. Hell, Kid, you'll be just fine. Why you so worried? You look like you just lost your best friend."

Sundance looked up from the fire and gazed at Butch. "It looks like I am about to, Butch. Wherever we go from here, I don't see how we can go there together. We're just too easy to spot that way."

"True enough." Butch looked pensive for a moment until a thought came to him. "I've never seen you carrying a lot of loot. Where the hell you been hiding all that money, Kid?"

Sundance looked at his friend with a sheepish grin. "I've been keeping some of it in the Tupiza National Bank."

Butch began to laugh. Soon, he was laughing so hard he fell over backward off the log he'd been sitting on. Sundance started to laugh as well.

When Butch could talk again, he said, "No wonder you didn't want to rob it."

"Hell, Butch, that wasn't it," Sundance smiled. "I knew we'd get mine with all the other money when we robbed the bank."

Butch nodded but kept on chuckling.

Sundance stopped smiling. "I figure it'll be safe to withdraw it in a couple of days. After that I can get the rest from the other banks I have it in. Then, what I want to do is split it with you."

Butch looked hard at his friend. The smile faded from his lips. "You can't do that, Sundance."

"I've already made up my mind, Butch. Half of what I've got is enough to last me. You might have to be a bit more thrifty than usual with your share. But, I figure, since you know the money came from me, you might be a tad more careful how you spend your half."

When Butch started to protest again, Sundance cut him off. "It's the only practical thing to do. If we split up and you don't have money there's only one thing you'll be able to do. And, that'll get you caught or killed. I don't want that on my conscience, so you'll actually be doing me a favor by taking half of the money."

Butch stayed silent for quite a while. Finally he said, "You've been a mighty good friend, Kid. Better than I been to you." He smiled. "Must admit, bein' responsible has never been what people admire most about me. Maybe time for a change."

Sundance nodded, but kept his silence.

"Where you going to go?" Butch asked.

"Don't know. Thought maybe Mexico. How about you?"

"I was thinkin' Costa Rica."

"Where?"

"It's in Central America. Kinda primitive but cheap to live there. I could buy a little plantation, grow bananas."

"Now I know you're puttin' me on, Butch."

"No, really. There's good money in bananas and I'd just lie back on a beach and let hired locals do the work."

"Whatever you say, Butch." Sundance gave him a skeptical look.

The fire had burned low and Butch stuck another log into the coals. "So ... when we leave, I suppose it won't hurt none to take the train together to the port at Mollendo."

Sundance wanted to prolong the inevitable also so he nodded. "We can wait to split up 'til we get there."

Sundance was a bit sad and low on hope when they lay down that night to sleep. As they dozed off, he didn't know it, but things were already happening that would change their chosen destinations to the one place they never expected to go.

* * *

After his posse had killed the two bank robbers in Tupiza, Samuel Stillman was feeling like a hunter who had set a bear trap only to catch a rabbit. Diego tried to console him by saying that catching these two unknown bank robbers in the act was better than nothing, even if they were the wrong ones. But Stillman was not so sure. It was far from what he'd been hoping for and there was the chance that Butch and Sundance would learn of the trap he had set.

The day after the robbery, Stillman returned to La Paz to plan his next move and to do what he could to diminish any damage that killing the wrong robbers might cause.

That afternoon, he entered the Director General's office with his hat in his hand. He could read the disappointment in the Director's eyes. With a slight nod he sat down.

"I'd like news of this here incident to be kept quiet as possible, Director. I'm hoping our quarry has not got word of it. They find out we set a trap an' they're likely to go t'ground."

The Director nodded. "We will ask the newspapers to put the story in the back of the paper or perhaps to not write the story at all, yes?"

"Not likely they know I'm here an' it's best kept that way." Stillman stood up. "Sooner or later I'll catch up with these two."

With that the lawman put on his hat and left the office.

The Old Gun

Stillman had begun plans for his next trap when he got word of rumors that Butch and Sundance had been seen in Tupiza less than a week after the attempted robbery of their National Bank. This was disturbing. If they were there, they might have learned about the trap from the locals. At any rate, the lawman decided to take Diego and travel down there again to check things out.

Chapter 30

THE DEATH OF BUTCH AND SUNDANCE

~ ~ ~

The day after retrieving his money in Tupiza, and at about the same time as Stillman and Diego were heading for that town, Sundance rode with Butch to La Paz. They registered at a different hotel than usual and took the precaution of using new aliases. With Stillman in Bolivia, they thought it best to be extra careful.

Sundance still wasn't sure if Butch was serious about going to Costa Rica, but he was sure about his own decision to go to Mexico. At least in Mexico he'd be close to Texas and he had a firm suspicion that Etta might be there. He knew she had a cousin in Texas and knew Etta and her cousin had been close. Maybe it would be possible to sneak across the border and look up the cousin.

The next morning, dressed in their vested suits and derby hats, the two outlaws left the hotel and took a carriage to the train depot. As they cautiously entered the station, Sundance and Butch scanned the platform and the ticket area for any sign of lawmen. Butch nodded to Sundance and casually the Kid approached the ticket office.

"Two tickets to Mollendo," Sundance said in Spanish. The tickets would take them to Lake Titicaca where they'd cross by ferry and then transfer to another train for the final leg of their journey to Mollendo.

"Do you want a private compartment, Señor?" asked the ticket master as he appraised Sundance's fine clothes.

Sundance considered the question. They would be less exposed in a private compartment, but would looking that affluent attract unwanted attention?

While Sundance wrestled with buying the tickets, Butch purchased a La Paz newspaper. He had been reading the papers regularly for years.

During their time in South America, both men had made it a chosen task to learn to speak Spanish. Butch had also learned to read Spanish well enough to muddle through the local newspapers. It was considered exceptional when they came across a paper in English. Unfortunately, on this day, he was not to be blessed with such a find. Sundance joined Butch as he bought La Tribuna de La Paz. With the newspaper tucked securely under his arm, the two men hurried along the busy platform and boarded the train.

Sundance had made the decision for the two of them to be in a private compartment. He figured privacy outweighed any other considerations. The two men settled back in the spacious, but rather uncomfortable wooden seats.

A few minutes later came the first chug of the engine and the inevitable jolt signaling the start of their journey. Soon after, Sundance was gazing out the window as the countryside drifted by to the sound of the wheels clacking along the iron rails.

* * *

Butch was seated across from The Kid reading his newspaper. With his face buried in the paper, Butch tried to concentrate on the words, but try as he might his mind kept returning to thoughts of his future. Hidden from Sundance behind the paper curtain, he stared absentmindedly out the train window. Sighing, he shook his head. Someday he'd pay his friend back for the money he'd bestowed upon him.

Butch had decided to go to Costa Rica as planned and buy a plantation with the money. Still, it wasn't something he was looking forward to. Living in a primitive jungle did not seem like an alluring prospect for a man who thrived on saloons and a glitzy lifestyle.

After a few minutes, he lowered his newspaper to peer over the top at Sundance.

"I won't miss South America all that much," Butch said. After a pause he added, "We'll get on separate steamships when we get to Mollendo."

Sundance took his eyes away from the outside scenery and gazed at his friend.

Butch could read his mind. "I know. I'm repeating myself."

Sundance opened his mouth to make a comment when something caught his eye. An article on the front page of Butch's newspaper had a heading that read: BANDIDOS NOTORIOS DEL YANQUIS MATADOS EN SAN VICENTE.

"Butch, you see this?"

"What?"

"This article. It says, Notorious Yankee Bandits Killed in San Vicente."

Butch smiled, but didn't look immediately. "When did you learn to read Spanish?"

"I know enough to know what that says," Sundance said as he pointed at the headline.

Butch closed the paper and turned it so he could look at the front-page. Slowly, he deciphered the text.

"San Vicente. Isn't that where those two idiot were going to hide out after they robbed that payroll?" Sundance asked.

"That's what they told us," Butch said as he kept reading. "Those two poor stupid..." Another few moments passed as he read on. "It has to be them. They were caught after they robbed the payroll because the locals recognized the mules they had with them."

Sundance looked sad. "They kept the mules. Now I feel bad. Maybe we should have advised them a little, like you said. I mean, not work with them, but give 'em a few suggestions." Sundance shook his head and sighed. "How could they be so stupid as to keep the mules from the robbery?"

"The locals saw the brands on the mules and sent for the authorities," Butch said as he read on. "Killed 'em in a shoot out."

Butch stopped reading and looked at Sundance. "I don't think it would have helped one damn bit if we'd advised those two nit wits. And I'll tell you why." Butch lowered the paper.

"I've been reading about this young guy in Europe somewhere, Germany, I think. His name is Bernstein or Einstein or something like that. Any way, people call him a genius. That's a guy who's real smart about somethin'. You see he's got answers to things that most people didn't even know there were questions about. Now, the way I see it, if this guy is a genius about science and stuff like that, those two guys were geniuses at being idiots."

Sundance's smile was almost imperceptible. Then it was gone. "Well, too bad about those fellas anyway."

After a pause, Butch picked up the paper and continued to read. "Funny they'd write so much about those two, and on the front page, too."

As Butch read, his eyes widened and his jaw dropped.

"NO! Oh, no!" That ain't right. They can't think that, someone's got to set this straight."

Sundance looked puzzled. "What? Set what straight?"

"They think it was us."

"Think it was us, what?"

"Right here. Muerto. Butch Cassidy and the Sundance Kid, muerto! That asshole Clifford kept calling himself Cassidy. He registered at the hotel in San Vicente under the name Cassidy. We gotta tell someone, Sundance. We can't have people thinkin' we were that dumb to get caught that way!"

Sundance stared at his friend as this news began to sink in. "Wait a minute, Butch. You're not seeing the big picture here. This is good."

Butch gave Sundance a hard stare. "What the hell can be good about lookin' stupid?"

"I can't believe you don't see it, Butch. Everyone's going to think we're dead. Once the word is out, nobody will be looking for us anymore. This is good. Believe me, this is good."

"Don't much like lookin' foolish though, Sundance."

"You're thinkin' with yer ego, Butch."

After a while Butch reluctantly nodded. "I guess so. I mean...I understand what yer sayin'. It's...It's just that I hate for people to think we were that stupid."

Sundance began to laugh. "I will miss you, Butch. What else does it say in the paper?"

Butch shook himself out of his funk and picked up the paper again. "They buried them in the town cemetery after they had their bodies on display in front of the local cantina for three days. I imagine they were pretty ripe by then."

"Anything about Stillman in there?" Sundance asked.

"Not directly. Just says that a lawman was sent from La Paz to view the bodies, but it took him a week to get there. Don't imagine he had much to look at once he got there."

"That's good. He might'a been able to tell it wasn't us if the bodies were fresh. As it is, we're dead. We still can't go back to the States together, too risky. But, if we lay low in Mollendo for a few months, wait for the word to spread, we can pretty much go anywhere we want."

"Where you going, Kid? As if I didn't know," Butch asked with a knowing smile.

Sundance smiled back. "What about you? Still going to Costa Rica?"

"Don't believe I will. Might try Oregon or maybe Washington."

After a short pause, Butch asked, "Where you going to look for her, Kid?"

"She has a cousin in Fort Worth. Might start there."

* * *

Samuel Stillman was feeling frustrated. His trap hadn't worked and his trip back to Tupiza to check out the rumors that the two bandits had been spotted there was turning out to be a wild goose chase.

It was while Stillman was in Tupiza that word arrived at the Director General's office in La Paz that Butch and Sundance had been killed in San Vicente. The officials there had not seen any need to rush when sending the news, so it was two days after the bandits' deaths that word was finally sent. It took the Director a day to contact Diego and Stillman in Tupiza and another day for Stillman to return to La Paz. From La Paz it took him three more days to reach the remote village of San Vicente: seven long days after the two bandits were taken down.

Even though the corpses had rotted in the sun for three days and had been buried for some time, when Stillman arrived in San Vincente, he ordered the bodies exhumed.

It took four locals the better half of the next day to unearth the two crude wooden boxes.

Stillman moved in close as the first of the coffin lids was pried open. The fetid stench hit him like a punch to the gut. One of the diggers dumped his breakfast next to the casket before he could clamber away from the smell. The others threw down their shovels and scrambled out of the grave right behind him.

In order to get through the opening of the second coffin, Stillman had to cover his nose and mouth with his handkerchief and do the deed himself. Struggling to control his gag reflexes, Stillman gazed upon the two cadavers. They were so badly bloated and decomposed that they were unrecognizable. Since he couldn't begin to identify them, Stillman ordered the bodies reburied and the next day he returned to La Paz.

Even though the bodies he'd seen in San Vicente were of the approximate heights of Butch and Sundance, Stillman wasn't convinced that the two bandits killed there were indeed the famous outlaws. But, he had nothing to prove they were not. It just seemed strange to him that the two experienced bandits would suddenly become so careless. In Stillman's mind, the only option was to continue on as though the two were alive. If they didn't surface in the next several months, then he'd have to accept that they were truly dead and return to the United States.

Whatever the case, Samuel Stillman was full of conflicting emotions. He had expected to capture or kill Butch and Sundance himself and this was not the outcome he was hoping for. It was, of course, the objective of the Director General to rid the country of the two outlaws and the Director was now satisfied. Still, Stillman secretly hoped that the two would show themselves again so he could have one last stab at their capture.

Four uneventful months went by and finally a dispirited Samuel Stillman reluctantly returned to the United States resigned, but not convinced.

* * *

While taking the ferry across Lake Titicaca, Butch finally came to the conclusion that the false news of their demise was extremely fortuitous. He agreed with Sundance that they could not take any chances. To be resurrected by a random encounter with someone who might recognize them together would be disastrous.

Upon reaching the town of Puno on the shore of Lake Titicaca, Butch gave Sundance an address in Oregon of a relative where he might be reached. Then he bid his friend a fond goodbye.

Butch missed the Kid almost immediately after they parted company. Nonetheless, when he arrived in Mollendo a week later he lodged in a separate hotel and avoided running into his friend.

They figured that laying low for two months should provide ample time for the word of their deaths to reach most of law enforcement in the United States.

Chapter 31

THE PROMISE

~ ~ ~

Two months later, to the day, Sundance left by steam ship for the U.S. It had been planned in advance that Butch would wait one more week before beginning his voyage. During the cruise to San Francisco, Sundance began to experience a strange feeling. His uneasiness had come on him slowly, but had grown as he approached his destination. The sensation was alien to him and it took a while to realize it was fear. He'd been in situations before where he could have experienced the emotion, but in those instances he had simply reacted. He never had time to do much else. Bullets flying, Sundance went into action. No matter the situation, Sundance had never before been gripped by any kind of overwhelming fear.

Sitting on the ship as it cruised the waters off the coast of California, Sundance was a prisoner to his own thoughts. What if he couldn't find Etta? It had been almost three years and he had not heard a word. The thing that brought on the most intense foreboding was what would happen if he did find her. What if she had a new man or, even worse, if she refused to see him?

Sundance had a hard time understanding what was happening to him. In the beginning of their relationship he'd enjoyed being with her, but it hardly consumed his thoughts. At least, that was how he remembered it. If Etta stayed, she stayed, and if Etta went, she went. He was sure that back then he hadn't really cared that much. When had that all changed? When had Etta become the most important thing in his life? Even now, as his ship steamed toward the port at San Francisco, he tried to convince himself that whatever happened, it wouldn't matter all that much. But that was when the fear snuck in and grabbed him by the gut.

When he arrived in San Francisco, he stayed in the city for a night. The following morning he boarded the Union Pacific train to start his journey to Texas. Settling into his seat, he was aware that he was riding on the same train line that had been the object of a number of his robberies in years past.

He slouched down, pulled his hat low to shade his eyes, and snuck a look at the assortment of travelers seated around him. A man across the aisle stared back. Sundance froze until the man smiled and gave him a friendly nod.

Word of his death had made it to the United States six weeks before he reached San Francisco. It had been big news for a day or two. Because of that, it was unlikely that anyone on this train would suspect that they were traveling with a notorious outlaw.

Sundance settled back and watched the countryside as it raced past his window. In spite of the apparent speed of the train, the journey itself seemed to never end. The train took him south to Los Angeles, on through Arizona and New Mexico, and finally into Texas.

Sundance couldn't relax. The same fear that had dogged him on the steam ship made itself his pestering companion on the train. He was exhausted from the worry by the time the train chugged into the station at Fort Worth.

The Texas town had changed a good deal since he was last there. The boarding house where he, Butch, and the Wild Bunch had hung out was gone. In its place was a modern six-story hotel. He stood gazing up at the amazing brick structure for a time before he finally stepped inside and booked a room.

The next day he went to the address where Etta's cousin, Elsie Roberts, had lived. He and Butch had been there only once with Etta and that had been a long time ago. He wandered around, searching for a while before he finally stumbled across the place. Mounting the steps, he lightly rapped on the door. After what seemed forever, the door opened a crack and an elderly man peered out.

Sundance smiled. "Mornin' sir. I'm wonderin' if a Miss Elsie Roberts is still livin' here.

"Don't live here no more, young fella." The old man's eyes looked Sundance up and down. "Moved out almost two years ago."

"Any idea where she moved to?" Sundance asked.

"You a friend?"

Sundance nodded.

The old man rubbed the grey stubble on his chin and looked hard into Sundance's eyes. "Try the lady in the front apartment across the street there. Seems to know everyone."

When the lady across the street answered her door, she told Sundance that she did remember Elsie but didn't know were she'd gone.

"I believe she married a railroad man. Don't know where they moved to, but I do remember she had a friend lived in an apartment building on the next block. Let me see.... Believe her name was Carol."

There was only one Carol living in that apartment building and she turned out to be the one who had been friends with Elsie. She told Sundance that Elsie and her husband had moved to Dallas. She'd kept in touch and gave Sundance the address.

The next day Sundance traveled by train the fifty miles to Dallas. He began his search there immediately after he booked his accommodations. Surprisingly, he had little trouble finding the address. Elsie was not at home when he knocked on her door in the late afternoon, so he settled in on the front steps of the apartment building and waited.

Around 6:00 p.m. Sundance saw Elsie approaching her apartment carrying a sack of groceries. She recognized him as soon as she spotted him sitting on the stoop in front of her building. She paused and stared, then she shook her head and walked past him.

"I guess I know why you're here," she said without a smile.

Hat in hand, Sundance followed her up the steps. "Might I come in and talk with you, Elsie?" He held the door open for her as she entered the building.

Once inside, Elsie turned at the foot of the stairs leading to the upper floors. "She's doing just fine without you, Harry," she said as her eyes looked him over from head to foot.

"When I read it, I figured it was too much to ask that you and Butch were dead. You're too good at what you do to get shot and Butch is too ornery to die." A slight smile touched her lips as she spoke Butch's name. "Where is the scallywag?" She looked behind Sundance as though she might see Butch lurking somewhere in the hallway.

"We split up. All of that's behind me, Elsie." After a pause he added, "It would please me greatly if you'd allow me to talk with you some."

She looked him over as he stood there with his bowler hat in hand and his shoulders slumped. "Come on up. My husband will be home soon. He works for the railroad. You can have supper with us if you have a mind to."

Supper was a little strained. Elsie's husband spent most of the meal glaring at their guest. It was obvious that the man did not feel kindly to the notorious train and bank robber. Finally he spoke up. "My wife invited you to join us and I ain't about to go agin her. Jist want you to know I don't much approve of yer profession." Having said this, he returned his attention to his meal and spoke no more.

As for Elsie, she talked little of her cousin during supper, only enough for Sundance to gather that Etta was in good health and doing well enough. It took a great deal of convincing, but eventually he managed to wrangle an address from her. Etta was living in Dallas. Her apartment was not far from where Sundance sat at that very moment.

A little after eight o'clock that same night Sundance approached the door to Etta's place. It seemed as if a ball-peen hammer was pounding on his chest as he reached out to rap on the door.

* * *

Etta was absorbed in the evening paper. Dressed in a warm cotton robe, she lounged on the couch in the single room serving as both living room and kitchen. Etta didn't usually stay up past 8:00 p.m. She'd decided that night to spend a few minutes by herself reading before she went into the bedroom where the new male of her life was already slumbering away.

The knock on the door startled her. Seldom did anyone visit and almost never this late. She set aside the paper, moved cautiously to the door and turned the knob. If the President of the United States had been standing in the hall, she would not have been any more surprised.

The sight of the Sundance Kid standing in her doorway made her knees buckle. She caught herself from falling by clutching the doorframe. A split second after she regained her balance, she had to catch herself again to keep joy and relief from showing in her face. She was ecstatic that he was alive and, at the sight of him, the old feelings came rushing back. But, that life was behind her now.

The two stood looking at each other before Etta opened the door to be able to see past Sundance. She looked up and then down the hallway.

Sundance followed her eyes. "It's just me, Etta."

A concerned look crossed her face and she asked, "Is Butch ... ?"

"No, no, he's fine. Just figured it was time to split up. Less likely to be recognized that way."

Etta still hadn't stepped aside to allow Sundance to enter the apartment. "I ... I thought you were ... I read in the paper."

"I know. Can I come in?"

Etta looked over her shoulder toward the door to the bedroom and hesitated. Finally, she motioned for him to step inside. After closing the door behind him, the two stood looking at each other while an awkward silence filled the room.

* * *

Etta didn't seem to have changed much and Sundance had trouble taking his eyes off her. She was wearing reading glasses that she'd forgotten to remove. Her auburn hair was a bit disheveled, which somehow made her look even more desirable. Sundance realized he was staring and finally forced himself to look around the apartment.

Etta discovered she was wearing her glasses and slipped them into the pocket of her robe. "Would you like something to drink?" she asked.

Sundance would have liked a whiskey, but he was sure that Etta was offering something a lot less potent. "That would be nice," he managed to say.

"Have a seat." Etta motioned to the couch as she stepped into the kitchen area. She poured two glasses of lemonade from a pitcher sitting in a small icebox.

"What happened? Why did they report that you two were dead?" she asked as she finished pouring the drinks.

"Long story, Etta. Just a mistake is the short of it. Two other guys who they mistook for us."

Etta brought him the lemonade and sat with her glass at the other end of the couch. The distance was not lost on Sundance.

For a while they caught up on what had happened in South America after she left. Sundance told her about Stillman and the failed attempt to get them in Tupiza. He explained how even before they were mistakenly thought killed in San Vincente, he and Butch had come to the realization that the game was up.

"How did you find me?

"Went looking for Elsie. Had dinner with her and her husband."

"Surprised she told you where I was."

"Guess it surprised me some, too. Especially the way she acted when she first saw me. Felt like maybe I was carrying the plague." Sundance's smile melted away when he saw Etta's somber face. "She said you were tutoring. You doing all right?" he asked.

"I'm fine. Students who need a little extra help come here in the early mornings and in the afternoon."

"That can't make you much."

Etta looked at him with steel eyes. "Why did you come here, Harry?"

He stared at his boots, struggling with the answer until he looked her in the eye. "Life without you just ain't no life at all, Etta." He let out a sigh. "Thought you'd come back. Then, as time went on, I prayed you would. When Butch and I got killed...I mean, you know. Well, then I knew I had to come lookin'."

Etta stared at him for what, to Sundance, seemed an eternity. "It's no good, Sundance. I can't live that life anymore. Besides, I've..."

Sundance held up his hand. "That's just it, Etta, neither can I. Ever since we had to leave the Cholila ranch it just wasn't the same. It all seemed so right while we were on the ranch. Going back to the old ways wasn't the same."

Sundance fumbled with his hat. Realizing it made him look nervous, he set it aside. "Before, in the States, it wasn't just the money for me and Butch. It was something else: adventure, excitement, maybe even the danger. I don't know. But, after Argentina and the ranch, the thrill part of being an outlaw was gone. When you left, it just slammed me like an angry old ram."

"You could have stayed with me when we came back to the States," Etta voice softened but still had an angry edge.

Harry felt the bite and opened his mouth to protest.

She cut him off. "I know what you're going to say. But we didn't have to stay in the States. You could have asked me to go somewhere like Canada or Europe. Somewhere that people wouldn't recognize us."

Sundance knew she was right. "Can't argue that. Guess I was just too bullheaded. I thought you'd come back. But, Etta, I need you. It's like I'm walking around half dead. We can go wherever you say."

There was a long silence as Etta sat on the couch gazing at him. She eyed the outline of his Colt bulging inside his suit coat. Her quick glance at the door to the bedroom made Sundance uneasy, but then Etta hit him with a question that took him totally by surprise.

"If I asked you to, would you cut off your right hand for me?"

Sundance was confused by the question. Was it some kind of joke or riddle? Etta's stare was unwavering.

Finally he responded. "You're serious. I ... yes, yes, I guess I would, Etta. If that's what you needed, I guess I would." Sundance looked straight into her eyes as he spoke.

Etta nodded. Then she reached across the distance between them and opened his suit jacket. Sundance's Colt .45 sat snuggly in its leather holster.

"This is your right hand, Sundance. It always has been."

Sundance looked down at the gun. It had been a part of him for decades. Etta was right. Without the gun, he would feel like a part of him had been chopped off. But the part of him that he'd lost when Etta walked out of his life was far greater. It was no contest.

He unbuckled the gun belt, pulled it from around his waist, reached over and set it on the lamp table next to the couch. "I promise you, Etta, I'll never use it again. There will be no more guns in our life."

Etta kept her eyes on his and closed the distance between them. Harry reached out, took her in his arms and looked deep into her eyes. "I promise." Their kiss was long and passionate.

Then she gently pushed him away.

Harry saw the hesitation. "We can make it work Etta," he whispered.

"I'm not so sure. Things have changed," she said as she looked back at the bedroom door. "I'm not alone here; there's someone else.

Harry felt the cold fear returning. This is what had been haunting him during his long journey. Etta had found someone else. He glanced at the gun on the table.

"Come with me, Harry. He's sleeping, but we'll have to deal with it sooner or later so it might as well be now." Etta took him by the hand and led him to the bedroom door.

As they stepped inside, Etta took a match from a cast-iron matchbox attached to the wall and struck it. She lit a lantern on the table next to the bed and the dark room flooded with a flickering yellow glow.

Harry waited for his eyes to adjust to the dim light, increasingly aware of how strange he felt without his gun. As his eyes adjusted, he realized the bed was still nicely made and there was no one on it.

His eyes shifted to Etta now standing next to a structure in the corner. She motioned him over and, as he got closer, Harry realized he was looking at a crib.

Peering down, he saw a child wrapped in a blanket, peacefully sleeping. Harry could only stare at the handsome baby boy. He looked at Etta and opened his mouth to speak, but she cut him off by placing her fingers on his lips.

"Don't wake him," she whispered. "We'll talk out there." She led him by the hand back into the living space.

"Who ... who's ..." Harry stammered, looking from Etta back to the bedroom.

"Now, who the hell do you think, Harry?"

"But ... you never said ... why didn't you tell me?"

"I didn't want to tell you, Harry."

"Why? Why not? I would have stayed with you, Etta, if I'd known about him."

Etta raised her eyebrows and nodded. "If you were going to stay with me, Harry, I wanted it to be because you wanted to stay with *me*, not because of some sense of manly responsibility. I didn't want a life with you based on something you felt forced into."

Harry took a minute to wrap his mind around what she'd just said. He halfway understood, but still felt angry that she hadn't been honest with him. After all, it was his kid, too, he had a right to know. But, he didn't say that. Instead he said, "He's got your nose. I bet he's got your eyes too."

"No, those he got from you." She smiled and led him to the couch.

They spent the next hour joined together, making up for all the time they'd been apart. And then, they stayed locked in each other's arms.

"I never want to lose you again, Etta," Harry whispered into her ear.

She smiled and looked at him. "What are we going to do, Harry? Where are we going to go?"

"I've thought on it some. I have some money, not a lot, but enough to put a good-sized down payment on a small ranch. I was thinking about Oklahoma. We never robbed any banks or trains there and, if I lay low some, I don't think anyone will recognize me."

"We'll have to have new names. Maybe we should keep our first names," Etta pondered. "It might be easier that way, not so likely to slip up."

"What about a last name? Any suggestions?" Harry asked with a smile, thrilled that she was already making plans to be with him.

Etta thought for a minute and then she smiled. "Kidwell."

"Kidwell?"

"You came back to me alive and well, Kid."

PART III

ARRIVAL OF THE GANGSTERS

Chapter 32

PROVOCATION
Oklahoma 1921

~ ~ ~

The tack room in the Kidwell barn smelled of leather and saddle soap. Harry picked up the whiskey bottle sitting between Butch and him and once again took a light swig. Way off in thought, he stared through the tack room door into the darkness of the barn beyond.

"What you thinkin' about, Kid?" Butch asked as the two sat in the yellow glow of the flickering lantern.

Harry smacked his lips and passed the bottle to his friend. "Nothing ... everything. Life's been pretty good, Butch, since I left the old ways behind. Miss it a little sometimes, but I don't know just why I do. More bad than good. Guess the good times seem to stand out a little more. Maybe because a man's mind plays tricks on him some as time passes. What about you, Butch? We've been harpin' on my troubles so much I haven't thought to ask about you. You talked a little about your new lady and such, but how about you? You been fairin' all right?"

"Been just fine, Kid. Not much is different since I was here last time. Hell, doesn't seem like it but that was probably seven or eight years ago."

Harry nodded. "Still got the money you invested from before?"

"You thought I'd go through it in a week, didn't you?"

"Crossed my mind," Harry said with a smile.

Butch leaned back and puffed out his chest like a preening rooster. "Gotta say, even made myself proud. I been livin' off that bundle and the proceeds for all these years. Have some o' what I owe you with me right now."

"Wasn't plannin' on yer payin' me back, Butch. Comin' here to help now is pay enough."

Butch gave a slight shrug. "Mighty glad the boy wrote the letter, Sundance. I can use a little excitement. Miss the dance."

Harry was about to respond when he heard footsteps outside the tack room door. Butch heard them, too, and reached for one of his Colt automatics. A small figure stepped into the frame of the door.

"Mind if I join you?" Etta smiled as she entered the room. When she caught a glimpse of Butch's .45s, he covered them again with his coat.

Harry saw the flicker of discomfort flash in her eyes.

In spite of it, she smiled as Butch stood up politely and gave her a hug. Etta sat on a sawhorse that Harry used to hold saddles when applying saddle soap.

For a few seconds there was an awkward silence until Butch spoke up, "You only get prettier, Etta."

Her eyes went from Butch to Harry and back. Glancing at the guns partially-visible in Butch's waistband, she frowned. "Don't you try to sugar me up. I know what you two are up to. I've known you too long. You're trying to cook something up and I don't want any of it."

Harry and Butch looked at each other, but neither said a word.

"I want to try to solve this by legal means, Harry," Etta continued with a meaningful look at her husband.

Butch and Harry rolled their eyes.

"Etta, we know Brooks is behind all this and the law is in his pocket," Harry said with a bit more irritation than he had intended.

"I'm not talking about local law," Etta snapped back.

"I know, I know. You want me to go to the Governor," Harry said with a calmer voice. "We talked about this too, Etta. I go to him I might be recognized."

"So, I'll go," Etta said. "No one will recognize me."

"I don't know, Etta. What do you think, Butch?"

Before Butch could get in a word, Etta continued, "I'm leaving for Oklahoma City at first light. I'll be back in a day or two. In the meantime, I want you to promise you won't do anything stupid."

"We weren't planning to do anything *stupid*, Etta," Butch said with a smile.

"You know what I mean."

Harry held up his hand. "We know. We're just talking, Etta. We have no plans. We'll wait and see how things go with the Governor in Oklahoma City."

With squinted eyes, Etta gazed at the two men for a second. "I'm going to turn in," she said.

As she turned and headed for the door she added, "Leroy, I fixed up a place for you to sleep in the sitting room, on the divan."

"Thanks, Etta."

After she was gone, Butch shook his head. "Doubt she'll accomplish much, Kid. Brooks is a powerful man in this state right now. He might even have the Governor in his pocket."

Harry nodded. "Maybe, but best let her try."

A few minutes later the two men left the tack room and walked out of the barn. Harry led the way as they headed for the house.

In the moonlight, dew sparkled like gold dust on the inky dark grass. They crossed the barnyard mounted the porch and entering the back door. Neither of them was aware that they were being watched.

* * *

Ratt Wilson had his pride. He was not going to let some old farmer and his black lackey get the best of him and he certainly wasn't going to stand for being replaced by some city slicker from Chicago. So what if Brooks had already sent for the killer? When he arrived he'd find the job done and would have to turn around and go back. Wilson would take care of this situation himself and he would start by teaching Harry Kidwell a lesson.

The Old Gun

The first thing he did was to replace Pony McCauley, whose wounds were too severe to make him useful. He found a man out of New Mexico named Arlyn Springer. Josh, who'd worked with the man while in Texas, had recommended him. Wilson wired Springer and he'd arrived a day later.

With Springer was a man named JW Jessup. He was an out-of-work friend of Springer's who claimed to be handy with firearms.

When these two arrived, Wilson was inclined to dismiss Jessup because he'd only sent for one replacement. After thinking about it, he decided that another gun wouldn't hurt.

With his newly-acquired reinforcements, Ratt decided it was time to pay Harry Kidwell a visit. He and his men arrived near the Kidwell ranch as the glow of the setting sun melted below the horizon. Leaving their horses a quarter-mile from the barn and house, they stealthily approached on foot.

The chirping of crickets broke through the ominous silence as the six gunmen crouched in the darkness, surveying the Kidwell property. A light was shining through the cracks in the barn walls and they could see a lantern glimmering in the bunkhouse window.

They had been there only a few minutes when Wilson observed Harry's wife walk from the barn and head to the house. A few minutes later, the barn got dark and Harry stepped out in the company of a stranger. In the gloom of night, Ratt couldn't make out the stranger's features, but he felt that there was something familiar about the fellow.

The Old Gun

* * *

Clarence had retired to his room for the night. The wall that separated his bunkhouse from the barn was not a sufficient barrier to prevent him from hearing the conversations taking place in the tack room. He hadn't been eavesdropping. The voices had come to him uninvited.

So many questions were answered for Clarence as he listened to Harry and Butch reminisce: Harry's reluctance to use or own a gun, his desire to maintain a low profile and to avoid conflict as well as his distrust for the law. Now it all made sense. Clarence had always recognized Harry's courage and strength, but had been puzzled when Harry constantly suppressed it. Now, it was as clear as freshly-distilled corn liquor.

As he sat in his bedside chair, Clarence heard Etta say her "good nights" and it wasn't long before he heard Harry and Butch leave the barn. Still seated, Clarence caught a glimpse of them strolling by his window.

Like everyone, Clarence had heard the stories and the legends of these two men, none of which had lost anything in the telling. He knew they'd been wanted men and that they were supposed to be ruthless outlaws. Still, he'd known Harry for too long to see him as anything but a kind, decent man. He smiled and shook his head as he heard them in the distance, mounting the porch steps and closing the door to the house.

A little later, with sleep eluding him, Clarence lay quietly on his feathered mattress. Memories of Harry over the years kept filling his mind. He'd been working for a famous outlaw all these years and neither he nor anyone else had suspected it. Not even Alva, who considered himself well-versed in matters of that kind.

Finally, he drifted off with the images flickering in his head of Harry expertly dispatching the rustlers at the Jackson ranch.

The nighttime quiet was disturbed by the creaking of wood. It wasn't part of any dream. Clarence opened his eyes.

* * *

Ratt Wilson had planned on catching Harry alone and hopefully unarmed, but the appearance of the stranger caused him pause. Before he could decide on a plan of action, Kidwell and the stranger had walked to the ranch house and disappeared inside.

Trying to formulate his next move, Wilson heard movement in the bunkhouse. He motioned his men to wait while he moved silently toward the barn. Removing his hat and slowly raising his head, he peeked through the bunkhouse window. Seeing Kidwell's black lackey, he realized his hatred for this bastard was greater than for Kidwell himself.

With a wicked smile, he silently crouched down and leaned against the bunkhouse wall. Wilson remained there until finally he heard the sounds of the black man snoring. Standing up, he motioned to his men to join him as he eased open the bunkhouse door and slipped inside.

* * *

The Old Gun

It was the creaking of the wood floor of his bunkhouse that had awakened Clarence. He heard the unmistakable click of a revolver being cocked. It took half a second to clear his foggy mind, but when he did he saw a shadowy figure leaning over his bed, holding a pistol to his temple.

"Just try something. I'd like that," Wilson hissed.

Clarence knew exactly where he'd left his gun. It was sitting on his chair more than six feet away.

In the dim light, Ratt Wilson followed the black man's eyes and spotted the dark shape of the revolver on the chair. Smiling, he took a step back and picked up the old .32. "Lookin' fer this?"

Clarence watched as Wilson made a display of opening the cylinder and dumping the bullets on the floor. Like the slow ticking of a grandfather clock, the cartridges, one by one, hit the wooden floor. With a flick of his wrist, the gunman tossed the empty weapon into a corner of the room.

Taking count of the men standing around him, Clarence was painfully struck with the hopelessness of his situation. Fear was building inside him as he looked into Wilson's eyes. Still, Clarence decided at the first opportunity, he would fight.

Wilson gave a nod and his men yanked him out of bed. Noticing a lariat hanging on the wall, Ratt grabbed it and holstered his gun as he prepared to tie Clarence's hands behind his back.

Clarence could feel the confidence of the thugs and he knew that they were not expecting resistance.

Like a bucking bull bursting loose from the rodeo gate, Clarence went on the attack. Grabbing

Wilson with his huge meaty hands, he lifted the gunman like a sack of cornmeal and used him as a weapon to swat the other men. Bodies slammed against the bunkhouse walls and crashed and tumbled over furniture.

Clarence lifted Wilson above his head and slammed him to the floor. Grabbing another gunman, he pulled him so close he could feel the man's terror. Rage fueled Clarence's strength. He hurled the man across the room where he landed on one of the other thugs just as he was regaining his feet.

* * *

Wilson gazed up from where he'd landed and felt blood trickling into his eyes from a gash on his forehead. He shook his head,trying to clear the daze. Struggling to stand, he used the wall for support. Fury filled him as he focused on the black behemoth now heaving his men about like scarecrows. He pulled his revolver, cocked the hammer, and took aim.

Before he fired, common sense stayed his finger. The noise from the ruckus alone could have alerted the people in the house but a gunshot would awaken them for sure. Wilson would have been pleased to get a chance to put a bullet in the head of the old farmer, Kidwell. But if he killed Kidwell he'd likely have to take care of the rest of those in the house as well. That would be too hard to explain or cover up.

Instead of pulling the trigger he eased up behind the black tornado and brought the butt of his gun down hard on the man's wooly-white head. The sound of the resulting thump filled the small room.

Clarence wobbled and then toppled forward until his body slammed down on the wooden floor.

Bruised and bloodied, Wilson's men stumbled to their feet. Panting and wheezing, it took them a minute or two to catch their breaths.

Wilson kicked the unconscious black man with his sharp-toed cowboy boot. Seeing no response, he tied Clarence's hands behind his back, and then directed his men to lift and drag him outside.

* * *

Once in the cool night air, Clarence began to regain consciousness. He struggled to keep down the dinner that wanted to push up from his stomach. His noggin felt like someone had dropped an anvil on him. As his head began to clear, he glanced at the ranch house only sixty yards away.

Wilson saw him glance. "Go ahead. Give a big yell and maybe that old man you have for a boss might come runnin' to help you. Who knows, maybe his woman and kids will come out, too. Go, on. Call out," he hissed in Clarence's ear.

Clarence said nothing.

Wilson shoved him toward the door to the barn. "I didn't think so."

Clarence searched his mind for a means of escape. He was afraid to call for help. Maybe Wilson was bluffing when he said he'd kill the whole family, but he couldn't take the chance.

Light from the moon snuck through the cracks in the barn walls and cast slender shafts of gold in the dark interior. As Clarence was pushed through the open door he stumbled, kicking up dust that hung in the air and was caught in the glowing beams.

Wilson looked around and spotted another rope hanging on the wall inside the tack room. Clarence watched as the gunman slipped it off its hook and stuck it in his face. "Looks like we have all the fixin's for a little necktie party."

One of the men grabbed a lantern sitting on a barrel near the stalls. He produced a match and lit the wick before he carried the lantern over to the group gathered around Clarence. A flickering glow pushed back the darkness and illuminated the center of the barn.

Wilson stepped over to the barn door and looked toward the house. Grabbing the door, he pushed it shut.

"Get that barrel, Josh," he said as he walked back to where his men were holding Clarence.

Due to his wounded hand, Josh struggled with the empty twenty-gallon barrel.

"Murphy. Jessup. Give'm a hand," Wilson hissed.

Turning the barrel on its side, the men rolled it to the center of the barn.

Wilson took the rope he'd been waving in Clarence's face and slipped the noose around his thick neck. He tossed the other end over a rafter and pulled. He kept pulling until it bit into the skin of Clarence's throat.

"You don't look so uppity now, Nigger." Wilson spat out the words. "Did you think you and your boss could shoot up my men, leave us trussed up in that corral like calves fer brandin' and then just go on about your business?"

Clarence looked him in the eye. "Do what ya wants. But you'll be regrettin' it."

"I will? Why's that, old man?"

"You don't know who you's messin' with." The words came cold and without fear.

Wilson looked in Clarence's confident brown eyes. For a second the gunman gave pause; then looking at his armed men versus his tightly-bound victim, he laughed.

"Whoooo, you got me scared, old man. Who am I messin' with? You? You don't look so dangerous right now. Are you talkin' about that old man in the house? Who am I messin' with?"

"Kill me and likely you'll find out," Clarence whispered ominously.

Again Wilson gave pause as he looked into his victim's eyes. After a moment, a smile crept onto his thin face. "It's *you* didn't know who *you* was messin' with," he said as he pulled the rope even tighter. "Choke on that, Nigger."

Wilson pointed to a spot next to Clarence. "Put that barrel right here, Frank."

Frank rolled it over and started to stand it up.

"Leave it on its side." Wilson ordered. He pulled a bandanna from his pocket. "Hold him," he ordered as he stuffed the rag in Clarence's mouth. "Give me your neckerchief," he said to Frank. When it was handed over, Ratt tied it around Clarence's head, securing the gag in his mouth.

With the gag in place, Ratt Wilson had his men hoist Clarence up on the unstable barrel. Once they had him balanced on it, they pulled the noose tight and secured the other end to a post. The barrel began to rock to and fro. With his hands tied tightly behind his back, Clarence had to struggle to keep his balance.

"Wonder jist how long you can stand there before this barrel rolls out from under you?" Wilson's lips curled into a cruel smile. "Like to stick around and see jist how things turn out but we got to be *rollin'* along ourselves."

His men laughed. The ruthless smile was still etched on Wilson's lips as he led the gunmen from the barn.

Clarence listened as their footsteps faded into the night. Once he was sure they were gone and there was no chance of bringing Harry and his family into a deadly situation, Clarence attempted to cry out. But he could make only the most muffled of sounds. The rag stuffed down his throat and the rope tight around his neck greatly restricted his ability to get air.

He strained to balance himself on the barrel and the effort produced an even further need for oxygen. He tried to stand on his tiptoes to relieve the tension on the noose. That made balancing on the barrel more difficult. He tried to relax and thus reduce his need for oxygen, but that only tightened the noose. He strained to slip free of the ropes that bound his hands, but they were too well tied. The effort nearly caused the big man to lose his balance as the barrel rocked back and forth. If it rolled out from under him he would hang.

Still, he was determined not to give up. It would be at least five or six hours before he was missed. If

he were going to survive he would have to find a way
to persevere until he was found.

Chapter 33

DISCOVERING CLARENCE

~ ~ ~

Outside, a predawn glow brightening the horizon as Etta lit the lantern in Harry's and her bedroom. The rest of the house was dark and quiet under the sapphirine velvet sky.

Harry stirred and opened his eyes.

"It's early, Harry. Go back to sleep."

Harry rubbed his eyes and stretched. He watched as Etta finished dressing. Then slowly he rolled out of bed. "Since your mind is made up, I might as well see you off," he yawned.

A few minutes later, Harry was dressed and had joined Etta in the kitchen. She poured them each a cup of coffee from a steaming pot then sat with him at the table. "Sorry about breakfast," Etta said. "You and the others will have to fend for yourselves this morning."

Harry swallowed a sip of coffee and set down his cup. "Still don't think much will come of this idea, Etta."

"I know that's what you think, but nonetheless, you're glad to see me go."

Harry gave her an innocent "what-do-you-mean?" look.

"You don't fool me, Harry Kidwell. After all these years, I think I know you better than you know yourself. You and Butch can't wait to see me leave. Well, just you remember your promise."

Harry took another sip from his cup and kept still.

Etta finished her coffee and took the cup to the sink. Together they walked outside to the Model T. Harry stepped to the front of the vehicle, turned the crank and the Ford sputtered to life.

"I'll be back in a couple of days," Etta said as Harry leaned into the vehicle to give her a kiss. She looked into his eyes then put the truck in gear and drove away down the lane.

When she was out of sight, Harry turned and walked back to the house. On the porch he paused and looked over at Clarence's bunkhouse. He had expected the noise of the Model T to elicit some early morning activity from Clarence, but maybe it was still too early.

As he opened the back door and stepped into the kitchen, he was surprised to see Laura fixing breakfast.

Harry smiled. "What are you doing up so early, Pollywog?"

"Paaa…"

"Sorry, I mean, Miss Laura," Harry corrected.

She sparked an impish grin. "I figured you might need someone to fix breakfast since Ma left so early."

Ten minutes later Lee entered the kitchen. "Need any help with breakfast?" he asked, looking over his sister's shoulder to see what she was cooking.

Harry was accustomed to doing a few chores before breakfast, but Laura was going to have a nice meal ready in a few minutes. Harry didn't have the heart to tell his daughter that her timing was off a bit.

If breakfast was going to be early, he thought it best to call out to Clarence. He was sure to be up by now, but probably not expecting breakfast so early.

Harry stepped out onto the porch. "Clarence!" he yelled. "Breakfast! Come 'n get it!"

When Harry re-entered the kitchen, Butch was strolling in from the sitting room.

"How's anyone supposed to get any sleep around here when the whole household is up at dawn and clomping around in the kitchen?" Butch teased with a smile.

"Likely you'd sleep the day away if you had your way," Harry shot back.

"You can sit down," Laura beamed. "I have breakfast ready."

She carried a plate of scrambled eggs and another piled with thick-sliced bacon to the table. Lee brought over the biscuits fresh from the oven and set them next to the other dishes.

"This could be the finest breakfast I ever sat down to," Butch said, pulling back a chair.

Laura gave him a shy smile. "I think you're lathering it on a little thick, Uncle Leroy, but thank you for the compliment."

Harry smiled, too. Butch's compliment reminded him of something Clarence might say. Where was he? Surely he'd heard the call to breakfast.

Harry, Leroy, and Lee stood behind their chairs waiting for Laura. She blushed when Lee held her chair as she sat down.

Butch winked at Harry before he eased into his seat. Harry hardly noticed the wink. His mind was pre-occupied. "Can't understand what's keepin' Clarence. I expected him to be roused by the truck engine when Etta left this morning. Step out and give him another yell, Lee."

Lee opened the back door and stepped out on the porch. "Clarence!" he yelled. "Breakfast is on!" When there was no reply he descended the stairs and called again, "Clarence!"

Harry could hear Lee call out several more times as his voice became more distant. Then he heard nothing.

Several minutes later the door opened and Lee entered the kitchen with a puzzled look on his face. "He's not in the bunkhouse."

"That's strange. Did you check to see if his saddle is in the tack room?" Harry asked.

"I never thought to do that, Pa. I'll go look." Lee opened the door to go out again.

"No, wait," Harry blurted. "Let me check. Sit down and eat." Harry stood and gave Butch a look as he headed for the door. "Butch?"

Butch followed Harry out.

* * *

"Why did Pa call Uncle Leroy, Butch?" Laura asked Lee as she watched them leave. "Don't know," he said absentmindedly. He was pre-occupied with his dad's sudden desire to check on Clarence himself. It wasn't like his dad to take on a chore so mundane.

He went out onto the porch where he could see his father and Uncle Leroy nearing the barn. The rapid way they were walking further piqued his interest.

Harry stealthily approached the barn. Following just a step behind, Butch pulled back his coat jacket and touched one of his Colts. Harry gently pushed open the barn door and peered inside.

* * *

Clarence had lasted almost four hours before his legs began to tremble and spasm with the stress. He was a strong man, but even in his youth he would not have been able to endure that kind of strain.

Finally, the muscles had given way and the barrel slipped out from under him. The noose tightened and his airway squeezed shut. He'd struggled vainly to find footing, anything to lift himself and ease the pressure, but the more he struggled the more the rope tightened. As his lungs burned without air, he thought of his friend, Harry. By allowing this to happen, he'd let his friend down. When a cold blue haze crept over him, and just before all went dark, he felt his daughter reach out and put her arms around his waist.

* * *

The Old Gun

Before Harry's eyes could adjust to the dark interior of the barn, he heard a faint creaking sound. It took him a couple of seconds to realize the sound was a rope swinging gently in the center of the barn. His breath was sucked from him when he realized what was hanging from the rafters.

"God, no! No!" he screamed as he ran to his friend. He grabbed Clarence by the legs and tried to take the pressure off his neck. Tears welled up as he struggled to lift the limp, heavy body.

"Get the rope, Butch! Untie it!" he called out.

Butch sadly shook his head, but rushed anyway to the post where the rope had been fastened. He began to work at the knots. As he struggled with the rope, Lee and then Laura entered the barn.

Through his bleary eyes Harry saw his son and daughter silhouetted against the light from the open barn door.

Laura screamed. Lee stood frozen.

"Lee! Get Laura out of here!" Harry yelled. "Take her to the house! Do it! Now!"

It took a few seconds for Lee to come out of his daze. Tears streamed down his face as he grabbed his sister by the hand and led her back to the house.

Chapter 34

ETTA'S QUEST

~ ~ ~

Etta had never driven in traffic like the kind she encountered when she reached Oklahoma City. Aooga horns blared and shod hooves clattered on brick pavement. Autos and carriages intermingled on the streets, causing horses to buck and prance nervously from the noise of the honking, sputtering, oil burners. Blending with exhaust fumes was the pungent odor of horse manure. Amid this bedlam of confusion it took all of Etta's nerve to keep from going into a panic.

Before she left home, a neighbor had suggested a hotel and gave her directions. She'd found it after several wrong turns and missed landmarks. Parking the Model T in front of the hotel, she walked inside.

There were several men in the lobby and their eyes followed her as she strolled by.

A house detective was seated in a soft leather chair reading a paper. He set it aside and watched Etta approach the registration desk.

It was somewhat unusual for a single woman to register in a hotel, so Etta wasn't surprised when she got the once-over from the man behind the desk. "A room, please?" she inquired.

The man hesitated as the house detective stood up and approached. "By yourself, Ma'am?" The detective asked. There was a suspicious tone to his voice.

Etta turned to look at the man. "There a problem?"

The glare Etta gave him caused the detective to wilt. He cleared his throat. "Uh no, no, of course not." A nervous smile painted his lips. "Just wonderin' what brings such a lovely lady alone to this hotel."

Etta gazed at him for a few seconds before she decided to answer. "I'm in the city to see the Governor."

"Oh. I uh, I see," the house dick stammered. "Sorry for the bother, ma'am. Just doin' my job. No offense meant." He nodded to the receptionist who quickly offered Etta the book to register.

"I'll have a porter show you to your room," he said as he rang a bell on the desk.

Etta's accommodations consisted of a single room with a bed. The bathroom was down the hall and was shared with several other guests. It wasn't the best of situations, but the price was right and, after all, she only planned to spend one or two nights.

After she settled in, she went down to the lobby and inquired about public transportation and how to reach the Governor's office. It was already midafternoon so she found a little restaurant where she settled in for an early supper.

* * *

The next morning Etta arrived at the Governor's office a few minutes after eight. She was somewhat surprised to learn that the office hours didn't begin until nine.

Finally, at five minutes to nine, a woman arrived to open the door. By this time, several other people had joined Etta to wait for the Governor. Etta politely introduced herself to this woman as she unlocked the office. The woman glanced at her, but said nothing. Etta and the others followed her into a large walnut paneled waiting room. The room smelled of wood, leather, and tobacco and was lit by electric lights suspended from an ornate chandelier hanging from the middle of the ceiling.

* * *

Mary Frantz had been the secretary to Governor Walton since his election. She was an attractive woman with grey hair that arrived too early for her thirty-six years. She could have colored it but she was a no-nonsense woman with not a hint of vanity. The Governor depended on her because of her efficiency and her ability to deal with the petitioners and politicians that descended upon his office every day.

As always, upon her arrival at the office, Mary took note of the visitors waiting to see the Governor. She sized them up with a single glance and expressed very little interest in the people who showed up.

The Old Gun

Since she knew most of them would leave without seeing her boss, she didn't see any reason to give false hope or the impression that she might be able to smooth the way for any of them.

On this day, she had observed the usual group gathered at the door. For some reason, Mary took particular note of the woman who had introduced herself as Etta Kidwell. She had tried to feign disinterest in this woman, but there was something intriguing about the attractive lady who seemed to hold herself with a certain strength and character.

As always, Mary motioned for the people to seat themselves along the wall in the finely-crafted wooden chairs that were padded and covered in rich brown leather. As Mary took her place behind a massive walnut desk, her diminutive frame seemed to become even smaller.

Etta and the others had just seated themselves when the Governor entered the reception room from the hallway. Two State Senators flanked him as everyone in the waiting room tried to get the Governor's attention. Without a turn of the head, he and the Senators made the way to his office. At his office door the Governor paused and turned to face the crowd. "Nice to see everyone," he said. "Afraid it's a very busy day, but I will do my best to see some of you. Give your names and a brief description of your concerns to Mrs. Frantz."

As his eyes quickly looked over the crowd, they paused on Etta. Turning, he ushered the Senators into his office.

Mary Frantz looked at the visitors for the first time. "The Governor was being polite," she said. "He leaves it to me to deal out the bad news. If you don't have an appointment your chances of seeing the Governor today are very slim. Nonetheless, I will be happy to get your names and a brief description of your concerns."

When her turn came, Etta gave Mary a summary of what had been going on with the small ranches in her county. Mary looked at her with interest and even though intrigued, she made no comment. It seemed incredulous that a pillar of the community such as Brooks would be involved in murder and cattle rustling, but Etta seemed far too sincere to be making up the story.

As the morning wore on, people with appointments came and went. At 12:30 p.m. the Governor stepped into the reception room and spoke quietly to Mary. Once again the Governor glanced at Etta before returning to his office.

Mary stood and addressed the people in the room. "We will be closing the office for lunch, ladies and gentlemen. You will have to leave for one hour and then you may return. I suggest that you take the time to get something to eat. I am sorry that none of you have had a chance to visit with the Governor this morning but, as I said earlier, he has a very busy schedule today."

Grumbling but resigned, the people began to shuffle out the door.

* * *

Etta wasn't sure but she thought she sensed some kind of connection between her and the secretary.

She paused as the others filed out. When the room was empty, Etta decided to take a chance.

"Ma'am, if you are going to lunch, I'd be pleased to have you join me."

Mary reacted with a sharp expression. "I'm afraid that would not be advisable, Mrs. Kidwell. Some might look upon it as inappropriate." Then, she added in a softer tone, "But, thank you anyway."

Etta turned to leave.

"Mrs. Kidwell, do you know Oklahoma City at all?" Mary asked.

Etta turned back. "Not really."

"There is a nice restaurant with reasonable prices and good food not far from here. If you leave the building, turn right and walk two blocks then turn right again, you will find it in the middle of the block on the right-hand side."

"Thank you. That's very kind," Etta almost whispered.

Ten minutes later, Etta was seated at a table in the small restaurant. Coffee was poured as she studied the menu.

While ordering the lunch special of liver and onions with mashed potatoes and green beans, she spotted the secretary, Mrs. Frantz, enter the restaurant.

The woman nodded at Etta, but said nothing as she was seated at a table nearby. Picking up her menu, she began to look it over.

In a low voice Etta addressed her. "It would be much more pleasant for me, Ma'am, if you'd join me. Dutch treat of course."

The secretary looked up at Etta for a moment before she smiled and approached Etta's table. "Don't think that this means I'll be giving you any special favors, Mrs. Kidwell," she said somberly as she sat down. Glancing around she added, "When you go back to the office, however, you will notice that a large percentage of the people will not return after lunch. So, even though I can't do you any favors, your chances will have increased significantly."

Mary turned out to be pleasant company. They conversed on many subjects, but Mary suggested they not speak of the business that had brought Etta to the Governor's office. "It would not be appropriate to discuss your plea before the Governor has a chance to hear the details himself."

Mary asked Etta where she was staying and then suggested a small bed and breakfast that was closer and a better alternative to the hotel she now occupied.

When they returned to the office, Mary's prediction proved to be accurate. Still, it didn't help much. The day wore on while Etta and the remaining people waited. As five o'clock approached, Etta became painfully aware of why Mary had suggested a place to stay for the night.

* * *

On the day that Clarence was found murdered, Harry spent the afternoon making arrangements for his funeral. The local undertaker agreed to provide a custom-made coffin and Harry spoke with his minister who agreed to prepare a grave for Clarence in the church cemetery.

Later that afternoon, Alva rode up to the Kidwell ranch on his big roan gelding. "Hello, in the house!" he yelled as he climbed down from the prancing animal. He'd come by to offer his sympathy.

Harry thanked Alva for his thoughtfulness as they settled in on the porch steps together.

"If'n it's all right with you, Harry, I'll let some of the neighbors know about the funeral, in there."

"Obliged, Alva," Harry muttered as his sad eyes gazed at the empty bunkhouse.

"I'll start with Slim. That's one man I know will be wantin' to pay his respects," Alva suggested.

A few moments later, Lee came out of the house in time to see Alva mounting his horse. Lee's shoulders were slumped low as he nodded to their neighbor.

Harry looked at the boy and then called out to Alva. "Hold up there a minute, Alva. Mind takin' the boy with you to help spread the word? Might do Lee some good to get away from here for a bit."

"Sure, Harry."

For the rest of the afternoon Harry agonized over the absence of Etta. She had mentioned a hotel where she might stay while in Oklahoma City but he had not paid much attention. He hadn't expected to have to contact her while she was gone.

That evening after supper, Butch sat with Harry on the porch.

"Think Etta will be back in time?" Butch asked.

"Hope so, but can't say. Funeral's day after tomorrow. Woulda waited another day or two but, even on ice, 'fraid Clarence won't wait that long."

The next day the undertaker arrived with the casket. It was a finely-crafted walnut coffin with a padded silk lining and a pillow for Clarence's head. Harry held back his tears as he helped the undertaker place his friend into the casket. Looking down on his friend, Harry decided he would weep no more. Now, it was time to look for justice.

Before Harry closed the lid, he placed a bible next to Clarence that he'd found in the bunkhouse near his friend's bed. The evening before, Harry had been going through Clarence's effects when he'd run across it.

Inside the good book he'd found a picture of a young girl of nine or ten. Clarence had never talked much about his life before the Kidwells. He'd once told Harry that his past was best left there. But when Harry saw the picture he realized instantly that it had to have been Clarence's daughter. The photograph had been torn. It would seem there had been someone else standing next to the little girl, but that part was missing. Harry had returned the photo to its resting place inside the bible before placing it inside the coffin.

Looking at the bible laying next to his friend, Harry couldn't help but wonder what had happened to separate Clarence from his little girl. Was she still alive? Would she be sad if she knew her father had died? Harry realized he would never know.

* * *

The bed and breakfast Mary had suggested for Etta was much more homey and pleasant than the hotel.

The next morning, she arrived at the Governor's office at five minutes to nine. This time Etta brought along reading material to while away the time.

When Mary arrived to unlock the office, she gave Etta a slight nod. Opening the door, she motioned Etta and the new conglomerate of visitors into the reception room.

As he had done the day before, the Governor arrived shortly after nine o'clock. Again several politicians accompanied him. He nodded and smiled at the hopefuls who had come to beg an audience. Pausing, the Governor gave the same short speech he'd given the day before.

Etta could have been imagining it, but once again, it seemed that his eyes connected with hers more than once before he gave his apologies and entered his office.

Lunchtime rolled around and for the second time, Etta found herself eating her meal at the little restaurant with Mary Frantz.

"Yesterday before he left his office, I had a chance to mention to the Governor your reason for being here. He seemed interested, but I certainly can't guarantee anything," Mary told her as they waited for their orders to arrive.

"You've been more than kind, Mrs. Frantz."

Mary looked at Etta with a warm smile. "Mary."

Etta smiled back, "And you may call me Etta." She took a sip of her coffee, set the cup down and looked earnestly at her new friend. "Mary, I'm determined to wait as long as necessary to see him. He's my only hope. If I can't get help from him I'm afraid of what my husband will do and...."

"I understand, Etta. You're afraid he might get in over his head against these dangerous men."

Etta tipped her head and reflected before she replied. "My concern is that it will lead to bloodshed."

Mary placed a hand on Etta's arm. "We'll keep working on His Honor, Etta."

After lunch, as before, the crowd in the Governor's reception room had thinned. Etta sat all afternoon watching important people come and go and hoping the contingency of drop-ins would dwindle. It was almost five o'clock when Etta began to give up hope for a meeting that day. With the minute hand on the oversized wall clock ready to reach straight up, Etta stood and began to gather her things.

The door opened and the Governor stepped into the reception room. Etta expected him to tell Mary that he was leaving for the day. Instead, he looked at Etta and whispered something to his secretary before returning to his office.

Mary smiled. "He will see you now, Mrs. Kidwell."

Mary gave Etta a wink as she ushered her into the office.

* * *

Even as he and Butch harnessed the horses for the wagon that would carry Clarence's casket to the cemetery, Harry kept looking down the lane, hoping for any sign of Etta. He continued to hope as they drove the wagon away from the ranch.

Harry wasn't sure how it would play out at the cemetery. He knew there were those who would not be happy to have a man of color buried next to their kin, but that would not deter him. Clarence deserved to lie in a place of honor and respect. If there was trouble, Harry was determined to meet it head on.

Under a cloud-dotted sky, Harry drove along the rough gravel road leading to the church. As the wheels turned, the coffin in the back of the buckboard jostled and bounced like it had life of its own. Butch sat next to Harry while Lee and Laura sat brooding and silent on a wooden box behind them.

* * *

Lee gazed with damp eyes past the casket to the horizon in the distance. Beside him was Laura, her eyes red and swollen. Both could see the sinister black oil derricks that punctuated the horizon. The sadness in Lee's eyes slowly changed to anger.

Finally, Lee broke his silence. Speaking loud to be heard over the rattle of the wagon and clomping of the horse's hooves he cried out, "Pa, we can't let them get away with this. We have to go after them, make 'em pay for what they did."

Harry looked over his shoulder at his son. "Right now, Lee, we're going to see to it that Clarence gets a proper burial."

Lee stared at his father with a mixture of disappointment and contempt. He turned to Butch. "Uncle Leroy, give me one o' your fancy guns. If Pa's afraid, you and me can go after that man, Wilson. I know it was him."

Butch turned and fixed his eyes on the boy. "Listen to me, Lee. You asked me to come here and help. Now, if *you* want to help, you'll calm down and do what your pa says."

Lee glared at his uncle. His frustration and disappointment was almost more than he could bear. Finally, realizing his protests were futile, he gritted his teeth and lowered his head.

* * *

A short time later, Harry turned into the lane leading to the church. Alva, Slim, and Austin were already at the cemetery. The minister was there, too, and he helped direct Harry to the gravesite.

Shadows from the slowly drifting clouds wandered ominously over the grounds. A hole had been prepared and Harry maneuvered the wagon alongside. With help from their friends, Harry, Butch, and Lee unloaded the casket. Carrying it to the grave, they placed it on two stout planks spanning the hole.

As Harry drove the wagon back to the parking area, he noticed that more people were beginning to arrive. He was stepping down from the wagon when three men trotted up on horseback. Harry quickly recognized Buford Bauer and his friends, Martin Bowen and Darnell Hutton. He had hoped they would stay away. They certainly weren't here to pay their respects. Harry glanced in the direction of Butch, who picked up on his partner's request and sauntered over to join his friend.

The three men road up to Harry with Buford in the lead. "Harry." Buford nodded as he pulled his horse to a stop. Martin and Darnell sat defiantly in their saddles on either side of him. "I understand that you're fixin' to plant yer colored boy here in the church cemetery alongside my pa 'n ma and the other regular folks."

Harry stared up at Buford and the other two men. The steel in his eyes told more than any words Harry could have uttered. Butch stepped closer to his friend.

Buford and the other two began to look uneasy. "Now it ain't that I don't think your...darky don't deserve a Christian burial." Buford continued nervously. "It's jist this here...."

Harry cut him off, "You know, I'm mighty glad to hear that, Buford. For a minute there, I thought maybe you'd come here to keep me from giving my friend a Christian burial. If that had been the case, I'm afraid someone would have gotten hurt."

As Harry spoke, Butch opened his coat to reveal the two colt automatics stuck inside his belt.

From the corner of his eye, Harry saw Alva talking with Slim. Slim nodded in his direction. "That could be trouble, Alva. Maybe we best get Austin." A few moments later, all three strolled over and stood behind Harry and Butch.

Buford was still staring at Butch's guns when Alva and the others arrived. Now, he looked at the group of men facing him. When Buford looked from side-to-side for support from his two friends, he did not seem encouraged. He looked back at Harry and nervously touched the butt of his own gun resting in the holster on his hip. Sweat formed on his brow as he stared into the eyes of the men before him. After a long minute, fat with tension, Buford motioned to Martin and Darnell to follow as the three men wheeled their horses around and rode away.

Unaware of the confrontation that had just taken place, Lee and Laura strolled over to join their father.

"Where are Mr. Bauer and the others going?" Lee asked.

"They weren't able to stay, Son."

Lee nodded. "Ma will be sad she wasn't able to be here too."

By this time, a small crowd had gathered for the service. The minister delivered a fitting eulogy and a solemn prayer, then the boards were pulled away and the coffin was lowered with ropes into the grave. The sound of the ropes being slid from under the wooded coffin was unsettling considering Clarence's cause of death.

With the coffin resting at the bottom of the grave, Harry plunged a spade into the mound of dirt beside the hole. As he slowly let the red earth rain down on the casket, it echoed with a hollow clatter. When the shovel was empty, he set his teeth and stabbed it angrily back into the ruddy mound of soil. Then he strode away.

Lee retrieved the spade and sadly dumped a shovelful of Oklahoma dirt into the hole. Soon others followed suit.

As the crowd began to disperse, Harry and Butch led Lee and Laura back to their wagon. Harry came to an abrupt halt when he spotted Ratt Wilson and Melvin Howell standing next to his rig. Harry hadn't seen them ride up but now he saw Melvin Howell's fancy automobile parked close by.

Wilson leveled his gazed at Harry as the Kidwell's approached. When he spotted Leroy, for a second a puzzled expression crossed his face. Then, returning his attention to Harry, Ratt cracked a wicked smile. "Too bad about your nigger, Harry."

With eyes blazing, Harry took a step toward the murderer but Butch stopped him with a touch to his arm. "Not the time," he whispered.

Harry calmed himself. "You don't belong here, Wilson." Harry glanced over Wilson's shoulder and saw his gunmen loitering near Howell's automobile. "Your men don't belong here, either." Looking pointedly at Howell he added, "And that goes for your oily pet snake, as well."

"What? We can't pay our respects? I'm all *choked* up about this," Wilson said with exaggerated sincerity as he grabbed his throat. "Ain't that so, Mr. Howell?"

Lee's face had turned crimson at the first site of the gunman. Now, with Wilson's mocking tone, the boy snapped. "I'm gonna kill you for what you did," he screamed and rushed forward.

Harry pulled him away.

"Hey! Your boy's quite a pistol there, Harry. Do believe he's got more spunk than you," Wilson sneered.

Ratt looked at Butch. "Who's your friend, Harry? Don't believe we've been introduced. He come by to hold your hand?"

Harry ignored Wilson and touched Laura's shoulder. "Time to leave, Laura." To his son he said, "Let's go, Lee."

Lee's eyes pleaded with his uncle to do something, but Butch shook his head at the boy. With a disappointed sigh, Lee followed his father and uncle as they walked away.

"That yer little girl there, Harry?" Wilson shot after them.

Harry paused, but didn't turn around.

"Lookin' real fine." Wilson whispered with an emphasis on the last word. "Should ripen out mighty good...if she gets the chance. Shame if'n somethin' was to happen to her."

The muscles tightened in the back of Harry's neck. After a long pause, he hustled the kids into the back of the buckboard. He and Butch climbed onto the wagon seat. Harry snapped the reins.

"Seen you somewhere before, Mister," Wilson shouted at Butch as Harry drove away. "Can't figure just where, but it'll come to me."

* * *

Governor Robertson was standing behind an ornate walnut desk. He smiled as Etta was ushered into his office.

"Mrs. Kidwell, his Honor, the Governor." Mary made the introductions before stepping back into the reception room and closing the door.

The Governor extended his hand and Etta reached out in kind. Gazing into a strong but kind face, she liked the fact that his handshake was hearty and firm.

"Please, have a seat, Mrs. Kidwell. Mary has told me a little about you. Seems you are a persistent lady. Hope I will be able to be of some help," he said as he sat down. "Now, tell me what is troubling you."

"It's a rather sensitive matter, Sir. It concerns an oilman named S.C. Brooks." Etta began.

A few minutes later, having finished her story, Etta sat before a pensive Governor James Robertson. He peered at her over his wire-rim glasses as he pondered what he had just been told. "The circumstances of Mr. Jackson's death and the theft of those cattle are extremely troubling."

The Governor stared up at the ceiling fan that lazily turned above his head. Finally, he asked, "You've gone to the local law?"

"Yes, but the sheriff appears to be bought and paid for by Brooks."

Again there was a pause. "You're certainly right about *one thing*, Mrs. Kidwell. This *is* a sensitive matter. Don't take this wrong. It's not that I don't believe you. Or, let me phrase that another way. I do believe that you are sincere."

The Governor rubbed his chin and took off his reading glasses. "*But,* if you're mistaken about Mr. Brook's involvement in this business or even if you're right and we can't prove it...." He looked sad and shook his head. "Well, to accuse him or to start an official investigation could be political suicide for me. You see, this man has gained a lot of political power in this state. To be quite candid, he even helped me get elected."

"Then you won't help?" Etta seemed to melt as she spoke.

"I didn't say that. I can see that you're desperate and I want to help. To tell you the truth, Mrs. Kidwell, I don't care one bit for S.C. Brooks. He's a viper."

"But you said you couldn't take the chance of opening an investigation."

"I said, 'an official investigation'. I didn't say anything about unofficial. You see, I have a man who sometimes does personal business for me. He's a private investigator and I trust him completely. He's experienced, used to be a pretty good lawman when he was younger. What I will do, Mrs. Kidwell, is send him out your way to check into things. If Brooks is behind any of this, believe me, this man will get to the bottom of it." The Governor stood and offered Etta his hand. "That's the best that I can offer."

"You've been very kind, Governor. I just hope it's not too late. You see, my husband is like a locomotive's boiler that has been stoked to the bursting point."

"You go on back to your ranch and I will get my man right on it. I'll even wager he'll be on the job before you get home."

Etta left his office but stopped to say good-bye to Mary Frantz and to thank her.

"I'm glad I could help, Etta." Mary replied. "By the way, are you going back home this evening? If not, I'd be pleased to have you at my home for supper tonight."

"Must admit, it's a bit late to head back home." Etta pondered for a second. "Yes, I'd like that. I'll spend one more night and start back tomorrow morning."

"I'll come by your boarding house to pick you up at seven o'clock if that's all right."

"Sounds just fine."

Mary gave Etta a hug and walked her to the door.

Shortly after Etta had left, the Governor called Mary into his office.

"Mary, I want you to get in touch with Samuel Stillman for me. I have a job for him."

Chapter 35

THE BURIED GUN

~ ~ ~

After the funeral, Lee still looked sullen as he helped Harry unharness the horses from the buckboard in front of the barn.

Butch left them to their work and went to his automobile where he retrieved a box of ACP .45 bullets. Taking them into the barn, he slipped into the tack room, set the box on the workbench and checked the clips of both his Colt automatics. Seeing that they were fully loaded, he stuck the guns in his belt.

Stepping from the tack room, Butch watched as Harry and Lee put the horses in their stalls.

Harry looked at his son. "I want you to take Laura to the house, Lee. Uncle Leroy and I have some business to talk over."

"Pa, if you're going to make plans to do something about that Wilson fellow and his hired guns, I ..."

Harry cut him short. "You do what you're told, Lee Kidwell."

"You leave this to me and your pa, boy," Butch said as he approached the two.

Lee looked at Butch and then at his father. Lowering his shoulders, he reluctantly led Laura toward the house.

Harry and Butch watched the kids enter the back door before exiting the rear of the barn and stepping into the small corral there.

Butch took a plug of tobacco from his pocket and cut off a chunk with his pocketknife. He stuck it in his mouth and offered Harry a chew.

"No thanks, Butch. Gave it up some years ago."

Butch nodded and said, "I take it you know where to find 'em."

"Pretty sure they're staying at Gilbert Jackson's place. Clarence and I had a little run-in with them out there a while back."

"Appeared to be seven at the funeral if ya count that Howell fella." Butch observed.

"Wouldn't count him. Six looks like the full of it."

"You know the setup?"

Harry nodded.

"What do you think? Morning or night?" Butch asked.

"They're likely to be in the ranch house both times. But it faces east."

Butch nodded his understanding. "So, morning. Tomorrow or the next?"

"Tough call, Butch."

Butch gave Harry a questioning look.

"The way Wilson goaded me today, I think they'll expect us by tomorrow," Harry began to

338

explain. "If we don't show by tomorrow night they'll probably think we're too scared to do anything. So, if we wait, we'll likely have more surprise on our side."

"So, why's that a tough call?"

Harry looked at his boots then up at Butch.

Butch had seen that look before. "Etta," Butch whispered.

"She's likely not to be home by tomorrow morning, but by the next ..."

"Sundance," Butch interrupted. "Things are different now. They killed Clarence and rubbed it in our noses. Then, to top that, Wilson threatened your little girl. Etta will understand we have to act now."

Harry seemed to ponder for a bit. Finally, he shrugged.

"You want to try out one of these?" Butch pulled the two Colt automatics from his waistband.

* * *

Back in the ranch house, Lee was peering out the kitchen window toward the barn.

"What are you looking at Lee?" Laura asked.

"Just wondering what they're up to. Stay here. I'm going to take a look," Lee said as he opened the back door.

"I want to come, too."

"You stay!"

The order was so final that Laura gasped a little. She slumped down in a kitchen chair and watched as her brother left the house.

Approaching the barn, Lee could barely hear his father and uncle talking. He entered the barn through the main door and looked around. Voices were coming from outside in the corral. He tiptoed past the horse stalls and paused for a second at the place where Clarence had been hung. Skirting the spot, he continued through the empty cattle pen and moved quietly to the open door that led out back.

Pressing his cheek against the worn wooden frame, Lee peeked around the edge of the door. About forty-feet away, Butch was setting up four bean cans on the top rail of the fence circling the corral. Harry stood several feet from the door with his back to Lee.

When his uncle turned around to face the barn, Lee pulled out of sight and waited. He cocked his ear and listened to the footsteps as his uncle returned to where his father stood. When Lee was sure both men faced away from the barn, he peeked out again.

Standing next to Harry, Butch handed over one of the shiny Colts. "I know you ain't all that familiar with these, but see what you can do."

Lee rolled his eyes as he watched and listened from inside the barn door. *"Ain't all that familiar with these,"* he thought. That had to be the understatement of the decade.

Harry took the Colt. He hefted it for weight and balance. "Never fired one of these. Feels kinda strange," he commented.

Butch nodded toward the cans. "Give'r a try."

Harry held it out and made a move with his left hand to fan back the hammer. He stopped in mid-motion and looked at Butch.

"Take off the safety catch and then slide back the rack," Butch explained.

"Safety catch? Rack?"

"Yeah, safety, that little doohickey there to keep someone from shootin' off his foot by accident." Butch pointed at the catch on the .45. "Here, watch me," Butch took out his other gun and demonstrated by flipping the catch and racking a round into the chamber.

"How the hell would anyone shoot a gun by accident?" Harry asked.

Butch shrugged. "I don't know. It's just a safety thing. They seem to be big on that stuff these days."

Back in the barn, Lee shook his head in embarrassment. Even he knew about a safety catch. He could see that his father was going to be no help at all in a gunfight with Ratt Wilson and his men.

Outside, Harry clicked off the safety, racked a shell into the chamber and took aim. He fired. The cans remained where they sat.

Butch shook his head. "Like this." He took a quick aim with his gun and fired. The can on the far right flew up into the air and landed beyond the fence.

Harry made a move to fan the gun with his left hand and again stopped in mid-motion.

"There's already another bullet in the chamber. All you have to do is squeeze off another round," Butch instructed.

Harry tried to shoot with a quick move of his body and hand in a failed copy of the way he'd normally fire a revolver.

It looked quite silly to Lee and he almost laughed, but this was too sad to be humorous. Lee watched as Harry's second shot missed. His father fired twice more with the same results. Then he angrily emptied the gun without hitting a thing.

"Damn it," he swore. "Take this damn thing. I need a real gun." With that he thrust the automatic into Butch's hand, turned and headed toward the barn.

Lee was surprised to see his father heading toward him, but he quickly ducked back and scurried out of sight into one of the stalls. He could see his father enter and march over to the tack room where he disappeared inside.

A second later he re-appeared with a short-handled spade. Lee gazed on with curiosity as his father stepped over to one of the support posts near the tack room door and pace off several steps. Then he plunged the spade into the ground and began to dig.

Butch came wandering back inside and watched as Harry angrily attacked the dirt.

"What ya doing, Kid?" Butch asked.

Lee was startled when he heard the word, kid. For a second he thought he'd been discovered and his uncle was talking to him. Then he realized Uncle Leroy had been talking to his dad. He'd never heard his uncle call his dad "Kid" before. He guessed it must be some kind of buddy thing.

Harry didn't answer. He looked up for a second and then went on digging. A couple of feet down, the spade made a thumping sound. Harry got on his knees and began to dig with his hands. Butch sauntered over and watched with curiosity.

"Don't tell me you kept it!" Butch said.

Again Harry said nothing as he pulled out a bundle wrapped in rotting burlap. He peeled back the decaying woven material to reveal a layer of oilcloth. He unwrapped several thicknesses and a well-preserved holster and a .45 Colt revolver appeared. From a second small roll of oil cloth, Harry produced a box of cartridges.

"How long has that been there?" Butch asked.

Harry glanced at Lee's uncle as he strapped on the holster and checked the gun. He spun the cylinder and took bullets from the box to load the weapon. Once loaded, he twirled the revolver on his trigger finger and, still spinning, slid it into the holster.

Lee watched all of this in wonder. He was especially amazed by the ease and speed with which his father loaded and handled the weapon.

Butch walked alongside Harry as the two headed back to the corral. "Thought you told Etta you got rid of it," Butch said with a little edge of sarcasm.

Harry looked at him. "Couldn't do it, Butch. Buried it instead. Never planned to dig it up though."

Lee was puzzled. Why had his father called Uncle Leroy, Butch? Lee slipped out of his hiding place and reached the door as his father and uncle came to a stop a few feet from the barn. Crouching inside the door, Lee peeked around the frame. A change seemed to come over his father. It was in the way he stood, in the way he held his body.

Three cans still sat on the top rail thirty-five feet or so from where his father stood.

If Lee had blinked, he would have missed what happened next. His father snatched the gun from its holster and fanned it with his left hand. The shots were so close together Lee had to think about it afterward to realize that, in a flash, six shots had been fired.

With the first shot the tin can on the left flew into the air. The second shot caught it in mid-air and tossed it higher. The third and fourth shots did the same to the middle can. The fifth shot launched the third can but the sixth shot missed hitting it the second time. "Damn," Harry cursed when he missed on the last shot.

"I guess you ain't completely lost your touch, Kid," Butch commented with a smile.

"Never woulda missed that last shot in the old days," Harry snapped.

In the barn, after the last shot, Lee fell on his butt. He quickly regained his feet and looked to see if he'd been heard. Evidently, the loud report of the .45 revolver that was still ringing in his uncle and father's ears had covered the sounds he had made when he thumped down on the floor. Lee quickly brushed the straw and dirt off his backside and slipped back though the barn and ran to the house.

Laura was waiting for him as Lee burst into the kitchen.

"I heard gun shots. What were they doing?"

Lee looked at her with a blank expression.

"Is everything all right?" Laura persisted.

He didn't know what to say. After a pause he said, "I don't know. I don't understand. I never saw anything like that before. And it was Pa."

Lee left Laura puzzled and wondering and went upstairs to his room. He needed time to think. As he sat on his bed and reflected on what he'd just seen, other things he'd seen and heard over the years came to mind. He thought about his uncle calling his father, Kid. And his father calling Uncle Leroy, Butch. He thought about the way his father always tried to keep out of any kind of trouble and his distaste for lawmen.

The truth seemed to be slapping Lee in the face, but he couldn't quite accept it. There would only be one way to find out for sure and that would be to ask. But he wasn't sure if he would be able to find the nerve to do it.

* * *

Etta came home early the next afternoon. She parked the truck near the fence and approached the house. Laura had seen her drive up the lane and burst through the door. She cried out and leaped down the porch steps. "Ma, Ma!" Tears welled up as Laura ran into her mother's arms.

"That's quite a welcome. I'm glad to see you too," Etta declared.

Looking toward the house, she saw Lee and Harry step through the back door. The smile on her lips faded. The sorrowful look on Lee's face and the tears that were streaming down Laura's cheeks were sure signs of trouble.

"What is it, sweetheart? Why are you crying?" She looked at her daughter and then to her husband on the porch. "What's going on, Harry?"

Behind Harry, Butch stepped out of the back door.

"Take the kids for a walk?" Harry asked his friend.

"Come on, kids." Butch put his hand on Lee's shoulder and the two walked down the porch steps. They took Laura by the hand and led her toward the barn.

Etta stood alone looking bewildered. "What's happened, Harry?"

"Come in the house," Harry said softly.

A cold shiver ran down Etta's spine as she walked up the steps and followed Harry inside. The door shut behind them.

* * *

Lee stopped walking and turned to look back at the house. He could see his mother through the kitchen window. His father was not in view but he could tell from the intense look on his mother's face that he was standing in front of her, just out of view, talking.

Lee watched as the look on his mother's face changed from questioning to confusion, from shock to horror. His strong mother seemed to be shrinking before his eyes. When Lee could no longer watch, he joined Butch and Laura as they went into the barn.

Chapter 36

THE BROKEN PROMISE

~ ~ ~

It was after seven that evening when a lone automobile motored into the town of Hobard. It cruised slowly down the nearly-deserted Main Street of the sleepy little town. Light from the street lamps reflected off its shiny green surface as it pulled to a halt in front of the sheriff's office.

The driver's door opened and a tall, powerful-looking man stepped out. He was dressed in black and held a black four-cornered western hat. When he placed it on his head, Samuel Stillman, though somewhat older, was every bit as imposing as he'd been a dozen years before. Stretching his large frame, he looked around before walking up to the sheriff's door and thrusting it open.

Sheriff Rafter was leaning back in a padded wooden chair with his feet comfortably planted on his desk. A whiskey bottle sat near him as he peacefully sipped from a half-empty glass.

"Hey, what the hell!" Rafter cried out as he shot upright and put down his glass. "Ain't you ever heard o' knocking?" Somewhat flustered, he pulled a newspaper over the glass and slipped the whiskey bottle in his desk drawer.

"You Rafter?" Stillman's steel-grey eyes bored into the startled man.

"Wh ... who the hell are you?" Rafter wanted to know.

The slight trepidation in his voice told Stillman that the man was unnerved. "Name's Stillman. I want you to answer a few questions."

"Stillman, Sa ... Samuel Stillman, the Marshal?"

So, Rafter had heard of him. Good. It was important to make this man feel intimidated.

Stillman placed both his hands on the sheriff's desk and stared into the lawman's eyes. "I'll be wantin' straight answers and I'll know if they ain't."

"Look, Marshal, you shouldn't be comin' in here talkin' to me like this. I'm the law in this county," Rafter blustered.

"Nonetheless, you'll answer my questions and answer 'em straight." The implied authority in Stillman's voice had the desired effect.

"Well... I ain't sure what gives you the right to ask me anything, but if I was to answer, I wouldn't have no reason to lie." Rafter turned his eyes away from Stillman as he spoke.

"I figure that to be one lie right there. Don't do it again."

Fifteen minutes later, Stillman left Rafter's office. He'd learned less than he'd hoped, but enough for a start. Rafter had been evasive and even untruthful. The lies told him as much as the truth. One thing he'd learned troubled him greatly: Rafter had mentioned the death of an elderly black man. Evidently, the sheriff assumed that Stillman knew about it. It was a suicide according to Rafter. Stillman could read a lie better than most any man; now there were apparently two murders. Tomorrow he'd continue his investigation by canvassing the ranchers.

* * *

At the Kidwell ranch, the evening sun had turned the sky pink and gold. Harry sat with Etta, rocking in the swing on their back porch. The chain that held the seat gave out a rhythmic creak as they gently swayed back and forth. Etta took Harry's hand and, with a profound sadness in her eyes, looked out toward Clarence's bunkhouse.

"I know that, for you, this changes things, Harry. But revenge will not bring back Clarence."

Harry said nothing.

"The Governor's sending a man, an investigator, to look into what's going on here. He believed me when I told him about the gunmen Brooks sent. What's more, he doesn't like Brooks." Etta voice was forceful and confident. "In time this investigator can get to the bottom of things."

"That's just it, Etta. We don't have time."

"You made a promise, Harry."

Harry looked in his wife's eyes and touched her face. There was one thing that he had not told her and he didn't want to worry her even more by telling her now. He silently nodded and then looked away and sighed. Standing up, he walked into the house. Tomorrow morning he and Butch would act.

* * *

Slim was finishing a long day of riding fence. He was much more vigilant since his cattle had been stolen. The nervous man stayed contently on the lookout for the kind of trouble that had taken the lives of Gil Jackson and the Kidwell's hired hand, Clarence. Now, Slim rode with a revolver on his hip and a rifle on his horse. For him, the rifle was standard, but the revolver had been recently acquired.

He was about to head back toward home when, in the distance, a glint from a glass windshield caught his attention. An automobile was bouncing over the field in his direction. He didn't recognize it and it was trespassing on his property. The closer the vehicle got, the more nervous Slim became. His fingers touched the butt of his new revolver.

* * *

Samuel Stillman had learned from one Mr. Austin Peese where Slim Moore's ranch was located and it had taken him very little time to find it. He'd seen a lone rider near a fence line about half a mile from the ranch house and he'd pointed his Ford in that direction.

As Stillman grew closer, he knew that this stick of a man seated on a buckskin gelding had to be Slim Moore. Mr. Peese had told him Slim Moore was the man whose cattle had been stolen.

Stillman had not swallowed the story Rafter had tried to feed him about a bill of sale. There was no doubt in Stillman's mind that the cattle had been rustled. He wanted to know how they'd been stolen and who were the rustlers. And there was something else. Austin Peese had spoken of the rancher, Harry Kidwell, who'd helped to get the cattle back. This was the husband of the woman named Etta who'd appealed to the Governor for help. Stillman really wanted to know more about that man.

As he approached, Stillman could see that Mr. Moore was apprehensive. When he stopped the automobile, he stuck both his hands out the driver's side window.

"Good day to ya, Mr. Moore. Don't be alarmed. I ain't here to cause you no trouble," Stillman said as he reached down with his left hand and opened the door of his vehicle from the outside.

Slim pulled the revolver from his holster. "Maybe you best stay in that automobile, Mister. And keep those hands where I can see 'em."

Stillman hesitated. A smile touched his lips. He was more amused than irritated that this farmer would challenge him. "My name is Stillman, Mr. Moore. I'm an investigator sent by the Governor. Jist came from Austin Peese's place."

Slim climbed down from his horse still holding the revolver. He cautiously approached the vehicle and the man inside.

Stillman made a mental note of the awkward way in which Mr. Moore handled the weapon.

"Feel a bit more easy if'n you'd holster yer weapon, Mr. Moore. Wouldn't want it goin' off by accident."

"Maybe you should just ease on outa that auto and let me get a better look at ya."

Stillman did as directed and with two fingers pulled back his coat. He reached slowly into his inside coat pocket and pulled out a badge. It was just his private investigator's badge, but it looked official and Stillman found it useful in situations like this.

Ten minutes later, Slim was squatted on the ground holding the reins to his horse. Squatting in front of him, Stillman absent-mindedly prodded the ground with a stick as he listened to Slim tell of the loss and return of his cattle.

"So, you got all your cattle back?" Stillman confirmed.

"Sure did, but if you want to know more about that you'd have to ask Harry Kidwell. Was Harry what got 'em back." Slim shifted his gaze to look Stillman in the eyes before he continued. "Harry and his hired hand, Clarence, the colored man them Brooks' men hanged."

"When was he hanged?"

"T'other day."

"Any proof it was the Brooks men?"

"No, but who else? They did it 'cause him and Harry made 'em look foolish. I mean, if'n ya ask me."

Stillman nodded, but remained silent. Men liked to fill silence with words and often they said much that was useful.

"There was five rustlers, all well-armed. Clarence and Harry took all five without killin' a one of 'em and Harry and Clarence only had one gun a'tween 'em. Harry said it was all Clarence, but I think he was bein' modest."

"Sounds like quite a feat. Only one gun. Whose gun was it?"

"Had to be Clarence's cause Harry don't never carry a gun. Far as I can tell, he don't have much use for 'em."

Stillman pondered this for a moment. Then he stood up and shook Slim's hand. "Much obliged, Mr. Moore."

He was still pondering all that he'd heard as he climbed into his vehicle and drove away.

In the morning, he'd visit the one rancher that everyone claimed knew most everything that went on in the county.

* * *

The morning sun had not yet risen when Harry and Butch slipped out of the Kidwell house. They made their way quietly to the barn and began to saddle their horses.

Harry's Colt revolver was in its holster and Butch's two Colt automatics were stuck snuggly in the belt of his trousers. Harry took a second to tighten the cinch on his saddle. As he did, Etta entered the barn. Harry had thought he'd slipped out of bed without waking her, but he realized now he should have known better.

The sun was beginning to peek over the horizon, but the dark interior of the barn required two kerosene lanterns to create enough light by which to work. In the dim glow, Etta looked at the guns that stuck out from Butch's waist belt. She looked accusingly at the two men; then her eyes alighted on the gun worn at Harry's side. Shock, betrayal and then sadness scrolled across her face: Harry saw it all.

"Harry ..."

Her unfinished sentence cut him like broken glass. "I ... I buried it, like it was dead. Never would a ..." Harry looked helplessly at the woman he loved.

Etta stood with tears forming in her sad hazel eyes. There was a deadly silence until Lee entered the barn.

"What are you doing up so early, Son?" Harry asked the boy with a bit more irritation in his voice than he wanted to show.

"Guess I could be askin' you the same question, Pa, but I figure I already know the answer. I figure I know who you are, you and Uncle Leroy. And I'm bettin' the two of you are going to go after that Wilson fellow and his hired guns."

For a second Harry was at a loss for words. Etta stood speechless as well. Butch was the one who finally spoke up. "What do you mean, you know who we are?"

"I saw you yesterday, Pa, you and ... Butch. I saw what you did. You're them, aren't you, you and Uncle Leroy? Everyone thought you were dead. But, you aren't dead. You're them."

Harry took a deep breath. "I'm your Pa. That's all that's important. Whatever else you think you know doesn't matter. Now, go on back in the house."

"I want to go, too, Pa," Lee pleaded.

Etta brushed away the tears that had been forming. "You aren't going anywhere, young man, and I don't want your father going either." She glared at Harry and Butch. "There has to be another way. Harry, you made a promise." Anger had begun to replace the sadness in Etta's voice.

"It's different now, Etta," Butch interrupted.

"Why, because of Clarence?"

Harry stepped close and put his hand on Etta's shoulder. He gazed into her eyes. "Wilson threatened Laura," he whispered so that Lee couldn't hear. "I can't let that go and I can't wait for him to make good on the threat. He has to be stopped. Now!"

Etta's eyes went wide, first with shock and then sparked with anger. She looked at Harry for a second then turned and left the barn.

Harry and Butch finished adjusting their saddles before leading their horses outside. Lee followed quietly, but once outside he made one last plea to go along. He was about to get a harsh answer from his father when Harry saw Etta step out of Clarence's bunkhouse. She was carrying Clarence's revolver.

"Saddle my horse, Son," she directed Lee with a bark.

Lee hesitated. "Pa, if Ma is going why can't...."

"Do it now!" Etta cut him off.

He looked questioningly at his father and uncle.

Butch spoke. "Do as your ma says, Lee. She knows better than you can imagine how to use that weapon she's carrying."

Harry spoke calmly, "Your Uncle Leroy is right. Now go saddle your mother's horse. I need you to stay here and watch after your sister. At the first sign of trouble, you take her down in the fruit cellar and lock it from the inside."

Lee glared at his parents and uncle. Finally, he nodded and went into the tack room to get his mother's saddle.

Ten minutes later, for the first time in years, Butch, Sundance, and Etta rode together, heading for the Jackson ranch.

* * *

After downing a quick breakfast, Samuel Stillman set out for the one rancher who was suppose to know more about the goings-on than anyone else in these parts.

He arrived at Alva Bevan's ranch a little after seven-thirty. Alva opened the door with a Winchester rifle in his hands.

Stillman gave a small sigh and raised his hands as he got out of his vehicle.

"You Stillman?" Alva asked.

A wry smile touched Stillman's lips. Maybe they were right, he thought. This man does seem to know what's going on in the county. "That's right, Mr. Bevan." Stillman slowly opened his coat to show that he was carrying no guns.

Alva set his rifle against the doorframe and motioned Stillman onto his porch. There were two chairs and Alva offered one to the investigator.

"You the same Stillman who used to be a US Marshal?" Alva asked as they settled in.

Stillman nodded.

"Heard you ain't been a Marshal for some time."

"You heard right. Now I do private work fer the Governor of Oklahoma, him and a few others."

"You here to clean up this mess that Brooks has caused, in there?"

Stillman smiled. Alva Bevan didn't mince words. "I plan to get to the bottom of what's goin' on 'round here, Mr. Bevan."

Alva nodded and began to fill him in. After about an hour, Stillman had gained a good deal more information than he needed, but some of it was useful. As always, Alva's propensity for hyperbole was undiminished.

Stillman was about to leave when he decided to ask one more question. "One other thing, Mr. Bevan; this Harry Kidwell and his wife, Etta, when did they come to live in this part of the country?"

"Harry and Etta? Let me think. Believe it must'o been around ought-eight or ought-nine, in there. Had the young'n Lee with them when they showed up. The girl, Laura, come later. Sweet girl that one, in there."

"And the brother?"

"Leroy? Well, now, I ain't sure he's an actual blood brother. Jist that the kids call him Uncle, Uncle Leroy. He don't look none like Harry or Etta, so I wouldn't swear he was kin. Showed up after the trouble started, in there. Although, as I recall, he came by once for a visit a few years back. Nice fella, that one is. Can't help but like him first you meet him, in there."

Stillman nodded as he pondered this intriguing information. Walking back to his auto, he couldn't help but think about the man they called Harry Kidwell and his brother/friend named Leroy. Stillman didn't believe much in coincidences and this one was ripe.

Chapter 37

THE PLAN

~ ~ ~

The Jackson ranch was quiet and peaceful in the pale glow of the morning sun. Harry, Etta, and Butch sat on their horses atop the hill that overlooked the ranch house, barn, and corral. The corral was empty now; Harry and Clarence had seen to that. But smoke drifting lazily from the ranch house chimney suggested it was not empty. Harry knew that this was the headquarters for Wilson and his crew. Just how many there were Harry was not sure. He'd spotted two new recruits with Wilson at the funeral. He was pretty sure the one they called Pony was out of commission, but with the new gunmen, Harry guessed that there were now at least five or six all told.

The trio pulled back below the ridge of the hill and dismounted. A light dew still clung to the tall grass and dampened their boots as they stood peering over the rim.

"Got a plan, Butch?" Harry asked.

"You mean you haven't talked about a plan?" Etta exclaimed.

Butch gave a small shrug. "We had one for the two of us, Etta, but ..."

Etta cut in, a bit testily. "With me along you're afraid it might be too dangerous. That's annoying, Butch. I didn't come along to be in the way. What were you planning?"

Harry answered her. "It was going to be a bit direct but it could be modified a little. Not to protect you, Etta, but because now there are three of us."

Etta turned to Butch. "All right, let's hear it. You're the planner. Just hope your anger isn't clouding your judgment."

Butch smiled. "I don't generally get that angry, but I wouldn't want to be those guys when Sundance gets hol' 'o 'em. Anyway, we think they won't be expecting us. We didn't come yesterday or the day before. They're probably thinkin' we're scared of 'em."

"We're counting on them underestimating us," Sundance said. "They did it before and I think they'll do it again."

Butch's horse gave a whinny and he rubbed its muzzle to calm it. "We're going to try to lure them out of the ranch house with the morning sun behind us," he said as the horse settled down. "If we can do that, we have a pretty good chance."

Etta nodded. "How do you plan to do that?"

Butch was about to answer when Harry cut him short. "Someone's coming."

Harry and Butch dropped to the damp ground, crawled forward, and peered over the rise. In the distance a lone vehicle bounced along heading for the ranch. They watched as the driver pulled up in front of the house and got out.

"Recognize him, Kid?" Butch asked as he rose up for a better view.

Harry squinted. "Can't quite make him out."

"You're going blind in your old age, boys?" Etta had crawled up next to the two men. "That's Rafter."

"Well, that's damn inconvenient," Butch said.

Harry nodded. "Let's hope he doesn't stay. I don't want to do anything with him here, but we'll lose the morning glare in about half an hour."

* * *

Wilson sat next to the kitchen window of the Jackson house, sipping whiskey from a tin cup. The room smelled of fried eggs and burnt bacon. The cat that the Jacksons had left behind jumped into his lap. He stroked his hand down the feline's back and it began to purr.

Wilson's men were seated around the kitchen table eating the breakfast that Josh Howard had fried for them. It was being kind to say that Josh wasn't much of a chef, but Wilson had laid out a schedule and it was Josh's turn to cook.

Frank Murphy gave a chuckle as he glanced over at Wilson. "Where'd you get that mangy cat?"

Wilson glared at the man. "You got a problem with cats, Murphy?" Wilson challenged.

The smile faded from Frank Murphy's lips. It was replaced with a look of apprehension. "No, guess not. I mean...I like cats. Jist didn't expect you to be likin' 'em is all."

360

Ratt Wilson continued to glare. The others stopped eating to shift their eyes from Frank to Wilson and back. Wilson finally looked away from Frank and stared out the window. "Had one when I was a kid," he said softly. "My old man wouldn't let me keep it."

Frank nodded. "He gave it away, huh?"

Wilson sat stroking the cat until he finally answered. "Killed it," he whispered just loud enough for Frank to hear. Then he turned and glared at Frank again. "He don't kill cats no more."

A cool silence fell over the room. Ratt turned his head and looked out the window. In the distance, he caught a glint of sunlight reflecting off the windshield of an approaching automobile. He stood up, causing the cat to jump from his lap.

"Someone's comin'." Drawing his gun, Ratt stepped to the door and watched the vehicle come to a stop in front of the house.

Chair legs squawked along the wooden flooring as the gang of gunmen pushed back from the table and rose in unison.

"Is it the old rancher?" Josh asked with fire in his eyes. He pushed his way past the others and headed for the door. "Pony won't never be able to use his arm again after what that shit-kicker did to him."

"It's Rafter," Wilson spat out the words as he holstered his gun.

"Damn," Josh cursed as he and the others turned to go back and finish their breakfast.

Rafter mounted the steps, took off his hat and wiped his forehead with a handkerchief. He nodded nervously when Wilson stepped onto the porch. "Morning, Mr. Wilson."

"What the hell brings you out here, Rafter?"

The sheriff looked around. "Kidwell and the other one, did they come after you? Expected them to by now."

Wilson's eyes blazed. "Does it look like they come after us? Do you see any dead bodies lyin' around?"

In spite of himself, Rafter couldn't help looking around for a dead body or two.

Wilson rolled his eyes. "You're pathetic. Listen here, they ain't comin'. We got that rancher shakin' in his boots. He's so scared he can't spit."

Rafter changed the subject. "That fellow Mr. Brooks hired; the killer named Serpente? He's supposed to get here tonight. Just thought you should know."

"Too bad. Looks like he'll make a trip down here from the big city for nothin'. When he gets here, tell him to turn around and slither back to Chicago. I got Kidwell ready to fold and, once he does, them other cow-humpers will drop one right after the other like leaves in October."

"Yes, sir, I'll tell him. But I doubt much he'll be leavin' so easy."

"Doesn't much matter to me what he does," Wilson sneered. "That all you came out here for?"

Rafter lowered his head and scraped his boot on the top step of the porch. He paused before he answered. "Had a visitor at the jail. Fellow by the name 'o Stillman, Samuel Stillman."

"Stillman? That old lawman? I thought he was dead."

"He didn't look dead to me. Far from it. Wanted to know about what happened to Gil Jackson and Slim's cattle. Also seemed to know about the darky gettin' hung."

"What ya mean 'seemed to know'?"

"Well..."

"What did you tell him?"

"Me? Why...I didn't tell him nothin'. Gave him the story about Jackson's accident and how the darky hung hisself. Told him the cattle were bought and paid for, saw a bill a sale. You know, just what I was supposed to say. Ain't sure he bought it. Seemed to already have in his head what he thought."

Wilson stared at Rafter with those cold rattlesnake eyes. "You're worthless. Go on back to town. We'll handle things. If Stillman gets in the way, we'll take care of him, too." When Rafter hesitated, Wilson stepped close and hissed, "Go on, GIT!"

Rafter turned and stumbled down the steps. A few seconds later, his auto was kicking up dust as it headed back toward town.

* * *

On the hill, Harry and the others watched as Rafter drove away.

"Sheriff's leaving," Etta said. "Better hurry if we want the sun. Now, what were you planning?"

"With you here, I thought front and flanks." Butch said as he stood and wiped at his damp shirt.

"All right, so who's front?" Etta asked.

"That would be me," Harry answered for Butch.

Butch gave him a look as if to ask why was he taking the most dangerous position.

"My mess," Harry answered.

"Be more surprise if I was to be front," Butch said.

"Nope. My job."

"You may be outa practice." When Butch got no reaction he persisted. "You're not as young as you used to be."

"You're older than me."

Etta cut in. "Keep arguing, we'll lose the sun."

Harry nodded. "We'll flip. You call it, Butch."

Harry pulled a silver dollar from his pocket and spun it up in the air. The coin flipped head over tails, glinting in the morning sun. "Tails," Butch called.

Harry grabbed the coin from the air and slapped it onto the back of his left hand. He took a quick peek and put it in his pocket. "Heads. You lose."

"I didn't see it," Butch complained.

Harry glanced at his wife. "You saw it, didn't you?"

Etta shook her head.

Harry reached back in his pocket and pulled out the coin. He showed the head side to Butch. "There it is."

Butch smiled and shook his head. "Let's dance."

Chapter 38

THE SHOWDOWN

~ ~ ~

Ratt Wilson was once again sitting in the chair near the window. The cat was back, rubbing against his legs as Ratt cleaned his Smith & Wesson revolver.

There was a yell from outside. "Hello in the house!"

Wilson's men were still at the table finishing their breakfast. Once again their chair legs screeched against hardwood as they jumped to their feet.

Wilson squinted out the kitchen window.

"Who is it, Ratt?" Josh asked as he pushed his way past the others.

"Son-of-a-bitch." Wilson turned to grin at Josh and the others. "It's old man Kidwell!"

Tobacco-stained teeth were exposed as Josh smiled back.

Still grinning, Wilson expertly jammed cartridges into the cylinder of his .38 and slipped the gun into its holster. A second later, he and the others heard Harry call out to them again.

"Come on out! I have business with you and your men, Wilson."

Wilson stepped to the door and used his hand to shield his eyes against the morning sun. He could make out the lone silhouette of a man standing a dozen yards from the porch. Twisting his head around, he saw no other challengers. With a wink back at his men, he grabbed a twelve-gauge, short-barreled shotgun leaning against the wall. He motioned to the others, "Follow me. This should be fun."

* * *

Harry's stance looked deceptively like a cowering amateur. Under the façade, every fiber of his being was alert.

He sized up the killers as they followed Wilson onto the porch. From their demeanor, Harry judged the two new men to be experienced fighters.

Harry stood with the morning sun glaring over his right shoulder. He had Butch and Etta to back up his play. But, as he looked at the six men before him, he began to wonder if it would be enough.

Wilson was still shading his eyes as he spoke. "I really didn't think you'd have the grit to show up here, old man."

To further disarm his opponents, Harry spoke with a slight tremble in his voice. "Y...you have to pay for what you d-did to Clarence."

Wilson smiled. "What did I d...do to your nigger?"

His men laughed.

Wilson glanced at his crew flanking him on the porch before smiling. "Kinda stupid comin' out here by yer self...don't ya think, Harry? One agin six. Don't look like good odds for you. Or, did you bring your kids to help you?"

Butch stepped into view on the left side of the porch. "He brought me," He opened his coat and exposed the two .45 Colt automatics in his waistband. "And I brought my two friends."

On the right side of the porch Etta stepped into view. In her hand was Clarence's revolver. "I decided to come along, too, and I brought this." Etta cocked the weapon as she spoke. "It belonged to Clarence."

Anger replaced the false tremor in Harry's voice as he tapped his gun-butt with his finger. "You add them to me, and my friend here, and that makes seven. Kind of evens things out a bit."

Harry was sure that, if Wilson had not been underestimating his opponents, he would have just started shooting, but the killer was enjoying the situation a little too much.

Wilson sneered. "You got me shakin', old man." He cracked a wicked smile. "But the way I see it, you count pretty damn bad. Two old men and a woman don't add up to much.

He shook his head in mock sadness. "It's a shame. You came here lookin' for trouble and me and my men had to defend ourselves. There was just no way to avoid killin' you." He leveled a deadly stare at Harry. "That's the way I'll be tellin' the story."

"We've been dead before." Butch said.

Harry smiled. Wilson's bluster had allowed for a few valuable seconds to appraise the gunmen. In spite of his overconfidence, Wilson was a very dangerous opponent. As for the Murphy brothers, they would be competent gun fighters, as well. Harry recognized Josh Howard as the rustler he'd shot in the hand. He could see the desire for revenge in the man's eyes.

Josh's gun had been cocked and in his uninjured hand when he'd stepped onto the porch. Now he began to bring it to bear.

Under normal circumstances, Harry would have tried to take out Wilson first, but Josh's threat changed that. What happened next took less than seven seconds.

Harry drew and fired. Almost simultaneously Wilson lifted and fired his shotgun. Perhaps it was surprise at the speed of Harry's action, but whatever the reason, Wilson pulled the trigger on his weapon a fraction of a second too early. As Harry's bullet smacked square into Josh's forehead, the ground in front of Harry exploded in a burst of earth and grass.

Six feet to Harry's right was a horse trough filled with water. Harry had situated himself so he could use the trough for cover. Diving behind it, he fanned off a second shot that caught Wilson in the left arm and sent him spinning.

With his .45s already cocked, Butch pulled them from his waistband and began to fire. JW Jessup fired at the same time. Two of Butch's bullets tore into his throat and chest. The bullet Jessup fired buzzed past Butch's head, causing him to dive to his right behind the corner of the house.

Arlyn Springer was well-tempered by gunplay. Not shaken by the deaths of the men on either side of him, he fired two shots.

As Butch dove for cover one of Springer's bullets smacked into the heel of his boot. The other grazed his left leg.

On the other side of the porch, Etta was dealing with the Murphy brothers. Initially, their attention had been focused on Harry. Wes Murphy fired as Harry dove behind the water trough.

Harry had seen Etta start shooting as soon as he'd fired at Josh Howard. He knew she had never fired at a live individual, but she had always been proficient with firearms. Now, in her excitement, her first shots went wide-right missing all of the men on the porch.

With Etta's first shot, Frank turned in her direction. He fired and the shot took a nick out of Etta's neck. His second shot was a miss. He was cocking his gun for a third time when Etta finally managed to calm herself. She deliberately aimed and fired. The bullet hit him in the fat of his belly. His cry of pain caused Wes to look his way. Still screaming, Frank gaped at his shirt and a rapidly-expanding stain of crimson blood.

When Wes saw the wound that his brother had suffered, he swore and took aim at Etta. At that instant, Harry fired and the bullet slammed into the side of Wes Murphy's head. The killer crumpled to the deck of the porch.

By this time, Wilson seemed to realize the folly of his overconfidence.

With his wounded arm, he was unable to accurately wield the shotgun. He dropped it, drew his revolver, and fired at Harry behind the water trough. Springer was also firing at Harry, but the Kidwells and Butch had them in a three-sided crossfire. The precariousness of their situation was obvious.

Harry saw Etta take a final shot at Wes Murphy before rushing for cover around the corner of the house. That last shot caught the already wounded man in the throat. He fell back and slid down the porch wall, sputtering and spitting blood. With bulging eyes, he gurgled a final breath before he died.

Ducking low, Butch reached out from behind the corner of the house and fired blind in Springer's direction. Springer was dodging bullets both from Harry and from the wild shots taken by Butch. "What the hell, Wilson! What did you get us into?" He screamed out.

Wilson didn't answer. Instead, he dove for the door to the house. Still firing, he landed on his back inside the Jackson kitchen. Bullets from Harry's revolver flew through the door after him.

The abandoned cat howled in fear as it hunched its back and stood in the doorway. Wilson swore and kicked it out of harm's way.

Springer fired a final shot before he ran for the door. A bullet from both Harry and Butch found him at the same instant. Harry's hit him in the left side; Butch's bullet caught him square in the back. Springer fell to the porch and left a trail of smeared blood as he crawled into the kitchen. Harry could faintly hear him gasping, "Who, who are ... these ..." Then there was silence.

Harry and Etta made their way cautiously onto the porch. Butch, limping slightly from his wound, followed them up the steps. Staying low, they checked each of the four bodies that lay there. All were dead.

Without words, the three turned their attention to the two men who had made it into the house. Harry snuck a quick look through the open door and spotted Springer lying in a pool of blood on the kitchen floor. "One dead in the kitchen. Don't see Wilson," Harry reported.

Butch stepped closer to the door. "Hello in the house," he shouted. "Empty your hands and come out. We won't shoot no more!"

Harry gave Butch a steely look then yelled, "My friend doesn't speak for me, Wilson. He'd surely keep his word but I have other plans! Fill yer hands and come out shootin' or I'll come in after you! Either way, I plan to kill you for what you did to Clarence!"

Butch raised his eyebrows as he looked at his old friend.

There was no answer from the house. All was eerily quiet. The silence was broken by the sound of hooves pounding dirt as a horse bolted from the barn.

Harry turned to see Wilson high-tailing it on horseback away from the Jackson ranch.

Butch cursed, "Damn! He snuck out the back, Sundance!"

Gun in hand, Harry bounded down the steps. He fired a shot, but Wilson was already out of pistol range.

They had left their horses back on the hill above the ranch. It would take Harry several minutes to reach them.

"Son of a ...!" he yelled as he started to run toward the rise.

"Harry, stop!" Etta shouted after him. "It's too late! He'll have too much head-start by the time you get to the horses."

Harry slowed to a walk.

"We'll get him later, Sundance," Butch said as he limped down the steps.

Harry holstered his gun, but continued on up the hill to collect their mounts.

Ten minutes later when Harry returned with the horses, he found Etta standing in front of the porch with a shovel in her hand and one at her feet. He also saw blood from Etta's neck wound staining her blouse.

"Let me look at that."

"I'm fine, Harry. It's already stopped bleeding." Etta then held out the shovel.

"What's this?" Harry asked.

"We killed them. Least we can do is bury 'em. I can't see letting them rot here on Gilbert's porch."

Butch was sitting on the porch steps with a devilish smile. "I already put in my two cents, Sundance. Seems she's determined to do the Christian thing here. Too bad my leg wound won't let me help you none."

Harry grabbed the spade from his wife. "You're not hurt much." He tossed the shovel to his friend. "Hand me the other one, Etta."

* * *

As Harry and Butch toiled away digging a large community grave for the dead gunmen, twenty miles

372

away, four black Cadillac Phaetons were ominously and relentlessly making their way toward the small town of Hobard.

Chapter 39

THE GANGSTERS

~ ~ ~

Sheriff Rafter looked up with a start as the door to his office burst open. Exhausted, Wilson stumbled in. He sat down in a chair and gazed over at the puzzled look on the sheriff's face. "What the hell you gaping at?"

"You're shot," Rafter said as he gawked at the blood dripping from Wilson's arm.

"No shit. You must be some kinda Sherlock Holmes. You never cease to amaze me with your brilliant powers of observation. Now, why the hell don't you do something useful and get me a doctor?"

Rafter could not stop staring at Ratt Wilson and the blood dripping on his floor. All he could think about was how Wilson and his men had been waiting at the Jackson ranch for Harry Kidwell to walk into their trap.

"You going to get me a doctor or are you going to just sit there with your mouth open?" Wilson's eyes shot bolts of lightning at the sheriff.

"S-sorry. I'll c-call him on the telephone," Rafter stuttered.

He rushed to the Western Electric magneto telephone that hung on the wall. Rapidly turning the generator crank with his right hand, he put the receiver to his ear with his left. After a few seconds he got the local operator on the line. A minute after that he was shouting into the mouthpiece at Doctor Jonas Nordham. Although it was not necessary to shout, Rafter was one of those many people who still thought it was the only way to be heard several miles away. "No, he needs you to come here!" Rafter yelled. "Yes, yes. You'll come right away then?"

After he hung up the receiver, Rafter turned and nervously inquired as to what had transpired out at the Jackson ranch. He knew before he asked that it couldn't be anything good. He also knew that he would have to endure a barrage of insults and profanity before Wilson would divulge the details of what had happened out there.

"This is bad, real bad." Rafter said after hearing Wilson's version of the morning's events.

Wilson told him there had been ten local ranchers with guns who had conducted a cowardly sneak attack on the unsuspecting inhabitants of the Jackson house.

"We're in real trouble," Rafter wailed after hearing that all of Wilson's men were dead.

"Shut the hell up, Rafter. This can be fixed. I just need some men who know how to fight."

A while later there was a light knock on the door. It swung open and Doctor Nordham stepped into the office. He nodded at the two as his eyes fell on Wilson's wounded arm. "You best sit down here while I take a look at that," he said, placing his kit on the sheriff's desk. Taking out a pair of scissors, he cut away Wilson's shirtsleeve.

"This will need some stitches, but it doesn't look too serious. How did it happen?"

"I ain't payin' you to ask questions, Doc," Wilson snarled.

Sheriff Rafter gave the doctor a look that said, "Just do as he asks."

Nordham shrugged. "At least we should take you to my office so I can give you a shot of procaine to dull the pain."

"I ain't goin' nowhere. Jist stitch the damn thing up and do it before I die of old age."

Doc Nordham was a decent sort, but his penchant for a little more than an occasional nip was something that had kept him from being a highly-respected doctor. Nordham had learned that sometimes it was best to turn a blind eye to suspicious wounds and to ask few questions. That was why Rafter had called him.

Looking at the thin, surly and obviously-dangerous man before him now, Doctor Nordham closed his mouth and began to examine the wound.

The bullet had plowed a nasty gash in Wilson's upper arm but had done no damage to the bone. Nordham cleaned the wound with antiseptic before he started to stitch.

Wilson grimaced from the pain, but said nothing.

"You'll need rest and time to heal," Nordham said as he dressed the wound.

"You stick to fixin' the damn arm, Doc. I ain't payin' for advice."

Nordham nodded diffidently. "I'll return in a few hours to see how you're doing." He hurriedly packed his bag and scurried out the door.

Wilson settled into Rafter's chair and soon fell asleep.

* * *

Lee was eating supper with his sister when he heard horses. Jumping up from the table, he hurried to the Kidwell's kitchen window. His father, mother and Uncle Leroy rode slowly into the barnyard and dismounted.

"Stay in the house, Laura," he ordered his sister.

Laura got up from the table. "I want to come, too."

"Just wait here for now until I find out what happened." Lee directed as he stepped outside.

Laura reluctantly sat back down, placed her elbows on the table and rested her chin in her hands. "Don't see why I always have to stay in here," she pouted.

The sun was low on the horizon as Lee followed his parents and uncle into the barn. They all looked worn and tired but safe...and alive. Lee sighed with relief. His father was lighting a lantern and his mother and uncle were unsaddling the horses.

"What happened, Pa? Did you get 'em?"

Harry set the lantern on a barrel. "Where's your sister?"

"Told her to wait in the house. What happened? Is it over?" Lee persisted.

Etta began to curry her horse. "We hope so," she sighed.

"I doubt it." Butch said under his breath.

Etta glanced at Butch before she spoke to her son. "Lee, you should go back into the house."

Lee looked at his mother and in the dim light saw blood on her neck and the collar of her blouse.

"Ma, you're hurt!"

"Just a scratch, Lee. I'm fine."

After a second, Lee turned to his father. "Can't you tell me what happened, Pa?"

"Everything is fine, Son," Harry said. "Go back in the house."

Trying to stall, Lee grabbed his uncle's saddle and carried it into the tack room. When he returned, he caught a glimpse of blood on Butch's lower leg.

Lee was about to comment when Harry saw him looking at the wound. "Go back to the house and tell your sister it's time for her to get ready for bed. We'll be along directly."

Lee continued to stare at Butch's wounds. "But, Uncle ..."

"We're all right, Son. Go!" Harry barked.

Lee lowered his head and walked slowly out of the barn.

* * *

Etta watched through the barn door as Lee clumped up the porch steps and entered the house.

"What do you think will happen now?" she asked.

"We killed off everyone but Wilson." Harry carried his saddle into the tack room. "But, I don't think it'll end here."

"Not likely," Butch said. "Brooks is not the kind to give up easy. He's also not the kind to put all his eggs in one basket. We may have beaten that bunch today, but I feel like a bigger storm is gathering."

Butch sat down on a sawhorse and pulled up his pant leg to look at his wound.

"Let me get something to clean that, Butch," Etta said as she headed for the house.

"Don't bother, Etta. I had hedge thorn scratches worse'n this." Butch pulled down his pant leg and started walking to the house.

Harry turned the horses out to pasture, then he and Etta followed Butch. "Hate to admit it, Etta, but our bed's going to look mighty invitin' tonight."

* * *

Ratt Wilson was still asleep in the sheriff's chair when the doctor returned that evening. Ratt awoke to the sounds of knocking and the door opening. He grabbed his gun, but relaxed when he saw it was the doctor.

Sheriff Rafter had spent the last several hours in a back room. He hurried into his office when he heard the doctor return.

Standing in the doorway, Doctor Nordham stared nervously at the gun in Wilson's hand. "I ... I brought some laudanum for you, Mr. Wilson. Thought it might help a little with the pain."

"Do I look like I'm in pain, you gin-soaked quack? You can take..." Wilson stopped mid-sentence and crossed the room to the window. It was late evening and the dark street outside the sheriff's office was nearly deserted.

The Old Gun

Wilson had heard the unmistakable sound of automobile engines and tires on the brick street. He peered through the lead glass window and watched as a precession of sinister black vehicles approached. Sheriff Rafter peered over his shoulder and together they watched four Cadillac Phaetons pull up in front of the jail.

* * *

The men in the sheriff's office were not the only ones watching the procession of black vehicles. Down the street, from an upstairs window of the Hobard Hotel, a lone figure watched as the four shadowy black Phaetons came to a halt. Donning his four-cornered black hat, he slipped out of his room and left the hotel.

Chapter 40

SERPENTE

~ ~ ~

Wilson stepped out of the sheriff's office and into the glare of the headlights from the four Cadillacs. Rafter and the Doc followed close behind. The shadowy vehicles sat idling ominously in the middle of the gloomy street.

Shading his eyes from their bright beams with his left hand, Rafter looked at Wilson. "Looks like he's here."

Wilson shook his head and rolled his eyes.

The lead car cut its engine and a second later the others did the same. A chilly, dead silence filled the night.

Wilson watched as the rear door of the lead automobile slowly opened. Dressed in a long black coat and a sleek ebony, wide-brimmed fedora hat, a shadowy figure stepped from the vehicle. He looked around then reached back into the Phaeton and pulled out a Thompson sub-machine gun. He gazed for a second at the weapon as he lovingly stroked its sleek shimmering barrel.

The Old Gun

* * *

For Silvio Serpente this particular weapon had become his constant companion over the last two or three months. He trusted few people and was not inclined to make friends; the Thompson was his new friend. In a shoulder holster under his coat, he also carried the newly-developed Browning 9mm Hi-Power semi-automatic pistol. This was his back-up. Killing was his profession and he enjoyed it.

Serpente had committed his first murder when he was twelve. An orphan, he'd made a living on the streets of Chicago, stealing money from men who came to the Rush Street area looking for loose women. Young Serpente often lurked in the shadows to watch. He learned quickly how to spot a John on the prowl. Choosing his prey, the innocent-looking boy lured them into the dim recesses of an alley with the promise of a liaison with his older sister. Then he'd pull out a thin, sharp stiletto and demand money.

Most men turned over their cash without a fight and went on their way without reporting the incident. Silvio knew the circumstances of the robbery were too embarrassing for the Johns to explain to the authorities.

The young thief's first murder took place when one of the victims had not taken the mugging seriously. Serpente had never forgotten the shocked look on the man's face when he'd plunged his stiletto into the fellow's chest. He also had not forgotten the thrill he felt when the blade had stuck for a second on one of the man's ribs before he gave a second shove and felt it slip past the rib and into the heart.

In time, killing for hire replaced robbery as his main source of income. For years the stiletto was like a cool silent companion. He liked the closeness that the blade afforded him in his work. The gun was efficient, but keenly-sharpened steel was more personal. He liked the way it felt when he slithered up on his unsuspecting victims, grabbed them from behind, and slipped the thin blade between their ribs. He never tired of the uncomprehending look in his victim's eyes as he lowered their limp bodies to the floor and waited for the cold, dead stare that he loved so much.

Many years later, Serpente's reputation came to the attention of the mobster, Johnny Torrio, who had moved from New York to Chicago. Torrio recruited the killer and placed him under the immediate control of his top lieutenant, Alphonse Capone. During this time Serpente switched his allegiance from the blade to the Thompson.

The weapon had recently become available to the public and Capone had purchased two of them. The price tag was excessive and the money Al spent on his two Thompsons could have paid for a new automobile. But, when Serpente saw what Al's weapons could do he immediately deemed the cost acceptable. He still had a soft spot for the blade, but he couldn't deny the terminal finality that the Thompson produced when he touched the trigger and made it roar.

At Al's bidding, Serpente and his men had traveled the long journey to Oklahoma City where he met with Brooks. The oilman explained the problem and assured Serpente that he would have an open hand to resolve the situation. The local law, he said, would not only stand aside for him, it would back him in his actions.

Overkill was the unspoken word that came to Serpente's mind when he learned from Brooks that the "situation" was an old rancher and maybe one or two others. *This could be too easy to be fun*, he thought as he left the office of S.C. Brooks.

Now, Serpente stood silently in the inky darkness of Hobard's Main Street. He lifted his head slightly and gazed from under his wide-brimmed fedora at the men who'd just come out of the sheriff's office. He assumed the thin man, armed with a revolver and sporting a bandaged arm, was Wilson.

With a voice that sounded like a hiss, Serpente spoke. "Brooks said you had a gang. Where are they?"

Wilson glanced over his shoulder at the doctor and said, "You're done here. Beat it."

For a second, Nordham stood gaping at the menacing dark figure silhouetted against the Phaeton headlights.

"I mean now!" Wilson barked.

Shaken from his trance, the doctor quickly shuffled down the street.

Serpente watched him leave and returned his attention to Wilson. He was not in the habit of repeating himself so he gazed into Wilson's eyes waiting for an answer.

"They're dead." Wilson returned the cold stare.

Serpente showed no emotion, nor did he ask any other questions. He made a gesture toward the

Phaetons sitting motionless on the street and the doors to the automobiles opened in unison.

Dressed in three-piece suits and armed with pistols and rifles, three men emerged from each Phaeton. The driver of Serpente's auto opened his door and stepped out. In all, there were ten well-armed men.

Serpente nodded toward the sheriff's office and led the way as Wilson and Rafter followed him through the office door.

Serpente's soldiers stood silent guard next to their vehicles.

Once in the office, Serpente settled himself in Rafter's chair. He gazed coolly at the two men before him. He judged Wilson to be an experienced and deadly killer and Rafter to be spineless and weak. He'd taken Rafter's seat to show the men who was in charge.

During Serpente's meeting with Brooks, he was told he could use Wilson and his men as extra hands when dealing with the situation. Now he was puzzled, but not unduly alarmed by the fact that Wilson's men were dead. He was curious how it had happened.

He looked Wilson in the eyes. "How?"

For a second, Wilson looked back at him with a blank stare. Finally, comprehension lit his face. "Oh, my men."

He then relayed the story of the ambush by a mob of ranchers in much the same way he'd told it to Rafter.

When Wilson finished his narrative, Serpente nodded his head. The story almost made sense. How else could Wilson have lost five good men and got himself shot. But Serpente was skilled at reading people. There was something missing; Wilson was not telling the complete truth.

"The other ranchers still with this man, Kidwell?" Serpente asked. He wasn't concerned about a few more shit-kickers. He just didn't want a body count that was too high.

"Only Kidwell and his family at his ranch," Wilson replied. "His brother, or friend, or whatever he is will probably be there too, but that's it."

Serpente turned to Rafter. "You'll come along, Sheriff. This should look like an arrest that went wrong."

Then he eased himself out of the chair and walked to the door. "Come or stay, Wilson. No matter to me." He didn't bother to look at Wilson as he spoke.

"This is unfinished business for me," Wilson said as he followed Serpente out the door.

A moment later the raven-black Phaetons drove away.

* * *

Hidden in the shadows of a nearby alley a tall lone figure watched the caravan melt into the dark night. He stood for a moment in thought then he made up his mind.

Chapter 41

UNWELCOME COMPANY

~ ~ ~

Harry Kidwell was running franticly down a railroad track. He could see a tunnel up ahead. Sweat soaked his shirt as he plunged into the darkness of the stone-carved entrance. It was difficult to see where he was going but he knew he had to keep running. Somewhere ahead his family was in trouble.

In darkness he raced on, stumbling from time-to-time on the railroad ties that were nearly impossible to see. His foot snagged on a rail spike that was not fully-seated in one of the ties. Hitting the ground hard, he rolled to a stop. There was a rustling sound and he sensed movement near him. A sizzling rattle told him it was a snake. Then came more movement, more rattles; snakes were all around him. He reached for his gun, but it wasn't there.

Fear gripped him, not so much for himself but for his family who needed him. He had to reach them. He screamed for help, but no sound escaped his lips. Then he heard his name being called. The voice was far away, a whisper like wind through fall leaves. He could hear footsteps heading his way, but they sounded hollow, like boots on wood.

"Sundance! We got company," Butch called in a flat whisper as he bounded up the steps to the second floor of the Kidwell house.

Harry opened his eyes. Sweat soaked the sheets around him. It took him a second to realize where he was. Etta sat up in the bed beside him.

Butch was gently knocking on their door. He spoke from the hall in a loud whisper. "You awake? We got company."

Harry sprang from the bed as Etta threw back the covers and climbed out on the other side. Harry looked out the bedroom window and saw a parade of headlights moving along the lane toward the house.

"I see 'em. Butch, go back down. We'll be right behind you. Etta, you better wake the kids."

Etta looked out the window over Harry's shoulder and then grabbed her clothes.

Harry was still buttoning his pants as he bounded down the stairs. His gun and holster were thrown over his shoulder. He entered the kitchen to find Butch, .45s in hand, gazing out a kitchen window. "Looks like four big black automobiles, Sundance."

Under his breath Harry cursed. At that instant, Etta entered the kitchen. Behind her were Lee and Laura. "I want you kids to go with your mother to the fruit cellar," Harry ordered as he gave Etta a nod.

"Come on, kids," Etta turned and began to herd them from the room.

Lee gently pushed his way back in. "If there's going to be trouble, Pa, I want to help."

Harry was in no mood for diplomacy. "You'll do as you're told!" he barked. When he saw the look on his son's face, he calmed a little. "I need you to stay with your sister, Son. I know you want to help but I can't be looking.... Just go with your mother."

Reluctantly, Lee turned, grabbed his sister's hand, and followed his mother to the pantry where the trap door led to the cellar.

Harry could hear his son protesting in the pantry as he helped his mother lift the cellar door. "Pa doesn't understand; I can help. I don't want to hide out."

Through the kitchen window, Harry watched the automobiles as they roared to a halt outside the house.

Butch ducked down and crawled to the window that was on the left side of the back door. Harry buckled on his gun belt and checked his Colt revolver. "I figured on another batch of 'em showin' up, but not so damn soon."

Sitting on the floor with his back to the wall, Butch ejected the clips of his 45s and checked to see that they were full before he slid them back in place. "I shoulda figured it," he said. "That Brooks is the kinda guy that would use a stick of dynamite to kill an ant. He probably hired these guys several days ago. That's how they got here so fast."

* * *

Sheriff Rafter had been relegated to the second vehicle when the procession of Cadillacs left Hobard. Wilson, on the other hand, had slipped into the front seat of Serpente's Phaeton next to the driver.

As the luxurious vehicle motored along, Wilson had time to ponder. That was when it snapped in his mind like a spark from dry flint. The man in Brooks' office, that's who he was. Kidwell's brother or friend or whatever was the stranger in Brooks' office. What the hell? Why had he been there? What was he doing here? It made no sense, but then it really didn't matter. He'd be dead before morning. Wilson put it from his mind.

* * *

With the Phaetons parked facing the Kidwell house, Wilson and Serpente exited the lead car while the sheriff climbed out of the second vehicle.

Serpente watched Rafter cautiously approach and motion him off to one side. "There's something I should tell you, Mr. Serpente."

The gangster's eyes reflected impatience and he almost dismissed the man, but intuition told him this might have something to do with what Wilson had left out of his story. Serpente nodded for the sheriff to speak his piece.

Rafter glanced at Wilson and stepped closer to Serpente keeping his voice low. "There's something ain't right about this Kidwell, him and his friend. Wilson had two run-ins with him. Had half-dozen men each time and was bested each time. Wilson'll tell you it was luck or some other excuse, but there's something ain't right here."

"Anything else?"

"No, guess not. Just thought ..."

"He got a gang o' some kind in there with him?"

"My guess, just him, his friend, and his family." With a slight tremor Rafter, added, "Won't be easy to explain if the kids and woman get killed."

"Go back there and keep outa the way for now," Serpente whispered through his teeth.

When Rafter retreated behind the vehicles, Serpente reflected on what he'd said. So, the rancher was a tough old bird. That was good to know. It might make this a bit more fun.

Wilson had strolled over in time to hear Rafter's caution about killing the whole family.

"This old man and his friend are going to die tonight." Wilson spoke to Serpente but glared after Rafter's retreating form. "And if anyone gets in the way they'll be dead, too."

Serpente went to his Phaeton and retrieved his Thompson from the back seat. He slapped a 100-round drum in place and racked the slide. Then he motioned to his men.

In unison the killers exited their vehicles and positioned themselves between the headlights of each Phaeton facing the house.

* * *

Harry had watched as the vehicles formed a semicircle facing them. Their headlamps lit the porch like a Broadway stage. A few seconds later, doors to the lead auto opened and two men stepped into the light of the waning moon. A rear door of the second auto opened and someone else climbed out.

Glare from the headlamps made it difficult to make out anything but outlines of men. Still, Harry recognized Wilson by his thin frame and swaggering walk.

"I think I can make out that sheriff fellow," Butch whispered.

"And I see Wilson," Harry whispered back. "Don't recognize the other, but no surprise there. Seems to be some kinda parlay goin' on."

The creaking of the trapdoor to the storm cellar caught Harry's attention. He turned from the window and saw Etta enter the kitchen.

Butch's attention was focused on the men outside. "Look out! It's startin'!"

Harry sensed it, too; a strange millisecond of silence that always came before the first shot. "Get down, Etta!"

Etta dove to the floor as the windows exploded and a deafening roar erupted. Wood splinters and flying plaster filled the air around them. Bullets punched holes in the walls and shattered dishes and splintered furniture. All three hugged the floor as they waited for the barrage to subside.

"How the hell many are there, Butch?" Harry shouted over the din.

"Figured ten, maybe twelve of 'em, Kid."

The barrage continued. "Gotta be more than twelve," Harry said as he tried to look through the broken window. "Seems more like an army."

Butch snuck a glance. "One of 'em has a 'chopper'."

"A what?"

"A 'chopper', a machine gun. Where you been, Kid?"

"I've been right here on this damn ranch! I guess I haven't been keepin' pace with all the new-fangled killin' machines!"

In the middle of his last sentence the gunfire abated, leaving Harry's shouted words echoing in the dust-filled kitchen.

Etta crawled back toward the door to the hallway.

"Where you going?" Harry asked.

"Upstairs, to get Clarence's gun."

"Maybe best if you went back to the ..."

"Not a chance," Etta shot back.

When she was gone, Harry turned to Butch. "I want to draw them away from the house...and them," he said, nodding in the direction of Etta and the kids.

Butch nodded. "The barn?"

"Our best chance."

A moment later, Etta slipped back into the kitchen, carrying Clarence's revolver. Keeping low, she joined Harry.

Outside, several of the killers started to move cautiously toward the house. The glare from the headlamps made it hard to see, but Butch and Harry sensed them coming and fired off a few rounds. One man went down, a bullet in his chest. A second man spun and fell with a flesh wound to the leg. Crawling, he pulled back with the others as they retreated.

* * *

Serpente was surprised when gunfire erupted from the bullet-riddled house. With as much firepower as they'd directed into the place, he felt sure anyone still alive would be cowering behind the perforated walls. Instead, they'd fired back and accurately enough to hit two of his men. He turned to look at Wilson. "Those hay-rakers know how to shoot."

Rafter came out from behind the autos and took a couple of steps closer to Serpent. "It's like I said. There's something ain't right about these two old guys."

Wilson was reloading his Smith & Wesson. "Shut the hell up, Rafter. Kidwell's just a farmer; I checked him out."

"Somebody in there can handle a gun," Serpente said. He nodded at his men and they opened up with a second barrage.

* * *

Inside the house, the trio glued themselves to the floor once again as the walls splintered and white plaster rained down.

"We get a break in this, we'll shoot out their lamps," Harry yelled in Etta's ear. "Then Butch and I are going to dash for the barn." Just as he finished shouting the gunfire subsided again.

Harry saw a flash of fear from Etta when he said they were going to try to make it to the barn. He gazed into her eyes. "It'll be fine. You shoot the two lamps on the auto to the right, Butch can take the two to the left and I'll get the four in the middle. And, Etta, after we break for the barn, I don't want you to shoot anymore."

"But ... Harry ..."

"When we run for the barn, I want you to join the kids in the cellar." Nodding toward the killers outside, he added. "They should leave you alone. They'll be busy after us."

Tears began to well up in Etta's eyes; she looked away. Harry understood the conflict going on inside her. After a moment her motherly instincts won out and she nodded.

Harry lifted her chin and kissed her cheek. "We're gonna be fine, Etta. Once we reach the barn we'll have a good chance."

* * *

Etta had seen the firepower that the men outside possessed. There was little chance that Harry and Butch would make it to the barn, but she knew the killers needed to be drawn away from the house and the kids. Cocking her gun, Etta peered through the kitchen window. There was movement behind the shining lights but she couldn't quite make out the forms. Etta swallowed her concern for Harry and Butch and tried to focus on the job at hand.

* * *

After Serpente ordered a halt to the gunfire, he directed his attention to the house. With two of his men shot, he knew he needed to be cautious. That was when he got another surprise.

In less than two seconds, eight shots rang out accompanied by muzzle flashes from the windows of the house. Glass shattered as the automobile lamps were blasted into darkness. Serpente's men as well as Rafter and Wilson dove for cover.

The Old Gun

Serpente stood looking at the ruined lamps on his four Cadillacs. In the still aftermath, Wilson, Rafter and the others slowly rose from the ground.

Serpente turned to gaze at the house. It had been plunged into darkness. "Those guys aren't simple farmers. Who the hell are they?"

Rafter peered out from behind one of the Phaetons. "That's what I been tryin' to tell ya."

* * *

Harry reloaded his Colt before looking once again into Etta's eyes. He gave her a kiss. She hugged him back as if she'd never let go. After a few seconds, Harry gently pushed her away. "We have to go. We need the dark and dawn is coming. Harry turned to Butch. "Ready?"

Butch nodded. "Let's dance."

Chapter 42

THE LAST DANCE

~ ~ ~

The door to the Kidwell house burst open. Serpente was disengaging the empty 100-round drum from his Thompson when he saw two shadowy figures dart from the house. "Get them!" he yelled to his men as he dove for the back seat of his Phaeton and a replacement drum of ammo.

* * *

Sundance and Butch sprinted along the porch and jumped the rail on the left side. When he hit the ground, Sundance fanned off a couple of shots in the direction of the killers. At the same time, Butch began firing both his .45s.

There was confusion in Serpente's ranks. A couple of valuable seconds passed before Wilson started firing at the fleeing quarry. Then the others opened up.

At first Sundance and Butch were shooting blind. But when the killers began to fire, their muzzle flashes became targets. Racing through the backyard, the aging duo aimed at the flashes. Two of the killers cried out in pain. Both were mortally wounded.

Sundance and Butch sprinted all-out for the barn door while bullets buzzed past them like angry bees.

Butch was trailing Sundance when he was hit. The bullet plowed a clean path through his left thigh. He went down and skidded to a stop in the damp grass. A millisecond later he cried out from the pain. His former wound at the Jackson ranch was a pinprick compared to the pain he was experiencing now. Nonetheless, as he lay on his back, he kept firing with both automatics.

Ahead of him he heard Sundance skid to a halt.

"Keep goin' Kid!" he yelled over the gunfire.

But, seconds later, Sundance was at his side.

* * *

The beating of Etta's heart pounded franticly inside her chest. She'd watched from the house as Butch and Harry sprinted for the barn. The roar of gunfire broke out and the earth exploded all around them.

When Butch went down she froze. Then, when he kept firing from the ground, she let out a quiet sigh.

Seeing Harry turn toward Butch and slide to a stop, she sucked in her breath. "No, no, no. Don't stop, keep running, Harry!" Panic clutched at her throat as she watched Harry go to Butch's aid.

Bullets buzzed past them and plowed into the ground around them as Sundance struggled to pull Butch to his feet. Etta watched as Butch put his weight on Sundance's shoulder. With the damaged leg dragging through the damp grass, the two stumbled toward safety.

* * *

Butch's defensive fire from his Colt automatics had helped to keep the killers from shooting accurately. Now, neither he nor Sundance could fire as they stumbled toward the barn.

More shots rang out. Sundance let out a gasp as both men tumbled to the ground.

With bullets still buzzing around them, they struggled to their feet again. In the early dawn light, Butch's eyes zeroed in on one of the shooters. The man was taking careful aim and Butch knew he was about to be shot again.

At that instant, a crimson mist exploded from the gunman's head and he fell like a dropped marionette.

This inexplicable death of one of their gang seemed to cause momentary confusion among the killers. This gave Butch and Sundance a second of respite. Together they stumbled for safety. Reaching the barn, they dove through the open door. Once inside, the two crumpled to the floor and out of the line of fire.

Butch still wasn't sure why they'd both fallen while struggling toward the barn. At the time, he surmised they'd just stumbled. As Sundance gingerly adjusted himself on the floor, Butch began to suspect that he wasn't the only one who got wounded. "You hit, Kid?"

The answer came a little too curt. "I'm all right." Then, with less rancor, "How's your leg?"

"Horse flies bite worse." Butch had to grit his teeth to keep from letting the pain show.

Once again Sundance shifted his position to get the weight off his wounded buttock and Butch noticed the grimace as he moved. Then, he saw the bloodstain on the rear of his friend's trousers. "Looks to me like you were hit." A smile touched his lips as he realized Sundance had taken one in the buttock. "You sure you're all right?"

"I told you ... I'm all right!" Sundance barked.

Butch leaned forward so that he could more clearly see the location of Sundance's wound and began to chuckle.

"It jist grazed me, but still, it ain't funny, Butch."

Still trying to suppress his amusement, Butch cautiously crawled to the barn door. He peered out toward the killers. "Get any kinda head count on 'em?"

"Best guess is around a dozen," Sundance said through clenched teeth.

"My guess too. Got at least one before we broke. Then got three more on the run."

Sundance looked puzzled. "Three?"

"Yeah, the one you shot, the one I shot, and the one Etta musta shot."

"Etta? Etta wouldn't a done any shootin' once we left the house. She's got the kids to think about. Besides, I told her not to."

Butch peered into the predawn gloom. "Then who the hell shot him? I saw his head get practically blown off." He looked back at Sundance. "Now that you mention it, it would be damn near impossible for

Etta get off a clean shot from the house in the dark with that old pistol."

"Like I said, wasn't Etta." Harry shifted so he could extract fresh cartridges from his gun belt. He winced from the pain as he reloaded his revolver.

Butch strained his neck to get a better look outside. The early morning sun was beginning to peek over the horizon. As he surveyed the scene, he caught a fleeting glimpse of a shadowy figure moving along the side of the ranch house.

Gunfire blasted up dirt and splintered wood near Butch's face. He jerked his head back. As the dust settled, he gave a puzzled look in Sundance's direction.

Sundance saw the look. "What?"

"Can't be ... " Butch tried to get a look again, but more gunfire forced him back before he could get even a glance outside.

"What did you see, Butch?"

Butch shook his head as if to clear an impossible picture out of his mind. He tried again to look outside but once again was driven back. He looked at Sundance, who was still gazing at him expecting an answer.

"What ever happened to Samuel Stillman?" Butch asked.

* * *

Etta was watching through the window when Butch and Harry fell for the second time during their dash to the barn. That was when she heard a shot ring out from near the house and saw one of the killers go down. She also noticed the confusion among the rest of the gunmen. That was when she realized that Harry and Butch were going to make it.

She was able to breathe again. But, who had fired that fatal shot? Etta moved to the other window to get a better look, but could see nothing. She went into the sitting room and looked out the window there. Again there was no one. Soon, realizing that no more time could be wasted, Etta headed back to the storm cellar and her kids.

Slipping noiselessly into the pantry, she eased up the trap door and descended the wooden steps, quietly closing the door behind her. Lee and Laura were waiting anxiously in the dim glow of a single lantern.

Laura thrust herself into Etta's arms. "Ma!" she cried in a soft, frightened voice. Etta set Clarence's revolver on a fruit shelf so she could hold her daughter close and brush away the tears.

Lee put his hand on his mother's shoulder. "What's happening, Ma?" Where's Pa? They all right?"

Etta gently covered Lee's hand with hers. She gazed into his eyes. "They're all right. They made it to the barn." She smiled encouragingly. "They're going to hold up there."

Just as she finished speaking a new volley of gunfire broke out. Laura clutched her mother even tighter. All three listened, their eyes drifting to the floor above and, in their mind's eye, to the barnyard beyond.

* * *

Serpente wasn't sure where the last shot had come from that had killed one of his men. But he realized that, with the morning sun easing up, he needed to get his men better deployed and under cover.

He was surprised and more than a little aggravated that four of his men were already dead and another had been wounded in the leg.

He stopped firing and his men did the same. His drum was near empty anyway, so he retrieved two more from his vehicle.

During the reprieve, he decided his best option was to flush out his quarry. To this end, he sent two of his killers around to the back of the barn. The remaining four of his able-bodied gangsters, plus the one with the leg wound, he stationed in positions around the front of the building. He gave them instructions to shoot at anything that came out the door. For the present, he left Rafter and Wilson to their own devices.

Rafter was cowering behind the autos while Wilson stood in the open near Serpente's Phaeton, firing periodically into the open barn door.

When Serpente estimated that the two men he'd sent to the back of the barn were in position, he ordered the men stationed in front to open fire again.

With bullets blazing at the front of the barn, the two Chicago gangsters slipped quietly in through the back door. Moving low and quiet, they made their way toward where Butch and Sundance were holed up.

* * *

Sundance looked at Butch with bewilderment. "Stillman? He must be dead by now. Why?"

Butch glanced out the barn door and then back at Sundance. The look was unmistakable.

"You gotta be kiddin', Butch. There's no way. No, no. It doesn't make sense. What the hell makes you think it's him?"

"For one thing, the hat. That damn hat."

"Lots of guys have hats like that."

"Name one."

Sundance could only stare at his friend.

Butch raised his eyebrows. After a few seconds he looked at his two automatics. "Empty. I left a box of .45s in the tack room. Guess I best get it."

Sundance was about to say something when a new barrage of gunfire broke out. At the same instant, he saw movement in one of the stalls. Shots rang out from inside the barn. A hole opened up in the wall next to his head and a bullet plowed into a post next to Butch. With both his guns empty, Butch was helpless. More bullets hit the dirt next to him.

Sundance spotted the two men slinking low in the horse stalls and rapidly fanned off four shots. One gangster got off a final shot that sliced a piece of flesh out of Sundance's shoulder above the collarbone.

The Kid's bullets hit their mark. Both men stumbled forward. One had two wounds in his chest; the other had taken one bullet to the neck and one to the head. They flopped down to lay lifeless in the straw and dung of the horse stalls.

"You all right?" Butch asked.

"Would you quit asking me that!" Sundance barked. He gingerly touched the wound to his shoulder. "Of course I'm not all right. I'm shot again."

"You didn't used to be this irritable when you got shot."

"What the hell would Stillman be doing here?"

Butch ignored the question and crawled to the tack room where he retrieved his box of .45 cartridges and crawled back.

Sundance glared at Butch as he sat loading his clips. "Why would you bring up Stillman at a time like this, Butch? Aren't we in a big enough jam? You gotta bring him into it?"

"I didn't say I was sure it was him. Look, just forget it."

Before either could say more, a new volley of gunfire erupted. Evidently, the men outside had surmised that the two men they'd sent to flush Butch and Sundance out had been less than successful in their venture. That was when the Thompson cut loose again.

The entrance of the barn had a sliding door. In the open position, it combined with the barn wall to make a double thickness of wood, giving added protection to Butch and Sundance. With the new eruption of the Thompson, that protection started to weaken as splitters began to fly.

"That damn thing ain't natural. There's no skill or honor using a gun like that." Sundance complained.

Crawling on hands and knees, he and Butch retreated into the dark interior of the barn.

* * *

Serpente was furious. Who the hell were these guys? In frustration, he'd let loose with his Thompson and sprayed the barn in anger. Al had sent him down here with a team of ten soldiers to take care of a small problem for an old friend. This was supposed to be a piece of cake.

In less than an hour, six of the soldiers were dead. Now he was left with four plus Wilson and Rafter. Serpente surveyed the situation. He considered Wilson proficient and obviously a professional killer. But Rafter was another matter. He'd been brought along to make the killings seem legit, but Serpente had no illusion about Rafter's usefulness beyond that. He motioned for Wilson and Rafter to join him.

Wilson fired two shots at the barn. Then moving in a crouch, he covered the distance to reach Serpente's side. "What now?" he whispered.

Serpente looked at him like a snake about to strike. "I ain't no Wyatt fuckin' Earp. This ain't my kinda fight."

"We could come at 'em from all sides," Wilson suggested.

Serpente studied on the proposal before he nodded, more to himself than to Wilson. He beckoned to Rafter again.

The sheriff cowered behind Serpente's parked Phaeton. He stared wide-eyed at the dead bodies of Serpente's men. Then he looked nervously at the door to the barn.

Serpente called out once again.

Rafter stared at Serpente and once again looked anxiously at the barn door. Finally, he bolted from behind the automobile and scampered across the barnyard to the gangster's side.

Serpente glared at Rafter for a moment before turning his attention to Wilson. "You know where the windows to the barn are?" he asked

"You can see the one on this side. There's another behind the bunk house on the other side."

Serpente nodded. "I'm going to have one of my men go through this window and two of my men go around to the window behind the bunk house." Lovingly, he stroked his Thompson. "I'll take this and one man to the back entrance."

He gave the orders, instructing his men to take only their handguns. Slipping through the small windows with long guns would likely cause more noise than desired. Besides, handguns would be more useful in close quarters.

Turning his attention back to Rafter and Wilson, Serpente said, "I want you two to fire into the barn from the front."

Rafter shook his head and looked at the ground. Timidly, he mumbled, "Not sure I should be takin' part in ..." He stopped in mid-sentence and froze as he glanced up to see the threat in Serpente's eyes.

Wilson waived his revolver in Rafter's direction. "Don't worry. He'll do as you say."

Serpente continued to stare coldly at the sheriff. Finally, his eyes shifted to Wilson. "I need a distraction. I want them to think we are all still out front." he hissed.

"We can do that," Wilson whispered.

Chapter 43

AN OLD NEMESIS

~ ~ ~

Hidden from view among the bushes near the house, a lone figure watched as Serpente's men dispersed to their assigned positions.

Earlier that night, from his hotel room, Samuel Stillman had seen the gangsters arrive in Hobard. It hadn't taken a genius to realize why they were there. A few minutes later, from a dark alley, he watched as the parade of Phaetons drove out of town. Retrieving his automobile, he followed them, keeping at a distance.

Stillman heard the barrage of gunfire before he actually reached the Kidwell ranch. Parking his vehicle some distance away, he grabbed his Winchester and approached on foot.

When he arrived at the ranch, two men from inside the house were making a break for the barn. It was obvious to the old lawman that these two were the victims of a vicious attack. As such, he felt compelled to help them.

During the confusion of the break, with the two victims wounded on the ground, he saw that one of the killers was taking a deadly bead on them, so he took aim himself and killed the shooter.

After that, he was forced to lay low. To fire again would give away his position.

He watched as two gangsters were sent to the back and he heard the gunfire when they were presumably killed. Waiting to see what tactic the gangsters would use next, he didn't have to wait long.

Hidden in the brush near the house, Stillman desperately looked around for some means to aid the trapped men inside the barn. It was obvious they were about to be rushed from all sides. They needed to be warned. His eyes alighted on the Kidwell truck parked on the west side of the house.

* * *

Lee huddled together with his mother and sister in the cool, damp fruit cellar, listening to the cracks of gunfire outside. He could hear the distant roar of the Thompson. Images came to him of that day not so long ago when he'd accused his father of being a coward. He felt ashamed and sick to his stomach.

"I gotta go help him, Ma. Pa needs me," Lee pleaded.

"Your pa wants you to stay here. They don't want your help, Lee."

"But I gotta! I gotta tell him, Ma!"

In the dim light Lee could see the question in his mother's eyes. "Tell him what?" she asked.

"That I was dead wrong. I know who he is now, who they both are. I gotta help 'em and tell Pa that I understand now."

"Your Pa realizes that, Son. You need to stay here. You can't be of any help to them."

Lee wasn't listening. He'd spotted Clarence's gun sitting on the shelf and grabbed it. Bolting up the stairs, he heard his mother shriek his name as he pushed back the trapdoor and vaulted into the pantry room. Lee could hear her scrabbling after him, so he slammed the trapdoor and threw the wooden latch that locked it shut.

With his mother pounding on the door beneath his feet, he called down to her, "I have to help him."

Listening to the gunfire outside, Lee cautiously made his way through the house. Entering the kitchen, he stood paralyzed. Early morning sunbeams pushed though hundreds of holes in the perforated walls. Plaster and broken glass were everywhere; even the furniture was splintered and nearly destroyed. How had anyone lived through this?

He was shaken from his daze when the gunfire outside suddenly ceased. Coming from the barnyard, a male voice was calling his father's name.

* * *

In the barn, Butch was sitting on the floor tying an old rag around his leg to stop the bleeding. Harry was reloading when he heard the firing stop and Wilson call out.

"Give it up, Harry! You and your friend come on out! You won't be shot!"

Butch looked incredulously at Sundance. "Now that's brass," he said with a shake of the head. "Come on in *here*, Wilson!" he yelled back. "We won't shoot you much either!"

Wilson answered with his Smith & Wesson and Rafter finally began to fire his revolver, as well. Seeking better cover, Sundance and Butch moved to the corner of the granary where they crawled to the left and settled with their backs to the granary wall.

* * *

On the west side of the barn, one of the gangsters quietly crawled through the window. When he looked around, he found himself inside the tack room.

At the back, Serpente, carrying his Thompson and accompanied by the wounded gangster, slipped through the door and moved quietly into the barn. He motioned for his companion to separate from him and work his way along the stalls while he crept into the implement section of the barn. Like a snake he weaved his way among the harrow, plow, and farm implements.

* * *

At the same time, the two gangsters behind the bunkhouse helped each other to slip quietly through the east window of the barn. The gunfire coming from the front covered what little noise they made as they alighted on the straw-covered dirt floor.

Not far from the window one gangster saw a ladder leading to the loft. Quietly he climbed the rungs, one cautious step at a time. When he reached the loft, he crawled along the floor. There were small quarter-inch cracks between the boards and he could just make out the layout below.

As he moved silently along the floor, he constantly peered through the spaces searching for his quarry. Through the cracks he spied a portion of a man's bloody leg right below. He brought his gun to the crack but decided he needed a better shot. Two boards over should give him a head or chest shot. With a smile, he made the adjustment. He could hear the old men whispering below. *This will be easy*, he thought as he peered down once again. But this would be last thing he ever saw.

* * *

Sundance was in pain. Given the nature of his wounds, he found almost any position to be agonizing. Sitting was out of the question. Butch sat with his back against the granary wall, while Sundance crouched by his side. He and Butch suspected that the full strength of the killers was not reflected in the gunfire from outside, so their senses were on the alert.

Butch gave Sundance a nudge and nodded toward the loft floor above their head. Gazing up, Sundance saw a single chaff of hay float down from a crack in the floor of the haymow.

Butch nodded at the chaff. In a whisper he asked, "You got a cat?"

Sundance watched the chaff swirling in the air and shook his head. "Had one. Died last year." Both men looked up and concentrated on the cracks until they saw another bit of chaff float down.

Sundance and Butch fired at the same time. Five holes were punched through the loft floor causing a muffled thump and blood to ooze from between the cracks.

On his left, Sundance sensed movement and turned his head to face the tack room. The gangster appeared in the doorway. Sundance fanned off two shots and dove to his right. Remarkably, his bullets missed their mark and the killer in the tack room pulled back out of sight.

At the same instant, Serpente opened up with his Thompson.

Butch dove to the left, separating himself from Sundance. Bullets flew in all directions as the two former outlaws returned fire.

Over the din of the gunfire, the roar of a racing vehicle reached the men in the barn. With headlamps glaring, the Kidwell's truck burst through the barn door thundering past Sundance and Butch.

In the dimly lit interior, the truck's lights illuminated the gangster who'd accompanied Serpente into the barn. For a second, Serpente was also spotlighted, but he quickly dove out of the glare. The other gangster wasn't so lucky. Unable to move with dexterity because of his wounded leg, he took the full force of the Model T. It plowed into him and threw his body ten feet toward the back of the barn. The man was dead before he hit the floor.

The Ford slammed to a stop when it collided with a twelve-inch support post. Dust and debris rained down from above as the whole barn shook from the impact. The engine of the Model T shuddered, rumbled, and died.

The Old Gun

Sundance stared in disbelief at his Model T as a dust cloud settled around the battered vehicle. This shocking apparition had momentarily dumbfounded him, but his gunfighter instincts helped him to keep his focus on Serpente.

As the gangster dove out of the light, Sundance fanned off two shots. One missed, but the other hit Serpente's Thompson and slammed the weapon against the gangster's chest. The impact caused him to fall backward, where he rolled to a stop among the farm implements.

With dust and chaff still hanging in the air, the gangster hiding in the tack room once again started to fire. Another, who had taken cover behind a large wooden barrel to Butch's left, began to fire, as well.

As the truck shuddered one last time, the driver's door burst open and Samuel Stillman rolled away from the vehicle. Revolver in hand and with bullets blasting up dirt and straw around him, he crawled toward Sundance. Still crawling, he fired at the gunman in the tack room, causing that man to duck back out of sight.

If Sundance had been shocked by the appearance of his Model T Ford charging into the barn and slamming into one of his enemies, the sight of his old nemesis crawling toward him with a gun in his hand was stupefying. Sundance kept his weapon trained on the old adversary. Instinct told him to shoot. Common sense told him otherwise. Against all logic, it appeared that the old marshal was there to help.

With Sundance's .45 pointed at him, the lawman nodded and smiled. "Sundance, hope you don't mind my droppin' in," he said with a deadpan look.

Harry pointed his gun away from Stillman long enough to fire a shot at the gunman to his left. "Samuel." He nodded at the old lawman. "Thought you were dead."

"Reckon I could say the same about you and Butch, there."

After a pause Sundance replied, "That was the idea, Samuel."

Butch fired several times at the gangster behind the barrel. The shots made the man pull back. In the brief respite, Butch called over to Sundance and Stillman. "Hate to break up the heart-warming reunion, but this ain't the best time to reminisce. Not that I ain't glad to see you, Samuel."

Butch fired in the direction of the implement section. "The one with the Thompson seems to be movin' around in there, Sundance."

* * *

When Serpente regained his composure he realized that his favorite weapon would never roar again. The damn farmer's bullet had slammed into the firing mechanism, rendering it useless. Cursing it to damnation, he tossed the shattered weapon aside and drew his Browning automatic. As he staggered to his feet, Butch fired in his direction. Bullets whizzed past his head and he squeezed off several shots before diving for cover behind a manure spreader. One of his bullets hit Butch in the right side below the rib cage.

Cautiously, Serpente began to worm forward. He was looking for a clear view of the rancher who'd destroyed his precious Thompson. The obstacles between them protected Serpente from gunfire but also impeded his ability to get a clear shot at the old shit-kicker.

* * *

Sundance saw the gangster behind the barrel reappear and take aim. With Butch nearly incapacitated from his wounds, Stillman sprang into action. Firing his revolver, he dove over Butch, landing between Butch and the killer. A bullet hit Stillman in the right shoulder, knocking him backward where he fell on top of his old adversary.

Butch let out a grunt, but managed to slowly raise his right hand and fire. The gangster behind the barrel took the bullet square in the chest and fell dead.

Sundance was trying to get a glimpse of the man with the Thompson in the implement section when bullets kicked up dirt and straw near his right leg. The gunman in the tack room was firing again.

It was becoming increasingly difficult for Sundance to use his right hand. The wound to his shoulder was causing the muscles to tighten. Nonetheless, he whirled and fanned off a shot that hit the man in the stomach. Screaming in pain, the wounded gangster fell back into the tack room.

Butch was unable to rise and Samuel seemed to have lost the use of his gun arm. Realizing it was up to him to get the man hidden amidst the farm implements, Sundance fell to his stomach and crawled forward. Searching, he saw nothing. Then a wicked smile touched his lips. He was looking at the shiny plow blade that he'd personally cleaned to a mirror surface when he'd put it away at the end of the spring season. He could now see a dark figure reflected in the blade.

Sundance eased himself up until he was in a crouch and then fanned off three shots at the plow blade. Sparks flew. The sound of the bullets ricocheting off the blade echoed through the barn.

A scream was followed by a muffled curse. Serpente lurched up and stumbled forward. Blood flowed from the wounds in his chest. He tried to raise his gun hand, but his muscles wouldn't obey.

* * *

Serpente had seen the sparks from the bullets as they hit the plow blades a fraction of a second before he felt the slugs ricochet into his chest. A look of shock froze on his face. This wasn't happening. Never in his life had he experienced even a flesh wound. He staggered and his vision began to blur. The realization that he was dying began to sink in. A goddamn shit-kicker from Okla-fuckin'-homa. How could that be? These were his last thoughts before his world went black and he fell — face-down in the manure and straw that were waiting for him on the floor of the Kidwell barn.

* * *

Sundance watched the dust billow up around the well-dressed gangster as he thumped to the floor. The morning sun shining through the cracks and holes in the barn walls cast eerie beams of light across the settling dust. Everything was silent except for the moaning of the wounded killer in the tack room.

Sundance crawled over to Butch and Samuel. "How bad, Butch?" He lightly touched the wound in his friend's side.

"I'll live." Butch gritted his teeth as he breathed out the words.

Sundance looked at Stillman. "Samuel?"

"Won't be shootin' no more today with this arm, but could be worse."

Then a shout was heard from outside.

"Harry! Come on out ... or I'll kill your boy!"

Chapter 44

HELP ON THE WAY

~ ~ ~

When Lee stepped through the back door and onto the porch of the Kidwell house, his father's Model T Ford truck was speeding toward the barn. There was gunfire and flashes inside the barn and, out front, two men were firing indiscriminately at the open door.

With the truck bearing down on them, the two men in front of the barn dove out of the way. The Model T sped past them through the open door. A second later, there was a crash and the barn shook as the vehicle slammed into an interior support post.

The two men in front of the barn were still lying on the ground when Lee jumped from the porch. With gun in hand, he quickly closed the distance between himself and the closest gunman. The man was on his knees and dusting himself off when Lee came to a halt and loomed over him. "Drop your gun!" he demanded.

Sheriff Rafter looked up with surprise. A gun was pointed at his face. When he saw the boy who was holding it, he smiled. "Put the gun down boy. You're aiming at an officer of the law."

For a second Lee was confounded. He'd thought all of the killers were just that: hired killers. He was unaware that the sheriff was one of them. What was he to do? He was prepared to fight the men threatening his father, but how could he go against the law?

It was during that second of hesitation that Ratt Wilson, still on his knees, took aim and fired.

Lee felt the sting just a fraction of a second before he heard the shot that hit him. The bullet grazed his hand between the thumb and forefinger as it ricocheted off the butt of the gun. He let out a yelp and the weapon flew from his grasp.

Wilson smiled and stepped forward to claim his prize.

* * *

Alva had wakened to the sound of gunfire in the far distance. He wasn't sure at first if it was real or part of a dream. Sitting up in bed, he listened to the still, quiet night. Then it began again. He dressed quickly and ran downstairs. From his back porch he could hear the gunfire more clearly and he determined it was coming from the direction of the Kidwell ranch.

A short time later he was galloping his large roan gelding for Austin's place.

Austin was eating breakfast when Alva reined his horse to a stop behind his house.

"Hello in the house! Austin, I think Harry's in trouble!" Alva yelled.

A few seconds later, still buckling his gun belt and chomping on bacon, Austin burst through the back door. It took him less than two minutes to saddle his horse. He mounted up and the two men rode toward Slim's ranch.

When Alva and Austin thundered into Slim's yard, the thin young rancher threw open his back door and ran outside. He only needed to hear the words, "Gun shots at Harry's" and he sprang into action. Soon the three were thundering at a full gallop for the Kidwell ranch.

* * *

Etta charged after Lee when he ran from the cellar. She screamed at him as she bounded up the steps. When the trap door slammed down she pounded on its underside with her fists. She heard Lee slide the wooden latch and tried to lift the door; it wouldn't budge.

Laura clambered up the steps and stood next to her mother. She lent her weight to the effort and the two pushed on the trap door with all their strength.

"What's holding it, Ma? Is Lee standing on it?"

"It's the latch. Use your back, Honey."

Etta turned around on the steps and put her back against the door. Laura did the same. Together they began to push. With legs straining and backs throbbing, the latch stared to splinter and the door started to move. Finally, with a snap, the latch gave way and the door flew open.

Cautiously Etta peered out before she climbed the last few steps. Behind her, Laura's head rose from the cellar. Etta put out her hand to hold her back. "I know you want to come, but I need you to stay in the cellar. I need you to be brave."

Laura hesitated but then she seemed to understand. She nodded and climbed back down the steps.

Etta closed the trap door and made her way through the house and into the kitchen. The gunfire outside had stopped. Peering through the shattered window, she sucked in her breath at the sight that met her eyes. Lee was standing next to Wilson. The killer's gun was cocked and held next to her son's right ear.

She searched the room for a weapon and saw a butcher knife on the floor among debris. Picking it up, she quietly made her way outside.

At the foot of the steps, she saw her garden hoe leaning against the porch. She'd been using it just the day before to weed her vegetable garden. Etta dropped the knife and hefted the hoe. With a set jaw, she headed for the man holding her son.

* * *

"I mean it, Harry. I'll put one right in his ear!" Wilson yelled.

Harry peered around the corner of the granary and through the open door of the barn. He could see Wilson standing beside his son with a cocked gun held to the boy's ear. On Lee's other side stood Rafter. His gun, too, was drawn and pointed at the boy.

Sundance knew the danger. When a man got shot while holding a cocked gun, his reflex often caused the weapon to discharge even as he died.

The Old Gun

Killing Wilson from the barn was not the answer. Slowly, Harry struggled to his feet.

Butch saw him get up. "No, you can't go out there."

It was Harry the father, not the Sundance Kid, who looked back at Butch. He smiled at his friend lying wounded on the barn floor before he limped to the door.

Butch tried to get up but fell back.

Stillman managed to rise on wobbly legs. Then, leaning over, he helped his old enemy struggle to his feet.

Standing just inside the barn door, Harry held his Colt at his side and glared at the two men holding his son.

"Drop the gun, Harry!" Wilson commanded.

Harry stepped outside. Behind him, Butch clutched his two Colts as he and Samuel stumbled toward the door.

Wilson squinted at Harry with cold, angry eyes. "I won't ask a ..."

Something moved behind Wilson. He turned to the sound of rapid footsteps.

Harry heard them, too, and looked beyond the men holding his son. Etta was charging with a hoe held high above her head.

Wilson turned in her direction. Removing his gun from Lee's head, he tried to take aim at the crazed mother.

Etta let out a scream of rage as she closed the distance. Rafter saw her and also turned his gun toward the charging woman.

When Wilson's gun was nowhere near his ear, Lee twisted away from the killer's grasp and dove to the ground.

Harry lifted his Colt and fanned off two shots. The first hit Wilson in the shoulder, spinning him around facing Harry. The second bullet hit him square in the chest.

Sheriff Rafter saw Wilson take the two bullets and turned back toward Harry. Mortal fear clouded his face as he began to drop his gun. He never finished the task. Harry fanned off a third shot that hit him in the forehead. Mortally wounded, the sheriff stumbled backward and his gun discharged. The un-aimed bullet found its way to the center of Harry's chest.

* * *

Butch, with Stillman's help, reached the barn door as Harry crumpled to the dirt. He saw Etta throw aside her hoe and run screaming to her fallen husband. When Lee got to his feet, he looked toward his father lying on the ground with his mother kneeling over him. He rushed to them and fell to his knees by their side.

"Pa!" Lee cried out as the tears started to flow.

"Harry! Harry!" Etta lifted her husband's head and placed it in her lap.

Stillman and Butch stumbled from the barn. The old lawman helped Butch to reach his fallen comrade and eased him to the ground.

There was movement to Stillman's left and Butch spotted Wilson struggling to sit up. Blood flowed from his chest. As he breathed, bubbles formed at the wound.

Stillman approached the dying man.

Ratt Wilson gazed at his wounds with confusion. Then he looked at the old lawman standing over him. "Hooow...whhoo are...?" he coughed and blood flowed down his chin.

Stillman gave him a cold glare. "Who are they? You ever hear of Robert Leroy Parker or Harry Longabaugh?" There was a blank look on Wilson's face. "Probably not. Might be easier if I tell you that Harry Kidwell is the Sundance Kid and his friend over there is Butch Cassidy."

Shock, then comprehension registered on Wilson's face. Slowly, he fixed his glassy eyes on the two old outlaws. He cursed then coughed up more blood and died.

Kneeling next to Sundance, Butch watched his friend slowly open his eyes and blink a few times. Harry's eyes focused on his wife and son. Blood flowed from the wound in his chest.

Butch could see tears flowing down Lee's cheeks.

"I ... I'm sorry, Pa. Pa, don't die. It was my fault. Pa, please ..."

Harry looked up at his son. "Not...your fault. Take . . . care of your Ma . . . and . . . sister.

Butch watched as the life left his old friend. Sadness fused with anger. He saw the silent wail that came from Etta's open mouth. Lee's sobs were almost mute as well. The only truly audible sound was that of the moans of the wounded gangster in the tack room, the only surviving killer.

Hearing the moans, Stillman looked over at the barn. "Guess someone should look after that man."

With a superhuman effort, Butch struggled to his feet. "I will," he whispered. Slowly he limped back into the barn.

Samuel called after him. "Butch, you're in no condition to be trying to help the poor devil."

A second later, there was a gunshot. Then silence. Finally, Butch appeared at the barn door. Smoke drifted from the barrel of one of his Colts.

Samuel gazed questioningly at him. "What happened, Butch?"

"He died."

* * *

Riding at full gallop, it took Alva, Slim and Austin a full fifteen minutes to reach Harry's ranch. There seemed to be no more gunfire by the time they rode into the barnyard.

Several bodies were lying near the barn. Standing alone was a tall man. Alva quickly recognized him as Samuel Stillman.

When they reined in, Alva spotted Leroy leaning against the barn door. Blood covered his trousers and soaked his shirt. Etta and Lee were kneeling next to a motionless man on the ground.

Alva urged his gelding closer to Etta and recognized the man she was kneeling over. It was obvious that Harry was dead.

"We came as soon as we could," Alva said as he and the others jumped down from their horses. He knelt by Etta and put his hand on her shoulder. "I'm sorry, Etta."

Still sobbing, Etta looked at Alva and nodded.

"What happened here, Marshal?" Austin asked Stillman as he took in the bodies lying in the morning sun.

Stillman stood holding his wounded arm. "S.C. Brooks sent a bunch of killers out here." He looked at the bodies scattered around. "Guess you could say he didn't send enough."

"What now, Samuel?" Butch asked. He was still leaning against the barn door.

Stillman gazed back at the old outlaw. "I figure the first thing to do is get you to a doctor, Mr ... what was your name?" Butch smiled and Stillman continued, "Then I plan to make a report to the Governor."

Slim and Austin could see that Leroy was weak and about to collapse. They took hold of him and lowered him gently to the ground.

"What about Brooks?" Slim asked.

"He's a powerful man and has a lot of influence in this State," Stillman said. "Not sure we can pin any of this on him. But, if it's any consolation, doubt he'll be bothering any of you people around here any more. With what I have to report to the Governor, Brooks will, at the least, have to curtail his activities in this area."

* * *

Laura had waited as long as she could in the fruit cellar. It was silent outside when she eased open the trap door. That was when she heard a single gun shot. She wanted to duck back into the cellar, but her curiosity overcame her fear. She crept into the kitchen.

Jolted by the condition of the room, she halted at the door. Eyes wide, she surveyed the devastation before finally breaking free of her shock and making her way to the window. Alva, Slim, and Austin were riding up to the barn. Her mother and brother were kneeling in the barnyard.

She rushed from the house. As she drew close to her mother and brother, she recognized her father lying motionless before them. The look on their faces told her the awful truth.

Etta looked up as Laura approached. "Lee, take Laura back into the house. Laura, go with your brother."

But Lee didn't respond. He seemed to be in a daze.

Etta called to him again, "Lee. LEE!"

Chapter 45

OLD LEE
Oklahoma 2001

~ ~ ~

"Lee! LEE! Mr. Kidwell! Sir!" Sheriff Barton Shepard tried to rouse old Lee from what seemed to be a trance. The police cruiser was pulling up in front of the county jail. The sheriff had left Lee in his apparent daze for the past twenty minutes as they sped along the county roads.

He'd run a check on the old man and learned that there were no outstanding warrants, nor did Lee Kidwell have any record of any kind. The whole thing was a puzzle to Shepard. Why would a seemingly peaceful, law-abiding old man suddenly go berserk and shoot up a local tavern?

Lee still seemed to be lost in a daze as the deputy pulled him out of the car. The treatment was just a little too rough for Shepard's liking and he said so to the deputy.

"Sorry, Sheriff, but he just don't seem to be respondin' to nothin'."

"No reason to manhandle him, son."

They led Lee into the jail where Shepard read him his rights. Lee stared straight ahead and said nothing.

He was escorted to a cold empty cell with a stainless steel bench, stainless steel toilet and stainless steel sink. Shepard nodded for Lee to sit down on the bench, but the old man stood staring into space.

Leaning forward, the sheriff looked into Lee's eyes before speaking in a gentle voice. "We'll have an arraignment yet this afternoon, Mr. Kidwell. I'll see to it that you have a lawyer present. You should be able to get out on bond yet today. Given your lack of any record and given your age, I doubt if the judge will want you to stay in jail over night."

Slowly, Lee unbuttoned his breast pocket and pulled out his precious old silver watch. He gazed at the timepiece and gently rubbed the worn cover.

The deputy stood holding the cell door. "I don't think he's hearin' a word you're sayin', sheriff."

Shepard looked at his deputy and, as he started to leave the cell, he slowly shook his head. He had just stepped out of the cell door when Lee looked up from his silver watch and spoke for the first time.

"He wasn't a coward, you know."

"Whoa, the zombie speaks," the deputy exclaimed.

Shepard gave his deputy a stern glare. Then he turned back to Lee. "Who wasn't a coward, Mr. Kidwell?"

"My Pa! My Pa was the bravest man I ever knew."

"Well, I'm sure he was, Mr. Kidwell. But now maybe you best sit down there and get some rest." Shepard motioned toward the bench.

"He wasn't a killer, either. Those people got it all wrong. They weren't anything like that man on the TV said — Uncle Leroy and my Pa." Lee finally sat down on the bench and stared at the ceiling.

"I know that, Mr. Kidwell. Everyone knows your Pa was no coward," Shepard said reassuringly as he locked the cell door. "Just try to relax."

The deputy followed Shepard as they left the lock-up and entered his office. "Who the hell was his pa, Sheriff?"

Shepard looked at his deputy with sad eyes. "Who the hell knows?"

Epilogue

THE CLEAN UP
Oklahoma City 1921

~ ~ ~

It was 1:12 a.m. when the telephone on the downstairs wall rang. Detective Edward Buescher'd had a love/hate relationship with the new-fangled invention ever since he installed one in his house. There was no denying the convenience of the damn contraption but it just seemed to ring at the most unsuitable times.

Obviously, this was one of those times. He had gone off duty several hours before and there could only be one reason for a call at this hour.

Buescher gently slipped back the bed covers in a vain effort to keep from waking his wife. As he lifted his six-foot, two-hundred-and-twenty-pound frame from the creaking bed, he could see that his wife's open eyes were staring at him. He turned to her and shrugged his shoulders. Then he put on his robe and left the bedroom.

The telephone continued to ring insistently as he stumbled down the steps. He'd never received a call this late and he knew it had to be an important and high-profile case in order to prompt such an intrusion.

His suspicion was confirmed when he lifted the cone-shaped receiver and heard the Oklahoma City Chief of Police on the line. He brushed his hand through his shortly-cropped blond hair and listened to the Chief outlining the situation.

Buescher had a reputation in the city as being the very best at what he did. So, it was not a surprise that he'd been called out of bed for this one.

Thirty minutes later he arrived at a grand, though somewhat gaudy, mansion situated in the richest section of Oklahoma City. He stepped from his shinny black 1920 Dodge Model 30 Sedan to find the area crawling with uniformed police; so much so that, once inside, he had to order most of them out of the residence to prevent further contamination of the crime scene.

He found the victim in the den, lying in a pool of blood. Gazing down at the body, he could see that the man had been riddled with so many bullet holes that Buescher, at first, thought he'd been killed with a sub-machine gun.

Upon further examination, he concluded that this theory didn't hold up. The pattern of holes made by the weapon or weapons was not consistent with that of a sub-machine gun. What's more, a Thompson or similar weapon would commonly miss almost as many times as it would hit the target. In this case there were thirteen distinct holes in the victim's torso as well as one well-placed shot to the forehead. This had been very deliberate and very personal.

There had been a witness. She'd been living in the residence with the victim at the time of the shooting. The uniformed police had asked her only a few basic questions before they'd made her comfortable in the parlor to await the lead detective.

A uniform motioned Buescher aside. "She's in there," he whispered. "Says she's been living here for more than three months." Then in an even lower voice, he added, "She's not his wife."

Buescher found the woman dressed in a nightgown and seated on a divan in the parlor. She appeared to be in her early twenties or late teens and she was quite lovely. She was also quite shaken.

She told him that she had gone upstairs to prepare for bed at around 9:00 p.m. She said that the victim, as was his habit, had remained downstairs to read the paper and do "what ever else he did down there".

She was in the bathroom when she heard the doorbell ring. Because it was such a late hour, she'd gone to the head of the stairs to see who it might be. There was a staff of servants that tended the house but they did not live on premises. They'd all gone home so there was no one but the victim to answer the door.

She was sure that the man who rang was not a stranger because the victim had peered through the peephole before opening the door.

"There's no way he would have opened the door if he didn't recognize the man," she explained. "And

I heard him comment to the visitor that it was a pleasure to see him after so many days."

"Did the stranger say anything?" Buescher asked.

She thought a minute. "Yes, he apologized for coming at such a late hour."

She went on to say that she'd watched from the top of the stairs as the two men walked into the den. Then she had gone into the bedroom to finish preparing for bed. That was when she heard the shots. She knew what the sound was because she'd heard a gunshot before. But never had she heard so many and in such a short time.

She told Detective Buescher that she had immediately been fearful for her life. She'd locked the bedroom door and hid. She was sure the stranger would come for her, too, so she remained in the room shivering in fear for what seemed like hours.

In reality it was less than twenty minutes.

She explained that, when she was convinced that the man must have left, she gathered her courage and ventured slowly down the stairs and entered the den where she saw the body. She didn't have to get very close to see that he was dead.

For a while she hadn't known what to do. She considered running, but finally decided she would have to telephone the police.

Detective Buescher assured her that she had done the right thing. Then he asked her if she could describe the stranger.

She paused and looked at the ceiling as though there might be a picture of the man painted there. Finally she looked back at the detective. "He was wearing a very nice suit and a bowler hat. I didn't see what his face looked like because, from the top of the stairs, the brim of his hat covered his face."

After another pause she told Buescher that there was one other thing. "He walked with a bad limp. You know," she said, "now that I think about it, when they were going to the den, Scotty asked the man what had happened to him. And the man said that was one of the things he'd come to see Scotty about. Scotty seemed real puzzled when he said that."

A week later, the new science of ballistics revealed that the victim, one Scott C. Brooks, owner of Brook's Imperial Petroleum Company, had most likely been killed by two .45 cal. Colt semi-automatic pistols, wielded by an unknown assailant. Not that this information would turn out to be of any help. Even with a massive search, the stranger was never found.

Made in the USA
San Bernardino, CA
19 June 2014